Prisoner of Passion

As his four comrades looked on, the drunken Jamieson held Elsa Jane tightly, a glint of anticipation in his eyes. Desperate to free herself, the young beauty raised her knee forcefully, catching him directly in the groin.

"Bitch!" Jamieson roared as he yanked at her petticoats, pulling them down around her ankles to subdue the wildly kicking legs.

One of his men, Dunbar, locked her wrists together with a single bear paw, as Jamieson tore away the remaining tatters of sack cloth, leaving Elsa Jane quivering in nothing but her chemise and stockings.

Jamieson's hand crept under his sweater. Suddenly it reappeared and there was a flash of steel. With a single upward thrust, the knife severed the chemise lacing, and the material fell away from her young breasts and virginal body like a descending theatrical curtain.

"Me first! Me first!" Caldwell shouted as he began to remove his clothes.

Jamieson raised his hand. "New rules, gentlemen. With her we may get but a single chance—so we'll take her all at once!"

&❧

The
WOMEN WHO WON THE WEST
Series

TEMPEST OF TOMBSTONE
DODGE CITY DARLING
DUCHESS OF DENVER

WOMEN WHO WON THE WEST

Duchess of Denver

Lee Davis Willoughby

A DELL/JAMES A. BRYANS BOOK

Published by
Dell Publishing Co., Inc.
1 Dag Hammarskjold Plaza
New York, New York 10017

Dell ® TM 681510, Dell Publishing Co., Inc.

ISBN: 0-440-02172-3

Printed in the United States of America
First printing—April 1982

1

"The RIVERBOAT's leavin', li'l missy. Y'all best be findin' yore folk."

Elsa Jane looked quizzically at the black man. When she realized that she had been looking nostalgically at the *River Queen* and had been mistaken for a passenger, she couldn't help but giggle. Her "folk," if one could call them that, were already up river. She had not seen them in two years.

A stern hand grasped her by the elbow and spun her about.

"Child, I do declare you are a caution. Now get yourself back with the other girls and wait for Bishop Landry."

The twelve-year-old curtsied and sauntered back to the knot of pupils from the Saint Rosa Lima Convent. Each wore the same black dress, white dickey

5

and straw sailor hat as Elsa Jane, but she alone stood out. It was not merely that she was a head taller than her classmates; there was something in her face, in her eyes, that was unique. The other young faces were animated. The children felt a thrill being out of the stuffy convent classrooms for the morning. Elsa Jane, however, was solemn. Her green eyes lacked their usual brightness. She was disinterested and discontent.

"Here they come," Sister Martha Mary said happily, clapping her blue-veined hands together. "Line up girls! Line up! Elsa Jane, the flowers. Where are the flowers? Hazel, give those flowers back to Elsa Jane."

"But Father Dubois said . . ." Hazel began in protest. However, the expression on Sister Martha Mary's face caused her to bite her lower lip rather than continue. The old woman could stop any argument with a single look.

"Prune," Elsa Jane thought, watching the nun's face.

"*I* decided," Sister Martha Mary replied in a thin, even tone, "that Elsa Jane would be best suited to present the bishop with the flowers."

Ten pairs of eyes turned to Elsa Jane with knowing disapproval. The Bender family was the largest contributor to the school. Elsa Jane was, therefore, constantly being granted embarrassing little extras not given the other girls. The attention had set her apart and kept her friendless for the two years she had been a student at Saint Rosa Lima, and there was nothing she could do about it.

The girls were still glaring at her when the bishop's carriage arrived. Father Dubois bounded from the coach and turned to help the frail old man. A single raised eyebrow from Sister Martha Mary sent Elsa Jane forward with her greeting.

She dipped into a curtsy, held out the beribboned nosegay of flowers and mumbled a memorized "thank-you" for the bishop's visit.

Bishop Landry grasped the flowers and her fingers between his hands. They felt cold, like parchment, and Elsa Jane wanted to pull away.

"And what charming little maiden have we here, Father?"

Father Dubois shot a questioning glance at Sister Martha Mary. His black Creole eyes danced with hatred. He had given strict orders for Hazel DeFontaine to meet the old man, and yet there was the Bender girl with the flowers. Calvin Bender might be a steady and large contributor, but he was a long way from New Orleans. Henre DeFontaine was local, had the finest wine cellar in the city, set a remarkably fine table—and was Father Dubois's constant host.

"This is Elsa Jane Bender, Your Grace. Calvin Bender's niece."

The wrinkled, parched face came to life.

"To be sure," he chuckled. "It was my pleasure to lunch with your uncle at Bender's Landing while the downriver steamer was refueling. I was under the impression that his niece was a far younger being."

Elsa Jane smiled blankly. She would have loved to have shocked them all with a few eye-opening facts. To begin with, the noble Calvin Bender was not her uncle, but her real father. The bachelor plantation owner had raised his illegitimate daughter in his mansion as his niece and had enrolled her in Saint Rosa Lima under the same ruse.

"Yes, yes," Landry continued, "much younger, I thought. What would you be, my girl, fourteen, about?"

"Twelve," she answered, casting a daring look at Father Dubois.

The younger priest blushed deeply. A few months earlier, when he had noted that Elsa Jane was developing rapidly, Sister Martha Mary had implied that such observations were lecherous. She then ordered the other nuns to bind the child's blooming breasts flat so that they wouldn't be apparent to the priests or any other man in that "hotbed"—New Orleans. Her efforts had obviously failed when the bishop expressed curiosity about the girl's age. Father Dubois cringed when he thought of what measures Sister Martha Mary might now take to hide Elsa Jane's subtle curves.

"Well, my child, I shall inform your uncle that we met," Bishop Landry said as he patted her hand. "A most charming place, Bender's Landing. Most charming. Father," he continued as he turned away, "let's see to my ticket and luggage. We seem to be holding up the departure. Goodbye, Sister Martha Mary. Goodbye, girls. Most charming."

Elsa Jane was unsure if the bishop was still referring to Bender's Landing, herself or all the schoolgirls.

She almost wished that he had not mentioned Bender's Landing. It was a world apart from New Orleans. The wharf area was foul, and, although it was the same river that engulfed the shores of the plantation, there was no other connection.

Elsa Jane could remember the strong, clean smell of the mighty river drifting across the island plantation. There were rolling fields scattered among forests of white birch and pine, fir, spruce, maple, and hemlock that whispered in the breeze. Spring and summer flower gardens added a sweetness to the air, and the colors were as bright as the rainbow.

The ten years that Elsa Jane had spent on the plantation had been as friendless as those at the school, although she had never really thought of it as a lonesome life. The island forests provided a place for her youthful spirit to soar as free as a bird. There were, however, some restrictions, as Calvin Bender had strict ideas about the upbringing of a female child in the middle of the nineteenth century.

First and foremost, Elsa Jane was forbidden to associate with the "darky" children. During her childhood on the plantation she had never been within the slave compound. Of course, this rule was slightly bent in the summertime when her Uncle Calvin went off to Europe and the governess got sick and tired of having the child constantly under her feet. It was then that she was allowed to roam free, and would meet the "darky" children.

Often the children would be along the hillsides and fences picking wild raspberries, strawberries or gooseberries. It was one of their chores, and Elsa Jane delighted in seeking them out.

Most of these children were illegitimate and thought nothing of sharing their common knowledge. When Elsa Jane first learned her own status, she assumed that it was simply the way all babies were brought into the world. In her precocious way she had broached the subject with her governess to learn if the same was true for the four Harrison children.

Mattie Goldunk had gulped and colored. As a spinster, there were some things she just never let enter her pious brain. Anything to do with Harvey and Helen Harrison—or their four urchin sons—she never cared to think about. To her way of thinking, even though Harvey Harrison was the plantation overseer, the family was worse than "white trash." She couldn't bring herself to look upon the mulatto children that Harrison had sired, and she couldn't bring herself to honestly answer Elsa Jane's curious question.

A wrong answer would have been better than no
answer at all. Elsa Jane became even more curious,
and began digging for an answer from the black
children.

At first they were mostly timid, although as slaves
they tended to know all there was to know about
what went on in the main house.

When she finally got an answer, she was shocked
and disturbed. It was hard for her to understand.
How could Calvin Bender be her father and not her
uncle—and Helen Harrison her mother? The slave
children couldn't help her solve that riddle; they just
knew what they knew, and that was all.

Elsa Jane just couldn't dredge up the courage to
broach the subject with Helen Harrison. In the first
place, she seldom saw the woman, in the second place,
she was scared to death of her when she did see her.

"Thurd-ay minutes! Ribba Queen delayed thurd-ay
minutes!"

The voice of the black wharfman who had first
spoken to Elsa Jane echoed over the gathered throng.
Elsa Jane turned to see the battalion-like lines of her
classmates marching away behind the commanding
back of the nun. She ran to catch up but stopped
short. With no plan in mind, she quickly stepped behind a towering stack of baled cotton.

The bishop had all but said that he would be seeing her Uncle Calvin again. That had to mean that
the *River Queen* would refuel at Bender's Landing.

"Lord, how I would love to be home!"

"Where's dat?"

Elsa Jane spun around and stared into large blue
questioning eyes. The girl could not have been much
older than she, although she was a size smaller.

"Bender's Landing. Who are you?"

"Eliza. Eliza Cartwright. You goin' on dat steamer?"

Elsa Jane looked back at the *River Queen* wistfully and shrugged.

Eliza shrugged back. "Guess we ain't either. My paw's been trying to raise the fare or pay less for a stowaway berth. Ain't doin' much good on either. Right pretty hat."

"What's a stowaway berth?"

Eliza pinched her scrawny face into a scowl. "You with that school bunch, ain'tcha?"

Elsa Jane nodded.

"Then they don't teach you much," Eliza said as she preened. "Stowaway is when you can con a crewman into sneaking you aboard for less than the fare. A right pretty hat. Ain't never had one like that."

The young girl seemed to be enamored of the flat-brimmed straw hat with its trailing ribbons of blue and red.

"Would you like to try it on?"

The girl looked dubious. "Would . . ." she said slowly.

Elsa Jane picked up Eliza's train of thought before she finished the sentence.

"Seems to me," Elsa Jane interrupted matter-of-factly, "that I might wish to know more about this stowaway business. Would you like the hat for keeps . . . for telling me?"

The girl's eagerness almost made Elsa Jane laugh. The information came pouring forth as she removed her poke-bonnet and took the straw hat in trembling hands.

"How do I look?"

Elsa Jane pursed her lips and frowned. "Most fine . . . except you'd be most proper if you had this dress to be going with it. I'm most partial, myself, to calico and poke-bonnets."

"You be?" Eliza said with a gulp, not believing her luck. Her flour-sack dress was homemade, fading, and fraying at the hem. It was hideous when compared to the black uniform and white dickey.

"Are you suggesting a trade?" she gulped again.

"Yes. But we will have to do it quickly. Any minute they will be getting back to the school and will note my absence."

Eliza Cartwright had her own reason for wanting to do it quickly. She was afraid the schoolgirl would change her mind. In almost a single movement she had the simply cut garment over her head and was thrusting it forward.

It took Elsa Jane a few minutes longer to undo the neck-to-waist bone buttons of her uniform. She hesitated a moment before stepping out of the skirt. It was not like her to be so impulsive. The strict code of rules on the plantation and at school had allowed for very little individual thinking. She began to giggle at being so rash. She imagined the look on Sister Martha Mary's face when she discovered Elsa Jane's absence, and in defiance of that look as well as at all the dictates of the nuns, she reached into the petticoat, untied the breast binding and pulled out the long swaddle.

When she put it on, the calico dress was far too short and revealed several inches of her high-button shoes.

Eliza nudged her.

"That whistle means the 'all aboard.' You ain't got much time. That looks like your only possible choice, if you're aiming to get home on this steamer."

Through a little corridor in the baled cotton stacks Elsa Jane saw the figure of a crewman. His back was to them and he kept peeking out of his own hiding spot in a furtive manner. She could see why he was being so cautious. Every few seconds he would tilt a clay corn liquor jug upward and let a stream of the clear liquid trickle into his throat.

His drinking made her hesitate. Ever since she could remember, Calvin Bender had preached on the evils of "spirits."

"Good luck, and remember all I told you."

Elsa Jane was just about ready to give up on the wild notion of being a stowaway when she heard the commotion on the other side of the bales. Sister Martha Mary had run back and was shouting at Father Dubois.

Elsa Jane didn't wait to hear his reply. She quickly donned the poke-bonnet, waved a silent goodbye to Eliza and went running to the sailor.

"I need to be stowed away on that steamer," she gushed, trying to ignore her fear.

For a long moment they stared at each other.

"Cap'n Allard don't allow his crew to do such."

"But I must get home and don't have the money. I can see that you get paid when we stop at Bender's Landing. My uncle owns it."

Daris Jamieson shrugged and looked at her questioningly. The wealth of Calvin Bender was a legend on the river. No niece of his would be roaming about in flour-sack calico. He shook his head.

"I traded clothes," Elsa Jane stated simply.

Jamieson shrugged his shoulders again. Then he looked at her more closely. The mass of spiral brunette curls that reached halfway down her back were out of keeping with the poke-bonnet, as were the high-button shoes of unscuffed black leather.

"You in trouble or something?"

"Not real trouble. It's just that there is a man who will be on the trip who must not see that I am aboard."

Now she puzzled Jamieson. He couldn't determine her age, but the face and "little girl" curls suggested she was too young to be "involved" with a man. Yet her body could suggest otherwise. The calico dress clung to her young breasts, thin waist and flaring hips like the most provocative silk.

"Why are you hiding from him, miss?"

There was not enough time to explain the truth to him, and even if she had, she wondered if he would help. Men were a bit of a mystery to her, having known only her Uncle Calvin, Harvey Harrison and the priests. Daris Jamieson was not like any of them. He was shorter than Calvin Bender, but more muscular, with a rich, olive complexion and midnight black hair. His cotton twill trousers and shirt sensuously hugged his frame, and his rugged face was quietly handsome. He looked as if he had seen much more of life than he would reveal, and Elsa Jane's intuition told her to play upon that aspect.

"He wishes to keep me in New Orleans, sir. I—I do not wish to discuss the reasons he wishes to keep me here. I wish only to discuss them with my Uncle Calvin."

Her directness aroused Jamieson's interest. For ten of his twenty-five years, the Mississippi had been his home. He had left a string of broken hearts from St. Louis to New Orleans. He courted until he made his conquest. Then he instantly lost interest and sought out a new victim for his collection. Here, indeed, was quite a challenge. A young, pretty and well-bred girl had never crossed his path before.

"Well," he drawled, "a favor done means a favor in return."

"Get me home and I'll see that you are rewarded by my uncle."

That, too, interested Jamieson. Captain Amos Allard scowled with disapproval when his crewmen involved themselves with the riverboat gamblers, and on the trip south Jamieson had heavily involved himself right into debt.

"That would be most kind of your uncle, miss," he said, thinking of how to pay off the gamblers, "but can you think of some way that you might be able to personally reward me?"

"I don't understand."

The final whistle shot a plume of steam high into the air.

"Never mind. I'll spell it out for you when we are on board. Now, don't say a word and keep your face tucked into the bonnet. I'll carry you from here."

"Why?"

"Just shut up and try to look limp. You'll understand when I get you up the gangway."

Jamieson scooped Elsa Jane up into his strong muscular arms. He carried her as if she weighed nothing, and she turned her head into his shoulder so that only the back of her bonnet would show.

She peeked over his shoulder at the people they were passing on the wharf and nearly giggled aloud. When they passed within three feet of the frantically searching Sister Martha Mary and Father Dubois, the nun let out a funereal wail that made Elsa Jane cringe in Jamieson's arms. Her heart stopped beating. She was sure she had been discovered.

But Sister Martha Mary waddled off at such a fast gait that it made Father Dubois's robes flap around his ankles as he tried to keep up with her. They headed down the wharf to where they saw Elsa Jane's black uniform and straw hat being dragged along by a rough looking man and woman. Elsa Jane watched their chase until she too saw Eliza with her parents. The man and woman looked like Creole gypsies, and when she realized that Sister Martha Mary probably thought they were kidnapping her for ransom, she couldn't help but giggle.

"Hush!" Jamieson warned, as he started up the gangplank. "This is going to be hard enough as it is."

Elsa Jane stifled her giggles and buried her face deeper in his arms. A sweat crawled up her spine. The reality of what was happening hit her like a cold wave. It was madness. She might be thrashed like a runaway slave for such a brazen thing. Yet, her fear diminished the farther she was carried up onto the stern-wheeler. She could think of only one thing: she was in the arms of a real man!

It was quite an experience. The only time any man had ever touched her was to pat her on the head. But now she was wrapped in strong arms, next to a steely chest, with neck muscles like entwined lengths of rope within reach of her lips. There was also the most incredible aroma.

She couldn't recall what Calvin Bender smelled like, but she would always remember that Harvey Harrison had a strange scent of horse and cow manure, and that the priests smelled of incense and lavender water.

But the smell of Daris Jamieson was purely masculine. She had never before encountered the odor of corn liquor and tobacco, but found it delightful.

"The sick girl for Natchez," she heard Jamieson growl at someone. "Which cabin? She ain't light, you know."

There was a slight pause. "I thought she was aboard already, Jamieson."

Jamieson cursed. "Come on, Logan! This ain't no sack of grain I got in my arms. It may be your first trip as a purser, so let's not make your mistakes known to Allard."

"Is there a problem? May I be of some help?"

Elsa Jane froze. She didn't have to see to recognize the wheezing, nasal tones of Bishop Landry.

"Sick girl, Padre," Jamieson said. "I just want to get her to her cabin."

"To be sure, to be sure," the old man clucked in sympathy. "I've medical experience if it is required. Purser?"

"Cabin nine," Lawrence Logan stammered.

Logan was sure that one of the crewmen had already brought the sick girl aboard. But then, again, could he be sure? He hated his job, he hated the river and he hated Captain Amos Allard. He had been content as a dry-goods salesman in St. Louis. He had been content living with his private, secretive life. For him it had been exciting and daring, but it had come to an abrupt end the very night he had hoped to start an even greater adventure.

It had taken him a full year to build up enough courage to bring a young lady into his bachelor quarters. Oh, how his expectations for that evening had soared! For a year he had plotted the end of his virginal state.

His state was still most virginal. After a romantic dinner, he had arrived back at his quarters to find his mother, father and Uncle Amos Allard awaiting the couple. He quickly dispatched the young lady. His minister father then preached for three hours, using carefully selected Biblical quotes, and demanded that he put his life in care of the puritanical Captain Amos Allard.

With that kind of history, Lawrence Logan was not about to reveal to his Uncle Amos that he couldn't even keep track of the passengers coming on board.

Jamieson had no intention of taking Elsa Jane to cabin nine. He had already delivered a very young girl to that cabin before he had gone back to the wharf to nip his corn liquor. He couldn't take her to his own cabin, as he shared it with three other crewmen, so he carried her deep within the hold.

As an old hand on the river, first as a bargeman and then as a crewman for stern-wheelers and side-wheelers, he knew that the freight load would be heavy coming downriver, but very light for the return trip. Back in the stern were cage-like sections that could be locked up and would go undetected until their arrival at Bender's Landing.

It was cold, dank and dark. Jamieson put Elsa Jane down and lit the wick of an old oil lamp embedded in the hull.

"Don't make a sound. If anyone comes, hide behind those old crates. I've got cast-off chores to do and then I'll rustle you up some blankets and food. Don't answer to anyone but me."

Elsa Jane nodded and looked around. She had not expected such dungeon-like quarters. Somehow she had just assumed that she would be traveling in the same luxurious style as on her trip to New Orleans. The twenty-by-forty wire-caged room was normally used to store bundled pelts that would find their way to the hat factories of Europe. It had no accommodations for a human being.

A sharp hissing noise erupted around her as steam was forced through the lines to drive the stern-wheel pistons. The sounds were amplified as if in a cave, forcing her to cover her ears with her hands. The whole stern shook as the driving arms began the rotation of the paddle wheel. Then came the most frightening sound of all as the two dozen paddles began to eat through tons of river water and splash it into the stern hull.

Not even her hands could keep out the noise. Elsa Jane cowered down beside one of the old crates and tried to wrap her arms about her head. The sound and the movement seemed to enter every fiber of her body, making her shake violently.

She tried to think of something else. She had always been left pretty much to herself, but had never felt this lonely. She tried to think of the birds and the tethered goats that came to the convent garden.

Suddenly she felt the pressure of a little nose sniffing and investigating her foot. Had she so longed for a friend that she had created an animal companion? She opened her eyes and looked down but saw nothing. She straightened up and took her arms away from her head, but still saw nothing.

She was instantly aware that the sound had diminished. The riverboat was now out in mid-stream and the paddle wheel was working with quiet ease at half-steam. The fierceness had been replaced by a lulling beat.

"That must mean his departing chores are almost over," she said aloud as she stood up.

It was still chilly in the hold so she began pacing. She tried to peer out of the heavily laced wire of the cage, but the single little lamp didn't cast enough light for her to see anything. It was like looking out of a window into a starless night. Suddenly she stopped short, shielded her eyes, and stared again between the diamond pattern of the mesh.

It was not totally starless. She could see little flickers of light that seemed to blink on and off in the distance. There was also a new sound mixed in with the wheeze of the steam pistons and the splash of the water. She closed her eyes and tried to divorce it from the other sounds.

Rabbits? It sounded just like the caged plantation rabbits gnawing on their grain. Was her imagination working overtime again?

When she opened her eyes the blinking lights had increased and drawn closer. Then, in the partial darkness she saw furtive movement. She stood still, and wondered if this was just a repeat of her constant nightmare—the only time she had really been frightened.

She tried to close out of her mind that horrible day two years ago, when she had rebelled against the orders of Mattie Goldunk and had been locked in the root cellar until the return of Calvin Bender. There she had met a vicious breed of animal unlike any other. She could still feel the stinging bites as their razor-sharp teeth had snapped at her stomping ankles. In her innocence she had not even been aware what they were, and the rats had preyed on her hysteria.

Now the shadows took on the forms she dreaded most. They silently glided up to the cage and squeezed their gray bodies through the mesh.

Elsa Jane could not breathe; she could not even gasp for air. She began to move along the cage wall, seeking an escape. Twice she circled past the gate without realizing it was made of the same wire mesh. The river rats sensed her fear and packed together. They were preparing to lunge for her ankles.

Elsa Jane began to run around the cage, shaking and banging on every section. Tears sprang to her eyes, but her throat was too dry and constricted to cry out. Then she saw what was keeping her prisoner and her heart went faint.

The wire door had been bolted from the outside. The mesh was such that a rat could squeeze through, but her hand and arm were too big to reach the bolt.

One daring rat leaped upon her calico skirt. With a cry of horror Elsa Jane tried batting it away with her hand, but it's claws sank into the cloth. Finally there was a sound of ripping material and the gray form crashed down into the gathering pack. Together as one, they began a squeaky hiss and showed their ugly yellow teeth.

Elsa Jane ran back to the crates and grappled to loosen a board. She opened her mouth to scream and stomped her feet until she had the weapon in hand. Then she began to brandish it wildly. The rats were no match for her adolescent strength. They now knew the enemy that they faced. She was like the sailors who periodically reduced their numbers with clubs. Now their piercing squeaks were of a different tone—they were fighting for their lives.

"What in the hell?"

There was a rasp as the bolt was pulled from its rusty case and the wire door banged back. The rats scattered.

Elsa Jane stared in terror. She could not focus, or recognize Jamieson through her fear.

He lumbered into the cage and dropped the articles in his arms down on a crate.

"Damn!" he snarled. "I thought I told you to keep quiet. I could hear your racket the moment I started down into the hold."

Elsa Jane burst into tears and ran to him. It was the third time she had cried in her life. She had tried to hide her tears when she was brought out of the root cellar; tried to hide them again from the nuns on her first night alone at Saint Rosa Lima, but this time she didn't care who saw her tears or knew of her fear.

"Hey," he said soothingly, enclosing her in his arms, "it was only a few rats. I'll take care of them."

"Don't leave me," she wailed, clutching at his shirt.

He pulled her hands away. "Now, just be still. I'll just be a few feet away for a few minutes. I've brought you some blankets and grub. See to them."

Elsa Jane had no desire to do anything but stay close to him, no matter who he was, yet when he vanished into the darkness she forced herself to stay within the cage.

He was as good as his word. He was back shortly with a sack and began to dump its contents into little piles around the outside of the cage.

"What's that?"

"Poisoned wheat. We use it this way when the hold cages are filled with things the rats like to gnaw on."

When he had completed his chores he came back and took the blankets from the crate. He spread one out on the rough-hewn deck and placed the others suggestively on top.

Elsa Jane's eyes flared. "I can't sleep here with . . . *with them!*"

"They will be more interested in filling their bellies with that wheat than with you."

"Please," she begged, placing her hand on his arm. "Is there no other way?"

She felt his muscles harden under the twill fabric. She tightened her grasp.

"Now don't worry," he said soothingly. "Just eat some of that grub and relax. I'll be here to spend the night with you."

"Thank you," she sighed, but did not remove her hand.

The contact with her flesh excited him and he longed to possess her, but to avoid questions he had to continue his duties until nightfall. He turned slightly away to hide his burgeoning excitement. However, even in his elation he sensed that he might not get back that evening. Charles Dunbar had been hounding him since the first turn of the paddle wheel. He had to raise the gambler's money or stand the chance of Captain Allard finding out how he lost it. His plan was to fleece Lawrence Logan, the Captain's nephew. The pale, effeminate young man never seemed to spend any money, so Jamieson assumed he would have plenty tucked away in his sock. To gain it, Jamieson was not above blackmail.

He left his young prize so he could search for Logan, but as his luck would have it, he never found him. He did spot "Charley the Ace" Dunbar on several occasions but carefully avoided him.

The night, black and blustering, descended on the boat, bringing a bone-chilling wind with it. Passengers and crew stayed within the warmth of their cabins and quarters, and Jamieson continued his search.

"Mis-tah Jamieson!" A deep voice shouted. "Are you, or are you not, the one who carried the sick girl aboard?"

Jamieson's heart froze as he turned and looked up the passageway into the glowering face of Amos Allard. No one dared lie, even a little white one, to that man.

"Aye, that I am, sir," he stammered.

The monstrous bulk moved down to the deck. Allard's uniforms were well-tailored to his barrel-chested frame. The square cut of his gray-black beard and his bushy eyebrows made him the living image of a Biblical patriarch. It was an image he was proud of.

"An' did not Mis-tah Logan check the girl aboard?"

"Aye, aye, sir."

"Then, looky here, mis-tah! Why does Bishop Landry now feel that the girl in cabin nine is not the same as seen in your arms? Find Logan, mis-tah, and get your arses back to report to me!"

There was only one place on the riverboat that Jamieson had not looked for Lawrence Logan, but he hardly believed he would find the young man in Dunbar's cabin. Still, he couldn't avoid Dunbar any longer. He flung open the cabin door without ceremony. There, hunched around a low, makeshift table, was Logan, watching an engine-room fireman play cards with Dunbar. Jamieson instantly thought of a new scheme to forestall the gambler, but there was a fourth man who he had not noticed.

"To the captain, Logan. To the boiler, Kramer!"

The fourth passenger lifted his head from his cards so quickly that his nose-nippers fell off. He clutched the pasteboards to his chest, fearing Jamieson would snatch them away. It was almost comical.

Taking note of the gentleman for the first time, Jamieson hastily continued, "This doesn't apply to you, sir. Captain Allard has no thoughts when it comes to the passengers, but he does not allow gambling by the crew aboard his ship."

"Have a heart, matey," the broad-shouldered fireman leered at him. "My deuces are backed by something that will take this pot."

Jamieson glared, waiting for more pleas. Logan sat, clean-limbed, clean-faced, and unsure of what to say. Jamieson cursed under his breath.

"Capt'n wants to talk to you about the sick girl, Logan. That purple-lipped padre says the girl in the cabin ain't the same one I brought on board. Now, you know that it is, don't you?"

"How could I know? I didn't see her face. What is this, Jamieson?"

"Yes, Jamieson," Dunbar growled. "What has that to do with my card game? Is this a scam to get you out of your debt? I gave you till sundown to pick up my marker."

"What the hell?" Kramer bellowed. "You friggin' capt'n licker! Stoppin' the game on his say-so when you've been just as bad."

The argument that ensued could be heard on deck. Jamieson knew he would lose everything if he didn't quiet it down before the captain got wind of it.

With amazing speed he caught the fireman by his collar, pulled him from the bench and held him against the bulkhead.

"The old man sent me looking for Logan," he shouted. "I ain't said I found him yet, have I? Just shut up! You help me and I'll help you. Dunbar, you're in on this. Logan, too. You loan me the money to pay off Dunbar, which I can repay you when I get my "passenger" safely to Bender's Landing. Do that and I'll just keep looking for *Mis-tah* Logan."

"How much?" Kramer asked, suspiciously.

"Forty bucks."

"*Jee-sus!*" Logan gasped. "That's a whole month's salary for you, Jamieson!"

"I ain't got but ten left," Kramer said quietly, "unless I win this pot."

Dunbar sat back, his gross red face filled with mirth. "From what you have revealed of your hand, my boy, you are not about to win. Admirable try, Daris, my boy. Admirable, but failing. As you can see, Logan is also down to about his last twelve to fourteen gold coins. The evening was about to come to a halt before your rude interruption. An interruption that Mr. Caldwell and I intend discussing with Captain Allard. Need I say more, Jamieson?"

Jamieson's thick torso trembled on legs that had suddenly gone soft. Everything was slipping away from him. He had to give it one more try.

"Bah! You would get me fired over a lousy forty bucks? I told you that I would make that much, if not more, in getting this girl to Bender's Landing. Can't you wait until then?"

"No," the gambler snarled.

Jerome Caldwell cleared his throat. He eyed Jamieson through the pince-nez with a naughty leer.

"Perhaps, sir, the girl could be of assistance in your plight *before* you receive your reward."

"I don't get your point." But Jamieson knew exactly what the fat old man was suggesting.

Caldwell lifted his huge head and looked at Jamieson with lecherous and passionate impudence.

"Don't be coy, sir. I'm well aware that all sailors are rogues. Did you not intend, on your own, to taste of her sweetness?"

"No! She is too young!"

"No woman is ever too young. What is your price for her?"

Jamieson did not like the man, but there are times when a man must act quickly on the idea of another. This scheme might be better than his original.

"Just a minute," Dunbar growled. "I am the one he owes money to and should have first crack if he is going to put her services on the line."

"Why?" Logan asked, so quietly it brought all eyes to focus on him. "Why must this little barter game be reduced to just you two? Perhaps Kramer and I might wish to get in on the auction."

Such a comment coming from Logan surprised them all. The boy looked like he would hardly know what the conversation was about.

"Nonsense," Caldwell chuckled. "Neither of you

have the capital to meet the debt. Besides, you both look as if you'd be better suited to each other."

Kramer was outraged. The insidious little man had openly put him in the class of men who had strange sexual desires. He fought to control his anger.

"You're wrong, mister. I learned early never to bring all my money to the gambling table. I've got enough to cover th gambling debt of Jamieson, but I ain't ever paid that much for a whore before."

"She's not a whore!" Jamieson insisted. Then he realized that Caldwell or Dunbar could possibly be the man she had not wanted to see on board. Hell, if either of them were, and won the right to be with her, he could still end up losing everything.

"No," he went on slowly, his mind racing, "she's better than that . . . too good for just one of you."

"Oh?" Dunbar said with a raised eyebrow. "What are you suggesting?"

"You each put ten into the pot, draw lots for your position, and that is that!"

"Good," roared Caldwell, who thought a quarter was better than none at all.

Dunbar grinned, thinking his turn would be free. He had never really hoped to collect from a dead-beat like Jamieson.

Logan looked pale, but oddly excited. One of his fantasies was about to come true.

Only the fireman took it all in stride. "Let's cut the cards. High, and then on down."

Only then did Daris Jamieson start to worry. He still had the odious task of preparing the girl for such acceptance.

"I would suggest," Dunbar said slowly as he shuf-fled the cards, "that we plan with a little caution. Midnight, I would say, is the proper hour. Until then life should go on as usual to avoid suspicion."

* * *

Elsa Jane tried in vain to hug warmth out of the thin blankets. She was still frightened of the rats, who had oddly stayed away from the poisoned wheat, but even more frightening was the prospect of staying alone. The hours of darkness seemed eternal and her stomach ached with hunger. The food Jamieson had brought was no more than an apple. She knew it was well past her bedtime but she dared not close her eyes. She cursed herself for having been such a fool to embark on this adventure. Then she cursed the sailor for having left her alone for so long.

Finally she heard footsteps echo through the hold. The oil lamps were burning low and, although she thought she had detected more than one footfall, only Jamieson unlocked the gate door and stepped inside. She could smell his corn liquor stench even at fifteen feet.

"Where have you been?" she pouted.

He mumbled a reply and busied himself with re-filling the lamps and trimming the wicks.

"Did you bring me anything to eat?"

Elsa Jane noticed the look of surprise on his face. "I forgot," he answered.

"Well, I'm starved. Can you still get me something?"

Jamieson leaned across the crate and whispered, scarcely moving his lips. "Later. First, you must do me a favor. There are some gentlemen immediately outside who wish to meet you. Each wishes a few moments of your pleasure. Grant them this and I'll bring all the food you desire."

Elsa Jane stood rigidly by the crate, her eyes staring at the blank wall of darkness beyond the cage. "Why would they want to meet me? What is this pleasure?"

"Don't be coy with me. You all but said that you

were running away from a man. It's that kind of manly pleasure they seek. They are all worked up over the thought of being with you, so it should be very quick for each."

"I don't understand."

Jamieson sidled around the crate with a suggestive swagger and blew hot, sour breath in Elsa Jane's face as he whispered, "Make it easy for all of us, little girl. Just take off your clothes and I'll bring them in one at a time."

Elsa Jane didn't know what he was talking about. The request to take off her clothing did not embarrass her, but she saw no reason for it.

A vicious cackle sounded from the darkness. Caldwell pressed his two-hundred-pound bulk through the doorway and into the pool of light. "By the ace that I drew, you're some looker. No wonder this drunken sailor wanted to plant his paws beneath your skirt."

"Will you just wait until I have her ready?" Jamieson snapped through his foggy haze.

Caldwell nodded his head slightly but never took his eyes off Elsa Jane.

"You do not seem to be making much progress, sailor."

"What would you have me do?" he asked challengingly.

"Undress her yourself," the shaking fat man replied, moving to unbutton his trouser flap.

"But . . . but . . . ," Jamieson blurted, unsure of what he really wanted to answer.

"Coward," yelled Charles Dunbar, stepping into the cage, "you are wasting our time!"

"What is going on?" Elsa Jane asked incredulously.

"Shut up!" the giant gambler who had stood in the background boomed with a barrel bass voice.

"And this is really misrepresentation of the first order. I doubt that she is strong enough to get pumped
four times."

Jamieson took Elsa Jane's arm and pulled her into
the brighter circle of light. The remaining two men
raced into the cage like dogs nipping at the heels of
a bitch in heat.

"No, I'll do it!" Jamieson bellowed. He moved to
the girl quickly and shoved the gambler aside. De-
murely he took the poke-bonnet from her head and
prayed that she would give him no trouble.

Elsa Jane stood stiffly, still unsure of his intent.
Then with an apprehensive glance over his shoulder,
Jamieson made a dive for her skirt hem and started
to lift it to her waist.

"What . . . ?" Elsa Jane gasped, but steely hands
grabbed her wrists from behind before she could
finish.

Dunbar's touch was rough. He pulled her arms
over her head and held them firmly. Jamieson had
the thin dress up to her shoulders and covering her
head when she realized her danger.

Her arms were useless but she screamed in protest and kicked wildly with her high-button shoes.

"Bitch!" Jamieson growled, as his shin exploded
with pain. He continued pulling the dress over her
head but to no avail. Elsa Jane twisted and turned
in hopes of escape.

She raised a knee and caught Jamieson directly
in the groin. His drunken rage turned to fury. He
clawed her petticoats down to her ankles to subdue
the kicking legs, and Dunbar, locking her wrists together in a single bear paw, tore away the remaining
tatters of flour-sack cloth. All that remained were the
chemise and the long black cotton stockings.

When she could not move, the stocking material

was inched down her shapely young legs in the flickering lamp light. This was done slowly so that each set of bulging eyes had an opportunity to send a message of excitement to the brain and then back to the growing members between the men's legs.

Elsa Jane whimpered and cried. Jamieson struck her so hard across the face that she staggered and kept her balance only because of the grip Dunbar still had on her arms. Jamieson's hand slid under his turtleneck sweater and suddenly there was a flash of steel.

"Put that damn knife away," Dunbar cried.

Jamieson ignored him and spun Elsa Jane around, pulling her free from Dunbar's grasp. With a single upward thrust he severed the chemise lacing from buttocks to shoulder blade. It slowly fell away from her coned young breasts, quivering belly and virginal forest of pubic hair. For a moment all was quiet.

"Me first! Me first!" Caldwell cackled as he started to denude himself. The other three were quick to follow suit.

Jamieson toted the clawing, scratching, screaming Elsa Jane over to the crates and, with one mighty effort, flung her onto the top of one.

She squatted on her haunches, stunned and mystified. She hoped he was putting her out of harm's way, but she could only glare with dismay at his next move.

Without seeking the others' consent, Jamieson tugged other crates and piled them around hers. Like a stage manager with props, he brought two to the side and a taller one to the back.

The completely nude quartet came to gawk.

"What is this?" Caldwell squeaked. The man looked ridiculous with nothing on his rolling pink flesh but his nose-nippers. "Bring her down to me!"

Jamieson shrugged his shoulders. "New rules, gentlemen. We may get but a single chance with her,
so we'll take it all at once. Caldwell, up on the crate
for the front. Dunbar, you may go up to taste of the
rear, and you two may use those side crates to expose yourselves to her hands."

"And what of the top crate?"

Jamieson's voice trembled as he answered—trembled with anger and pent-up jealousy at having to
share this prize. "The top crate is for me! I will sit
and enjoy the only portal left open to me. If she is
capable, we can switch around. Besides, we need her
mouth busy so that she can't scream and arouse the
night-watch."

The four other men mumbled but quickly accepted
his decision. They scrambled to their positions. For
a moment they hesitated, for they had seen what a
little hellcat she had been with Jamieson.

Reason told her to fight back; madness urged calmness against such odds.

Jamieson climbed to the higher crate and dangled
his long legs over the side. He barked orders for
Elsa Jane to be turned about for the positioning of
the bulky Caldwell and Dunbar.

Their corpulent bodies touched hers as they moved
about like two figures on top of a music box. She had
never before seen an unclad male body, but because
of their girth their real manliness was hidden from
view by rolling layers of fat. The sight so amused
Kramer that the fireman began to giggle. Elsa Jane
looked at him.

She openly gaped at the gorilla-like hair that covered his chest, waist and brawny legs. Then her eyes
riveted on the strange projectile between his legs,
and a long forgotten memory came flooding back.

The "darky" children had once made reference as

to how these "projectiles" were used. At the time
Elsa Jane had put it out of her mind, believing that
it was a practice used only by slave men and women.
Now her instincts warned her that somehow all five
of these strange white projectiles were to be used on
her in a like manner. Terrified, she reared back her
head and erupted with a piercing wail, stomped up
and down in her stocking- and shoe-clad feet and
thrashed about wildly.

The old crate was unable to withstand her actions
and weight as well as that of the two large men.
Without any warning, it collapsed with a single ex-
plosive crash. The two men toppled over onto the
crates bearing Kramer and Logan, who screamed and
cursed, fearful that their own crates would collapse
as well.

Elsa Jane had fallen unhurt onto the straw packing
at the bottom of the wooden box. She struggled to
get to her feet, thought better of it, and curled into
a ball, praying she would be out of reach of her
captors' hands.

Cursing, Jamieson rolled onto his belly, stretched
his arms down and shouted for her to grab them.
She curled her arms even tighter about her knees.

The other four men clamored for a position on the
side crates to peer down into her wooden pit. They
shouted and cursed in complete confusion.

Jamieson made an effort to rise, then rolled himself
quickly off the back of the crate. A cold sweat crawled
up his spine. Slowly he raised himself to his hands
and knees and crawled around the darker side of
the crate. Someone had heard all the noise.

The swinging bosun lamp cautiously approached
the cage from the far hold ladder. Jamieson prayed
he had not been seen and stayed close to the deck
until he was near the gate door. Then he scrambled

to his feet and made a dart for the shielding darkness.

He had forgotten that his trousers were pushed
down to his buttocks, and as they fell to his knees
he tumbled back to the deck with a crash.

The bearer of the bosun's lamp now broke into a
run. Jamieson rolled away from his approach, tug-
ging at his trousers. Then, just as the lamplight
reached him, he stretched out his long legs and
tripped the running legs. The night-watch crewman
somersaulted over him, and the bosun's lamp crashed
on the deck. Jamieson stood up and slammed his
boot into the crewman's face.

The broken lamp oozed oil and fingers of flame
across the dry wooden hold deck. In seconds the boat
could turn into a flaming nightmare. Someone had
to act fast.

Peter Forest grabbed the stocking cap from his
head and rolled toward the rising flames. In their
illumination he thought he recognized the back of
a departing crewman, but there was no time to go
after him. He beat the flaming tongues until he had
them confined to the small area around the broken
lamp. Then he covered the brass and glass rectangle
with his cap and smothered the remaining flames with
his hands.

Before he moved he let his hands roam over the
charred wooden planks to make sure there were no
live embers. Once assured, he turned his attention to
the lamp-lit cage.

For six years Peter Forest had been on the river,
rising from cabin boy to waiter to deck hand to
pilot, and he had never seen anything to equal the
four bare butts of various sizes, shapes and ugliness.
He automatically assumed that this was some weird
version of the sailor "in the barrel" act, something he

never dreamed would be attempted aboard a boat commanded by Captain Amos Allard.

Forest gulped for breath as he sought the words of disgust he wanted to shout.

"Cover yourselves!" was all he could muster as he rose to his feet.

He watched the four nude bodies stumble down from the crates, rush for their clothing and try to hide their faces. He made no effort to move toward them, but used those fleeting seconds to try and recognize faces. He was successful with two. Lawrence Logan's face was a pale mask of guilty trauma, and the passenger Caldwell was given away by his pince-nez.

Although Peter was unable to see the faces of the two others in the lecherous quartet, he was able to detect their identities. He had often seen the fire-man stripped to his waist in the boiler room. No other man on board was as hairy as Kramer. And no other man on board reeked of scented pomade for his sleek hair like the gambler Dunbar.

Peter would keep all such knowledge for the ears of Captain Allard. His present duty was to see about the poor fool of a sailor who had been confined with-in the crate, whether by force or submission.

He climbed up on to the lowest crate and peered down into the darkness. He could see nothing.

"Come out of there!" he commanded harshly.

There was no reply. He leaned over the rim and searched with his hands.

"Come out of there!" he repeated. "They have all gone."

Still there was no reply but he could hear someone breathing. To Peter, the refusal meant only one thing —the culprit was there of his own free will and didn't want to get caught or be recognized. The

thought angered and disgusted the young riverboat
pilot. He put his shoulder against the rough edge of
the packing crate and pushed. The box turned over,
spilling its contents, and from the lampless side of
the cage came a shrill frightened voice.

"Get away from me!"

Peter Forest blanched. It was the voice of a child.
He jumped down and picked up the balled figure.
It was impossible to tell whether it was a boy or girl,
as she had straw matted in her hair and was still
curled in the fetal position. She hammered blindly at
his face with considerable force but Peter paid no
attention to the blows as he strode around the toppled crates looking for the oil lamp. He put her down
and lifted her chin to the light to study the pinched
and frightened face. Elsa Jane kept her eyes screwed
up tight. The mass of spiral curls could have only
belonged to a girl—but no girl child like that had
been brought aboard for this trip.

"Oh, God," he whispered, thinking of Logan's involvement, "are you a stowaway?"

Elsa Jane stared at him with her round green eyes.

"Are you a stowaway?" he repeated. "Or do you
have folks aboard?"

She shook her head.

"How far to Bender's Landing?" she asked calmly.

"Almost three days."

She studied him with grave eyes. He didn't look
like the others. His sandy hair was already thinning,
his face was simple and common, and his body was
small-boned, although wiry and muscular.

"Are you like the others?" she asked simply.

Forest gasped and dropped down beside her.

"No," he grinned, "I'm not. Why?"

"Your trousers. Even with them on I can see you
got a thing like they did."

Peter blushed scarlet. His knowledge of women was almost as limited as her knowledge of men. Since putting her down into the lamplight he had been very much aware of her nudity, and nature had taken over. He rose and spun about, frantically looking for something to cover her with. He saw the blankets and raced for them.

"Here," he said nervously, tossing them over his shoulder, "cover yourself."

"They ripped off my dress," she cried suddenly, unexpectedly. "Then they pulled down my petticoats and used a knife on my chemise."

"Oh, my God!" Peter whispered. "Don't think on it. I will get you to a cabin and then you can tell the whole sordid story to the captain."

She was then silent for so long that he was finally forced to turn. Rivers of tears streamed down her cheeks. Although her mouth was open, she uttered no sound. Beneath the blanket her body trembled violently.

The sight was not new to him. Twice in his river experience, boilers had exploded and burned the paddle-wheelers. He had seen many such blanket-wrapped survivors in the state of shock.

"All right," he said despairingly, "so you are a stowaway. Forget the captain. First, let me get you safely to my cabin and then we will figure out what to do with you."

2

ONCE WITHIN the safety of Peter's cabin walls, the nightmare of Elsa Jane's experience became a reality. She kicked and screamed out her hysteria. Peter was, for the first time, glad that his cabin was right over the boiler room and far removed from passenger and crew.

He ignored her screaming and left on unstated errands. He knew there was nothing more he could do, but being locked within a cabin was no different to Elsa Jane than being locked within the cage, and her tears flowed so freely that she nearly exhausted herself.

When he returned, she imagined him as a Daris Jamieson. She didn't understand the effort Peter had gone through to secure clothing and food for her. She didn't know that he had had to rummage through the forward hold luggage like a thief to find something feminine and near her size. Getting food from the galley had been almost as difficult, as any leftover passenger food usually became mixed slop for the crew's next meal. Wordlessly, he gave her the bundle of clothing and tray of food. He left again so she could dress privately. His consideration puzzled Elsa Jane. This was no aloof Calvin Bender or rule-issuing priest. This man was gentle, soft-spoken and considerate—elements she was not aware that men possessed.

She doggedly fed and dressed herself, then waited. The waiting stretched until a gray dawn streaked the cabin porthole.

A knock at the cabin door roused Elsa Jane from her brooding. She winced helplessly in fear that it might be Jamieson. As the door opened, she drew the blanket up to her neck and dropped it only when she saw that it was Peter Forest.

Peter smiled wearily at her.

"I didn't want to wake you," he said timidly, almost apologetically, "in case you might have been sleeping. I'm just off the night watch."

"You might have told me," she pouted, "that you would be gone the whole night."

Peter brushed the morning dew off his slicker and came into the dingy crew cabin.

"Didn't you sleep?" he asked.

"No," she said sadly, "not a wink."

"I'm sorry. The way you were, I thought it best to just leave you by yourself. Do you wish, yet, to discuss how you got on board?"

"No," she answered fervently. The tears sprang to her eyes again.

"I see."

She noticed that he seemed slightly awkward, as if wondering what to do next.

"You been out there all night?"

"Yes. It's my job. The cabin boy will be here in a moment with hot coffee."

Her eyes flared in alarm. "He will see me!"

"No," Peter said soothingly, removing the slicker. "He knocks and leaves the tray outside the door."

"I can't take your coffee from you. You look cold enough to need every drop for yourself."

Peter chuckled and smiled. His expression brought a soft handsomeness to his otherwise stern and common face.

"For the night watch he always leaves a double ration of coffee, bisquits and cheese. There will be ample, I assure you."

Elsa Jane studied the sailor closely. He hardly seemed the same man who had rescued her the night before. Still, she did not fully trust anyone on that vessel, and hid when the cabin boy knocked.

She downed her coffee almost at a gulp, and consumed more than her share of bisquits and cheese.

"Didn't he feed you in the hold?"

"No, except for a tin of soup and heel of bread after we left New Orleans. Nothing since. Who *is* he?"

"You don't know?" Peter gasped. "You don't know the name of the man who stowed you away down there?"

"No," she shrugged. "It just never came up."

It was incomprehensible to the pilot. He had purposely not reported anything to Captain Allard until he could question the girl, and now he found she could not even give the captors' names.

"And the other men? You knew none of them?"

"No. None." Her slim body shivered.

Peter walked slowly over to where she sat on his bunk, and gently put an arm around her shoulders.

"It's alright, miss. I've just got all the questions out of order. First, I'm Peter Forest. Now, what is your name?"

She looked up. Then very slowly she pulled herself erect.

"Elsa Jane," she whispered. "Elsa Jane Bender. You're not going to put me off the boat, are you?" She sobbed against his arm.

"Hush," Peter crooned. "Hush and be still. I just want to learn how I can help you out of this whole situation which you seem to have gotten . . ."

"It was horrible," Elsa Jane said brokenly. "At least it seemed that way. Do all men act like that? Do they all have those things? Do they really stick them into girls somewhere?"

"Enough of that," Forest said, his own embarrassment returning. "You should forget about—"

"No," Elsa Jane said sternly, "I can never forget about it. Could you forget about it?"

Forest looked at her.

"I said forget it, Miss Bender," he said with gentle dignity. "It is not a proper topic between a young man and a young woman most recently met—no matter the circumstances!"

"Why?"

Peter sighed. "How old are you really, Miss Bender?"

"Twelve."

He cringed. He had thought her to be at least fourteen or fifteen.

"All the more reason not to discuss it," he said, sidestepping the issue.

A question formed again on her lips, but he held up his hand to ward it off.

"Please. It has been a very long night for both of us. I am tired and need some sleep. My duties require eight hours on and four hours off. That's really not much sleep."

"Four hours!" Elsa Jane was shocked. "At the convent school we were made to sleep from sundown to sunup—twelve hours, more or less."

"Lucky you," he grinned. "And a thread to your past. I take it the school was in New Orleans."

Elsa Jane slowly looked up. Her eyes pleaded for understanding.

"You won't send me back?"

Peter laughed openly. "How can I send you back, when I don't know where you are from or where you are going?"

"I think I like you," she said happily.

"Thank you, Miss Bender."

"Call me Elsa Jane. Calling me Miss makes me sound like my stuffy old governess. She had to be a hundred, if she was a day."

"All right, Elsa Jane," he laughed, "but only if you call me Peter."

"I like that. Peter was the rock that the church was founded upon, and I guess you are the rock that I found to cling to in my darkest hour of need." She giggled. "At least that old crate was dark after I fell into it."

"How," he asked, hesitantly, "did you get yourself into this pickle?"

The question startled her. She was not accustomed to being allowed to express herself.

"Do you really want me to tell you?"

Forest nodded grimly. "I'm waiting," he said.

Peter Forest sat enchanted and enthralled as Elsa Jane described her life. How similar, he kept thinking, their earthly experiences had been. He had been raised by a stern Quaker aunt in Ohio. His only youthful love had been the gently flowing Ohio River. Elsa Jane longed to get home; he had longed to get away from home. His wish was granted when his aunt had indentured him to a barge owner for a trip down the Ohio to the Mississippi.

Elsa Jane talked of the smells of the river; he had lived with the smells and loved them all. She didn't know men and he didn't know women, except in the secret reaches of his shy and sensitive heart. His secret desires were few and simple—to be the best river pilot on the Mississippi, and to someday have a wife and children he could love as deeply as he did the river.

"Wow!" Elsa Jane said a few hours later. "I don't think I've talked this much in my life."

"Don't stop," he whispered. "I could listen to you the whole night through."

Elsa Jane laughed naturally and comfortably. "Don't you mean the whole *day* through? You worked the night, remember?"

"I don't care. You have been far more restful to me than any few hours of sleep. Naturally, as I have said over and over, I will see you safely home. But I still wish revenge, in your name, against those bounders. Was the name Jamieson mentioned at all?"

She shrugged and shook her head.

"Pity," he said. "He is really a lowlife and I'm sure he was involved."

"Is he the type of man who would do those sorts of things to young girls?"

"Elsa Jane, please!" he gasped. "Must you continually keep coming back to that subject?"

"I guess so," she said innocently, "because I'm not aware of what is wrong with the subject. Is it like being illegitimate?"

"Well . . ." he gulped, turning red all the way up into his thinning hairline. "I . . . ah . . ."

The door of his cabin crashed open, forestalling his answer but not diminishing his embarrassment.

Amos Allard's face was an Armageddon of his emotions. Disgust battled with hurt pride. Hurt pride ranked supreme.

He clawed at his square beard and stalked to the center of the cabin. He quivered with a horrible fury.

"Infamy, Mis-tah Forest! My most trusted officer stabs me in the back with infidelity. Oh, what mortal shame!"

"Please, sir, you do not understand," Peter stammered.

" 'Understand,' he says! You forget where you are, Forest! This is my boat! My command! My eyes are seeing you sully them with a harlot in your cabin! Beached, sir. You are beached forthwith and without salary or pension!"

The pilot stood speechless. Elsa Jane knew that she had never heard words more dreadful. In those few hours Peter Forest had become her first human friend. Loyalty made her rise to his defense.

She moved from the bunk in a slow and graceful manner, extending her hand as she rose. She tried to sound mature.

"Captain, we have met before. I am Calvin Bender's niece, Elsa Jane."

Amos Allard paled. This was even worse than he had anticipated. He could not afford to lose Bender's Landing as a fueling stop.

"How? Why?" he demanded.

"She is my intended," Peter quickly blurted.

The lie was so obvious that Allard ignored it and

kept his steely gaze on the pretty young face of Elsa Jane Bender.

"I don't know what that fully means," she said cheerfully, "but Peter is not at fault, sir. May I explain what has happened?"

She could see the beads of sweat on the captain's forehead. His fingers nearly ripped his beard out by the roots, but he nodded.

The captain seemed to be an odd combination of Mattie Goldunk and Sister Martha Mary. Elsa Jane noted this and kept her narrative short, to the point, and with enough proper details to forestall any further questioning.

Allard looked as though he would double over in agony. It was a severe blow to his vanity that this could happen aboard his vessel. He turned to Peter.

"And you," he asked in a thin squeak, "were aware of this?"

Forest gulped. "I have been gathering her side of the story, sir. I'm sure that I can single out the quartet of men, but I only have a suspicion about the ringleader who brought her aboard."

"Then," he wheezed, "am I to assume that you have just lied to me, sir? Did you not call her your intended?"

Forest blushed crimson red. "It was no lie," he said quietly, "although it may sound somewhat strange. In these few short hours I have come to realize that I shall desire no other woman as the mother of my children. The subject has not been broached to her, sir, but that is the feeling of my heart."

Then, with a slow grin spreading across his face, Amos Allard thought of a way to save his riverboat from apparent scandal and disgrace.

"Man is born of woman," he intoned, "to cleave unto woman. Come, Forest, we have work to do on this matter. Miss Bender, pray rest. I shall have the cabin boy bring you an ample breakfast . . . to help make up for your ordeal." He grinned once more.

"Now what is this all about?" Elsa Jane asked herself as the cabin door closed and she was left alone again. "What does intended mean?"

Of course Amos Allard had the right to prosecute all of the men. In the middle of the nineteenth century a riverboat was a kingdom unto itself. However, since God and the law were on the side of Amos Allard, he would use fright and not prosecution to win his point. Under ordinary circumstances, he would have beached Jamieson and hired a new man. But what then? Jamieson would spread the story, and he, Amos Allard, would lose his reputation. Even the hint that such a thing could have happened upon his vessel would be damaging to his company as more and more women and children were becoming his passengers and their men demanded safety and protection for them.

Kramer, after all, wanted to be cooperative. In fact, Kramer needed to be cooperative to keep his job— so much so that he told the whole story quite truthfully and took upon himself what blame was due him.

He decided to be conciliatory toward his nephew for the time being. Later, when Logan felt he had redeemed himself, he would strike. Amos Allard was determined to make Lawrence Logan God-fearing. Back in St. Louis he knew a shy, if not pretty young lass who would make Logan an excellent wife— whether he liked it or not.

"Charley the Ace" Dunbar was the easiest to take

care of. He was given strict orders to disembark at the noon fueling stop and to never again board a vessel under the command of Amos Allard.

The next culprit would receive an entirely different kind of punishment. Mr. and Mrs. Jerome Caldwell were luncheon guests at the captain's table. Conversation centered around the freighting of the Caldwell Lumber Company material, but the corpulent businessman was well aware that the captain knew every detail of the preceding night. He did not want the equally corpulent Melanie Caldwell learning of his perversities. After all, the hardwood lumber company may have borne his name, but it was her family's money that kept it operational.

"Well, Amos," Caldwell cackled, "I have to admit you've got me. All right, I'll tell you my decision. Give me decent rates and I'll forget about our haggling over this last night. I'll ship exclusively with your company's steamers."

Melanie leaned forward, her piggy little eyes bright and eager. The decision was exactly what her father had advised Jerome to do for years. She would be eternally grateful to Amos Allard for making her husband see the light.

Only one problem remained—Daris Jamieson.

"Sorry, Captain Allard," he said quietly. "I'd like to oblige you, but I can't."

"You—you can't?" Allard gasped. "How can you refuse to tell me everything when I have the evidence from the others?"

Jamieson turned an amazed face toward the fuming captain. "Sir, it is just their word against mine. For one reason or another, they all have it in for me."

"Look, Jamieson, I am saving your neck from that gambler. Remember, he still does not have his forty dollars, and for that alone I could beach you with a snap of my fingers." Amos looked at the crewman and smiled gently as he continued. "And from what I hear, you were doing the girl a service by helping her get to Bender's Landing—although Bishop Landry might see it in a different light."

"Oh," Jamieson murmured, "so that's the man she didn't want to see her on board."

It was a thread of information Allard had not heard before, but he would find use for it to further safeguard the good name of his steamer.

"Wrong! The man she did not want to see her aboard was her intended."

"Intended? What are you talking about? How could she have an intended at her age?"

"Come, come, Jamieson," Allard grinned. "Age has nothing to do with it when a family intends a girl for marriage to the son of another family. Luckily for you, nothing happened to the girl to ruin her."

"I told you," Jamieson spluttered, "I had nothing to do with what you say went on last night."

"As you keep saying," Allard agreed, "so the girl's decision about last night should be a great relief to you."

"What decision?" he asked suspiciously.

"She and her intended shall be married by me forthwith."

"You thief!" Jamieson shouted. "You robber! If she's a married woman, how can I claim the reward from her uncle for seeing her safely home?"

"Exactly my point, Jamieson. This stowaway will turn out to be a blessing and not a disgrace."

Daris Jamieson fingered the brim of his work cap and glanced uneasily at the captain. By the sheerest luck he was being set free from his debt to Dunbar, but he was not about to have his reward from Calvin Bender denied him.

"Who is her intended?" he demanded.

"I am sorry, Jamieson, but I don't think that information is any of your business."

"I'll make it my business," Jamieson threatened. "If Calvin Bender doesn't owe me something, then that man does."

Allard frowned. Then his face cleared.

"You might, for your own sake, look at it in a different light. Her intended might just break your evil neck for what almost happened to her in the hold. Think on that!" he warned as he strode through the door.

Jamieson stood in the wheelhouse thinking. He never once suspected that the pilot who had been present at the discussion knew everything. Pilots were no more than an extension of the wheel they manned —unseen and unheard from.

He might have thought quite differently if he had noticed the rapture on Peter's face, but he was too busy thinking up a new scheme.

Jamieson would not be denied his due. He would find out who the intended man was and make sure he never left the steamer at Bender's Landing. Then he would go to Calvin Bender as planned, but he would present himself as the man who had saved Elsa Jane from the depraved quartet and demand such a reward that it would be possible for him never to return to Captain Allard's boat.

Captain Amos Allard made his rounds just before sunset. With his thick black Bible in hand and his square beard neatly brushed, he visited the sick girl and prayed over her with Bishop Landry. He stopped to say the blessing in the crew's mess quarters. He conducted a ten-minute prayer meeting for the ladies on the foreward deck, and then he went to look in on his pilot who had taken ill during the later part of the afternoon.

The cabin boy was coming down the passageway just as the captain arrived at Peter's cabin. It was not by accident that this young boy was serving the meal. He was yet another nephew and could be trusted. Amos Allard never did anything by accident.

"Well, my boy," Allard grinned, "as we discussed earlier, your last day as a cabin boy, eh? You'll make a fine waiter, I am sure. Now remember, no mention of this to anyone."

Paul Allard did not need to be reminded. If his uncle said to jump overboard he would have jumped without question. He was a bumbling fool who had been stuck as a cabin boy for five years. He would not mess up this opportunity.

Captain Allard opened the door and ushered the boy in. Having preened himself, he then followed. He wanted this over and forgotten as quickly as possible. Paul would serve as an excellent silent witness to the marriage.

The illness of Peter Forest had been a ruse, but just in case Jamieson came to his cabin during the late afternoon, he took his vows in his dressing gown and slippers. Elsa Jane stood dazed by his side.

Peter had tried to explain marriage to her, but it was still alien to her. Fearful that she would refuse to go through with the service, he explained that it was simply a means of safeguarding her until they reached Bender's Landing.

The ceremony was over as quickly as Captain Allard had wished.

When it was over Elsa Jane looked out the port-hole.

"You sure he won't find me here?"

"Quite. That's why Captain Allard had me pretend to be sick. No one will disturb us. We are quite alone."

"For the night? How will we sleep?"

"Together. That's another thing that marriage means. We can sleep together."

"In what?"

He wanted to say "in nothing," but was too shy. "I've put out an extra nightshirt. I'll turn my back when you are ready to undress."

The young bride sat down on the bed and extended her feet. "Will you help me with the buttons? I don't have a hook."

His hands upon the pearl circles turned clumsy and stiff. Finally he drew them off and she stood in her stocking feet. They were so close that he trembled.

Quickly he put his hands on her shoulders and began to kiss her softly, barely touching his lips to hers.

"Oh," she sighed, her eyes bright, "now I know what Helen Tregent meant by being kissed by a boy. It sounded horrible to me then. I think I like it. But . . ."

"But what?"

"Claudia Delaney says that it makes babies. Does it?"

Suddenly, convulsively, he pulled her into his arms and his soft kisses became more intense and insistent. She broke his grip.

"Well? Does it?"

"No, it doesn't." Then he was silent for a long moment. My wedding night, he thought, my wedding night! How am I to explain things that I hardly know about? He suddenly, softly, began to laugh.

"What those men wanted to do to you last night makes babies. But doing it last night was wrong. You only do that to make babies when you are married."

"You mean we can do that because the captain says we are married?"

"Yes," he gulped.

She thought a long moment. "Well, I don't think I want to do it married or not. I like the kissing better."

He decided not to explain further.

"Do you want to kiss some more?"

She shrugged. "I liked it. It made me feel tingly all over."

"They say that kissing is even better when you are lying down in bed."

"Don't you know?"

"Elsa Jane, honestly, you are the first girl that I have ever kissed or been alone with in my life."

She looked at him, her eyes widening in her pretty face. "Then you've never done that other thing . . . with your thing?"

"Never."

"Then how do you know about it?"

"Oh, God, you can really embarrass a guy sometimes, Elsa Jane. I know because when I was about your age my father sat me down and had a long talk with me about girls and marriage and the rights and wrongs of it all. If you had a mother she would be telling you near the same thing about now. You don't have a mother, but you do now have a husband. Me."

Elsa Jane heard his words, but they made no sense. Her world had been too confined and confused. Harvey Harrison had been her mother's husband, so it just didn't add up. But the kissing she had liked— a lot.

"Alright, let's try the kissing lying down. Turn your back and I'll get into your nightshirt."

Peter's heart swelled. He had won a battle, if not the war. When he turned around she was on the bunk with her hair spread out over her shoulders like coiled springs.

"We will have to find you a hairbrush."

"Yes," she agreed. "I want to brush out all these stupid curls and let it flow free. Never again do I want to stand for an hour with tears in my eyes while some nun pulls and tugs and brushes them around her finger."

Peter crawled in beside her. "You are free from that," he whispered. "Soon you will learn how free you are from many things."

He kissed her again. This time there was a response. She was learning rapidly. She nestled into his arms and drew him close.

He trembled. "This may sound strange to you, but I do so love you dearly, even in this short time. I hope you can love me some day."

"That doesn't sound strange, Peter, except . . . What is love, really?"

He propped up his elbow and rested his cheek in the cup of his hand. What a wonderful sight, he thought. Beautiful and pure and so innocent. He prayed for her to always stay the same.

"I really don't know if my idea of love is the same as other people's, but it's that warmth in your heart when you are with someone or something. Early in life I had the love of a mother and father. When they died I thought my world had come to an end. Then I found the river and it became my love."

"Oh," she beamed, "now I understand. It's like my forests and animals. When I am with them it's like my heart has music in it. I can run and run and run and still not get enough of them or their beauty. I wasn't aware one could have the same feeling for people."

Peter nearly wept. He scooped her back up into his arms, cradled her close, and made his kisses loving, tender expressions of what he felt in his heart.

All his life Peter had deeply wanted this pleasure. It was also true that he had never known a woman, and he was sure that she too was still virginal. However, she was as curious as a roué's daughter. He had expected denial, shyness, timidity. But as his kisses became more intimate, and he began to explore her body with his shaking hands, she followed suit. Her curiosity led to further embarrassing questions until suddenly, unexpectedly, the questions were no longer embarrassing and he was able to answer freely. They were children sharing, experiencing, and learning together.

Forewarning her that there would be pain, he entered her. He was so gentle, so loving, that the friction became intoxicating. There was such enjoyment and such emotion that for the first time Elsa Jane knew love.

The warm tingle that had started in the pit of her stomach had grown to a flaming canvas stretching over all her body. She felt like a new person as the hot sensations consumed her every thought.

She heard herself give a low scream. Her passions had ignited, exploding throughout her groin. She felt faint, but wanted to continue. She wanted to feel the explosions again and again and again.

They lay silent, his wet hair sticking to her cheek as they regained their strength.

"Would last night have been like this, Peter?"

"No, it would have been lust without love."

"I see," she said slowly, "and marriage is lust with love?"

Peter laughed and rolled over on his back. "That is a most apt description—lust with love."

She kissed him gently on the cheek.

"Then I think I love you, Peter Forest."

He laughed again. "Why do you say that now but not before."

"Because before I didn't know how much it would hurt me to lose you. I would get as homesick for you as I do for the island and the animals. It's nice to be able to love a person that way."

Peter turned away to shed silent tears of gratitude.

"Are you sleeping?"

"No. Why?"

She was as playful as a kitten, and during the rest of the night they tasted many of the fruits of marriage.

Peter Forest remained "ill" until he was needed to pilot the steamer through the difficult shoals of Bender's Landing.

Early that morning he had quietly left their bed. He did not have the heart to wake his sleeping beauty, nor could he find the strength to say good-bye. He had tried many times the night before, but Elsa Jane wouldn't listen. She only wanted to make love.

Finally, the floating hotel inched toward the island and the long wooden wharf. Peter had seen the landing a hundred times, and yet he seemed to be looking at it for the first time. It was beautiful, just as Elsa Jane had described. The wharf-side warehouses, now empty, could hold thousands of bales of cotton of the finest quality. At various times of the season crates of tomatoes, squash, pole beans, yams and black-eyed peas would be stacked for consumption in the river-boat dining rooms. Bender-smoked hams and chickens by the hundreds were favorites of the galley chefs. It was like a rich fairy-tale kingdom, with a three-story white colonial southern mansion instead of a castle.

What did he possibly have to offer her to compare with all of this? It would all be hers someday—the entire island and its eight hundred slaves. They alone represented more money than he could make in a lifetime.

No, he didn't have the right to deny her all of this, now or ever. He would never be more than a river pilot, and that he well knew.

"All secured and ready for disembarking, Captain Allard."

"And as smooth a landing as usual, Mis-tah Forest. Call down for a banking of the boiler and prepare to take on cargo and fuel, Mis-tah Logan."

"Aye, aye, sir. Is Mr. Jamieson to see to the wood purchase as usual, sir?"

"Why, of course, of course. See to it." Allard lowered his voice. "Are you prepared to go ashore and break the news to Calvin Bender?"

Peter lowered his eyes. "Sir, how can I equal what she would have here?"

"With love," Captain Allard answered simply.

Reluctantly, Peter left the bridge and went down to his cabin. He fully expected to find it empty.

Jamieson usually needed a direct order from Captain Allard to make the Bender's Landing purchase. Jamieson hated the business, as he had to deal with Moses Larder, an educated black man. A trip never passed that Jamieson didn't feel like a fool. He was sure the lumbering black man somehow cheated him and then laughed behind his back.

But this trip was different. Daris Jamieson was the first down the gangplank, eager to find Moses Larder.

Moses already had twelve wood loaders lined along the wharf and was ready to heft the heavy log. bundles on board. He always had them ready, and knew exactly how many each vessel would require. Young men on the river often made bets on his accuracy. The older men knew better. Many thought he used voodoo when making his calculations, but Moses knew better.

His system was so simple that it amazed him that the rivermen didn't figure it out. It infuriated Jamieson.

"Morn', Mass'ah Jam'son."

Jamieson grunted.

"Figure ya'all be needin' five cord ta Na'chez."

"Fine," Jamieson nodded, "get them started."

Moses blinked. Normally he would have to fight this arrogant man tooth and nail over every log. "Must be trouble aboard the *River Queen*," he thought, but he saw no signs of it.

Captain Amos Allard came down the gangway laughing at something Bishop Landry had said. They climbed into the landau and rode to the main house.

Jamieson took note of this and frowned. Where was the girl? What game was Allard up to at his expense?

"Moses, you been here some little time?"

"Yassah. Since I be sixteen."

"Nice place. I expect the Bender family really enjoys living here."

" 'Spect so, sah."

"Never could figure out rich folk. Why would a man like Mr. Bender send his daughter all the way down to New Orleans to go to school?"

"Didn't," Moses said flatly.

"Come on, Moses, don't lie to me. I've met her."

Moses Larder's expression did not change.

"Don't see how, sah. Massah Calvin ain't got no daughter."

"And don't give me that horse pucky! She's about twelve years old and is called Elsa Jane."

The woodman smiled. He didn't know the reasons for such questions and didn't want to know. Like all good slaves he did not involve himself in family matters.

"Ain't got no such daughter," he lied. "Him's a bachelor man."

Jamieson gave him a threatening look. "Are you sure you're not mistaken?"

Moses shrugged. "Sah, I'm here mos' forty year. My own Mammy done diaper Massah Calvin. Ah should know he ain't got no woman of 'is own—or daughter to go wid it."

"Damn me for being a lame-brain. Uncle! That's what she kept saying! So much has been happening that I just got rattled. Elsa Jane is Calvin Bender's niece. Right?"

The man was an outsider asking personal questions about his master. Elsa Jane's parentage was a family matter that the slaves were not allowed to discuss. "Wrong!" he said firmly. "Ah don't know where y'all hear dis, Massah Jam'son, but Ole Moses don't know nothin' 'bout it."

Jamieson fumed. He should have known better than to question the black man. It simply confirmed his belief that they were stupid.

"Where's Bender?" he growled. "I'll put it direct to him."

"Up the river at St. Louie," Moses replied evenly, but it was another lie. Calvin Bender was on the other side of the island *querling* with Helen Harrison.

"Then why did the captain and padre go up to the house?"

"Tah eat," Moses answered.

Daris Jamieson was beyond speech. He had been hoodwinked. Moses had not lied to him, but the girl and Captain Allard had. He was not a man to be treated this way. He was determined to get his due one way or another!

When the captain returned with Bishop Landry an hour later, Jamieson was still at the foot of the gangway. The old priest was chattering, but Captain Allard seemed preoccupied.

He, too, had been bothered by the absence of Calvin Bender. He considered it his duty to inform the man of his daughter's marriage. Unwittingly Bishop Landry had confused the issue by reporting his meeting with Elsa Jane in New Orleans to the housekeeper.

He was still pondering this when he entered the wheelhouse. Peter Forest, ashen and grim-faced, was at the wheel, ready for the departure.

"What decision on the girl, Forest?"

The pilot stared straight ahead. "Her own, sir. She wasn't in the cabin when I returned. I didn't think it proper to follow her onto the island."

Allard sighed. "Perhaps you are right, my boy. Bender wasn't there, after all. If she raises any questions with him, we will settle them when we return. Give the order to cast off, Mis-tah Logan."

Amos Allard could only be thankful that the girl was gone and that the sanctity of his vessel had been preserved. He thought he had handled the entire matter fairly well.

* * *

Peter refused to look back at the island. Once the steamer was midstream, he turned the wheel over to the daywatch and walked listlessly back to his cabin. Narrow as it was, his bunk seemed vast and lonely without Elsa Jane. He tried not to give in to his pain, but when he thought that he might never see her again, he wanted to curl up and die.

A gentle rapping on the door forced him out of his bleak thoughts. He got up and pulled it open.

"Well," Elsa Jane whispered, "may I come in?"

Peter was stunned. For a moment he could do nothing but stare at her slim form and radiant face. He silently stood aside as she came in and sat down on the bunk.

As he closed the door, another figure scurried up and pressed an eye to the keyhole.

Daris Jamieson was elated. He had seen Elsa Jane sneaking down from the aft deck and followed her. As long as she was on board he would have time to devise a new scheme.

"Elsa Jane . . ." Peter whispered.

"Yes, Peter?"

"Where . . . where have you been? I thought you had gone ashore."

"I had to say goodbye."

"To whom?"

A tear rolled down her cheek. "To the island. I stayed up on the aft deck until I couldn't see it anymore. It's . . . it's no longer home."

"You don't have to do this, you know."

She placed her hand gently on his cheek.

"Yes, I do, Peter. Don't you know how much I've grown to love you? I'm ready to go home with you."

He put his trembling arms around her. Now his heart was really breaking—but from sheer happiness.

"What will we do about your Uncle Calvin?"

"I don't even want to think about him right now, Peter. I just want to think about us."

She tilted her chin up and the cabin was silent as they kissed.

Jamieson grinned. "So," he thought, "the prissy do-gooder Forest was her intended. No wonder Captain Allard lied. That pilot is nothing more than a kiss-ass for the bastard." He laughed and strutted down the deck.   ⇜§

3

"MOVE YORE arse, lady!"

A whip cracked next to Elsa Jane's ear. She jumped back from the wagon being pulled by oxen through the mud of the St. Louis street. It rolled past, splashing mud on her skirts.

"Beastly people!" Laura Logan hissed. "Think they own the town. I liked it much better in the old days."

Elsa Jane laughed. "The old days. I fail to see how four short years could be called the old days, Laura Logan."

Mrs. Lawrence Logan pouted, pinching her thin lips and chinless face. "I am not speaking of your arrival, Elsa Jane Forest. When I was born here it had a population of about five thousand and now look at it."

Elsa Jane loved every bit of the town and its spirit.

St. Louis was the gateway to the West and the young woman loved its vitality.

A heavy-set woman called out to Elsa Jane from a donkey-drawn cart. They exchanged friendly greetings.

"How common," Laura simpered, "calling in a public street. Well, what else can you expect from a woman with ten children—and she's barely thirty."

"Oh, Laura, I envy her each and every one of those babies. I wish they were mine."

"How can you say such a thing? Don't you have quite enough to do with the two you already have?"

"You wouldn't think that way if you and Larry had some of your own."

"Law-*rinse*," (as she pronounced it, refusing to call her husband Larry), "and I decided on the day of our marriage that it was proper to wait awhile before we had children."

Elsa Jane refrained from commenting. She thought three and a half years was too long to wait, and she worried about Laura. After all, she had been twenty-eight when she married Lawrence Logan.

For Elsa Jane it was different. Annie had been born when she was thirteen and Charles when she was fourteen. She and Peter had wanted a third child, but had been unable to have any for the last two years.

"Yoo-hoo! Elsa Jane, Harry Schroeder has just gotten in some marvelous new gingham at his mercantile. One pattern looks just like you. Tata!"

Elsa Jane couldn't help but tease Laura. "Is it common for Melanie Caldwell to call out on a public street?"

"We can cross over here," Laura said with a sniff.

Melanie Caldwell, *née* Tregent, could trace her St.

Louis ancestry back to when the city was still under French control. She was well aware of the problem between the two women—jealousy over her.

When Elsa Jane had first lived in St. Louis, she had been housed with the Beaumonts. Laura Beaumont had been aloof, snobbish to the young bride and only "thawed" when she became engaged to Lawrence Logan. At Laura's fashionable wedding, Melanie Caldwell had come into Elsa Jane's life.

"You poor dear," she boomed at the wedding, "I know your problem. An expectant mother needs a home of her own for her new babe."

Within two days Melanie Caldwell had found a small two-bedroom house in a lovely section of the city. Elsa Jane could not have been more grateful, and the friendship between the two women began. During the next few weeks, furniture was begged, borrowed and nearly stolen from all of Melanie's friends. She became the mother that Elsa Jane never had.

Unfortunately, their relationship made Laura extremely jealous, but each, in her own way, had been helpful to Elsa Jane. And they proved their friendship again shortly before the birth of Annie.

"Let he without sin cast the first stone!" Melanie shouted as she placed her large hands on her hips. "Imagine the gall of the man to disown you. What sand-hole has he had his head in for seven months! Impossible! Seven months for a man to start screaming about his daughter getting married!"

"Please," Elsa Jane begged. "I made you promise that you would never let on that I had told you the truth."

"I will keep my promise, my dear girl, unless he

tries to give you grief—then I will shout his hidden secrets to the masses from the house tops. He'd dare not show his face in St. Louis, and that's a fact."

Laura's help had been more simpering. "My problem was just the opposite, Elsa Jane. My father despaired for years that he would never be able to marry me off. He danced a jig when Captain Allard proposed a union with Law-rinse."

Elsa Jane had gasped. "You hadn't met Lawrence up to then?"

"Never set eyes on him."

"Then why did you marry him?"

"Last chance, you might say. Oh, I shall come to love him, in time. But Father knew best."

"And you are saying that Uncle Calvin didn't?"

"He can't fight true love, Elsa Jane," Laura said tenderly. "Oh, it warms me so to see you and Peter together. So happy, so content, so perfectly matched. You may call it envy on my part, but it is certainly envy on the part of Calvin Bender. You have what he seems to have been deprived of all his life—love."

By helping her overcome the loss of her father's love, the two women had become the foundation of Elsa Jane's new life. Their friendship gave her comfort and a position of respect in the community. Her house became a favorite gathering place for afternoon tea, and the women of St. Louis were always pleased to be invited there.

Elsa Jane nearly ran home in her excitement. She had just bought some beautiful gingham and was determined to welcome Peter in it even if she had to sew all night. When she reached her little brick house, she found the children playing on the floor and a coatless, dirty Daris Jamieson bent over a bottle of dark beer.

"Hi beautiful," he said in a deep lustful tone, having surveyed her maturing body.

This was the fourth time Jamieson had come for Elsa Jane. In the first three episodes, he had come near to raping her in a drunken rage. Elsa Jane had fought bravely each time, but feared telling Peter. When his threats increased, she told Melanie, who arranged for her to have a live-in maid. "Where is Kitty?"

"Sent her for more beer and out to Drucker's for some of their excellent beef jerky."

The black girl would be gone for some time.

"I thought you were back aboard the *River Queen*. Has it docked?"

"Ah, yes, the illustrious steamer of Captain Amos Allard. I remember my days on it well."

"Remember? What has happened?"

Jamieson sat casually back in the chair and crossed his long legs on the table. He answered just as casually, but with a murderous intonation.

"Beached! The pious, Bible-thumping bastard beached me in New Orleans. I will save you asking the *why* of it. You, my dear, were the main reason."

"Why me?" Elsa Jane asked in amazement.

"Well, let me put it more exactly. Because I could not, and would not, stop sticking my nose into your family affairs, a request to get rid of me came from your father."

"I've no father," she whispered.

"Ah, but you do," Jamieson said, and smiled wickedly. "In the past few years I have made it my business to come to know him well—although he was never aware, until recently, of my connection with you. Interesting chap, to say the least. Hypocrite, however, is a more fitting title for him."

"Stop it!" she warned, remembering the children.

Annie was at that age when she repeated everything she heard.

"No, I will not stop it," he said darkly. "You owe me a full hearing on this matter and then a lot more. Send them away."

She deeply hated this man. She owed him nothing, yet she was curious to learn why Calvin Bender had treated her so horribly for the last four years. She sent the children to their rooms and sat at the opposite side of the table.

"That's better," he said, and poured another glass of beer. "Now, Calvin Bender has at times been a passenger on the various steamers I've worked. While on board he can preach against *demon rum* as stoutly as Amos Allard. But . . . do you know his favorite two stops? Ah, Natchez-under-the-Hill, and the seamier side of New Orleans. And drink? Oh, how that man can get drunk in those curious places. It's as if he were trying to change himself into a different person. Luckily for me, when he gets that drunk he cannot help but talk, and talk and talk."

"I don't wish to hear this, Daris."

He banged his hamlike hand down on the table. "But you are going to hear it all! Because of you my whole life has been turned upside-down these past four years. Because of you his whole life has been turned upside-down for sixteen years."

"I didn't ask to come into either of your lives," she said coolly. "And you didn't have to stay in mine."

"You are blind, aren't you? One look at you, my dear, and I understand why Peter is so enamoured. Frankly, you've never understood that my feelings were the same. My problem, like your father's, is that I only fully realize the fact when I am drunk—then I would tear down the gates of hell to claim you."

"And you keep forgetting that I am now a happily

married woman with two children, Daris. Why don't you just accept that fact and bow out of my life?"

"Can you plan falling in love, Elsa Jane?" he asked.

"Oh, Daris, you are not really in love with me. Admit it!"

"I will not admit it, Elsa Jane," he said sadly, "but I will consider walking out of your life forever."

Her head came up on a jerk. "Oh? Why the sudden change of heart?"

"It's not a sudden change. It's my main reason for being here. I need your help, but I have to tell you the whole story of why I need it."

She nodded. She would do anything to rid herself of him.

"As I was saying, I came to learn far too much about Calvin Bender during his drinking bouts. Of course, he was not aware of how much he was telling me. I did learn how you came about. He's a faggot. He went to the overseer's wife to prove that he was really a man. It did nothing more than disgust him. He ran away to Europe to escape his guilt and came back to find you born. The only thing he could do was to take you in as his niece, and become more or less celibate for the next decade . . . except for his little trips to Europe."

Elsa Jane was stunned.

"He started his drinking again," Jamieson continued, "when you left for school. But he had to lead a double life to do it. When you ran away, it made him fearful. He felt as if the bad seed in him was coming out in you. You couldn't be aware that he disowned you in a drunken fit of rage and has regretted it ever since."

"Really?" she pouted. "I've heard nothing from him and the mail packet comes up the river all the time."

Jamieson nodded in sympathy. He really didn't

want to pursue the point, as it had all been a bald-faced lie. Calvin Bender had disowned Elsa Jane as an ungrateful bitch and loved the fact that he was free of her.

"But, Elsa Jane," Jamieson said slowly, "therein lies the problem. Bender found out I was back aboard the *River Queen* and grew fearful that I knew far too much about his secret life. He got Allard to beach me and blackball me with the other captains."

"That's not fair," Elsa Jane stated angrily, "of him or of Captain Allard."

"I knew you would understand," he answered, letting his voice crack like an adolescent's. "That's why I am asking for your help. Please talk to Allard and get me reinstated."

"Of course," she readily agreed. "I'll go first thing in the morning, as soon as they dock."

Jamieson rose and put on his coat. Timidly, he put out his hand.

"Thank you, Elsa Jane. Then . . . then this is good-bye. I'll never trouble you again, once I'm reinstated."

She shook his hand and he left quickly.

Daris Jamieson whistled a happy tune. His lies to Elsa Jane had worked. He was sure neither she nor Captain Allard would ever learn that he had stopped at Bender's Landing and confronted Calvin Bender. Earlier, he had allowed Bender to have homosexual relations with him in order to blackmail him. Bender's original fear of the confrontation had turned to rage and Jamieson was thrown off the island.

Jamieson purposely had not told Elsa Jane that Calvin Bender had approached Peter Forest to get him beached. He had seen the two men drinking together in New Orleans, and although he could not prove that anything funny had gone on between them, once reinstated he could make insinuations. He wanted to ruin Peter in order to possess Elsa Jane.

"Steamboat, steamboat!" shouted Annie, hearing the distant whistle.

Elsa Jane watched with pride as her two children clambered up the stairs to see if they could spot their father's boat. She quickly motioned for Kitty to follow them and departed for the docks before the children noticed she was leaving.

As Elsa Jane approached the waterfront, she wondered if she were doing the right thing. She had wondered about it throughout the night.

The *River Queen* was docked, and Peter was in his cabin changing out of his uniform when she arrived.

"Hi, Larry," she called cheerfully, tripping up the gangway.

"Hello. Come to meet your old man?"

Elsa Jane laughed. "No. I've come to see *the* old man. Is Captain Allard in his cabin?"

Lawrence Logan nodded and frowned. "If it's not real important, Elsa Jane, I'd put it off. He was in a horrible stew when we left New Orleans and has not been fit to live with from Bender's Landing up."

"I'll chance it. Care to escort me to the lion's den?"

"My honor," Larry obliged. "That way you can warn me as to what my wife has been up to. I sure got into dutch the last time I was home. I didn't even notice that she had wallpapered the living room, and she will never let me forget it."

As they were talking, Daris Jamieson sneaked on board and followed them to the captain's cabin. A few minutes later he was fuming with rage.

He had been blinded to the fact that Elsa Jane would have trouble broaching such a delicate subject

to Amos Allard and that the captain would be equally
sensitive when discussing such topics in front of a
lady. Suddenly there was a hand on his shoulder.

"What the hell are you doing here?"

Peter's voice had been so quiet, so firm that the
blood rose and beat about Jamieson's ears.

"Is it any of your business, Forest?"

"Logan tells me my wife is in there, so I'm making
it my business."

"She is there at my request, if you must know.
She's going to get me reinstated with Allard."

"Oh, God," Peter groaned, "I don't want her knowing any of this."

Jamieson took advantage of Peter's statement. "You
mean you're afraid she will learn of your involvement with the faggot Bender?"

"*Involvement*? Jesus, that's a strange word for you
to use after what you've done to the man, you filthy
blackmailer!"

"My, my, my," Jamieson simpered, "you really must
have gotten most *intimate* with the man for him to
have revealed that."

"You scum!" Peter growled. "I've been trying my
damnedest to patch things up between Elsa Jane and
Bender, but you had to keep sticking in a dirty oar."

Two crewmen came down from the upper deck
and stood silently in the shadows as the argument
continued.

"Dirty?" Jamieson chuckled. "How many times has
he dropped his prissy head between your legs?"

Peter's eyes flashed. "I'm going to ignore that question, but for your information, Captain Allard was
with me at Bender's Landing when we learned of
your latest blackmail attempt, Jamieson. He will
never reinstate you. Now, get off of this boat and
don't ever try to see my wife or Bender again. Try,

you son of a bitch, and I'll kill you with my own hands!"

Jamieson shrugged and turned away. He took three steps, then turned back. He cocked the hammers of his owl's-eye pistols, short heavy weapons with two barrels.

"Now she will be all mine," Jamieson growled, and pulled the twin triggers.

There was no time to react. The blasts of buckshot lifted him off his feet and threw him against the deck stairs. His heart had been pierced.

The explosions echoed over the boat and waterfront. There was yelling as the two crewmen ran in pursuit of Jamieson and a mournful wail as Captain Allard saw what had happened. This was followed by shouts from Logan, informing all that they had captured Jamieson.

Elsa Jane emerged from the captain's cabin. No one dared speak. She pushed her way past the Captain and saw the bloodied body of her husband. A piercing scream vibrated across the deck. Peter was dead. ◄§

4

AFTER the funeral, only Melanie Caldwell remained
Elsa Jane's friend. Amos Allard's words had destroyed
her reputation with vicious rumors. "She was pleading
for the man's job when he shot her husband. It's obvious that she was lying and cheating on Peter."
Laura recalled seeing the man at Elsa Jane's house
and was no longer allowed to see her. "If I were you,
nephew, I wouldn't allow my wife to associate with
the woman. You know, bad apples and all of that."

Slowly, the reality of Peter's death sank in. His
salary had stopped and he had left no savings. The
money she had been tucking away for the next baby
was all that she had. She would soon be destitute.

"Excuse, miss," Kitty said, "but there's a young man
to see you. He's from the *St. Louis Dispatch*."

"I don't care to see anyone, Kitty."

Kitty hung her head and shuffled her feet. "Am about that Mistah Jamieson, Miss Elsa Jane."

"What about him?"

"He free," she whispered.

"*What?*"

Elsa Jane raced to the front room.

"I am Mrs. Peter Forest," she said.

"Maynard, ma'am. We would like a statement, if possible, on your reaction to the decision handed down this morning by the district court. It seems that the verdict against Daris Jamieson for your husband's murder has been overturned on a technicality."

She braced herself against the back of a chair and nodded for him to go on.

"I'm sorry, Mrs. Forest, but it seems that the two sailors who captured him after the shooting only gave written statements and did not appear at the trial as witnesses. In their statements they did state that Mr. Forest did threaten Mr. Jamieson. They can't be found, and the appeal judge looked at the whole thing as a case of self-protection. He's been released."

Elsa Jane paled with fear. "Thank you," she stammered, "but I would rather not comment. I—I'm . . ."

She ran from the house before finishing her sentence. Blindly she raced through the streets until she came to the Caldwell mansion. She needed Melanie more than she had ever needed anyone.

To her amazement, Jerome Caldwell answered the door. His mouth was slack, his eyes lost in shadowed sockets.

"Dear Elsa Jane," he gulped, "thank you for coming." He looked behind her. "Where is Harold? I just sent him with the carriage for you."

"Harold? I haven't seen him. What is it, Mr. Caldwell?"

His fat face altered as if some unseen hand were molding it. He took her arm and clung helplessly to it.

"She didn't want you to be bothered. Not with so many troubles of your own. She is here in the drawing room."

The casket sat upon four straight-backed chairs, banked by massive flickering candles. To Elsa Jane the figure lying there was no more Melanie Caldwell than it had been Peter Forest in that other casket. It was simply a cold, waxen image that could no longer talk to her.

"She seemed much better last night," Mr. Caldwell said dully. "But she must have known. She spoke of you and your loss. She said she wanted you to have the little house. Did you know she had purchased it so you and Peter could rent it? No, it wasn't her way to let people know the good she did in life. Then she just went to sleep. Peaceful as ever. Poor lamb."

He cried, but Elsa Jane had no tears. She felt that Melanie would not want tears shed for her. She had been a forceful, dynamic woman who had loved every moment of her sixty-two years.

"I'm sorry," she said to no one in particular, "that I can't thank her for the house. Leave it to Melanie to take that worry off my shoulders."

"Elsa Jane," Mr. Caldwell sobbed, "what am I to do? It never crossed my mind that she would be the first . . ."

"I ask myself the same question, Mr. Caldwell. At least, as a man, you are automatically granted part of the answer, and you don't have to find a way to support two children."

"Don't worry," he said, sliding his arm around her shoulders. "A young thing like you needs a man to take care of you and the young ones. I will see to that, and in time . . ."

Elsa Jane pulled away. She would not cause a scene, but she was sickened by his suggestion. She had often dreamed of that night on the boat, and Jerome Caldwell had always been the worst villain.

"I don't want charity, Mr. Caldwell . . . or another husband. I want work."

"Work?" He made it sound like a nasty word. "My dear Elsa Jane, unless you wish to become a charwoman or scrub lady, there is no work in St. Louis for a decent woman, let alone a girl of sixteen. Now you just listen to me, young lady, and do as I say."

She knew what he would say. "Mr. Caldwell, please, this is not the proper time. I'm imposing upon your grief. Another time."

She went quickly to the bier, closed her eyes so she wouldn't have to look down, and quickly left the house.

The days that followed were like a nightmare. Through the butler, Harold, Caldwell kept sending her messages. First, the papers on the house and an offer to help. Then just offers to help. All offers were refused, so he tried a different ploy. He sent Harold to bring Kitty back to the main house.

Now she was really in a bind. How could she possibly get a job without Kitty to take care of the children?

"Insufferable!" she fumed.

Each morning she wrote a half-dozen letters, asking for positions. By the end of the week, none of them had been answered.

"Damn!" she yelled, "Annie, take care of your brother!"

Elsa Jane went into the bedroom and grabbed a shotgun standing in a corner. She had never handled one before but Peter had always left it loaded in case she needed it while he was gone.

"Damn!" she repeated as she turned it over in her hands. "I'll put food on the table, one way or another."

She hid the gun under her shawl and walked south until the cobbled streets and brick buildings had given away to clapboard structures and a dirt path. She headed towards the summer picnic grounds.

Elsa Jane knew and loved this area. She and Peter had often brought the children for long afternoons among the trees. Peter had been gay and full of playfulness. Elsa Jane wept as she remembered how he had loved to frolic in the tall grass with the toddlers.

"Stop it," she scolded herself. "He's gone and you can't get him back. It's fine to keep the memory alive, but it's not going to help you right now, Elsa Jane. "You've got to go into that wood and . . ."

She became alert. She could see movement everywhere—a rabbit here, a grouse and chicks scurrying there, even a lazy rattlesnake slithering through the grass. Once the animals had trusted her—they had been her only friends. Now she would kill them.

She rationalized; wild rabbit might be a little too stringy, the grouse too dry, and she couldn't imagine anyone in their right mind eating rattlesnake.

The sun grew high and then began to drop. Still Elsa Jane sauntered on through the woods as though on a Sunday outing. A faun came within a hundred feet of her, but she could not shoot it. It's eyes were too brown and soft and it was too young.

"Face up to it, Elsa Jane," she said to herself, sinking down into the brush deep in the woods. "It's not that the animals are your friends, you are just not cold-hearted enough to be a hunter."

She shivered as she thought of the alternative.

Jerome Caldwell aged her by some fifty years; he was fat, ugly, bald and lecherous. Yet he had wealth, a mansion and a future for her children. As she slowly resigned herself she heard a noise.

In a clearing a few feet away she saw a fine turkey gobbler with feathers as scarlet as the autumn leaves prancing up and down.

"Lordy," she gasped, "that bird is big enough to provide meat for at least a full week."

She brought the cumbersome weapon up to her shoulder and aimed at the rapidly blinking eyes. Her fingers gripped the trigger, but the eyes stopped blinking and stared at her through the sight.

"Please," she pleaded, as she felt her famished stomach turn over, repulsed by the thought of killing this wild thing. "Do it! Do it!"

The gun slid from her grasp and fell to the ground. Elsa Jane sank back and cursed herself for being weak; for being a woman.

In the clearing, the brilliant plumage of the gobbler flared as he let out a throaty mating call to a dull-feathered hen who had sauntered by.

"Go ahead," Elsa Jane said, "make a bunch of eggs to turn into little chicks."

She noticed that for all his efforts, the hen was not really paying much attention to the gobbler.

"Yah, we're about the same, young hen. Old gobblers for us both."

As if understanding her, the young hen led the gobbler back within firing range.

"You trying to tell me to change my attitude or starve, young hen? All right!"

Allowing no time to think, Elsa Jane recovered the rifle, aimed and quickly pulled the trigger.

The gun kicked back and sent her sprawling. Other turkeys, hidden in the trees, flew away squawking.

Geese honked in a clatter from a nearby pond. Deer crashed through bushes and rabbits dove into their briars.

Tears streamed from Elsa Jane's eyes and she threw back her head and howled in dismay. She had once been a friend to all animals and now she was their murderer. She felt she was no better than a Daris Jamieson—perhaps even worse.

She jumped from the brush and ran into the clearing. Her resolve to survive without Caldwell grew as she bled and plucked the bird while it was still warm.

"Dammit, I will survive. I've got to survive. I want my 'eye for an eye' against Daris Jamieson."

On the way back to her house she crossed some recently harvested fields. Sifting through the mounds of dirt, she found potatoes and turnips; in another field, enough barley to make soup.

"Now you are being just like a slave woman," she said to herself. "This would be their job, their way of providing for their family." She laughed. "I wonder if any white woman has ever before come to realize that she is also a slave to canning, mopping, candle-making, diaper changing and husband feeding. Why is a man able to make money by his exertions and not a woman?"

Annie's bright green eyes danced with delight. "That smells yummy, Mommy!"

Elsa Jane gleefully tousled the child's naturally curly, honey-colored hair.

"Yummies for the tummy, my darling."

She watched Annie and Charles Peter play and counted her blessings. The children were healthy. She knew she could manage them.

The savory steam filled the kitchen as she basted the turkey.

"Glorious aroma!"

Scooping and pouring the drippings over the browning breast, she thought of how different her role in life had become.

"You're full of odd thoughts today, aren't you, Elsa Jane?" she said aloud to herself. "A hundred times in your life you have smelled this smell and thought nothing more of it than of the pleasure eating it would be. Never once did you think of the turkey as one of your forest friends. You thought of hunting as something only men did. Well, you have now accomplished both the man and the woman's chore. Why can't you continue to do the same?"

She returned the bird to the oven and stood before the little silver-backed mirror over the washstand.

Her face was maturing but still youthful. She ran her fingers through her long, waist-length hair and twisted it into a knot on top of her head. She grabbed the pinking shears off the sewing table, and began to cut the tresses to a short and mannish style.

Elsa Jane looked out over the autumn colors of the Sisters of Charity Orphanage playground. The room behind her was cold and austere, but did not seem nearly as cold as the reception she had received. She turned back toward the silent figure of Mother Catherine and prayed that she would help.

Mother Catherine tried to look stern. It was difficult. Elsa Jane looked pretty silly in Peter's Sunday suit. It made her look like a dwarf trying to fit into a giant's costume.

"I like your spunk and determination," Mother Catherine said flatly. "Most just drop their unwanted children with us in the dead of night and vanish. We are left to feed, clothe, educate them, and more often than not, name them. But your request, Elsa Jane, is most unusual. To pick your children up and take them home each evening would be difficult for the other children. Orphanage life is hard enough on them, I hope you understand."

"I understand, Mother, but have you any other suggestion?"

"Where do you expect to find employment?" she asked, hoping for some more facts before she suggested anything further.

"W-wherever I can, Mother Catherine," Elsa Jane answered evasively.

"I don't recall seeing you at mass at St. Louis Cathedral."

"I have not been to mass since I left Saint Rosa Lima," she admitted weakly.

"But now you seek our help?" the nun growled in mock wrath.

"Only help that I am willing to pay for when I am salaried. I am not seeking charity, even though that is your name."

Mother Catherine smiled slightly. She liked the strength that this sixteen-year-old showed.

"Alright, my dear, I shall give you my suggestion. As you have not been to mass, you will not be recognized by some of our Catholic businessmen in town. I will prepare a list for you of those who might have employment that would be suitable for your size and strength. Because I do not expect you to get employment immediately, let me suggest that you leave the children with us, day and night, for a period of, say . . . three days. When we learn the type of employment you have obtained, we will consider your suggestion quite candidly."

Elsa Jane gratefully kissed the Mother Superior's hand.

Elsa Jane reached the last name on the list that Mother Catherine had given her near closing time on the first day. It was not that the nun had not given her a most satisfactory list; it was simply that time and time again her disguise had failed her.

The dressmaker's shop was her last hope. She peered through the window and could see the owner, his back to her, busily putting away the partly finished dresses that the seamstresses had been working on. Inhaling deeply she stepped inside the door and walked toward him, thrusting out the badly tattered letter from Mother Catherine. She had learned at the very first interview not to speak first—her voice gave her away.

The man read halfway down the page.

"Ain't got no position open for a boy," he growled.

"What about a woman?"

"Might! Tell your maw to come see me. Start my seamstresses at twenty-five cents a day until they prove themselves. Most don't. But I pay by the piece if they do."

"I sew."

"Of all the damn tomfoolery . . ."

"I sew real good, mister."

The man glared at her with a dark, angry expression.

"Do you take me for a fool?" he exploded. "There's no way a woman would buy a dress if they thought a cow-eyed boy had made it. What's the matter with you? You queer in the head or something?"

She ran down the street giggling to herself trying to relieve the day's tensions. She was fast discovering that the business world was filled with many unfeeling creeps.

She went home by way of the wharfs so she could sit on the pilings and watch the evening arrival of the steamers. She had barely relaxed when she was seen by no less than three of Peter's former crewmembers.

"Damnation to hell!" Captain Allard thundered. "Can I never rid this boat of the shame she keeps bringing upon it? I married her off to cover her first shame. I beached Jamieson to still the shame of her depraved father. I got rid of the witnesses to keep this from being called a 'murder' boat. What now? Why is she dressed as a boy? Get me Mis-tah Logan. He can find out the truth from her."

Lawrence Logan had already disembarked, and by the time he was found Elsa Jane had vanished.

Sitting on the wharf, Elsa Jane had realized that she could tell, simply by looking at the crewmen's dress, what work they did on the steamer—cabin boys, waiters, firemen, cargo handlers, deck hands and officers—and that there was a certain age for each and every job.

"I've been going about this all wrong," she cried. "If I'm going to con a man into giving me a man's job, with a man's pay, then I have to know what I'm talking about. Thank you, Peter. Because of you I know just as much about the river as any of . . . any of those silver-bellied swabbies that went down the Miss," she said, imitating their rough way of speaking.

Once home, she locked the door, sorted through Peter's clothing and brought out the sewing table.

She took in the white duck trousers and black turtle-neck. Then with tweezers, she laboriously tied strands of her shorn hair to a net. It took hundreds and hundreds of tiny strands to fill the fine mesh. By the time she had finished making a stylish beard, her fingers ached and her eyes burned.

Tying the beard to her chin would be too obvious, so she took the last of her wheat flour and mixed it with water. She added dirt to make it darker and covered her chin, cheeks and neck with the paste. She slapped the netting in place and waited.

As it dried, it conformed to the structure of her face but had a tendency to pull her skin and pucker her mouth. When she tried to talk it gave her gravelly voice a lisping quality. She liked the effect.

Next came the trimming. It had to blend into her hairline as well as look shaggy and unkempt. This done, she brushed her eyebrows backwards to give them a bush effect and set to work on her torso.

She remembered how the nuns had bound her breasts, and completed the effect by winding a sheet around her waist. Now, even when wearing the tight-fitting turtle-neck, no one would guess she was a woman.

The white duck trousers fit snugly at the waist and hip. Elsa Jane sewed a roll of cloth into the crotch, suggesting manhood and flared the shortened legs out like bells.

With six pairs of wool stockings stuffed in her boots and a black night-watch cap propped on the back of her head, she left the house.

An angry, odd-mixtured crowd flooded out of the Delta Steamline Company office and packed the narrow street. Well-dressed ladies and top-hatted gentlemen screamed at a knot of surly, hard-cursing sailors.

Elsa Jane ignored both factions and pushed through the middle of the crowd to the door of the office.

"Where the hell do you think you're going, kid?"

An ironlike hand clasped her shoulder and swung her around.

"Where the hell do you think I'm going, scarface?" she bellowed back at the enormous man with a scar running from his temple to his chin.

"Scab!" he snarled. "Come to take our jobs, have you, scab?"

Elsa Jane frowned fiercely. "What the shit you talkin' 'bout? I'm here lookin' fur a berth, not trouble."

"Let the boy go through," a woman shouted. "They're hiring, lad. They're hiring because this bunch of hooligans won't work."

"Screw off, lady," the scar-faced sailor spat. "That ain't true, kid. They done got themselves a new non-smoking, non-chewing, non-drinking whippersnapper for a cap. He's beached all the crew that does smoke, chew or nip at the jug. Psalm-singin' som-a-bitch!"

"Sailed with one near the same," Elsa Jane answered flatly. "No offense, mate, but tabbacy and liquor ain't fur me neither."

"I'll remember your runty little face," he snarled, "and it will pleasure me to quash it if'n your hired on."

Elsa Jane tilted her head back and glared into his ugly eyes. "If'n you'll be lookin' down, scarface, ya'all will be seein' boots that have kicked in bigger balls than you got a danglin'."

With uncontrollable anger he started to grab for her. Fortunately, the woman who had been shouting quickly brought her parasol down on the back of his head. Elsa Jane shoved her way into the steamline office.

"Cabin boy here!" she called out.

Spider Beauchamp looked down his needle-sharp nose and squinted.

"You?" he asked with a chuckle.

"Get yore arse down here so I don't have to yell up yore step-ladder frame," Elsa Jane hissed.

True to his nickname, Spider Beauchamp squatted down on the desk top like a spider crawling down its web.

"Sharp-mouthed little twerp, ain't ye?"

"Not when it comes to passengers, the captain or the steward."

Spider grinned, giving a bit of width to his abnormally long face.

"I'm the steward on the *Delta Star*."

"Sorry, sor. Who could tell in this madness?"

"Experienced?"

"Were. Beached, now."

"Why and when?"

Elsa Jane had rehearsed this while she was making her disguise. "Near four year. Cap found out I'd lied 'bout me age. I were twelve."

The steward frowned. The face was near sixteen, but the beard puzzled him. He leaned closer.

"What yah been doing since?"

"Cookin' fur me old man and takin' care his two brats."

"Running away again?"

"Nope. He's dead a month and the brats are in an orphanage."

It seemed near enough to the truth that she wouldn't confuse her story later.

"Sorry. You recall much about the duties of a cabin boy and his cabin chores?"

Unbelievably, Elsa Jane sounded as if she had left a berth just the day before. It wasn't hard for her; Peter had often carped on all the things the cabin boys did wrong. She just recited the things they should have been doing.

Spider Beauchamp began thinking that he had stumbled onto a real find, but there was something about the boy that troubled him. He was too frail, too pale and almost too pretty to be a boy. Still, he was in desperate need to hire someone.

"What's your name?"

Elsa Jane gulped. She had forgotten to think of one.

"E.J., sor."

"E.J.? What kind of a name is that?"

"Ain't a name. It's me initials."

"Well, initials always stand for a name, E.J."

"Sor," she said slowly as her mind raced, "when I be tellin' y'all me name, y'all will be a-knowin' I ain't a smoker, a chewer, a nipper or a skirt chaser. But if you be a laughin' over somethin' right outta the Bible, I'll not be a workin' fur yah. It's Ezekiel Jethro."

Spider Beauchamp pulled the rest of his rangy frame off the desk and stood up.

"E.J. it shall be."

He motioned a tall uniformed young man over and whispered at length in his ear.

Based on what had been said about the man by his former crew, Elsa Jane had expected a fire-breathing patriarch like Amos Allard. Instead, Raymond Spurlock reminded her of one of the apostles in a painting at Saint Rosa Lima. She knew at once, given the opportunity, she would enjoy working for the man.

"Thirty-five a month and keep while on board."

Her disappointment showed. She had been anticipating forty and up.

"It's a little lower than normal, E.J., because the cap is a little worried about your age and . . . ah . . .

well he thought it best for you to have one of the smaller crew cabins to yourself. We don't want any of the older hands getting ideas."

That was worth the lesser salary, she decided, and nodded her acceptance.

"Get your kit and be at the *Delta Star* by four. Ask for me, Spider Beauchamp, and I'll show you the ropes. Oh, and a word to the wise. Captain Spurlock likes his cabin boys to be clean shaven."

The beard may not have fooled Spider Beauchamp, but it certainly fooled Mother Catherine.

"What is it you wish to see me about, my boy?"

Elsa Jane stood in the dimly lit foyer twisting the stocking cap in her hands. She dreaded this moment. Her babies were her life and now she would give them away. A sob caught in her throat as she began to speak.

"I've gained a position, Mother Catherine, and must abide by your original suggestion."

The elderly woman's hand flew to her chest. "Elsa Jane! Oh, child, what a start! You are . . . are . . . like a boy, to say the least! Come and tell me all about it."

"Mother, my time is limited. I'm to be a cabin boy on the *Delta Star* and must be aboard by four. I must prepare more clothing and . . . and *shave*."

Mother Catherine laughed. "And how, pray, do you propose to do that?"

"The same as loosening wallpaper, I gather. A lot of steam and hot water." They both laughed for a moment happy to see each other.

"We do need to dicuss if you will keep my children and what I shall owe you monthly. I will be making thirty-five and keep while on board. I'll keep my little house, for when we are in St. Louis. Will I—will I be able to see them when I am in town?"

"My dear, dear child, of course, any time. And there is no set fee, because this has never happened to us before. You just make whatever donation you feel is proper. I am very proud of you. It's odd; I have been with the church for forty years, and have performed many manly duties, but, my dear, I don't think I could apply them to the outside world. May the Lord always be with you, my brave little saint. Now, shall I take you to the children?"

"Is it wise?"

"Normally I would advise against it. I will not lie to you. They cried a great deal the first night, but adjusted quickly. Bright ones, both. They think you are off on a trip."

Elsa Jane took Mother Catherine's hand and stood quietly for a moment.

"My mind is made up," she said gently. "I will see them the next time that I come home."

"I think you are being very wise, for their sake."

"It's mainly for my sake, Mother. My arms ache for them. Once near them I might be tempted not to let go."

Tenderly the woman raised Elsa Jane's hand to her cheek. Hot tears fell upon it.

"I shall care for them as if they were my own." ⤳

6

WITH EACH return visit, the rustle of petticoats and the swish of skirts felt more awkward. She was afraid she would trip or tear the hems. The only things that gave her any semblance of security during these monthly journeys back into her feminine role were her boots. She utterly refused to put her feet back into the cramped little feminine high-button "pinchers," but she did wear the latest hats from New Orleans. They were wide-brimmed saucers piled high with plumes and violet flowers that gave the impression the lady wore her hair in a fashionable upsweep. However, the hat too would go sailing the moment she was alone with her children.

Annie and Charles Peter never seemed to resent their mother being away. They loved her and eagerly looked forward to each of her visits.

Christmas was always the best visit. Elsa Jane would scrimp and save and plan for it the whole year long. She then played Santa Claus for each and every orphan under the sisters' care.

"How ever do you do it?" Mother Catherine asked. "You already send us nearly every dime you make, child."

"My needs are simple. Twice a month I get off the boat; once in New Orleans to make my purchases, and once in St. Louis."

"How long can you go on with this masquerade, my daughter, really?" Sister Margaret Rose asked.

Elsa Jane also wondered. She looked at the children playing under the Christmas tree and was aware of the rapid passing of time. This was the fourth year she had spent with the sisters and the children. Annie was like a jumping bean. She had become a leader of the other children, and had a mind the nuns could not educate fast enough. And Charles Peter, who preferred to be called Charley, was every inch his father—not really handsome until he smiled, and just as quiet and shy and loving. Even at age seven, when he put his arms around Elsa Jane's neck, she would remember her husband so vividly that it sent vibrations right down to her toenails.

"How long?" she repeated. "A constant question, Sister. It I were to return to my female role I don't know how I could continue to pay for the care and education of the children. I count my blessings. I have a captain and steward who love and respect me, as I love and respect them. At times I think they suspect or even know the truth, and at other times I think not. To the rest of the crew, we are quite an odd threesome. They are both married men, you know. Although, I sometimes wish Captain Spurlock was not. He reminds me a great deal of my late husband. He's a gentleman. Sometimes when I am blue or depressed, and wonder if I shall ever really be a woman again, I can't help but think of him in a—"

"Hush!" Sister Margaret Rose warned.

Mother Catherine chuckled. "Ah, dear Sister, don't cut off this bloom of womanly youth. The thought was a pure one, I am sure. It is only natural for Elsa Jane to have normal desires and thoughts for another husband. Twenty is hardly the end of life. Although some of these new sisters we are getting from the East are already eighty at twenty. I declare, I don't know what is becoming of the order. But, enough of this. I wish to bring up a most distressing point— to me, at least. Elsa Jane, we are grateful, and Bishop Landry is more than grateful, but child, can you really afford so much each month? Thirty dollars must leave you next to nothing."

Elsa Jane grinned. "I was actually thinking of increasing it, Mother."

"But how?"

"I've now become a second waiter and make forty-five. I can easily live off the gratuities that the passengers leave."

"But the future," Mother Catherine warned, "you really must start thinking of the future and put away a sum each month. We are not really living in the best of times, my child. We here in St. Louis are an odd rim to three different worlds—the industrial East, the slave-holding South and the expanding West. Look at what has happened to us in the five years since they cried 'gold' in California. We've become a melting pot of people moving in for the winter and dashing west in the spring. And, I might add, leaving their unwanted parcels on our doorstep when they depart. I had thirty-four children when you brought me Annie and Charley. I have two hundred and sixty-four now. Frankly, you support more of them than the Bishop's own purse does. You should really be thinking of putting a bit more of your own money away for . . . oh, even a little business of your own."

Elsa Jane laughed. "Forgive me, Mother, but many in St. Louis already think I am in business, but in New Orleans. I'm sure they think I just return to my little house to cool my ardor. I'm sorry, Sister Margaret Rose, to make you blush, but frankly, after four years on the river, I wouldn't know one of these so called 'scarlet ladies' if I were to meet her face to face. Oh, look at the time! Captain Spurlock wants to leave as soon after sunup as possible. They say another nasty storm is coming our way. This has not been a pleasant winter on the river. I really need a good night's rest if I am to face all of those passengers who get upset over a rolling boat."

Her chattering was a signal that she must leave. She would silently slip away, leaving the children to play.

Mother Catherine hugged her and held her out at arms length, gazing at her wistfully.

Here is a certain strength, she thought, of body, mind and attitude. Elsa Jane's hair was neatly trimmed, her face had developed a youthful male handsomeness and her five-foot-seven inch frame was muscularly hardened by work from neck to ankle.

"How long?" the nun repeated, and smiled sweetly. "As long as the good Lord deems necessary, for who dares question the path he will have us walk? Go with God, my dear, young sweet friend."

Elsa Jane had walked less than a block from the orphanage when the snow began to fall. The massive flakes nearly blinded her, but against the backdrop of the gaslamps she could see their intricate patterns. For an instant, she felt the white swirls brought her closer to Peter and Melanie Caldwell and . . .

She spun around. The orphanage was lost in the white of the storm.

"Mother Catherine," she whispered.

She somehow knew that she had looked upon the loving woman's face for the last time. How marvelous, she thought, that these three would become great friends somewhere.

Did she really believe in a life after death? Was she really that good a Catholic? She honestly wasn't sure. Of only one thing was she very sure—it might be a very, very long time before she saw her children again.

She wondered if she should go back while she had the chance.

"Idiot," she growled, realizing she was just being sentimental.

"I beg your pardon," a man said drunkenly.

"It is your pardon I beg, sir. I was not calling you an idiot. I'm just a little lost in the swirling snow."

"No one should be lost in the snow, should they, duckey-poo?"

The painted lady he escorted giggled inanely.

"Where are you going, pretty little miss?" he stammered, and nearly fell.

"Olivette Street. I shall find it, don't worry."

He grabbed hold of the lamp post to keep from falling and pushed back his top hat. The ghostly light illuminated his face.

"I don't think I know where that is. Do you, duckey-poo?"

"I only know the way to my place, lovey-poo," she simpered. "Let's get going."

Elsa Jane had turned away, ashen and shaken.

The man was Raymond Spurlock, the captain, but the woman was hardly his wife, whom she had seen on many occasions.

"Oh, Lord," she cried, "did he recognize me? I'm ruined if he did. Naturally, he's too much of a gentleman to make a scene in front of a stranger. I've got to be ready for it in the morning. I'll deny it. I know; I'll go home, change clothes and go back to the boat tonight. Mr. Hennessey has the night watch. He'll vouch that I came back aboard."

Back in uniform, E.J. boarded ship.

"Seen the Cap?"

She nearly fainted. "Nope."

Spider Beauchamp looked down at the decks and wharf. A foot of snow had fallen during the night, and the crew was valiantly trying to shovel it away, but it was still coming.

"Let's grab a mug of java, E.J. We might have ourselves a wee problem."

She followed him down to the galley.

"Didn't know where you stayed in town," he began, "or I would have looked you up during the night."

Elsa Jane twisted her hands behind her back.

"They got me out of bed around midnight," he continued, "to go get the old man out of jail."

"*To what?*"

"E.J., keep it down! I don't want the whole crew knowing. The Cap really tied one on and all hell broke loose in a bordello over on the east side."

"But . . . but . . ." she stammered, her voice slipping into it's natural, feminine tone.

"I know! I know! But you don't know. While we was enjoying our Chritmas Eve and day, he was going through hell. I ain't ever told you this, E.J., but that cunt of his is a real bitch. He came home from Orleans to nothing more than a cold note saying she'd left him. Everyone but the Cap knew that she dicks around on him when he's on the river. You knew, didn't you?"

"Ain't ever thought," she murmured.

"No, you wouldn't, E.J. You keep your nose clean. Well, she told him all and he went crazy. Probably did no more than sniff a cork to get drunk and lost his head when he saw a strange woman in bed with him. But the problem is now ours. The madam of the whorehouse is screaming her tits off that he's been sprung. We've got to get the boat downriver to let things cool off. The crew ain't ever that sharp right after Christmas and a few nights on the town, so I'll have to keep a watch on them. You see to the passengers. They'll bitch about leaving in a storm like this, so just keep them warm, filled with spiced cider, and the thought that the Cap's at the helm."

"Will he be?"

"I was a drinker fore I married, E.J. He's going to have a head on him bigger than the Mississippi's delta."

It was a madman's decision to embark. They assured the passengers the captain felt it was safe to leave in the storm, although the captain was snoring soundly in his bunk.

In the blizzard darkness of the mid-morning, the *Delta Star* plowed along in the ice floes out into the main currents. Then it was all alone. The pilot turned the wheel over to the helmsman in mid-river and retired, but the young helmsman couldn't see a foot beyond the bridge.

The blizzard created fantastic images—islands, shoals and overhanging trees—and in his fear he reduced the paddle-wheel speed to one-quarter. He was lost on a river he had traveled a hundred times. Passengers now demanded an immediate docking.

At noon a very red-eyed and grumbling Raymond Spurlock took over the bridge. He knew every current of the river and could navigate it blindfolded. As the blizzard got worse, he would not allow the boat to be brought near to shore for anchoring till nightfall.

At dawn the skies cleared over a fairyland of icy splendor. No one, however, was interested in nature's gift of beauty. The river had turned into a churning cauldron of danger. Ice chunks as big as rowboats crashed into each other and threatened to hit the boat. All hands were pressed to keep the mini-icebergs from getting caught up in the paddle wheels and destroying them.

Captain Spurlock was determined to keep as near schedule as possible. For two days he swore viciously at the crew. His face was mottled from his nightly bouts with liquor, and he became as unreasonable as the river. The crew grew silent, a protest worse than open defiance.

At Vicksburg things seemed to settle down. The local company official advised a day's delay in departure. Here the snow had turned to rain, and it was still raining on southward. The river was swelling to near flood conditions. Spurlock quietly accepted the official's decision on the matter and took to his cabin.

No one knew how he kept getting the jugs, but his supply was steady. He was constantly drunk—almost as drunk as he could get but not quite drunk enough. He wanted to drink until he could no longer think about his wife, or until the liquor shipment ran out. He wanted to drink himself into unconsciousness—until he couldn't stand, couldn't see, and didn't care.

The pilot and Mr. Beauchamp covered for him until the Vicksburg departure. It would be a two-day run to Natchez-under-the-Hill, and no passengers or cargo were due to disembark until then. From there, they would not stop until they reached Tennessee, so they prayed he would sober up in the next two days.

Their worry, however, would soon turn from the captain to the crew. After four years of Spurlock's strict rules, there were those among the crew who were ready to quietly rebel. The liquor cases were broken into and their nightly drunks began.

"I'm going to have me a little lie-down," the pilot yawned as they headed for the Tennessee shore. "Pipe me up when we are about fifteen minutes out, Shyler."

The helmsman nodded curtly. He was afraid to say anything because his head throbbed viciously. He was thankful that Mr. Horner had been so tired that he had not noticed his condition. It had been the second night in a row that he had partied with his three firemen cabinmates, and his stomach felt like a pit of writhing snakes. He picked the pipe tube off the bulkhead and blew into it.

"Boiler room," came the instant and wheezing reply.

"Smitty, Shyler here. Shit, man, I need fuel."

"You got full steam, Shy."

"For me, you asshole! I'm hurting bad!"

An eerie giggle came through the tube. "You should be down with us, Shy. We're still stokin' it away. Come on down."

"Come on, man. You know I can't leave the bridge. I'm all alone. Come on, man, bring me up one of those jugs."

E.J. heard the last sentence and banged into the wheelhouse. Shyler Manson quickly popped the speaking tube back onto its hook.

"Morn' Shyler. Damn, it's sure starting to get cold out there."

Shyler grunted.

"Mr. Beauchamp needs a reading on the schedule, Shy. We got time to open the dining room for breakfast 'fore we dock?"

He grunted again. "Do, if any of those bastards want to eat at this hour. We'll be in a little after six."

"That early, huh?" She stood right next to the wheel and peered out of the large glass windows. She wanted to be close enough to get a good sniff of the man, and when she did, she almost wretched. Too many days without a bath and too much liquor made his sweat ferment. "Where's Mr. Horner?"

"Resting. He'll be back to take us in."

"You want breakfast or coffee?"

"Naw." He just wanted to get rid of the goody-two-shoes. Smitty would come bounding in at any moment with his jug and he didn't want E.J. to see it. However, he almost giggled when he thought of the night before.

E.J. had always been resented for having a private cabin and being so close to the captain and steward. In their drunken night, they had wondered what the "pretty boy" was doing for the captain and steward to win such favors. They had almost decided to roust E.J. when they remembered that they would all be getting a piece of ass the next night at Parasol Sally's at Natchez-under-the-Hill.

"Hey, Shy, I got—" Harold Smith stopped short at the sight of E.J. They glared at each other. Smitty still claimed that it was E.J. who ratted on him when he brought a girl aboard in New Orleans. He had tried to pick a fight with her and she had foolishly backed down. He hounded her unmercifully for months. Finally a fight broke out and she was actually getting the best of him when Spider Beauchamp came along and broke it up. Smitty had been beached without pay for ten days but nothing had been said to E.J.

". . . got some bad news for you. The rain is turning to sleet."

E.J. shielded her eyes with her hands and peered out the windows. "Sure as hell changed fast. Shall I pipe up Mr. Horner?"

"Not yet. We'll probably be in before it gets too bad, but I think the Cap should learn of it, and how close we are to Natchez. He don't answer his pipe though."

"I'll go. My chores are finished in the galley till we start serving."

E.J. stepped out of the wheelhouse into a downpour of ice pellets. The rain-soaked decks had begun to freeze, and she had to cling tightly to the rails as she stepped down the ladder on her way to the captain's cabin. For the moment, action upon her suspicion that Smitty had brought Shyler a liquor jug would have to wait. She did, however, believe Shyler had erred in estimating they would dock before the storm grew worse.

Shyler Manson wasn't thinking clearly. Normally, when his visibility was reduced so dramatically, he would have ordered half or one-quarter speed. However, he was drunk and did nothing but nip at the jug while giggling with Smitty.

The two men did not notice the steady dip on the barometer. The storm clouds that had hovered for days over the length of the river were suddenly being forced down by a massive and rapidly moving arctic air mass. Further down, in the delta, some slave chil-

dren would wake up to the first snow they had ever
seen, but here, just above St. Louis, the mighty Mississippi had begun to freez and the *Delta Star* was
trapped.

E.J. banged and banged, but got no response. She
rattled the knob of the locked cabin door and shouted, but her attempts to wake the captain were in
vain. She raced back along the slippery deck and
down to the galley. She needed to find Spider Beauchamp. Only he had an extra key to the captain's
cabin.

As she entered the dining room, the sudden rush
of the steam heat made her shiver. Two daring passengers had seated themselves at one of her tables,
but she ignored them and raced through to the galley.

The cooks, cabin boy and kitchen helpers were
not alarmed by her entrance as they had grown used
to whispered conversations between E.J. and Spider.
They all knew they had to do with the captain, and
it pleased them to think he might disgrace himself.

"Here's the key, E.J. You look out for the Cap.
I think what you heard may be the key to where
he's been finding the stuff. He had another bottle
when I looked in around midnight. I don't think you
will be able to wake him, but try. I'll go down to
the boiler room and see if I can't catch Smitty red-
handed. I think we are going to have some crew
changes come New Orleans."

The odor of stale liquor and vomit made E.J. reel
as she opened the cabin door. The small room was
horribly overheated and, although the temperature
was now below zero outside, she had no choice but
to leave the door open and banging for a few seconds.

The combined office-living quarters was like a scene from a nightmare—clothing scattered everywhere, empty jugs rolling about, an eerie yellow illumination coming from the lamp above the bunk, and a pale and dissipated Raymond Spurlock sprawled nude on the bunk with one hand clamped weakly about his limp penis.

Gingerly, she touched his shoulder and tried to wake him. He felt like a dead fish that had been lying in the sun.

The room chilled rapidly. Holding her breath, Elsa Jane picked up the slop bucket and heaved it out into the storm. She slammed the door and went to the washstand for the pitcher.

The captain's quarters had the luxury of a steam radiator with a spigot for drawing off hot wash water. Elsa Jane drew half a pitcher and poured it into the basin.

"Just like a child," she thought, as she mopped Captain Spurlock's salt-sweated face with a washcloth. She applied the cloth to his neck, shoulders, arms and chest, and then she exchanged the hot water for cold and repeated the process. The cold applications made him moan. She lightly slapped his face.

Spurlock awakened. He opened his eyes, but the light seared them like acid and he shut them again. His head throbbed and his tongue was thick.

"Let me lone," he said.

"Captain, you've got to snap out of it. We are only about a half-hour out of Natchez and there is a terrible sleet storm."

He lay still for a few seconds and listened. He decided E.J. had to be lying. The engines were pumping at full steam. At thirty minutes out they would be down to one-half power. It was just a trick to sober him up before they landed, and he didn't want to sober up. He wanted another drink.

He put his hands to his head and groaned. "Christ! Christ and all the goddamn Almighty!" He slumped back on the pillow and ran his hands through his hair. His hair was sticky but his hands felt clean.

His mind churned painfully, trying to piece together some sequence of events. Had he gotten up and cleaned himself? Had he done that before or after he had gone to the hold for another bottle? He couldn't recall. Then he did recall that he had consumed a whole bottle and would have to go after another one. But he decided he needed to sleep a bit more before he made that journey again. He had almost fallen down the hold ladder and broken his neck on the last trip. But how did he get all washed up? he wondered.

"E.J."

"Yes, sir."

"Did you wash me?"

"Yes, sir."

"All over?"

"Almost, sir."

He giggled drunkenly. It had sounded so much like what his wife might have said. She would touch him "almost" all over. Bitch!

"You a good boy, E.J.?"

"I like to think so, sir."

"You've never screwed?"

E.J. gulped. "No, sir."

"And you've never played around with the sailors?"

"No," she barely whispered.

"I did, once," he said dully. "Before I was married and still a pilot. It was a cabin boy. Didn't go too far because he laughed at me."

"Laughed?"

Suddenly tears were rolling down his face and he was sobbing. "Laughed just like my wife. But we were already married and she couldn't do anything about it. Laughed just like that stupid whore in St. Louis, just before I broke the place up. Look at me, E.J. The great he-man captain—almost. Shit! I'm built like a runty dwarf. I'd have been better off with nothing down there at all. It's given me no children. It's only made me a laughingstock."

She didn't know what to say.

"I guess we are about the same, E.J., and yet different. I can at least overlook my small size and play with myself. But I've often wondered what you do to keep from going crazy."

"Do?" she gasped.

"Yah, do? How does a woman who has had two children not want it once in awhile?"

There was no trace of anger on his face. There was even a tinge of sympathy in his eyes.

"I've known almost from the first. Mr. Beauchamp a little later on. No others. Didn't you think I recognized you the other night?"

She looked at him blankly and gulped. "Scared the hell out of me, that you did."

"You are a very beautiful woman when you are all dolled up."

She dropped her eyes. "How did you know about my children?"

"Followed you once. Jesse Cito, Bishop Landry's secretary, went to school with me before he became a priest. He got me the rest of the information."

"Then why didn't you beach me?"

"First, because you were too damn good a worker to lose. Secondly, because you were the only thing that kept me going. If you could do without it will-

ingly, then I could do without it, being denied all
the time by my wife."

"It doesn't make sense then, Captain. Why all this
drinking over her leaving you?"

He chuckled drily. "That's but the tip of the ice-
berg, E.J. You don't deserve to be told this, but you
are a large part of the reason. I've wanted to come
to your cabin so many times it isn't funny. I couldn't
do it as long as I was still married. When she left
me I took up with the first whore I could find. But
then I saw you as you really are. I wanted to just
leave her standing and run after you, but my fear of
being laughed at had returned. It happened anyway,
didn't it? Now I just want to drown and forget."

Elsa Jane forced herself to speak. "There is something you can't forget, Captain. This boat and its
passengers. We must be getting very near to Natchez
now."

"Impossible."

"I was in the wheelhouse when Shyler told me we
were but an hour out."

He glanced at his desk clock. "Again, I say impossible, E.J. A good two hours. Can't you feel the beat
of the engines through your feet? Shyler may be an
idiot, but he would never run the engines full unless
we were midstream."

"Why don't you—" she started, but stopped when
she saw the hole in the wall. Now she realized why
they had been unable to raise him on the speaking
tube. He had pulled it right out of the wall.

"Why don't you just keep right on talking to me?"
he said. "Perhaps that is what I have needed more
than the booze. God, I feel horrible!"

"Shall I go get you some coffee?"

"No. Don't leave me. I can talk to you as a man
and a woman. That's odd, isn't it?"

"To some it might be, but not to me. After all, I've had to live and think like a man for four years."

"Tell me about it."

"Wait. I thought I heard a foghorn. There is a pretty bad storm out there."

He frowned and listened. "I don't hear anything but the howl of the wind. Besides, Shyler is such a chicken-shit bastard that at the first sign of any trouble he would have Mr. Horner racing for the bridge. I dread the day Shyler ever gets his pilot's license. He'll tear out every wharf he tries to dock at. Let me just rest a minute more and leave everything in the capable hands of Mr. Horner."

The capable Mr. Horner was sprawled fully clothed across his bunk. Even the engines with their fierce pounding on the other side of the bulkhead did not wake him.

Shyler and Smitty had tied the wheel into a stationary position and sat on the deck passing their jug back and forth. In the dining room, the first waiter was frantic. Over fifty passengers were demanding their breakfast and both the steward and second waiter had vanished. He cursed them both.

Spider Beauchamp had walked into the boiler room just as the firemen were finishing off a jug. He quickly hid in the shadows.

"Screw Smitty for taking that other jug up to Shyler."

"Quit carpin' and just go get another. Smitty said there was plenty."

"Hell, Smitty never said where he was getting it."

"Browning, you really piss me off sometimes. You heard as well as I did that it was in the middle hold. Oh, go to hell, you lazy bastard. I'll go for it."

Beauchamp followed. He wanted to see for himself where all of this mysterious booze was coming from, and he was not aware that Browning had seen him slip from the shadows.

The burly *mestizo* Domingo took three jugs from an open crate of Canadian liquor and headed back to the boiler room. He hid two of the three jugs to share with his wife in New Orleans.

Spider slipped into the hold. Thievery aboard a Delta Steamline boat was not tolerated. When the man had gone, he found where the crates were stored and started to count.

Browning watched him for a moment, but knew that the jig was up and slipped away.

Spider was aghast. Ten of the twenty crates holding six-gallon jugs had been broken into. The crew had consumed sixty gallons of the hundred-and-seven proof booze. He looked for the consignee on the shipment.

"That does it," he said aloud. "Anyone else but Sally Kallenbrough might have listened to reason, but she'll fry the company over the loss and the company will fry Raymond's ass. Well, I hope E.J. has him awake, because its going to be a rough landing."

Spider raced along the slippery deck. Time was limited. He could already see the double haze of shore lights through the storm—the lower ones of the brawling, seedy riverboat town of Natchez-under-the-Hill, and the higher ones, perched on the towering sandstone cliffs, of the more respectable homes of Natchez. He needed to get the captain to overshoot the landing and buy time.

"Mr. Beauchamp?"

"Yes," he answered, turning.

The grappling hook clawed into his neck and jerked upward so the rounded point could exit through his chest. Browning simultaneously raised his leg and booted him in the stomach. He didn't bother to re-move the hook.

Spider Beauchamp reeled backward and fell over the railing. He was aware of hitting the water for a second before he died.

"Wait!" Captain Spurlock shouted, suddenly acutely alert. "I hear it now. God, E.J., that's no foghorn. It's a turning warning. We're on a collision course! Quick, my pants!"

But before she could reach them she was thrown violently across the cabin. She threw up her arms to protect herself from the splintering wood and metal.

The *Memphis* ate through the center of the *Delta Star* like a saw. Death for many was immediate.

Mr. Horner's cabin was instantly flooded. He never had a chance to wake up from his nap.

Browning and Domingo heard the crash but prob-ably never realized it was the prow of another ship that pushed its way into the red-hot boiler.

Shyler Manson had jumped and grabbed for the speaker tube. He was greeted by a gush of steam from the volcanic boiler room that blinded him. He went screaming into a watery grave.

The front half of the *Delta Star*, passengers and crew, had already disappeared beneath the black waters of the river. The *Memphis* continued on into port, unaware that its splintered prow was taking on a dangerous amount of water.

E.J. left the captain to his hurried dressing. She pulled herself along the deck from door to door, banging and shouting to the passengers. She had just crossed the walkway when she ran into the cabin boy.

The fifteen-year-old lad stood and stared in bafflement at a strange phenomenon. The forward sinking of the vessel had raised the stern clear of the water, yet the massive paddle wheel continued to rotate like a riderless Ferris wheel.

"What is it, E.J.?" he asked numbly.

"It's trouble, Johnny," she answered quietly. "Get to the dining room and start bringing the people up on the port side."

"What do I do then?"

"Get them overboard and into rowboats. Mr. Beauchamp will be there to help you."

His face brightened a little. "All right, E.J."

At least it got him moving, Elsa Jane thought, but she knew it would be an impossible mission. There were hardly more than a dozen rowboats on the entire vessel. Several of those had been knocked off in the collision. She continued to gather the passengers until she reached the point where the steamer had been jaggedly severed in two. It was like a scene from hell. Steam rolled upward as the lapping waves bubbled with heat. Debris cluttered the water.

The shortest route to the wheelhouse was up and over the bridge on the port side. Elsa Jane inched her way forward but every few feet she had to stop to find a clear passage. Her journey through the jagged, twisted nightmare that was once a ship brought stinging tears to her eyes.

The windows of the wheelhouse had shattered inward. Sitting amid the glass was a benumbed Smitty. He did not respond to her shout, so she slapped him hard, took off her mittens and pinched him cruelly. His eyes were glazed, but he finally nodded.

"Get up! Grab a fire axe from the wall and follow me."

He obeyed like a confused child.

They had made it down the ladder to the third deck when the river itself seemed to erupt. The whole midsection of the *Memphis* blew skyward and the sleet which filled the morning air was pushed aside by a bright orange mushroom-shaped cloud. Now the screaming from both boats could be heard over the water.

Smitty's piercing wail could be heard above the others. He threw his axe to the deck and dove into the river. Several passengers from the lower deck followed suit.

Elsa Jane cursed the man's cowardice and grabbed the axe. She moved up the deck, chopping down cabin doors and tossing them into the water. She was exerting the strength of a man three times her size. Deck by deck she worked her way down to where Captain Spurlock and Johnny Ramey were frantically begging the remaining passengers to abandon ship. Many flatly refused to enter the water or take hold of anything that would float. Instead, they chose to yell and scream about the lack of rowboats, when the water was less than a foot from the deck.

E.J.'s anger flared and she forced two arguing ladies into the water. They called out in panic. Neither could swim. E.J. couldn't swim either, but dove in after them.

The icy water numbed her instantly and made her gasp. She had landed nearly on top one of the women and was met by stinging blows from flailing arms. Desperately, she gave the woman a blow on the side of the head that hurt her hand and staggered the woman. She wrapped the woman's arms around a shattered beam section and reached for her friend. Fortunately, her action had stilled the voice of the second woman, who had found that her bulk was

keeping her easily afloat. She calmly took Elsa Jane's
hand and allowed herself to be pulled over to the
beam.

Debris from both boats was everywhere. The burning hull of the *Memphis* gave ample light for the
oncoming rescue boats. Elsa Jane moved from floating object to floating object, encouraging panic-strick-
en passengers to grab hold and propel themselves
toward the shore.

All manner of little boats and steamers came out
from the shore. One by one the survivors were plucked
from the water. Finally Elsa Jane could encourage
no more. Her lungs felt like molten fire, the pain in
her arms was excruciating and she had used all her
energy. Bodies began to float by her. She closed her
eyes.

At last she felt herself being lifted over the side
of a boat. She sank down gasping. Silver lights flashed
in front of her eyes and her head was ringing. Something heavy and warm was thrown over her shoulders. She remembered nothing more.

Natchez-under-the-Hill was a muddied, one-street
jumble of hovels. Two warehouses, three steamline
offices, a mercantile store and a three-storied hotel
crowded the tiny space of land between the cliffs
and the wharfs. The narrow street curved along the
shoreline and was bordered on each side by an ugly
group of taverns, billiard balls, cheap boardinghouses
and no less than ten bordellos.

Natchez-under-the-Hill was the jumping-off spot
for the Ohio River bargemen. From there they began their trek back home along the Natchez Trace or
to new barges headed down to New Orleans. A good
deal of money was wasted in this hellhole. Still, the

harsh winter left the town in a state of poverty, crime and desperation.

Throughout the morning, Natchez carriages rumbled up the muddy street. They passed ruffle-skirted, gawking dance-hall girls, tavern fiddlers with dangling bows, and gaping drunks who couldn't figure out what had happened.

As the passengers were made welcome in the Natchez homes, the madams below locked their doors and sent their girls back to bed—they wouldn't be making any money from the crews of the *Memphis* and *Delta Star*.

The single hotel would only care for the surviving officers. The crew members were given cots and blanket rolls and sent to one of the vacant warehouses.

The warehouse was damp, unheated and drafty, but they hardly noticed it that first day. Their only desire was to get out of their wet clothing, crawl into blankets and forget. Under the circumstances, Elsa Jane had no problem slipping nude into the blanket roll and falling asleep instantly.

There was no written manifest of the passenger list, so the number of victims were determined by counting. This was made difficult by the fact that the survivors were spread out in a hundred different Natchez homes and were from two different boats. Even more difficult was the fact that the *Memphis* captain was dead, and his purser badly burned and unconscious. Captain Raymond Spurlock could recall no more of the journey than the rescue attempt, and the *Delta Star* purser kept changing his story.

Thus, throughout the night, the death count was continually altered. By morning it had reached a tentative one hundred forty-four.

With the morning came dry skies, dry clothing

and wet eyes. A riverboat crew was like a big family—they quarreled and had spats, but were close-knit. The crew of the *Delta Star* was devastated. They had been together for nearly five years, and now thirty-two were either dead or missing.

Elsa Jane was crushed when she learned that Spider Beauchamp was missing. She stayed in her blanket roll and tried to smother her grief.

When, at noon, the surviving twenty-eight learned they would be beached at Natchez-under-the-Hill without pay until the investigation was completed, their anger and frustration flared. But the damages incurred by each company were staggering. They wanted tongues loosened quickly to determine the fault, and threatened to withhold even more if the accident was not accounted for.

Bradford Thomas, the local agent for the Delta Steamline Company, was a merciless man. His assignment to work in the squalor of Natchez-under-the-Hill had soured him, and after three years among the "dirty Hottentots" he was determined to turn this accident to his own favor.

For three days, and late into each evening, he had the crew marched one by one into his office. The only other person allowed in the room was a clerk who recorded the testimony. Thomas acted as judge, jury and prosecuting attorney. He used one man's words against another man's words and believed only what he desired.

"I've been informed you were on the bridge, Mr. Smith. Why would a fireman be on the bridge?"

"The speaking tube wouldn't work, sir. The engineer sent me topside to learn why we were still at full steam."

"And why were you?"

"The helmsman informed me we were still three hours out and midstream."

"Another crewman has informed me that the helmsman had just stated that you were only an hour out. Who is correct?"

Harold Smith gulped. He didn't have to be told who the other crewman had been, and he thought it best to make both his and E.J.'s versions similar.

"Sorry to say it, sir, but the fact bears out that what the helmsman told the second waiter to tell the steward was nearer to the truth."

"Then why tell you something different?"

Smitty hung his head. "I don't like to speak ill of the dead, sir, but Shyler had been drinking all night and was still a little out of it."

Bradford Thomas had been hearing quite a bit about this drinking, but the stories were conflicting.

"A drunk helmsman without an officer on the bridge. Is that what you are saying?"

Smitty tried to look sheepish. "Yah."

Surprisingly, Smitty was excused and told to wait in the back office. Thomas smelled a cover-up.

The purser, E.J., and the first waiter were called back one at a time.

Most interesting, Thomas thought after having heard the three stories again. The purser was a weak fool who didn't want to be held to blame for the stolen liquor; the second waiter defended the captain with the knowledge that he was awakening him at the time of the accident; and the first waiter claimed a conspiracy between the second waiter and the steward to hide a drunken captain. But E.J. had mentioned something else which he had overlooked the first time around.

Smitty was brought back in and squealed like a

cornered rabbit. He tightened the noose around Raymond Spurlock's neck by confessing to bringing liquor on to the bridge. That night he took the winding switchback road up to Natchez and disappeared.

The bloated body of Spider Beauchamp was found a mile up river, lodged in a brush tangle, the grappling hook still embedded in his neck and chest.

Thomas preened. He now smelled mutiny, and it was confirmed by Smitty's disappearance. The company could be held blameless.

It was shocking news. The crew didn't believe it and Elsa Jane left them arguing as she slipped away to the hotel.

"What do you want?" a bearded and filthy old sailor asked as he sat with his chair tilted back against the hall wall outside Spurlock's door. He had a revolver in his lap.

"To see the captain."

"Can't!" He shot a stream of brown tobacco juice out from between his missing front teeth. "He's a prisoner."

"Prisoner!" her voice cracked with a note of femininity. "My God, why?"

"Ain't for me to know, sonny."

"Can you give him a message?"

"Nope! That Thomas fella says he ain't to see no one or talk to no one."

"What a stupid order!" Her temper was rising. She stormed down the stairs and out of the hotel. She was sure that the captain needed to be told about Spider, but she didn't know how to reach him.

Casually, Elsa Jane circled the hotel until she knew which of the rear windows was Spurlock's. She had just figured out a way to climb up to it when the rear door of the hotel opened. She crouched down behind a rain barrel.

A man in a low-crowned hat (made fashionable by the river gamblers) sauntered up the path to a bank of outhouses set against the bluff.

Elsa Jane dared not move until he had finished his business and had returned to the hotel. To her delight, he was very rapid, but as he returned, he angled off the path and stopped opposite her. He bit off the end of a cigar, carefully wet it between his lips and struck a match on the wood siding of the building. The flare of the match revealed his hideous face.

At long last Elsa Jane had crossed paths with Daris Jamieson. It was a glorious moment. All thought of Raymond Spurlock vanished as she swore to learn everything there was to learn about her enemy.

She was amazed at how calm she was. She let him disappear around the corner of the hotel, knowing he would not escape her—not this time—and circled back to the street.

It was nearly nine o'clock and Natchez-under-the-Hill's nightlife was just starting. Torches lit the winding streets and the sellers of "night-wares" appeared. Dance-hall girls stood on rickety platforms showing their legs and breasts and trying to lure customers to buy dances and drinks for their co-workers. Raucous music blared from every tavern and saloon. Shills hollered the names of their games of chance and madams took bids for their girls.

"Lookee! Lookee! Lookee!" an elderly madam with her face painted like a China doll screeched. She pointed at the windows of her two-storied house. "Each and every one is a talented creature straight from Orleans. You name your pleasure and I'll name the price."

Two doors down, another madam was shouting, "Free drinks! Free drinks, if you buy a beautiful Lucky Lady. Gotem by the hour or night, gents. No

Nigs or Mexes here, me lads. All prime virgins or double your money back!"

Elsa Jane neither saw nor heard any of it. Her eyes were glued to Jamieson's hat, which he doffed to each and every madam as he sauntered along. He touched the brim with a finger to every shill and tavern owner.

Gone were the days when he was a customer, or a broke sailor standing outside the brawling joints hoping to get in. He had been a nobody, but once free from jail, he had decided to become a somebody —and fast. The gaming tables were the quickest route to money, and in time he had been able to cheat even "Charley the Ace" without the cardshark catching on.

But he was too sharp to sink his money into just one flea-bitten joint. He worked them all, and fleeced any sucker stupid enough to sit at his table "for a friendly game."

The last three days his luck had all been bad. The hotel was filled with officers whose money had gone down with their boats, and other steamers were avoiding the town until they were sure the sunken boats were not a hazard to them. No one was doing any business.

He walked to the far end of town, where the road started up for Natchez, and entered the first of two identical houses. No torches lighted them. No signs announced their purpose. They looked like ideal family dwellings and that was exactly the way Sally Kallenbrough wanted it.

No riffraff or brawlers for Sally. She catered only to officers and passengers, and the occasional Natchez businessman who could slip unseen down the bluff and through her back door. She served only imported Canadian liquor, English gin and Scotch whiskey, and she charged plenty for it. She also charged a pretty penny for her bevy of twelve girls.

The forty-year-old widow was widely known in the brothel business for her eccentric ways. She was a cleanliness fanatic, would not let any girl work more than five customers a week, would never take on a customer herself, no matter how high the price offered, made all her girls sit down to a hearty meal each day and had an extensive wardrobe with a matching parasol for each of her flamboyant outfits. She was known best for her motto, which emphasized her desire to keep away the riffraff.

"I don't charge for the uniform, but the man beneath it."

"Parasol Sally" was well aware that most of the horse-studded sailors used stolen officers' uniforms to gain entrance to her establishment. She could spot the impostors the minute they entered her saloon. She let them stay as long as they acted like gentlemen and didn't argue when she charged them higher fees.

Her pet peeve, however, was hustling gamblers, but it seemed they were one of the necessary evils of her trade.

"Good evening, Miss Sally. Your maid sick?"

"Hardly." She never gave any more information than was necessary, especially to gamblers. Gamblers never bought, they only tried to get it for free.

"Any action?"

"Not here. Next door there's one table going, but the girls aren't working either house tonight."

Jamieson touched a finger to his hat. "I'll see if I can sit in, Miss Sally. Good evening."

Elsa Jane had seen Jamieson talk briefly with the well-dressed woman and then cross the small yard to the next house. He entered the second house without knocking. She couldn't figure it out. Was this where he lived?

She sat on a log across the road and waited for a light to go on in one of the windows. None appeared. She grew curious and ambled across the street and into the yard. The windows were heavily draped. She circled the house to check for an opening. She only found a crack of light where two drapes did not fit together properly.

She was barely tall enough to peek over the sill, but from what she could see, it was instantly obvious that this was not Jamieson's residence. Four men in shirtsleeves sat intently at the table playing cards. No one uttered anything more than an occasional mumble.

With hatred that had festered for years, Elsa Jane sat down in the shadow beneath the window and waited. Every fifteen minutes or so she would check to make sure the demon was there. The table of men would grow and diminish, but Jamieson remained, with piles of poker chips growing in front of him.

Eventually she returned to the street. She was sure that Jamieson would stay put long enough for her to bring about a plan that had been germinating in the back of her head. It took less than five minutes to get back to the hotel, but she noticed the changes. The dance-hall girls' steps had slowed, the tavern music was lagging and the voiceless madams stared desperately at the staggering drunks.

How could they sell what they couldn't even give away? Elsa Jane wondered.

Her hand trembled as she reached the back entrance to the hotel. The knob turned and she was quickly inside. She climbed the back stairs two at a time and casually entered the hall. She silently narched right up to the seated guard and stood before him.

Her excuse for being there would be the same, but her motive was quite different.

Her heart pounded. She could have walked right on into the captain's room, but that was no longer her desire.

Gingerly, she reached down, keeping her eyes on the guard's sleeping face and the dribble of tobacco juice that had trickled down from his gaping mouth, and closed her fingers around the barrel of the revolver. She slowly started to lift it out of his lap, but froze when he groaned and twitched in the tilted chair. He snorted, then rolled his bearded head to a more comfortable position, and sighed.

Quickly, she snatched up the weapon and hid it beneath her sailor's coat. She scurried down the hall and did not dare breathe until she had reached the back stairs.

Once back on the street, Elsa Jane felt as if she'd gone mad. A curious light glinted in her eyes. She had power at her side, and she would wait for Jamieson to finish his poker game and stalk him down like a rabid dog.

It was late. The brawling town that boasted that it never slept was putting out its street torches and closing tavern doors. Prostitutes cleaned their faces in rooms where they would sleep alone.

A kerosene lamp had been set on the porch of the house she sought. The gamblers were breaking up for the night and she feared she had missed Jamieson. Four men in pairs had already rounded the first corner of the climb to Natchez. Elsa Jane followed, hoping to see the single figure that symbolized her hate. However, none of the men's hats matched Jamieson's.

Her heart sank and she turned back. She was afraid she might never have another opportunity like this ever again.

Then down the road she heard a bright and cheerful whistle. Although she couldn't see the man, she would have known that whistle anywhere. She walked slowly, as if a despairing survivor, and came face to face with her enemy.

Daris Jaimeson was extremely happy. His night had been exceptionally profitable and he had been able to slip away without giving a "cut" to Parasol Sally. He now had enough stashed away to get him away from this depressed area. He would go where there was real money. Sailors were skinflints. They had too many ports of call full of women and grog to eat away their pay. Now, soldiers were something else, he thought.

That was his answer. The army had built forts all across the West to protect the wagon trains from Indians. Where did the fort soldiers have to spend their money?

Before he could finish his thought, he was looking directly into the barrel of a revolver.

"Now don't this beat all! I just sat on my butt for four hours winning a stake at gambling and some snot-nosed highwayman wants to take it from me."

"Don't want your money," Elsa Jane snapped.

Jamieson was startled. "What then?"

"Look close, you bastard! I want only for you to pay for the husband you took from me."

Jamieson looked but did not recognize her.

"I'm afraid I don't know you."

"I'm Elsa Jane," she screamed.

Jamieson's face paled in fright. He turned around, took two steps, grabbed for the derringer beneath his coat, and spun back.

She had made a gross error. She had forgotten to cock the hammer. The gambler's little pistol barked twice, catching her once in the thigh. She crumbled to the road, desperately trying to cock the hammer as she fell. With a sardonic laugh Jamieson raced past her.

"I don't know why I ever desired you. You can't do anything right!"

She aimed for his heart, but missed and hit his shoulder. The impact threw him but he remained on his feet and ran toward town.

Two other Natchez nighthawkers came staggering up the hill. They silently looked down at the bleeding young sailor, asked no questions, and speedily went along. They wished no involvement. Below was a lawless jungle. They wished nothing more than to climb back up to the top of the bluff and sleep in the security of their own homes.

The pain pierced her leg and thigh like a firebrand. She had been an idiot, a fool—and a very bad shot. Now she was the outlaw. At any moment she expected to hear the pounding of horses' hooves as a dragoon of lawmen came to drag her away as a common criminal.

"Oh, damn," she moaned, crawling to the side of the road, "why must I think that I know everything? Peter's shotgun is the only other weapon I've ever fired. I made a mess of it because I thought like a man and reacted like a woman. Well, that's what I am. Or am I?"

Everything seemed so lost—ship, friends, job and captain. Inch by torturous inch, she clawed her way back down the road, tumbling down an embankment and crashing into a tree. She knew she would never be able to crawl down the center of town to the warehouse without being spotted. Even if she did reach the warehouse, who of the crew would help her dress the wound? Not a single name came to mind. They were gone—all gone—all gone to watery graves.

Her wounded leg was nearly useless and drained her of strength with each pump of her heart. Her mind began to wander. The two houses she crawled toward seemed familiar, but she couldn't recall why.

Only one thing seemed important—she must get away before the lawmen found her.

Then, between the two establishments of Sally Kallenbrough, Elsa Jane fainted.

5

Missy Carver didn't know what to do. She wanted nothing with dead folk. She'd have to wake Sally, even though she knew she'd get her ears boxed.

Cursing like a sailor who had just burnt his hands on a tow rope, Sally stormed into the yard. She had heard the shots but had paid them no heed. It was none of her business then. Now it was, and she was furious. She figured it was a trick of some other madam who wanted to ruin her reputation.

"Humping whores!" she growled. "Look at those marks in the mud, Missy. Bitches dragged him here and dropped him. Roll him over!"

The thin little black girl shivered violently and screwed up her face, but one never countermanded an order from Parasol Sally. Gingerly she dug the toe of her shoe beneath Elsa Jane's shoulder and shoved. The limp body rolled over easily.

Elsa Jane's face was whiter than chalk and her blood had soaked her entire pant leg. Cold fear gripped Sally. How much blood could a person lose and still be alive? She bent her head to Elsa Jane's chest and could just make out a faint heartbeat.

"Alive, praise be. Seems small enough for us to handle, Missy. You take the legs and I'll handle the shoulders."

Missy blinked. "Which house, mum?"

"Mine," she answered without hesitation. "No use troubling the girls with this until we know how bad off he is."

Missy nodded and stepped forward. Together they were able to haul E.J. around to the back of the house and into a little unused bedroom off the kitchen.

Sally used a butcher knife to slit the trouser leg, while Missy started a fire to heat water. She examined the wound with the expertise of a doctor.

During her fifteen-year marriage, Sally Kallenbrough had seen and dressed many such wounds. Sam Kallenbrough had been a fighter. He fought men, animals and the elements, from the Blue Ridge Mountains to the Ozarks. His dreams were always just over the next hill, and Sally had doggedly followed him. It was the only existence she had known.

Sam then left her alone for two years in a Memphis shanty while he went off to pursue another dream —the independence of Texas. Texas won and Sam lost. For six years after he grumbled about his wooden leg, and what little marriage there had been, disappeared.

She couldn't fully recall how she went to work for Memphis Kate. She only remembered that she had been twenty-four and powerfully hungry. She could also recall that Memphis Kate had the filthiest house on the Memphis waterfront, although at the time Sally wasn't aware of it.

"A six-year nightmare," she would honestly tell her own girls. "I had always been barren with Sam, so that wasn't my worry. It was the disease, dirt and dreadful men. God, some of those bastards—you wanted to cut off their dirt-coated things and throw them into the Mississippi. The only thing that kept me sane was being able to take a bath at home. That's why I insist that you each bathe daily. But the bath was also my downfall. Sam got suspicious. I can still hear that damn wooden leg clomping down the hall at Memphis Kate's. Sam picked the wrong time to walk in on me. The bargeman also had a gun. That was the last wound I had to dress for Sam Kallenbrough. It was also the last time I worked for old Kate. They closed her down."

Sally Kallenbrough was thirty when she arrived in New Orleans. She was too old to work in any of the "fashionable" houses and stubbornly determined not to go back to a dive like Kate's.

Based on her previous experience and her dogged cleanliness, Myrtle LaRue gave her a job as a chambermaid. "A dash of salt among the pepper," Myrtle had chuckled, but Sally's friendliness and maturing beauty won her laurels with some of the clientele. Within a month Myrtle dressed her up and told her to serve drinks in the saloon. Sally became determined never to be without fine dresses ever again, and when parasols came into fashion, she took to them handily.

Myrtle LaRue noticed something else about Sally that she could use. Sally could act like a lady and blend in on the New Orleans streets. She became

Myrtle's personal errand girl, shopper, solicitor and banker. Sally began learning the business from an old master.

When Myrtle died, she didn't rebel when the house was turned over to someone else. She just casually went about New Orleans on errands of her own. Her nest egg was small, but she now personally knew Myrtle's bankers, lawyers and dressmakers. She also knew all of their dark secrets.

The lawyer drew up the proper documents for her for non-interest loans, the dressmakers gave her long-term payment agreements for her outstanding new wardrobe.

She returned to Memphis in triumph—but no one noticed.

Memphis had not been ready for a fashionable New Orleans "cat" house, nor had St. Louis or Vicksburg. Her dreams took a steady, five-year downhill slide to Natchez-under-the-Hill.

Her house was prosperous enough, but it was nothing like that of Myrtle LaRue.

Sally continued to cut away the trousers in order to cleanse the body and check for other wounds. Shocked, she quickly folded the slashed remnants back over E.J.'s femininity.

"I'll do the rest alone! Just get me more hot water, sheets and a nightgown. Move!"

The snapping order startled Missy. She sped away without a word. Sally took the duck fabric away from the wounded leg and began to wash away the dried blood.

"Well, my little mystery person, it's a nasty tearing of the thigh, but the bullet went right on through. I think you've bled away any lead fragments there might have been. Come on, little one, a lot of it will be up to you, now. You've got to live, because you've sparked old Sally's curiosity bone."

She worked swiftly and efficiently. She removed all Elsa Jane's clothing and marveled at the shapely, feminine frame that had been hidden. She cleansed her with soap and water first, and then with rinse water. She moved her back and forth gently on the narrow bed, careful not to start the wound bleeding again, as she removed the soiled sheets and placed fresh ones beneath her. Then she washed Elsa Jane's whole body with rubbing alcohol and went to work on the wound.

Pure Scotch whiskey was poured into the torn flesh until it dripped out of the other side of the thigh. The stinging caused Elsa Jane to thrash her head back and forth, groaning.

"That's it, little one, work your way out of the shock. I see a tinge of pink coming back into those cheeks now. Lord, I bet they called you a pretty boy."

Missy knocked gently and handed Sally her sewing basket.

"Got a touch of news, Miss Sally," she whispered.

"Yes."

"Natchez men been here searchin' for a body. Said I was de only one who awake 'n I ain't heard or seen nothing."

"Good girl, Missy."

"Knows who shot 'im, too."

"Oh?"

"Doc Frawley took a slug outta the gambling man's shoulder during the night and then he left on the dawn stage. Dat's why the Natchez men am lookin' for a corpse."

Sally chuckled as she closed the door. "Then let them keep looking, Missy. We don't know a thing."

Just as expertly and efficiently as she had been

cleaning the wound, Sally took silk thread and began
to sew the torn flesh together. She made tiny stitches,
as if she were working on a delicate embroidery pattern for one of her dresses. She tied the ends of the
thread long so that they could later be snipped and
pulled from the healing wound.

"Now you are even more of a curiosity, little one.
I wonder if it was an accident or if you knew that
vulture. You don't look like the type that would get
mixed up gambling with the like of Daris Jamieson.
Curious. But thank you. I've just been waiting for the
right man to come along and chase him out of town."

Then she laughed silently. She wondered if the
arrogant gambler had been aware that he had run
from a woman . . . which then made her wonder why
Jamieson had run. Shootings took place all the time,
but the Natchez law very seldom stuck their noses
into it. There was no law under-the-hill, except for
the law of the steamer lines when they wanted to
impose it.

Sally rightly guessed Elsa Jane's age to be about
twenty. She figured she'd been on the river a lot as
her face and upper neck were tanned far darker than
the rest of her body. Her equally darkened hands
confirmed this fact—they were work-hardened and
stub-nailed.

She was curious, however, about the odd, dark
strap marks around Elsa Jane's breasts. She wondered
if it was a permanent discoloration. Gently, she began
to knead and massage them to increase the circula-
tion. The flatness vanished as they grew and hardened under her ministrations.

Sally's hands grew sweaty and she shivered. She
let a hand move down to massage the belly and thin
waist. She knew nothing about this person, and suddenly she wanted to know so much.

She loathed being touched by Memphis Kate, but with Myrtle LaRue, it had been an intimate pleasure; they had been close friends.

She had never been intimate with any of her own girls. Motherly, yes. Caring, yes. But never intimate. She just couldn't do business that way. She needed someone like Elsa Jane to replace Myrtle. She needed someone to know the real Sally Kallenbrough; to look beyond all the fancy trappings, and she didn't feel a man could do it. To her, men were all nothing more than grunting clients.

She let her hand roam along the edges of Elsa Jane's pubic hair.

Nor did she want a woman who could be turned into a whore. Myrtle had never allowed her to have clients, and she had proved far more valuable to Myrtle, besides being a loving companion. Didn't she deserve something similar?

Sally softly put her cheek down on Elsa Jane's lower belly and rested. Tears rolled from her eyes. For years she had thought her life with Sam had been lonely and depressing, but she had not really known loneliness until now.

It had taken her five years to pay off all the loans. A house of twelve girls was not an inexpensive matter, especially when she fed and clothed them like they were all in New Orleans and was choosy about clients.

She never discussed business with her girls—it wasn't good policy. But damn, she needed *someone* to discuss it with!

Elsa Jane's skin was still unnaturally cold and clammy. Sally wanted to kiss it back to warmth. She shivered again, as she burned with desire. It had been five years. She quickly did what she had longed to do.

* * *

Elsa Jane quickly learned that the woman who had cared for her was both frank and honest. She was not nearly as shocked by what Sally had done to her as she was by the fact that she was a madam. Somehow, it seemed impossible that this beautiful woman, with her fine clothing, had anything to do with such a horrid profession. Still, Elsa Jane had no reason to doubt the woman's word. How could she?

Sally kept Elsa Jane a secret from Missy and her other girls. She told her everything she knew about Daris Jamieson, and was able to give her daily reports of the investigation and news about Raymond Spurlock. Not since the days of Melanie Caldwell had Elsa Jane been so well cared for.

She was therefore quite honest with Sally. She shared every detail of her life with her. It was as if Sally had become her confessor.

As the days passed the red marks on her breasts faded and the angry bullet wound healed. Her own natural strength and vitality returned. However, each morning she awoke to the misery of guilt and each night she vowed not to let Sally's passions continue.

At first, she had been only too willing to lie on the narrow bed and seek oblivion from her pain through Sally's patient massage. She could not return Sally's stored-up ardor, but sensed that the woman was really in love with her, and after that first night tried to forget that it was a woman unlocking her own long pent-up emotions. Then, with her gradual return of strength, she began to feel confined. Her meals were shared only with Sally. All of the news that she received came through Sally. She saw no one but Sally. It was as if Sally wanted to keep her in the little room forever and never let her be with another human being. Her mind, released from the pain of her wounds, began to question Sally's purpose. The forced inactivity and doubt caused her to long for a change, even a change for the worse. She wondered why they didn't bring the investigation to a close. She wanted to get back to work to support her children, and she wanted to end this tedious, never-ending confinement.

Sally knew she couldn't keep Elsa Jane a prisoner forever. She began to try and win her heart in other ways.

"Thank you. These are just like brand-new."

Sally preened at the compliment. "Missy washed them all, and I sewed them back as near original as possible."

It gave her a vicarious thrill to see Elsa Jane dressed again as a sailor. *Her* sailor.

"And this came for you—in care of me."

Elsa Jane read the letter from Sister Margaret Rose over twice before she put it down.

"You wrote her?"

"I thought your children needed to know that you were alright. The accident was reported in the papers, you know."

"But you sent money—two month's worth."

"One month has nearly gone by, E.J. I—I thought . . ."

"I know what you thought," Elsa Jane answered in exasperation. "I appreciate it, but I don't take charity. When I get back to work, if that day ever comes, I'll pay you back."

"I know that, little one," Sally said soothingly, "but I was glad to do it for you." Then she sobered. "I'm not glad to do this E.J. All of my information, for certain free favors given in return, have come from your purser, Mr. Carriday. He's sent a Johnny Ramey to see you. Do you know him?"

"Sure. He's our cabin boy."

Sally hesitated. The young man had refused to speak to anyone but E.J., and she was afraid to leave him with her girls for too long or they would gang rape him. For ten days she had allowed no man in her house but Ladlow Carriday, and she had had to force various of her girls to take on the simpering fool. She would just have to loosen her rein on E.J., or stand losing her altogether.

"I'll bring him in."

And that's what she did—and stayed.

"Geez!" Johnny gasped. "You sure look great. We feared y'all were dying."

"Hi, Johnny," E.J. greeted him with her gravelly voice. It suddenly sounded very fake to her.

"Geez!" he repeated. "Don't get mad, E.J., but you shoulda been born a girl. With rest and all, you're a better looker than some of her broads." Then he blushed and turned to Sally. "No offense, ma'am."

Sally roared in delight. The boy's statement had answered a serious question. E.J.'s masquerade was not known to the crew.

Johnny Ramey's tune changed. "Sorry to bring bad news, E.J., but you know how chicken-shit, excuse me ma'am, ole Carriday is about such things."

"What is it, Johnny?" She was completely alert.

"Was bad yesterday, and worse today. Yesterday they said that the crews of both ships would be held responsible for the accident and all our back pay held to compensate for the boats we lost. Sixty of us, from both boats, beached and declared unhirable."

"The rotten screwing bastards!" E.J. roared. "How can they hold us all accountable? I hope Captain Spurlock is screaming his bloody head off!"

"He's dead!"

She reeled as though he had slapped her, and sank to the narrow bed.

"That was today," he continued weakly. "They declared yesterday that they were going to hold him personally accountable for the murder of Mr. Beauchamp; that Spider would not have been murdered if the captain would have had control of his vessel. He—he did something horrible to himself during the night."

E.J. rose from the bed, green eyes spitting red sparks. "What?" she snarled, her voice mean and demanding. "I will hear every last goddamn detail!"

"He—he—," Johnny whispered, "he castrated himself and bled to death."

"Good God!" Sally gasped, horrified. "Why that way?"

E.J. knew and did not think it necessary for anyone else to know. Captain Spurlock had sent a message to his estranged wife.

"It no longer matters," she said. Her voice was so calm, so assured, so forceful that they each were stunned. "Sally, are you opened or closed tonight?"

"Closed," she muttered.

"Good! I'll need one of your two houses for a meeting. Perhaps as many as sixty."

Sally nodded. She couldn't help but feel that she was acquiescing to a very dominant male.

"Johnny, I will not let those slimy blood-sucking company bastards beach us just to save their damn profit margin. Tell the *Memphis* boys that they worked just as hard for their wages as did the *Delta Star* crew. Tell our boys that I am not thinking of Captain Spurlock, but of Spider. He would be doing the same thing that I am doing."

Johnny gulped. "What are you doing, E.J.?"

Frankly, she didn't have the foggiest. The news had been so shattering that she didn't trust her own emotions. One whiff of Sally's perfume could turn her female and crying but if she allowed that, she feared she might just be weak enough to become Sally's prisoner forever. If she could surround herself with people sharing the same woes she might be able to outlast this latest grief.

"Just get those who want to come here by seven and then find out!"

After the cabin boy left, Parasol Sally repeated the same question.

"What are you doing, E.J.?"

"Trust me," E.J. answered with sudden craftiness, "just trust me. I have listened patiently to your problems, and now you see mine coming to the forefront. In a way, Sally, we are all beached at this end of the world. Where is there a future for any of us? The sailors can't sail. Unsailable sailors don't make money. Sailors without money can't buy their favors from your girls. Shall we all just sit and watch each other starve? Not me! Each day I live teaches me to cope with life a little bit more. I've never let it get me down before and I'm not about to start now."

Sally could believe that. Suddenly, she loved this woman's maleness. Without comment their roles had reversed.

It was not so easy to win over the sixty fierce and determined men who had spent most of their lives on the river, but gradually, E.J. found herself in the role of spokesman.

"Are we married to this river?" E.J. asked, wondering whether she hoped for "yes" or "no" as an answer.

"No, not if we can't find work!" Ladlow Carriday

shouted. He was really the only officer present and felt he should have been in charge.

"You'll never get another berth on the Miss," someone sneered.

"Who will?" several shouted.

"Exactly," E.J. proclaimed. "Who will and why should we? They've got us in the barrel and sticking it through the hole at us. Oh, I know. You all think I don't know about those things. Well, I'm not blind and I'm not deaf. I'm just as river-wise as any man here. Think back, each of you. Has there ever been a time we haven't been in Orleans that one of those clipper agents hasn't been around making their offers?"

"Forget it, matey. I've heard tell of their cheatin' ways and that damnable passage."

"Right," she shouted back, "because they can easily cheat a single sailor on a single cruise. But what difference is one cruise around the Cape to the same fifty up and down the river?"

"Port calls," someone snickered.

"Rubbish! They've also got to make port calls for provisions and horny-handed sailors."

"Then get back to their cheatin' ways."

"I shall," E.J. said flatly, "because how can they cheat us if we are a solid unit? Sixty working crewmen carrying along thirteen paying passengers."

"Who the deuce are the passengers?"

"Need I tell you?" E.J. knew Sally was watching but did not look at her.

"And where would we be headed?"

"For some, the gold fields of California, for others the rich trade routes bringing Chinese goods from the Orient."

"Come, come now," Carriday said in good humor. "There is no place for rivermen on ocean vessels."

"Are you saying we are not qualified, Mr. Carriday?"

E.J. asked tartly. "Then, again, I have never been a purser."

She did not have to say more. The accusation was more crushing than a thousand words. Had Carriday done his job in a professional manner the captain and crew of the *Delta Star* would never have been able to get their hands on the liquor.

"How dare you?" Carriday snarled, turning purple.

"Easily," E.J. said, without batting an eye. "Because I don't believe in the innocent having to suffer for the petty inabilities of the guilty. I'm for California! Sally's girls are for California! Who else is with us?"

Sally's girls were not present to speak for themselves. They sat innocently in the next house, oblivious to what was transpiring. The men looked to Sally for confirmation.

Sally rose like a queen and smoothed her dress down over her ample breasts and hour-glass waist. There was not a man present who had not coveted her or one of her girls at one time or another. She was the epitome of their dreams.

"Why turn your questioning eyes toward me? My full faith in the matter rests with E.J."

Picking her skirts up to give them a tantalizing glimpse of her trim ankles, she left to break the news to her girls. That, she felt, would be an easy matter. Either they went or they were fired. She felt elated. E.J. would not have proposed this scheme unless they were meant to stay together.

E.J. was simply being river-wise. They would all rot in that hole before the companies would give them another berth. Parasol Sally was the only one with funds enough to get them downriver. ⟶§

7

E.J. HAD steeled herself for the indignities Sally would demand, but she had no idea it would go on for so long. It was a hundred-and-forty-day voyage from Havana to Sacramento via two seas and two oceans.

Fifty men had eagerly followed E.J. on the less expensive trip to New Orleans, and thirty had disappeared immediately.

It was there that she knew she had made a grave error. The Cape Horn route was well-advertised, but it was not out of New Orleans.

"Boston! New York! How the hell do we get there to be able to leave from there?"

Sally was livid. At least up North she had had a roof over her head that didn't cost her anything. What made it worse was that E.J. could do nothing about it.

The other men looked for jobs but their names were blacklisted with each and every river company. Only a Cuban-owned freighting line out of Havana would even talk to them.

Cautiously, E.J. spoke to some of the crew of one of the Cuban vessels. The pay was poor, the food was all Spanish and the return sailing dates could not be relied on. But she did learn something interesting.

"Don't you see, Sally, we can form a company like the shipping agents are doing. The agents want each member to pay three hundred dollars and give them an equal proportion of all profits made by the company either by mining or trading. Well, your girls are in trading, of a sort. I bet each of your girls have a few hundred tucked away. As for the men, we will reverse the process. We are a solid block of twenty-five, and that Diego fellow told me that many clippers sit for weeks in Havana harbor trying to build their crews back up from those who have changed their minds after sailing down from Boston."

"Well and good, E.J. But this is not Havana."

"We'll book aboard the freighter as passengers and crew."

"You're not thinking clearly. You said you had to book round-trip but only got paid on the return."

E.J. grinned. "Who said anything about returning? It will still be free passage for the twenty-five men to Cuba."

Their fortunes changed quickly. The barque-rigged *Lady Beth* had departed Salem understaffed and with only half its passenger list. Captain Josiah Perch said nothing about the fact that stout ships were already going begging at San Francisco for lack of cargo and passengers. The gold boom was beginning to diminish and he needed the thirty-nine-hundred dollar passenger fare.

As Mrs. Sam Kallenbrough, with parasol and Bible clutched tightly, Sally looked every inch the proper "lady" escort for her twelve "mail-order brides" destined for Sacramento, where men outnumbered women twenty to one.

The hard-driving Josiah Perch scanned the list of duties the various men had performed on the river steamers. They may not have been able to name every tag of rigging or every plank of a barque-rigged vessel, but they appeared to be men he could quickly shape into ocean sailors. Besides, he would be getting their services for free passage.

The problem was that the *Lady Beth* was only one-third the size of the *Flying Cloud*, which had set the record of eighty-nine days to San Francisco. It took the *Lady Beth* ninety-two days just to reach Cape Horn. There they met heavy gales and strong seas the like of which they had never experienced on the river.

"Oh, my God, E.J., I'm dying."

"Hush, Sally," E.J. mumbled. "Hush, please hush! Captain Perch says it will be calm once we hit the Pacific."

"I'm never going to reach it," she wailed. "I've nothing left to vomit up."

The smell of the two cabins attested to that fact. The women were packed three high on either side of the rooms. There was a cot in one for Sally. The arrangement had been a saving grace for E.J. as there was no privacy for Sally to make advances.

"Hush!" she repeated. "The other girls are just as seasick." And one even more so, she thought glumly.

Elsa Jane had begun to see the telltale signs in

Beth Larkin for several days and had paid close attention. When she was sure that Beth was with child she kept the fact to herself.

The Antarctic winds brought freezing temperatures and a sense of danger. The *Lady Beth* rolled and lurched, dipping in and out of the mountainous waves like a top.

"All hands!" Captain Perch hollered over the roar of the waves. "All hands man the sails!"

He had to bear down hard on the crew now to get them through the Drake Passage, otherwise they would be drawn down below the Antarctic Circle and into the Bellingshausen Sea.

In comparison, this storm made the river blizzards seem tame. Spars were carried away like pieces of balsam wood. Sails split and blew out. Men's fingers froze as they tried to sew the ragged edges.

"*Jesus!*" the man working above E.J. said, paling.

E.J. had felt it too. It was subtle but ominous. She took off her mittens and pressed her hand against the smooth wood surface of the mainmast. It vibrated as if alive. She put her ear to the surface.

"Down!" she screamed. "Everybody down off the mainmast! She's cracking." The crew did not have to be told a second time. It gave them an excuse to go inside for a few minutes, as they could do little but let her crack and pray that it wasn't taken overboard.

E.J. stayed on deck. If the mast fell overboard, the crew would have to be called out to chop it away before it could capsize the vessel.

A small figure came out of the forward passage and leaned against the starboard rail. E.J. cursed. This was no time for a passenger to be taking the air. She inched gingerly along the ice-coated deck toward the figure.

"*God!*" E.J. slipped and fell in her attempt to run. The figure was trying to climb over the rail. It was no use trying to call out; the wind drowned any sound.

E.J. crawled on all fours. The figure seemed to be hesitating. She was finally able to rise and move more quickly along the railing.

"Why, Beth—" she cried with anger and reproach, peering into the girl's stark face, "whatever are you doing?"

"Leave me alone!"

"No one is supposed to be on deck, Beth."

"Exactly. And no one was to see me."

"Do you wish to talk about it?"

E.J. scooped her from the rail and harshly pushed the girl in front of her.

After some feeble protests, Beth allowed herself to be taken to the cabin E.J. shared with five of the crew. Beth looked like she was going to be ill again.

E.J. flung open the wooden shutter of the deck window to let in the bracing air.

"Is it because of the child?"

"E.J.," Beth gasped, "how do you know about it?"

"I've been watching you. Your seasickness seems to come only in the morning and then you seem fine for the rest of the day."

"What luck—" Beth said morosely, staring out the little window at the black waters. "If an inexperienced person like you has noticed, then I'm doomed."

"Doomed?"

"By now you should know Sally's most famous motto—'If you start baking a bun in the oven get rid of it or I'll get rid of you.'"

"But you were trying to get rid of yourself, as well."

"Exactly," she declared, wagging her head so vigorously that her dark curls bounced. "Not being a woman, you wouldn't understand."

E.J. looked tenderly at the sweet comely face beneath the halo of dark hair. Beth was really more child than woman.

"I understand better than you think, Beth. Is it the first time you have ever been pregnant?"

Despite her profession, Beth was embarrassed that she was discussing such a topic with a male. She gathered her arms tight about her and whispered through her teeth. "Yes. I've always been careful before."

"Then why not this time?"

"Let me be!" cried Beth, loudly and sharply. Then E.J. sensed the problem.

"Sit down, Beth. I don't mean to embarrass you, but I'm not about to let you do something foolish. You must want this child very much."

Beth sat on the edge of the lower bunk with terror in her eyes.

"I'm going to tell you something, Beth. Something that will require your utmost secrecy. I am a woman. I also have two children. They are in an orphanage and I have had to pose as a man just to get work to support them. Now do you wish to discuss the whole matter with me?"

Beth couldn't believe what she had heard. She tried to smile up at E.J., that powerful, swaggering, handsome man in a foul-weather slicker, so masculine that even several of Sally's girls had been jealous of the madam keeping E.J. all to herself.

"But . . . but," she stammered, "what about you and Sally?"

"Sally learned when she took care of my wounds. She has kept my secret well."

That was all E.J. felt was needed to be said about the matter.

"I'll be damned. Were you a prostitute?"

It was a logical question but it made Elsa Jane laugh. "Hardly, Beth. I had the most marvelous husband for four years. He was killed."

"Do you ever think about getting a new one?"

"Someday I shall, Beth. Someday when I fall in love again."

"That's such a simple word, isn't it? Love."

"Complex as hell, Beth. Everyone eyes it differently, I am coming to find out. Is that your problem? The man was just a . . . ah . . . client?"

Beth rose and started to pace the narrow passage of the cabin.

"He wasn't that," she protested. "Oh, I suppose he was the first time, in New Orleans. It started as a dare from the other girls. He was so cute and young and bashful. Then it happened again while we were in Havana. I had to keep it secret from Sally because there was no charge. Oh God, she'll just kill me, I know."

"Sally is the least of your worries, Beth. The main question, because I am assuming he is one of our crew, is whether he knows about the child."

"Good grief, no!"

"Don't you want him as a husband?"

Her fingers twisted in the folds of her cloak. "More than anything."

"Ah, I see. You are afraid that he would not want you as a wife and mother of his children. You can't remain a whore all your life, Beth. And frankly, you're not forceful enough a woman to ever become a madam. None of Sally's girls are, when you get right down to it. I think she picks them that way so she doesn't have competition.

"Cute and bashful," she murmured. "Which one is it, Beth?"

"It will have to be my secret to you. It's Johnny."

"*Johnny Ramey*? He's a boy!"

"He's now sixteen and quite a man," she protested. "Oh, I know that he is awfully quiet, even in our moments of passionate love, and he has great plans for his future in California. That's what I can't ruin, his future, E.J."

"That's admirable, but foolish. What of your own future?"

"You mean my dreams?" she asked timidly. "When I saw that this ship bore the same name as myself I thought that was a good omen for the future. I could just see Johnny and me falling madly in love and being so happy."

"The child doesn't change that, Beth. It is something between the two of you. If you kept going back to Johnny, as you suggested, then the child was conceived in love. If you can share each others bodies in passion, then shouldn't you both share this problem you created equally?"

"But Sally will kill us," she insisted, near tears.

"Why don't you leave Sally to me? I have to go check on the cracking of the mainmast. Johnny was on that crew. I will send him down to you, if you promise to be forthright with him."

"What if he says 'no,'?" she wailed.

"Then you will know if he is still a boy just playing at being a man. Has he ever said that he loved you?"

"Not lately."

"Why not?" Elsa Jane asked with surprise.

"I've avoided him completely since I've known about the child. I feared that he would claim that it wasn't his. He's the only man that I have touched since we left Natchez."

"And you don't want to touch another?"

"How did you know that?"

"I guessed," Elsa Jane said gently. She examined Beth's quiet young face and saw that her hazel eyes were as honest and clear as brook water. She smiled.

"Yes, love is a simple thing for you and for Johnny. Just tell him that. I'll send him."

"Wait! I don't know how to thank you. I've always admired the way that you brought this all about for us and am now amazed that you did it all as a woman. I will be just as strong in this matter as you would be."

Elsa Jane blushed and fled. She was not used to flattery. Besides, she would have to be even stronger when Sally heard about Beth's condition.

After dispatching Johnny, she forgot about Sally entirely. The mainmast had cracked, but had not broken. Lengths of hemp had to be twisted about its base and buckets of pitch heated for a sealer.

All the while the *Lady Beth* was rounding the Cape and heading up the Pacific coast of Chile. Fifteen hundred miles to Valparaiso seemed short when compared with the seventeen thousand of the entire voyage.

Captain Perch made a sharp stamp, and stretched his hand above his head. "Not now! The bloody wind is slacking off!"

The crew followed his scowling gaze up to the sails. They were flapping fitfully, where they had been taut-bellied a few minutes earlier. Within hours they were totally slack.

For twenty-one days there was no wind and the boat drifted aimlessly, but there was nothing calm aboard the ship.

Sally wanted Beth to abort the baby. She was livid when E.J. told her she had nothing to say about the matter and that the captain was willing to marry the young couple. Sally carried on so that her face turned purple. She had never lost one of her girls to marriage.

"No," she shouted, the single syllable vibrating through the room. "No! If you help them go through with this, you damn runt, our deal is off! Fend for yourself when we get to California!"

Elsa Jane got up slowly and left. She refused to speak to Sally for the remainder of the voyage.

Beth put on her gown made of French serge, blue as the cornflowers in her farm home meadows, and her white lawn falling collar. The sea air made the collar limp but no one noticed. All they saw was Beth's jubilant face.

She longed for her mother to be there. One of fourteen children, she had run away from the Missouri farm at sixteen after her stepfather had crawled into her bed for the fifth time. She had come to Sally well experienced, but now that was over, and she wanted her mother to know she had turned out alright.

Johnny Ramey had asked E.J. to be his best man. It was a strange moment for Elsa Jane. The words touched a memory of her own marriage. She had had but a single witness. For Beth, everybody aboard, save for Sally, was in attendance. She wished the young couple the same love and happiness that her marriage had brought to her.

The ceremony and the following celebration made them all briefly forget their troubles. But the moment was short-lived.

The term "clipper" did not apply to the rig of a ship or to its size, but to the vessel's ability to sail swiftly—to "clip along the waves." The *Lady Beth* wasn't "clipping" and was dangerously low on food and water.

Thomas Roddenberry was the leader of a group of twenty men known as the *Beverly Mining Organization*. His was the largest passenger group, next to Sally's, on board.

"Mr. Roddenberry, we are all in the same fix."

"A deplorable fix, Captain Perch. The pork is rusty, the beef rotten, the duff half-cooked and the beans contain two bugs to a bean!"

"Which will be seen to at our next port of call."

"That has been your excuse for over twenty days, sir."

"And are we not moving again, sir? Granted it is not a fair wind. I can only suggest, sir, that if our speed is not to your liking that you get out and walk."

That gave the officers and crew something to chuckle about.

However, during the night Mr. Roddenberry took it upon himself to steal from the larder to feed his own group. He was caught in the act by the steward and thrown into the hold. His twenty men formed their own "mutiny" and nine crewmen died trying to control it.

Hoping for peace, Captain Perch ordered Mr. Roddenberry released. Unfortunately, someone had decided to give the man an opportunity to walk upon the waters. His chains had been sawed through and he could not be found anywhere aboard ship.

The passengers and crew were divided evenly about the course of action to be taken. The more verbal faction demanded the right to place the full blame on Captain Perch. The calmer faction, headed by Elsa Jane, cautioned against doing anything until they reached Valparaiso. Captain Perch wisely turned command of his vessel over to the first mate.

The first mate, just as wisely, gave orders that once they reached the harbor to allow nearly everyone to go ashore for three days.

After weeks at sea, the passengers and crew soon forgot the missing Mr. Roddenberry. Valparaiso was a gay port, with wide plazas, music, entertainment and beautiful women.

Only Sally's girls were unhappy. The Chilean men did not wish to pay for what they could get for free.

Elsa Jane stayed aboard and acted as supply officer for the new provisions. The amount of supplies purchased did make her curious, but not for long.

"It would pleasure me, Mr. Forest, if you would assume the duties of the third mate for the rest of the voyage."

"As you wish, sir."

Josiah Perch grinned broadly. "That's what I like best about you, Mr. Forest. No questions asked of my authority or of the fact that my third mate is being replaced. But, as you will learn, I am fair and honest with my officers. I've sold the remaining passage rights of Mr. Roddenberry's group to Captain Jessup of the *Morning Bell*. I have also sold the rights of those crew who in one manner or another supported him in their ill-fated mutiny. We still have nearly three months to California, lad. I'll not allow a repeat of what has happened in the past."

Only one event repeated itself during the rest of the voyage. Two more of Sally's girls felt their only salvation lay in getting pregnant and married. This further alienated Sally from Elsa Jane, as Elsa Jane was held solely responsible by Sally.

* * *

The April fog banks were such that San Francisco Bay appeared a ghostly graveyard for unmoving ships. The city could not be seen at all.

Captain Perch proceeded directly upstream to Sacramento. He had last docked there just after the fire of 1852, and now he had arrived just in time for another disaster.

The long, dry winter had turned into a wet, cold spring. The riverfront was bustling with life and despite the driving rain, the passengers and crew of the *Lady Beth* lined the starboard railing and cheered their arrival at the land of El Dorado.

They thought the returned cheers were a sign of welcome, but what was being welcomed was the vessel itself. The city had turned surly and wanted no part of newcomers. The financial depression of 1855 had left thousands with shattered hopes. The wealth they had wrested from the ground was swallowed up in spiraling inflation.

The lines formed quickly at the *Lady Beth* gangway. Desperate men were willing to offer any service they could for a berth back east. Captain Perch kept to his quarters and would consider no offers until he had disposed of his present consignees.

"She will lose more of her ladies," Perch told E.J. "The free-and-easy days of the gold camps are gone. Mrs. Kallenbrough will find that they have deteriorated into license and abuse."

"But . . ." Elsa Jane stammered.

"I am not blind, Mr. Forest. This is my seventh trip in as many years. However, I will admit this group of ladies has been the most well-mannered and least troublesome. I will give them first option to return, if they so desire."

"I doubt that she would accept, Captain Perch."

"I thought not. But what of you?"

The same question had been on Elsa Jane's mind since they had passed through Golden Gate. Again, she knew she was going to have to be honest—but not fully.

"Captain, I must stay and develop a livelihood. I have two children to support in St. Louis and they have not had a cent from me in five months. They are my first obligation."

"I fully understand, E.J., and admire your frankness. What say you for the rest of your crew?"

"They have all privately let me know their feelings, sir. Twelve will return with you as seamen. The rest still wish to try their luck in the gold fields."

Within a month they all wished they had sailed with the *Lady Beth*. The banks and gravel slopes of Deer Creek had yielded nobly to it's ten thousand inhabitants, and it soon became known as Nevada City. Ownership of a claim now included all the dips, spurs and angles of the vein, rather than just the area above ground. There were no new claims to be had, and the only work to be found was in the slush boxes for the well-established companies.

"Not even enough left for a glass of beer."

Elsa Jane couldn't have cared less about such nighttime activities. Her enthusiasm had been drained by the back-breaking work and slave wages. Her thoughts were of Annie and Charley and how to help them when she couldn't even help herself.

"Beth and I can't make it here, E.J. I've got to be thinking of the child," Johnny Ramey announced.

Johnny had foolishly thought he could strike it rich with the first shovel of gravel. Beth had not expected the luxuries of a Parasol Sally house, but was certainly not prepared for the hardships they had found in Nevada City.

"What do you plan on doing, Johnny?"

Johnny sighed. His blue eyes wandered past Elsa Jane to the dusty lane among the wooden buildings. "Not let her go back to Sally," he stated vaguely. "Never again that." There was anxiety in his eyes.

Elsa Jane had seen Sally talking with Beth. "Is she trying to get you back?" she asked softly.

Johnny blushed but Beth nodded and smiled.

"You know Sally, E.J. She claims I still owe her on our contract to get here. It was my own three hundred I put up, and you know it. She says I'm letting the other girls down and wants me to either go back to work after the child is born or buy my way out of the contract."

"How can you do either?"

Beth grinned. "You know I could never do the first, E.J., but Sally knows I could do the latter. I've still got a little kitty tucked away that my Johnny won't let me touch until the child is born. I want him to use that money right now to get us established elsewhere."

"Johnny?"

"I don't know, E.J. It just doesn't seem right to use Beth's money."

"It would seem that it is both your money now, Johnny. It took me a long time to learn that about marriage. It's another form of sharing."

Johnny blanched. "You married, E.J.?"

"And has two fine children in St. Louis," Beth quickly added.

Elsa Jane looked at the young woman with tenderness. Beth had been good to her word.

"Well I'll be damned," Johnny said excitedly. "Then I guess you're right about us getting out. Still . . . well, E.J., Sally scares the hell out of me. What if she still tries to hound us? I—I don't want people knowing about Beth's past. Would you have a talk with her?"

"Johnny," Beth scolded. "Hasn't E.J. done enough for us already?"

Johnny shrugged.

"It's alright," Elsa Jane said quietly. "I'll do what I can, although we haven't been too friendly lately. You just start thinking about your plans to get away."

But as she trudged up the path to where Sally had put her remaining girls to work, her heart was troubled. Any favors asked of Sally Kallenbrough meant favors in return. She just couldn't do that again.

A hundred yards up the slope from the town, Sally had found shelter for her girls. To get it, she promised the owner she would turn over a percentage of three months' profit. *Madame Moustache's* made Natchez-under-the-Hill look like fairyland.

It was a hundred feet long and twenty wide and was made with rough siding. The walls of the "living" quarters were covered with animal furs. The floor of the first fifty feet was earth—frozen hard, mushy mud or choking dust, depending upon the weather. The planked flooring was icy cold, muddied and splintery. Sailcloth hung from rope rods, dividing the back of the building into cubicles for Sally, her girls and the infamous Madame Moustache.

Elsa Jane had not yet met the celebrated lady-gambler, but had heard stories from those who had lost at her *vingt-et-un* tables.

Elsa Jane entered the dark and smoky establishment.

It had not occurred to her that Parasol Sally had been so hard up. She couldn't tell if it was the bad lighting or the situation, but Sally looked old and tired. Her fashionable shoes had been given up for cumbersome boots and the bottom of her gown was covered in caked mud.

Elsa Jane stood quietly and waited for Sally to acknowledge her. There was a scuffle of chairs as a game at the center table ended. An unkempt woman circled the table. Her hair was like a rat's nest and her gown was stained with claret. She stared sullenly at Elsa Jane.

Madame Moustache approached E.J. with a listless gait, giving herself time to size up this new customer.

"Might I have a word with Parasol Sally, if it's convenient?" asked Elsa Jane.

"*Mon Dieu!*" she answered, trying to look shocked. "You are but a baby for her!"

Elsa Jane shook her head. "It's not for that purpose."

"Is not?" The woman asked, squinting up her eyes until they were tiny slits. She could tell by the wind- and sun-weathered face that Elsa Jane must have been one of the sailors that came around the Cape with Sally. She was well aware that Sally had lost three of her girls and thought perhaps this was one of the husbands.

"Then," she asked, with gallant sweetness, "might I enquire as to the purpose?"

Elsa Jane was well aware of who was addressing her. If her heavy French accent had not given her away, the heavy growth of fine hair on her upper lip would have. She had thought the miners had been joking about her nickname.

"It is personal, ma'am."

Eleanore Dumont shrugged her humped shoulders. She didn't want any trouble, and was not opposed to using the four-shot derringer she wore strapped to her thigh.

"Sit! I geet her!"

Elsa Jane nodded and obeyed.

As she walked away, all aspects of the woman's plumpness seemed to vanish. She was as graceful as a swan.

Sally was talking to two seedy-looking prospects. Madame Moustache interrupted with a whisper. Sally turned and glared. Her eyes were full of bitterness. She turned away, but a sharp word from Madame Moustache brought her stomping towards Elsa Jane as though ready to do battle with the devil himself.

"It better be good," she growled, flinging herself down into a chair.

"It concerns Johnny and Beth."

"Screw them," she said with a low, hateful voice. "They owe me! You owe me!"

Eleanore Dumont came to the table with glasses and a carafe of claret. She sat as if she were the hostess, and poured them each a glass of wine.

Elsa Jane ignored hers. She felt intimidated by this intrusion.

"My former friend," Sally said sneeringly, "is here to talk about one of my girls, Eleanore."

"Oh? Which one?"

Sally laughed and slammed her parasol on the table.

"Not any of my present girls. It's the one who got married and started all this mess. And E.J. put her up to it."

"E.J.?"

"This is E.J. The Judas who stabbed me in the back!"

Elsa Jane swallowed. For a moment she could think of nothing to say. She was afraid Sally would reveal her secret. Finally, she decided to fight fire with fire.

"You only look at it in your own narrow selfish way, Sally."

"Selfish! You would be dead if it wasn't for me!"

Elsa Jane sighed. "And Beth would have committed suicide if I hadn't stopped her!"

Sally laughed. "Rubbish! A pack of lies!"

"No lies," Elsa Jane said softly, addressing herself to Madame Moustache. "The girl was with child and in love. She would not abort as Sally had commanded."

Eleanore Dumont gave a little cry and stretched out her pudgy hands.

"*Mon Dieu,* Sally! Of this you know I do not approve. Your girls must care for themselves so that this matter does not arise."

Elsa Jane had shamed Sally in the woman's eyes, and her anger flared.

"This is the first time the situation had ever occurred, Eleanore. The girl purposely got herself pregnant!"

"Ah, *mon cheri,* but for the *amour.*"

"Bah to love! You give it to someone and they only stab you in the back with it!"

Madame Moustache looked from Sally to Elsa Jane. The real problem had just revealed itself. Sally was in love with this *beau jeune homme,* but the handsome young man was still too youthful to reciprocate. It was the very reason why she herself had forsaken the life of the prostitute and concentrated on her success as a gambler—she always fell in love with the men who could not return her love. It gave her delightful sexual satisfaction to beat these suave and sophisticated men at the gaming tables. It emasculated them and destroyed her desire for them.

"Please, I would hear of this girl."

Sally scowled.

"It's simple. The man, or boy actually, is two years the girl's junior and was first taken as a client on a dare. As it happened again and again, he ceased being a client and became a lover."

"Hah!" Sally interrupted. "You don't have to marry a man just because you've become lovers."

"But the *bébe*," Madame Moustache chided. "That makes a big difference. And so they were married?"

"And broke my contract."

"To accept an even better one, my dear friend," Madame Moustache said quietly.

Sally pouted. "I hope her married life is as miserable as my own was."

"You are certainly trying to make it that way," Elsa Jane answered. "Can't you leave them alone? She will never come back to you after the baby is born."

"She's an embarrassment to me," Sally said unreasonably. "It gives the other girls ideas. And I've not —not yet—my own house to rule them properly. I just wish she would go away."

Elsa Jane smiled. Sally's words gave her hope.

"I can arrange that, Sally. If that is really your desire."

"You see," Madame Moustache chortled, "the solution is most simple."

"But what do I gain from it?" Sally asked.

"Why should you gain anything?" asked the woman. "Is it not the dream of every young miss who finds herself in our profession to be spirited away from it all in this manner? That is the hallmark, *mon cheri* —marriage, or a well-cared-for mistress. Now, run along and take care of those two customers before they decide my tables are more interesting than your girls."

Sally's jealousy soared. She rose haughty and arrogant, but did not move.

"Goodbye, E.J."

"He is not leaving as yet," Eleanore said seductively.

"Goodbye, E.J.," Sally repeated in warning.

Sally and Madame Moustache glowered at each other as Elsa Jane scrambled to her feet. She had what she wanted and it was a good time to depart.

"I'm sorry," she said gently to Madame Moustache, "but I should have made it known that I do not drink. I thank you kindly, though."

Madame Moustache looked up mournfully and Sally gloated. She took it as a sign that Elsa Jane had sided with her.

"When will I see you again, E.J.?" Sally simpered.

"Never."

Sally looked so astounded that E.J. smiled.

"I can't play man to your woman, and we've both known that since New Orleans. It's better that we just don't see each other. I've got nothing against you, Sally. As you said, I do owe you a lot. But please try to understand that I cannot repay you with my body. Someday I hope I can repay you in a proper manner."

Sally casually lifted the parasol from the table, unable to look at Elsa Jane.

"I could have easily forgiven you, E.J., but not now. I don't forget easily, you little runt."

She turned and greeted the men at the bar as if nothing had changed.

Madame Moustache put her hand to her breast and swayed a little as she stood up. "I wish no trouble here," she said in a whisper.

It was an easy enough request. Elsa Jane had no

intention of ever setting foot in the establishment again.

Before the week was out Sally found out where Elsa Jane was working and denied her boss the right to any of her girls until he did as she wished.

Howard Lusk had nothing against little men; he used three Chinese in his quartz mining, and they were smaller than E.J. But he was a single man with a heavy appetite for women. He had no reason to fire E.J., so he tried to hound her into quitting.

E.J. shook her head, and said, "No, I'm strong. Work is nothing new to me."

Her words seemed to please him. They were like the first toll of her death knell, for now the dirtiest most back-breaking assignments were given to her.

Blundering fool, cried Elsa Jane to herself. The work had become more than she could endure. Still, she couldn't afford to quit.

Sally, however, was unrelenting in her quest. At last Elsa Jane was fired, although Lusk could find no honest reason for it and recommended her highly to other miners.

She found one job after another but was hired and fired as quickly as Sally heard about it. The reasons were the same—she was just too small for the work; never mind that the Chinese were smaller.

A few sailors still left from the *Lady Beth* advised her to do what they were doing, and get out. Elsa Jane flatly refused, and was soon without any old friends.

The depression worsened and Elsa Jane found herself scrambling with the other men for any work that was available. It was an easy time for the mine owners. As the work force increased, the offered daily salary decreased.

"Miracles are wrought by prayer," Elsa Jane kept telling herself.

The miracle came in the form of Madame Moustache.

"Young man, I offer you the bartender job just to put a stop to an impossible situation. For two months Sally has acted like she was gnawing on wormwood. She's grown haggard and constantly carps at her girls. The girls are then not their best with the customers, which makes the customers surly at my gaming tables. If you are working for me, I think the two of you can patch up your differences."

"Thank you for your interest, but I think not." It was the first time she had realized Sally had been behind her troubles.

Eleanore, puzzled by her voice, and uncertain as to the true problem between them, persisted. "Why can't you just kiss and make up? She is really a woman with a heart of gold."

At this, despite her fears, Elsa Jane could not help but laugh. "Oh, you don't understand. I have to be candid, I suppose. Sally discovered my secret by accident. There is another I told to save her life. Now it is a necessity to tell you to save my own life. I am a woman. I am a woman who has masqueraded for five years as a man in order to support my two children. I cannot and will not give to Sally the only thing that she desires of me."

She watched the plump woman react. Her eyes widened and her mouth dropped.

"*Sacre bleu!*" she said, blushing, something she had not done since she was a young girl in Paris. "What a horrible old fool you must take me for. I am bad, most bad!"

Elsa Jane smiled.

"No, not bad, not at all. I was twelve when I married my husband and knew little or nothing of the world. He tried to teach me that the world is composed generally of three classes, good, bad and indifferent. In twenty-one years I have seen some of the good, a hell of a lot of the bad and on a few, rare occasions the indifferent. But here? Oh God, this place is the exception to all rules. I haven't made up my mind whether it is part of the earth, or an offshoot of some comet pulled here by gravitation. Oh, yes, my schooling was limited, madam, but my learning has never stopped. And my learning in this cruel world of men tells me that California is either very good or very bad. The soil is very wet or very dry, the land is very high or very low, the people very good or very bad. It is success or failure, and but small chance for in-between or indifferent. You are either good or good for nothing."

"Mon Dieu!" Eleanore said with a sigh. "My fate again is all bad. I think I am now honest, stating I did create the job for perhaps my own self-interest. But you would be less of interest to me than to Sally. I am French, to be sure, but not that French. But I am human and can offer in return something quite human. A slice of my friendship."

"Thank you, but I still could not accept the position."

"I know. I know this thing, now. My friendship is in the form of advice. Do you not think that Eleanore Dumont has no eyes to see you work? My amazement is that you are a woman. Nay, not amazement now. I have seen the women in my home province pick grapes until their fingers were raw and then carry two-hundred-pound baskets back to the winery. My own mother did this thing while I was still within her womb. We are remarkable when we wish to be. I salute you and then cry for you. *Mon cheri,* leave this place. How can you support your babes when you can hardly support yourself? But hear my words clearly. You were most honest with Madame Moustache when you could have remained silent. The favor is now upon my shoulders. When you have need of it, you need but ask." Then she roared with laughter. "Damn, what a horrible pity. As a handsome man you certainly can stir a woman's soul. To keep out of such trouble, I would subtly alter the disguise."

8

ELSA JANE quietly listened to Madame Moustache. She had seen a side of the legendary lady-gambler few knew existed—compassionate, loving and caring. Then Elsa Jane experienced a moment of *déjà vu*. Hadn't she thought the same of Sally Kallenbrough at one time?

Quietly, in the dead of night, she hiked out of the mining camp and down toward Sacramento. Each camp she passed through had a different name— Spanish Flat, Auburn Ravine, Murphy's Diggings, Sonora, Marysville—but they all looked the same. They were pits where men searched for riches and found only despair.

She slept outdoors along the way and purposely did not wash her face, hands or hair. She wore the same clothes until she couldn't stand her own smell.

This filthiness was a side of men she could hardly abide, but abide she would in order to survive.

She was tired and discouraged when she reached Sacramento, but was glad to be rid of Sally at long last. She wandered aimlessly, along with a thousand others, looking for work. But if anyone had a position available they were not advertising. She found herself gazing at a small sign in a dark window.

Free Lunch With Beverage Purchase!

The beverage was not important, but it cost less than the smallest amount of food she could buy in a café or boardinghouse. She was also interested in the man who pushed past her and entered the smoky tavern. He called for drink as if it were one of his regular stops.

The man was in his middle forties, rather short, and comfortably plump. His round face was clean-shaven, and his full cheeks were a healthy red, doubtless from a seafaring arrival. Elsa Jane found it disturbing that the face was somehow familiar.

As companions at the bar and buffet they fell into conversation. Elsa Jane was astonished to find that this Mr. Rod Berry was an official of the *Beverly Mining Company*. She gave him a closer look and decided that without the beard, without the additional fifty pounds and the friendly countenance, this man was the long-lost Thomas Roddenberry.

His conversation remained most genial, which convinced her that she had not been recognized. However, the tone of his conversation angered her. He was cleverly trying to recruit her to work in his Downieville mines for worse wages than she had been paid in Nevada City.

"Is it far from here?" she asked as he seemed to think she would jump at any offer.

"Only seventy-odd miles by pack trails up from

Marysville," he answered as if it were around the corner.

She was about ready to give him a piece of her mind when a new barman came on duty. Her heart beat fast as he rinsed the pewter beer mugs in a cask of water.

"Well—?"

Elsa Jane was too thrilled to be watching Johnny Ramey go about his work to answer. His training as a cabin boy was doing him well here.

"Well?" Roddenberry repeated. "My offer is most reasonable." He sidled closer. "However, under certain circumstances it could be improved."

Elsa Jane turned and looked at him. His peppermint-scented breath nearly choked her. "Oh?"

The man who now called himself Rod Berry smirked. "Downieville is isolated on the North Yuba. With a few scrubbings you might not be too bad under all that mud. As I said, we are most isolated, if you get my drift."

"I don't," Elsa Jane said sourly.

"Would making fifty to a hundred a night make you understand better?"

"Nope," she said innocently, although she understood his offer quite well.

"Well," he drawled, spreading his hands wide to let the diamond rings sparkle, "there are some miners who are just as willing to pay fairly for a young lad as they would a young lass."

"Do tell," Elsa Jane said in mock surprise. She bitterly thought of the irony of it all. Whether clean or dirty she was being sought out. "Is that the same as some men who are willing to pay for their mysterious disappearance overboard?"

Roddenberry leaned closer and his lips tightened. "What do you mean by that?"

"What do you think I mean?"

He didn't answer but glared.

Elsa Jane sighed and attacked. "But didn't you sail on the *Lady Beth*? You certainly bring a name to mind."

He grunted. "'If you desire work, you don't act like it.'"

Anger rippled through her. "Work I do desire," she shouted, "but not in the manner you describe. I would scrub the floors of this tavern before I would accept your offer."

"That's a glad sound to my ears," Johnny Ramey chortled without looking up. "I'm a new barkeep tired of being my own cleaning bode. If you be serious, grab the broom and show me your worth."

Elsa Jane quickly complied. It pleased her to see the fat man storm out. He had seen her turn down his "generous" offer for menial work.

The tavern was nearly as filthy as herself. It required not just a sweeping, but a scrubbing and polishing of spitoons and lanterns. She became so absorbed in her work that she jumped when a stout hand was placed on her shoulder.

"You do good."

She looked up from her scrubbing position into one of the most misshapen faces she had ever seen.

"Who are you?"

"Barkeep. Lonnie, by name."

"Where's the other one?"

"Home. Long time ago. He's gotta baby due. You want the job?"

"You the boss?" she asked suspiciously.

"Nope. He's new and thinks you're all right. Same here. You want the job?"

The slow sluggish speech, the cauliflower ears and the mashed face told Elsa Jane all she needed to know. Lonnie had fought his way back into a second childhood.

"I want it, sure. What's the pay?"

"Boss said thirty-five, bedroll by the kitchen fireplace and one take at the buffet board a day."

"Tell the boss I'll take it."

Lonnie grinned out of a toothless mouth. "I'm most glad."

"Why?"

He looked at her out of eyes that were so scarred they no longer looked human.

"I like things clean. You make things clean . . . except for . . ."

"Except for me, right? I'll take care of that before tomorrow. Frankly, I can't stand the way I smell either."

Lonnie beamed. "You gotta name and do you wanna drink?"

"The name is E.J. and I don't drink."

"Not even sarsaparilla?"

"What in the hell is that?"

"Lonnie show. Not powerful."

Elsa Jane liked the soft drink and she liked the soft-spoken, easy-mannered Lonnie. He was a giant in body and child in mind.

She almost had to like Lonnie, as once she started her cleaning duties, he was practically the only person she saw. She became addicted to the sarsaparilla he offered and overlooked the quantities of beer he could consume. Mainly he talked as she cleaned. He had been a prizefighter, sailor and barkeep. Hardly a past, present or future, but he seemed animated and alive when telling his tales.

When payday came at the end of the month, it came with a shock.

"Why?" she stormed. "Why didn't you let me know

you were the new owner Lonnie kept talking about?"

Johnny Ramey grinned. "Why didn't you let Beth and I know you were in town?"

"You know damn well."

"Then you know damn well why I didn't let you know I invested every one of Beth's dollars in this place. You never would have come to work for me."

"Bull!"

"And bull to you!"

They stared at each other and broke up in laughter.

"You idiot," Elsa Jane chortled.

Johnny sobered. "You adorable human being. I love you as much as I do my own wife."

Elsa Jane blushed. "You know?"

"Hey, that's your own fault. You taught us all about sharing in marriage. Yes, E.J., I know it all. It got to me at first, after coming to Sacramento. I thought back to the collision, the troubles in New Orleans and how you got us out of Havana. I resented that you were what you were and something different. I felt you had made me feel small and boyish. Beth screamed me out of that notion. Don't worry, your secret is safe and so is your job."

But safe for how long, she wondered. Too many people knew her secret. She forced the thought out of her mind. She was earning steady wages again, along with room and board. She could send nearly every cent back to St. Louis.

However, the depression had turned history back a page. The beached sailors created their own Barbary Coast in California. They plundered and pillaged ships in and out of the bay. It was unsafe to send money by sea, and just as unsafe to send it overland.

The lawlessness had turned inland, spreading terror

from San Francisco to Sacramento and up into the mining camps. There was no control.

Ramey's Tavern was fortunate in escaping robbery, but soon they were tormented by the malice and envy of their fellow businessmen. There were rumors that the saloon was housing the city's criminals.

"I hate to be telling you this, E.J., because you've been so faithful and all . . ." Johnny Ramey said while Beth nursed her son. "Well, we've decided to sell . . . as soon as we can find a fair buyer."

"What will you do?"

"You're going to think we've gone mad, but we are going back to the land. Beth and I were both raised on the farm, and the San Luis Valley looks most promising for such a life."

"Are you running scared?"

"To some degree," he openly admitted. "They hit Sam Duggan's place last night and killed him. He had a mere twelve dollars in the till. But it's not only that. We've doubled our investment here in these few short months and feel we should use that money to establish our future now. We don't want to raise our son in a tavern. Besides, California isn't going to vanish just because the gold is vanishing. People have always got to eat."

"Stop beating around the bush," Beth scolded. "Every time Johnny has disappeared this summer it's been to the valley. We've already got our land, equipment and a house started, E.J. Unlike Missouri, we can get two and maybe three crops a year off the land. We can move the day we sell this damn place. I'm sorry, but living over a tavern reminds me too much of the old days."

"We didn't want to tell you until we were sure the land was ours," said Johnny, understanding E.J.'s puzzled gaze. He laughed. "But don't worry about your job. With things being what they are around here, it might take months to sell out."

"How much are you asking?"

"We bought it for five and are asking eight."

Elsa Jane hesitated. "Seems fair. What might you be asking down?"

"Haven't considered it. Why do you ask?"

Elsa Jane lowered her head and stared at the crib. She didn't want her children raised in an orphanage forever. She was silent so long that Johnny began to wonder why the question went unanswered. When she did speak, her voice was so low that he had to lean forward to catch the words.

"I've put aside one hundred and forty dollars from my wages. Been watching the business quite close, other than just cleaning. Don't mean no offense, but I think I could save some money with a few changes. That way I could have you paid off in a month or two."

"But E.J. . . . ." he said frowning. "You running a tavern? What about the rowdies?"

She raised her head and looked at him with amused contempt. "You would never have dared asked such a thing if Beth hadn't revealed my secret. You can't help it, but your attitude has changed toward me. 'Don't move those beer barrels, they are too heavy for you. Let Lonnie change the tub water, E.J. Do you need more help with the cleaning?' My offer is made as E.J. Forest, riverman, sailor and mine laborer. Is it a valid offer?"

"A valid offer," he repeated slowly, relieved to have a simple solution to something that could have been complex. "But would it not be better if you made the payments over a six-month time period?"

"I think not." Elsa Jane smiled. "In six months time

I want to have made enough money out of the place to resell it and go feel my own children's arms wrapped about my neck."

Johnny stared at her. He knew that when she made a promise it was a promise kept.

"I'll leave the payments open according to your resources. Beth, finish the packing while I draw up the papers for E.J. and me to sign. It's hers from this moment on and we can leave whenever we are ready."

A half-hour later Elsa Jane stood in the taproom and looked about in wonderment. There was always a lull at about that time in the afternoon. The free-lunch crowd had finished cramming themselves full and the after-work crowd did not start filtering in for a couple of hours.

Lonnie stood polishing his beer tankards. A single customer was hunched over the bar.

She walked by the devastated trays on the lunch table. Here she could immediately save money. Johnny had just continued the practice of the previous owner. Beth had been too busy with the baby to prepare the sliced meats, cheeses and salads and Johnny had thought the prices charged by the delicatessen reasonable. Elsa Jane had considered them outlandish. A woman's touch was definitely needed, she wryly thought.

"Blood-sucking bushwackers!"

Elsa Jane frowned and turned to the bar. The customer was staring morosely at his drink, one foot resting on the brass rail, his jaws chomping on a plug of tobacco. She knew him only as Nat Reston, the muleskinner. It was hard to tell his age because of his undersized and scrawny frame, but the face beneath the beard was weathered to leather and his yellowish eyes were as wary and unyielding as those of an old lynx.

"What you carping on, Nat?"

"Bloodsucking bushwackers," he repeated, spitting toward the brass cuspidor. "Hit on one of my mule trains this morning. Killed two mules and made off with their packs."

"Why just two?"

His small eyes, cold as yellow glass, surveyed her with contempt.

"They somehow knowed those were the only ones carryin' gold. Varmints didn't even touch the rest. Damn skinner quit on me 'cause it, though. Freight's a rotten damn business."

Elsa Jane smiled to herself. Nat Reston had a reputation of being a damn rotten businessman."

"Hi, Nat!" Johnny called cheerfully, coming behind the bar. "You best start being nice to E.J. E.J. is now the new owner of the tavern."

Lonnie looked up and angrily smashed his right fist into his left palm. Johnny saw the warning sign and immediately knew his error. Lonnie should have been told before it was blurted out to a customer. He took the big prize fighter by the elbow and guided him to the back room.

"Lucky," Nat growled. "I'd give me left ball to get away from mules."

"What would you you do then?"

Nat shrugged and shifted the wad of tobacco to his other cheek. "Something like this. Ain't real new to me. I ran a shanty bar for Jim Bridger onest. Whole dang winter I ran it."

"You really want to get back into this business?" she asked quickly.

His yellow eyes shifted and rested on her. "I might." He took his foot off the railing and hunched farther over the bar. "Except I ain't got that kinda money,

E.J. You're a lucky young man. Lucky. I've lied so damn much I think I'll be fifty-five and nothing to show for it but thirty-eight mules, forty packs, a shanty office-live-in and a corral."

"What do you think they are worth?"

"I don't know. I guess five a head on the mules . . ." said Nat distractedly. "Maybe two each on the packs. That's it."

"You didn't mention the office and corral."

"Shit E.J., I'd be stealing if I got more'n a hundred out of the wind-whipped mess. Don't know nobody who'd want it in the first place."

E.J. had been making mental calculations. Mules one hundred and ninety dollars, packs an additional eighty dollars and a hundred dollars on the shanty and corral. That was only three hundred and seventy dollars. She also knew Nat Reston was a skinflint and one of the largest eaters at the lunch table when in town.

"What do you think I paid for this place, Nat?"

He looked around, screwed up his mouth and hit the spitoon again.

"More'n I got, I reckon. Maybe three . . . no, four thou at least."

"A thousand two hundred," she said quietly.

Nat nearly swallowed his plug. "You're joshin' me, E.J."

"Nope. I took it off Johnny's hands as a favor. He wants to set himself up in farming. I ain't partial to this business, but what the hell."

"What would you rather be doing, E.J.?"

She shrugged indifferently. All that mattered was that she had his undivided attention.

"Something outdoors, like I'm used to."

He hunched a shoulder toward the doors. "Know anything about the freight business?"

"Only that which came on and off the riverboats."

"Ain't much difference then between mules and boats, as I see it." He nearly stammered in his anxiety.

"Guess not," she answered casually. "Might be something for me to consider."

"Sure would, if'n you're hankering for some trading talk. What were those figures I gave you?"

She rattled them right back with the total she had summed up. "Even on a trade, Nat, that would leave a balance of about nine hundred and forty-four dollars. I'm afraid I wouldn't be able to do it on a payment plan."

"Shit E.J., you know I always pay hard cash and expect people I haul freight for to do the same." He rummaged inside his filthy buckskins and drew forth a heavy leather pouch. "Got it right here if your talk is serious."

Elsa Jane frowned. She drew out the paper Johnny had drawn up and turned it over on the bar. She found a stubby lead pencil and moistened it on the end of her tongue. She had no fear that Nat would ever read her contract with Johnny. He would never even read the one between them.

"I guess I'm serious enough to start writing, if you are serious enough to start counting."

He couldn't open his pouch fast enough. The gold pieces stacked up on the bar.

"What's up?" Johnny asked as he came back into the tap room with Lonnie.

Elsa Jane warned him with her eyes to keep quiet. "Lonnie, meet your new boss. Nat just bought the bar."

It was hard to tell which man showed the most surprise. Elsa Jane quickly left the gaping Lonnie to talk things over with Nat, while she ushered a stunned Johnny Ramey to the backroom.

In less than an hour, she had Johnny paid off in full, owned a freight line and had a two hundred and eighty-four dollar profit to invest in new business.

ఎర్

9

"Yeee-haw!"

The bright red wagons were a familiar sight along the road from Sacramento to the mountaintop community of Downieville. For the first six months of operation, Elsa Jane had poured every cent of profit into improving the freight line. There was constant talk of the building of a railroad, but until the first track was laid, she kept expanding. *Forest Freight* offices were erected in eight mining communities before the anniversary of her second year. Twenty-four bright red wagons, pulled by one hundred-forty-four mules covered every road and trail. Twenty-four mule skinners sat safely beside twenty-four heavily armed guards. The service was fast enough to bring up produce from the San Luis farms and ranged far enough to bring in heavy quartz mining equipment, furniture and even delicate glassware.

In two years, Elsa Jane lost only one customer—and that was in her first month of operation. The highwaymen had struck quickly, but unsuccessfully. They made off with two mules they thought were carrying ore. Fortunately, the packs carried only sacks of flour. Elsa Jane had learned from Nat Reston's mistake. Once out of sight of a mining community, she would switch the cargo or disguise it.

The dead highwayman was none other than Roddenberry, alias Rod Berry. Elsa Jane carted his stout body back to the Sacramento offices of the mining company and dropped it on their doorstep.

They might have been able to doublecross Nat Reston and hound him to pay for stolen shipments, but they'd be fools to try it with Elsa Jane.

A week later she was presented with a gilt-edged certificate that she would prize forever:

Committee of Vigilance
Fiat justicia ruat Coelum
This is to certify that
Mr. E.J. Forest is a member of the
COMMITTEE OF VIGILANCE OF THE
CITY OF SACRAMENTO
Organized for the mutual protection
of life, property & limb.

"Yeee-haw!"

Elsa Jane was riding shotgun on the first wagon. She stood up on the seat and shouted directions to the rest of the wagons. It was the first and largest caravan to arrive in Nevada City that spring. Twelve heavily laden wagons lumbered up the main street. Hundreds of people came out onto the board sidewalk to cheer and clap.

Many miners now brought their families to the digs, and the wives were anxious to see the new calicos, fresh barrels of flour and tins of cheese the general store would be offering. Miss Elsie Dutton was expecting a crate of books for the new school, and one of the wagons hauled a pump organ for the Nevada City Community Church of Christ. Lester Pike had two new barber chairs coming all the way from Boston. There was something for everyone, and more to take on to other communities.

"Mike, you know where Sally's house is. Tell her this furniture is cash on delivery. No screwing around like last month. If she bitches tell her to shove it up her ass and let her find someone else to haul her freight. If she asks why I didn't bring it personally, tell her to kiss yours."

Elsa Jane took the reins of the lead wagon and started up the hill. Sally Kallenbrough had not let up in two years. She had tried everything within her power to get Elsa Jane back, including trying to ruin her freighting business. But Elsa Jane had proven far too subtle a businesswoman to be thwarted. She now owned all three mule-train lines coming into the mining camps, so whatever Sally wanted, be it a jar of rouge or a new bedroom suite, she had to deal with E.J. or go without.

Cresting the hill, Elsa Jane grinned broadly. If ever a building looked out of place it was the palace of Madame Moustache. It was bright and gawdy, and had flower boxes and shutters at each and every window.

Eleanore Dumont had seen the caravan arrive and had sent her entourage out to accept her long-awaited shipment. Bartenders, card dealers, maids and cooks had been turned into furniture movers. She had waited nearly six months for this shipment from France and she was like a fluttering young child wanting to unwrap her Christmas gifts.

Elsa Jane had no doubt that Eleanore could afford such items. It was rumored, and for good reason, that half the gold that came out of the Sierra mountains found its way to the plump Frenchwoman.

She had become Elsa Jane's best customer and most-valued friend. "Of course you have seen my new treasures," she said enthusiastically.

"Eleanore," Elsa Jane chuckled, "I have seen nothing. They came off the ship crated and have remained crated for the wagon trip."

Her fleshy face fell. Then she brightened. "But, of course, *mon cheri,* that is how it should be. Can you stay to have a glass with me and see them uncrated?"

Elsa Jane nodded. She had secretly longed to see the crated treasures. Also, over the last two years she had learned that it was good business to stay and have a glass of wine while the merchandise was carefully inspected. Eleanore Dumont would not pay her bill until it was done anyway.

In public Madame Moustache treated Elsa Jane as if she were the most masculine male ever to cross a woman's path. Everyone was aware of Eleanore Dumont's penchant to be surrounded by the most virile, handsome men available. It was thus automatically assumed E.J. was one of them.

Alone, they let down their guard.

"What did simpering Sally order up this time?"

"It was crated," Elsa Jane answered evasively.

The relationship between Madame Moustache and Parasol Sally had become increasingly awkward. They constantly fought about E.J.—each of them wanting her friendship.

Eleanore was sensitive enough to know that Elsa Jane had closed the subject.

"And what do you hear from St. Louis?" she asked.

Elsa Jane brightened. With Eleanore she could discuss her children for hours, and not feel like a bragging parent.

Eleanore was a good listener. She simply sat there sipping her wine and following E.J.'s every motion with her small, knowing eyes.

"My friend," she said huskily in English, "you sound sad."

Slowly E.J. shook her head.

"No, Eleanore," she said, "I have no reason to be sad. In this last year alone, I have been able to send thirty thousand dollars to St. Louis. That is taking care of my babies, and the Sisters of Charity are holding the rest for me. When I return, Eleanore, I shall be a very wealthy woman."

"Woman? For so long have you played the man, how will you be able to revert?"

Elsa Jane sighed.

"You see too much, Eleanore. You see my thoughts as though they were written upon a page. Sacramento is becoming quite a city. I see the women in their fashionable gowns and carriages and I cannot help but feel envy. I could afford even finer than they, but then who would do business with me as a woman? People are so narrow. Do they not think that you must have great expertise to run this gambling establishment—or even Sally with her house? They are, in my opinion, harder enterprises to run than, say, a mercantile store."

Eleanore sipped her wine; her eyes, above the rim of the glass, never left Elsa Jane's face.

"Is it not time for you to spend a bit of your

hard labor upon yourself, E.J.?" She ran her finger around the rim of the crystal until it began to sing. "I am speaking of a trip home. A restful trip. It is spring. Do you not have someone you could trust to leave in charge?"

Elsa Jane stared at the Frenchwoman. It was as if she had heard her desire and put it into words.

"I just can't!" she whispered. "I can sit here and dream that dream quite wonderfully. Oh, Eleanore, I can't do it!"

"Can't," said Eleanore gruffly, "is not a word!"

"I . . . I guess it is, in a way," she said sorrowfully. "I suppose Mike would be capable. He's very good at keeping the books. He knows all the customers. He schedules all the drivers now."

"You are making him sound most capable."

"Well, he is!"

"Then where is the problem?" Eleanore asked gently.

E.J. gazed at her tenderly.

"Do me a favor, my friend," she said. "Keep talking me into this sudden and rash decision."

Madame Moustache tilted back her head and laughed. "Sudden and rash! Elsa Jane Forest, you have been a sudden and rash creature since you ran away to the docks of New Orleans."

It shocked her to hear her real name. It seemed a million years since she had heard it. She had forgotten how much of her history she had exposed to Eleanore Dumont. It amazed her when the woman, who was like a sponge that absorbed everything, squeezed it out when necessary.

"So?"

"So what?"

"So, when does this weathered old bag of bones get to say '*bon voyage*' and all that crap?"

* * *

From Sacramento to San Francisco Elsa Jane had remained E.J. Forest. In San Francisco the transformation began. She felt like an impostor boarding the sleek new Commodore Vanderbilt clipper ship as a woman. She was so self-conscious that she stayed in her cabin like a hermit for the voyage to Panama.

It was a relaxing trip. Elsa Jane slept deeply, as she had not slept in the last six years. There were no nightmares, no watches to rise and see over, no slush boxes to flume, no floors to be scrubbed, no mules to be driven. No nothing.

But there were surprises. The Vanderbilt lines did not go down around the Cape. They transported their passengers by stage over the Isthmus of Panama to their choice of waiting ships. In seventy-three days she was standing on the docks of New Orleans.

Elsa Jane breathed the river air deeply and felt at home. But she was still self-conscious. She felt a man in a woman's blue serge gown—plain and awkward. She decided to make some changes.

She accepted the designer dresses with a casual shrug, and allowed her face, hands and body to be creamed and massaged. Unfortunately, she saw no difference when she looked in the hotel mirror. She had played the male role for too long and could see nothing else.

But boarding the *Mississippi Belle* she felt quite different. She felt cumbersome. The heavily draped green velvet gown seemed an enormous weight to carry about, and the bustle made her feel like a beaver wagging its tail.

Daintily, so as not to trip and embarrass herself, she cautiously climbed the gangway. Suddenly she felt a hand come under the crook of her arm.

"Allow me, miss. These walkways were not designed for beautiful women."

She looked across at the face of her rescuer and then up at the deck. She had captured the eyes of every man about. She returned the gaze of one in particular. He was frowning, one hand supported his cleft chin, the other dangled over the railing. It was as if she could read his thoughts. He knew her face from somewhere, but couldn't figure out from where. Elsa Jane studied him just as closely. He had a dark-brown deep-curling mass of hair, sprinkled with silver streaks. His appearance was that of an aristocrat.

Calvin Bender thought she was one of the most strikingly beautiful creatures he had ever seen. Pretty? No, she was more than pretty. Her face was rare, very rare. It possessed character. Her skin looked soft, but the lines were firm. It was a face that might have been painted by an old master. It was a face that had experienced everything and yet still had dignity and grace. He probed his memory as he moved to the gangway to be within earshot of her boarding.

"Welcome aboard," the purser crooned, saluting.

"Thank you," she smiled graciously. "I am Mrs. Forest."

The purser quickly scanned his chart and frowned. "And would this be Mr. Forest?" he asked, indicating the man who had helped her aboard.

"This would only be the kind gentleman who helped me aboard, sir. I am alone."

Elsa Jane amazed herself. It was easy to sound like a helpless woman. And it was effective. A cabin boy was quickly summoned to escort her to her assigned cabin and every man doffed his hat as she passed. A sudden urge made her turn back to the man who thought he knew her.

"Excuse my forwardness, sir, but are we not acquainted?"

Calvin Bender bowed deeply. "I've thought the same since spotting you, miss, but I did not catch your name. I'm Calvin Bender of Bender's Landing, Louisiana."

She couldn't believe it. He didn't recognize his own daughter! Had ten years made that much difference?

"Then, I am sorry sir. It was my mistake."

"Please," he stammered, as she turned away. "I am entertaining the captain and a few passengers for dinner at my table this evening. We would be most honored if you were to join us, Miss ... ah, Miss ... ?"

"I shall consider it, Mr. Bender."

She quickly followed the cabin boy away before Bender could ask for her name again. She wasn't sure how she wanted to handle the situation. Too many ghosts from the past had suddenly appeared.

No, she swiftly decided, I shall not be attending that dinner.

The cabin boy abruptly stopped. "Excuse me, Captain, I am escorting this passenger to her quarters. May I present Mrs. Forest, Captain Herlock."

The Captain bent down and kissed her hand.

Herlock, E.J. thought, Emil Herlock from the *Memphis*?

Herlock straightened up and towered above her. He was indeed the same man who had refused to go on to California with them. Looking at him, she was reminded that she had been attracted to him. He seemed taller and more graceful than she had remembered. Her womanly interests had returned rapidly.

"My pleasure, Mrs. Forest," the Captain smiled graciously. "Is your husband already aboard?"

"I am a widow, Captain Herlock."

Now the smile became more intimate. "My humble error, ma'am. May I correct so gross a blunder by requesting your presence at the captain's table this evening?"

"I believe, sir, that Mr. Bender has already bestowed the invitation on your behalf. I shall be honored."

He bowed again. Elsa Jane watched him as he strode down the passageway. She remembered, with a mixture of regret and anger, how he had taken most of the *Memphis* crew and deserted them.

Elsa Jane knew she was the envy of every woman there as she entered the glittering salon. She felt strange but elegant in the gold faille with chocolate brown bowknots. She had a netted bun, with more bowknots, fastened to the back of her head to give the impression that the brunette curls were actually more massive. For this particular gown she had insisted upon shoes with a very low heel so that she could walk more naturally and without fear.

She did not desire a drink before dinner and had only a single glass of claret with the meal. She was therefore looked upon as a proper lady.

Several of the women did gasp when she dared to impose herself upon the dinner conversation.

"I'm sorry, Captain Herlock, but I think your information is a little dated."

Emil Herlock was not used to being corrected, especially by a woman, but he remained a gentleman. "And how is that, Mrs. Forest?"

"I have just returned from California and it is hardly a deserted wasteland."

"Just returned?" Bender asked. "My dear, you hardly look the pioneer type."

Elsa Jane smiled graciously. She had been studying him throughout the meal. He was like a complete stranger. She remembered him as old and gruff and always too busy for her. She remembered the horrible stories she had heard about him from Daris Jamieson, but did not now believe they were about the same man. He was twenty years her senior, but except for the graying hair, he looked to be in his mid-thirties. His aquiline face was firm and his eyes were clear and, contrary to the stories she had heard, he did not touch a drop of liquor or wine.

"You would be amazed, Mr. Bender, how cosmopolitan the cities of San Francisco and Sacramento are."

"But how can they survive when there is no more gold?"

"Another bit of bad information, I am afraid. The placer gold was quick to make headlines. Now it takes a lot of back-breaking work to get the gold out of the quartz rock. Work never makes headlines."

Mrs. Hollis leaned across the table anxiously. "Oh, my dear, have you actually seen a gold mine?"

"But of course. My husband has a freighting business that goes to all of the gold mining camps."

"Has?" Herlock asked impolitely. "I thought you said you were a widow?"

Mrs. Hollis turned and stared at him, eager to challenge such an impertinence.

"I did," Elsa Jane answered. "It is being run by a most able assistant."

"Can you trust him?" Herlock asked, trying to save face.

"Do you not trust the pilot of this vessel? Does

Mr. Bender not trust the overseer on his island-plantation?"

"What I meant . . ." Herlock stammered.

"I'm perfectly aware of what you meant," Elsa Jane interrupted. "Can I, as a woman, trust him not to cheat me? No, not unless I stay right on top of the situation. Just as you would watch over your vessel or Mr. Bender over his plantation. It's just common sense."

"Which we are not supposed to possess," Mrs. Hollis chuckled.

"Why? The home is the biggest profit-or-loss business in the world. A woman can make or break her husband by the cost of her food, clothing for the family, fuel purchases and everything else."

As a bachelor, Emil Herlock knew he could no longer carry the conversation and quickly broke up the dinner gathering. Calvin Bender helped Elsa Jane from her chair.

"Your knowledge of me is flattering," he gushed.

"Hardly, sir. I was born in Louisiana and have seen your plantation many times from the riverboats."

"Perhaps you will do me the honor of visiting Bender's Landing one day."

"Perhaps."

He hesitated. "It is a lovely evening. Might I have the pleasure of escorting you back to your cabin?"

Elsa Jane didn't hesitate. She was very curious about the man. "Thank you."

A slight thrill shot through her when he took her arm. It was the first time that she could recall that her father had touched her.

"California must have seemed a long way from Louisiana."

"I was only born here, sir. St. Louis was my home from age twelve."

"I see," he said thoughtfully. "I once had someone who moved to St. Louis when she was twelve."

"Oh!"

"Of course, you would never have run across her."

"Why is that? St. Louis is not that large a town."

"Different social backgrounds," he said dryly.

"Oh," she said softly. It gave her an odd feeling to discuss herself in this manner.

"To be sure. Look at you, the personification of a success in the social world and, from what you have said, a success in the business world as well. I'm afraid that the child I knew ran away from home at age twelve, married a river pilot, produced two children and then vanished."

"Vanished?"

He seemed to age before her eyes. "I'm sorry, Mrs. Forest, I did not mean to impose my grief upon a stranger."

"Are they not always the best to impose it upon, sir? They are the impartial listeners of the world. For example, I always thought that the church made a great mistake. How can a priest, who knows you from perhaps birth, be impartial in the confessional?"

He seemed to brighten. "You are, without a doubt, one of the most remarkable women I have ever encountered. Do you have an answer for everything in life?"

"Hardly," she chuckled. "I have seen much in my twenty-two years, but not everything."

"Twenty-two?" he mused. "You would be both the same age."

"Would be?"

"Would be had she lived," he said gloomily. "She died two years ago."

Although this raised many questions, Elsa Jane

knew better when than to ask them. She could only be the listener.

"Your cabin, Mrs. Forest." Calvin Bender raised her gloved hand momentarily to his lips. "Perhaps to-morrow?"

"Perhaps."

There was no perhaps to it. She had to find out why he thought she was dead. She shivered when she thought of how genuine his grief had been.

At lunch, and again at dinner, the subject did not arise. The conversation was general in scope, although she learned a great deal about the problems of the South. He told her of the growing slave problem and the necessity of replacing his overseer.

"You were wrong, Mrs. Forest, when you said I stayed on top of my overseer. I was a different man in those days. I left everything to him, a governess and the house staff. I was too busy with my own personal pleasures—as are most young men who are handed everything on a silver platter. Still, I did not wake up to his harsh handling of the slaves until after his wife died."

He continued talking about the replacement, but Elsa Jane barely heard him. Hearing of the death of her mother, even though she had hardly known the woman, was stunning. She tried, but she couldn't even imagine the woman. And how odd, she thought, that Calvin Bender had fathered a child by her and could speak of her death without a trace of emotion.

On the third day Elsa Jane did not see Bender until dinner time. No one else had noticed, but there was a subtle change in him. His cheeks were flushed, his eyes were glassy and he barely touched his food. Elsa Jane suspected that he had been drinking, but there was no proof of it.

He left the table before dessert, but was back in

time to escort her to her cabin. Now she was sure that he had been drinking; she could smell it on his breath.

This time, as he bowed to kiss her hand, he pulled her into a strong embrace.

"Oh, no!" she whispered. "No!"

"Take me inside with you," he moaned.

She struggled to get free. He was stronger than she had imagined.

"Please," he begged, his hands not relenting in caressing her. "No woman has ever stirred me like you have."

His hand molded over her breast and she knocked it away.

"Stop, before someone comes along!"

"Then take me inside," he giggled inanely.

"You're drunk!"

"And you drove me back to it. I've not touched a drop since I heard that my little girl had died. You made me break that vow."

She was torn between acting like a lady or fighting him like a man.

"It must have been a very weak-willed vow, sir."

He blinked at her stupidly. "Are you about to scream or something?"

"I see no reason to ruin your reputation with a scream that would bring other people. I recommend that you unhand me and go sleep this off."

"Why can't I sleep it off lying next to you?" he asked with drunken craftiness. "I promise to be good."

"No," she said firmly, and tried to turn away. His grip on her dress was tight and the sudden movement ripped it from her shoulder. Three-fourths of her breast was instantly exposed. Bender stood staring as if he had never seen such a sight.

"A gentleman would avert his eyes," she said quietly, as he started to raise his hand to touch her bare flesh. "Don't make me start thinking otherwise of you, sir."

It was like puncturing a blowfish with a spear. He deflated quickly, disgusted with his own actions. He turned and sulked away. Before she had closed the door behind her, she heard him sobbing.

Despite everything in the past and everything in the present, she wanted to run to him and tell him the truth. Still, she held back.

It wasn't revenge. Her wounds had healed so long ago that she couldn't find the scars. Pity? No, she was elated that after six years of posing as a man, she was again considered an attractive woman. It was simply that he had acted the cad and not the gentleman, as she would have expected of her own father.

A knock came at her door just after sunrise. She felt as if she had struggled through a million nightmares. The knock came again before she could get her feet into slippers and a robe drawn about her flannel nightgown.

She slid back the lock and opened the door.

"Please don't close the door on me," Calvin Bender pleaded. "I must talk with you."

She didn't respond.

"No words can express my chagrin over last evening," he rushed on. "You humbled me, as I needed to be humbled. I am sorry for the early hour, but Bender's Landing will be our next stop."

Still she did not respond.

"After last night I do not have the right to say these words, but say them I must. They have never been said to another woman. I desperately desire to make you my wife. No, don't give me a rash answer.

Go home to St. Louis and think upon it. Give me a chance to come visit you there and make amends. Please."

He could see her throat quiver with emotion. Slowly the door opened wide and she motioned him inside. Still she did not speak.

"Sit down," she finally said. "You are forgiven for last night."

Bender ran his tongue over his lips before he could speak again.

"Thank you."

"You are forgiven because you didn't know the truth." For a moment she hesitated, then continued. "You almost raped your own daughter last night."

"She is dead!" he said defiantly.

"Hardly," Elsa Jane said quietly and, turning, took a seat on the cabin bunk. "I am Elsa Jane. I am your illegitimate daughter by the overseer's wife."

"No," he blustered. "It's another damn blackmailing trick."

"By whom?"

"Are you in this thing with Jamieson?" he asked accusingly.

"Ah, the black devil comes back to roost. What did he tell you of my death?"

Gloomily, he shook his head.

"No," he replied. "I still do not believe this."

"Then go to hell," she flared. "I should have just slammed the door in your face. I thought I had seen some changes in you, but I should have known better. You've been selfish and self-centered your whole life. Where were you after Daris Jamieson killed my husband and left my two children fatherless?" Without knowing it, her voice had been dropping into its gravelly, male tone. "Drunk on your ass and sleeping with men."

"That was the first blackmail attempt I refused to pay for," Bender growled. "I knew nothing about your husband or children until Peter approached me in New Orleans."

"*Your?*" she snarled. "Does that mean you are starting to believe me?"

"No," he said stubbornly. "I've been through this too many times with the man. After her husband deserted her, I paid him for my daughter's burial and I have a death certificate to prove it."

E.J. sat fighting for self control.

"Did she die at Natchez-under-the-Hill?"

Bender grinned slyly. Only Jamieson was aware of that fact. "Yes." Then he added quickly to trip her up. "She died as a prostitute."

Elsa Jane roared with laughter. "Oh, the bastard! He never gives up. Do you really want the true story?"

He shrugged. He expected it to be nothing but a pack of lies. He seemed so preoccupied in disbelieving that she went all the way back to the first day she had met Daris Jamieson on the wharf in New Orleans. She spat the story out in bitter vengeance, and he sat stone-faced as every aspect of her life began to unravel. Had it not been for Jamieson's twistings, it would have sounded like a very farfetched tale.

"So," he said when she was finished, "what do you want from me?"

She stared at him with withering contempt. "You really are insufferable. I ask nothing of men because I have learned to beat them at their own game. What I have heard from you, and the lies put forth, should make me hate all men forever, but it only makes me feel sorry for your weakness."

Bender softened.

"Elsa Jane, my—I don't know what to say . . ."

"Then say nothing," she said gently. "You gave me life. For that I thank you."

"But, if you should ever need—"

"Don't say that, either. By today's standards I am a wealthy woman. I shall pick up my children, and the money I have left in trust, and return to California. You can leave Elsa Jane buried wherever Jamieson claims to have buried her, for I have not used the name for years. One favor you can grant me, however."

"Anything."

"Should you ever have chance to run across Daris Jamieson, tell him I'll shoot to kill the next time."

"Then you did have a duel with him?"

"Good God!" she cried in exasperation. "Have you taken this all as some fable I've been reciting? Look! Look here!" She jumped up and ran to him, thrusting out her hands. "There is the whole story. Oh, what tales those hands could tell you! You have only been kissing the gloves that hide the truth!"

Tears welled in his eyes and he gently took the work-hardened hands and placed them on his cheeks.

"I can never ask your forgiveness," he sobbed, "because I do not deserve it. I cannot ask to come back into your life as a father, because I was never really even a very good uncle. In time, and I pray we each live long enough to see it, I would at least like to become your friend."

Gently, she pulled her hands away. She was not ready to promise anything, not yet.

It took her several moments to realize that some things shrink with time. Her brick house seemed not small, but tiny, and very badly neglected. She chided herself for thinking she could walk right back into it as if she had only been gone a month. The yard was tangled by two years' growth and vandals had broken several windows.

"Sure yah got the right address, lady?"

"Quite sure, but let me give you a new address."

He was happy to oblige. She had already paid him for one trip and an additional one would keep him from returning fareless. But the new address puzzled him.

"You sure you want the orphanage?"

"Here is the fare," she said, not wishing to repeat herself. "If you will stay with my luggage, I will pay you a waiting time and a return fare. I shall probably be about twenty to thirty minutes."

He nodded in agreement. Three fares from one passenger wasn't bad. He was lucky to get three fares in a day.

As Elsa Jane pulled the bell cord at the entryway of the orphanage, a cold shiver ran up her spine. The door creaked open. It was badly in need of oiling. The interior was so dark she could barely make out the shape of a figure in a black habit.

"I am Elsa Jane Forest. I have children here. Please be good enough to inform Mother Catherine of my arrival."

Wordlessly, she was ushered into the foyer and the door creaked shut. The convent was far danker and mustier than she remembered. All the side doors, which had once afforded the windowless area some light, were closed tight. The only light was from four rosary candles flickering under a painting of the Madonna in a knave.

A withered old hand motioned for her to follow. Her heels clicked and echoed on the flat stones of the long passageway. It was the only sound. Elsa Jane remembered the sound of laughter coming from the classrooms. She wondered what had happened.

Again, without a word, she was motioned to wait. The nun slipped away.

Finally, a door opened and her heart brightened. In the sunlit room a familiar figure was hunched over a desk.

"Mother Catherine," she cried, running forward. "How marvelous to see you again."

The figure rose from behind the desk like a cobra right out of a basket.

"You intrude upon our silent period!"

Elsa Jane stopped short. Never had she seen a more hateful face. The hard gray eyes were like slashing swords.

"I was not aware," she mumbled. "I expected to find Mother Catherine."

"So it would seem," was the acid reply. "She has been dead for over a year."

Elsa Jane's knees nearly buckled. Mother Catherine had forewarned her, but to be told so callously was still a shock.

"I am informed that you are Elsa Jane Forest. I am Mother Xavier. What might we do for you?"

"May we call in Sister Margaret Rose? She's aware of my story."

"Unnecessary," the woman snapped, retaking her seat.

"But I would feel better . . ."

"Mrs. Forest," she interrupted, "how you feel is no concern to me or this institution. When I arrived here I found it being run like a private school. The nun in question has been transferred back to the mother house for retraining. Now, please state your business."

Elsa Jane remained standing.

"I have come for my children."

Mother Xavier looked up in surprise.

"And when would you like them?"

"Why, as soon as possible."

"Just like that?" she asked sternly. "Drop them off and pick them up whenever you take up with a new man. Women like you disgust me."

"Now, you look here . . ." Elsa Jane began.

"Get the Forest children ready," the callous woman sharply ordered the waiting nun. "We can use the space for children who might be adoptable."

"I will not be shut up!" Elsa Jane shrieked, losing her temper. "I have paid for my children to be here for these six years. I have not been a burden of charity."

Mother Xavier shrugged indifferently.

"And," Elsa Jane continued, "I also sent sums of money to be held in trust for me. I wish to collect that as well."

"Mrs. Forest," the nun said indulgently, "we, of the Sisters of Charity, handle none of our own funds. It is all sent directly to the Bishop's treasury. Every cent that we receive is sent directly there as a contribution to the cause."

"Even the money I sent for the care of my children?"

"Why should your children be treated any differently from the other orphans? That would hardly be fair."

"All right, I can understand that. Now, how about the rest of my money."

"I have told you."

"You have told me nothing! Oh, damn me for being a blasted fool. Look, I received one letter from Sister Margaret Rose in California, but I didn't bring it with me. She assured me that the money would be held for me."

"And as I told you, I brought this order back to

what it should have always been. I transferred that
money to Bishop Landry as soon as I learned of it."

"Good! Now we are getting somewhere. I shall just
go get it back from him."

"I wish you well," she said with acid sarcasm. "He
has left on a two-year journey to the Holy Land."

"On my money, I presume," Elsa Jane snapped.
"I'm amazed you didn't try to go along to warm his
bed."

Elsa Jane could see the spots of rage appearing on
the gaunt cheeks. But she could see something else
too, a tiny glow of fear in the woman's eyes. They
had stolen her money and never expected her to return for it. All this time she had been pouring out her
heart and her money in the parcels from California,
only to have this viper receiving them.

The door opened behind her and she spun. She
could have slain the woman behind her without a
second thought.

These were not the healthy, plump, carefree children she had left behind two years ago. Their clothing were rags, their faces thin, their eyes fearful. For
a moment they did not even recognize her, then Annie's eyes widened in total disbelief.

"Is—is it really you?" she rasped.

"Yes, my darlings, it is. Didn't Sister Marg—" She
stopped. "Weren't you told of my letters?"

"We never want to let one child . . ."

"Shut up," she growled, as though cursing a stubborn mule.

"We were told you were dead," Annie sobbed.
Charles Peter darted behind his sister, fearful such
a statement would bring about a whipping.

"That is a lie!" Mother Xavier snapped.

"Children," Elsa Jane said calmly, ignoring the
woman, "there is a carriage outside. Please go to it

and wait for Mommy. I shall only be a second or
two."

They did not need a second invitation. They had
been waiting six years to hear those words.

Slowly, Elsa Jane turned.

"Do you believe in God, Mother Xavier?"

"What an asinine question to ask of me."

"No, quite logical. For I do believe in God and
his judgment. Someday I pray that I may be standing near at hand when he must review your life. I
can smell the flames roasting your ankle flesh already.
Too bad you don't have as much fat as Bishop Landry."

As she exited, a faint whisper came to her ears
from the other nun.

"Bless you, my daughter."

The voice quieted her and for the next hour she
thought of nothing but her children. They needed
new clothing from head to foot. She couldn't believe
how they had each grown. But she reminded herself
that Annie was now ten and Charley nine and that
for more than half of their lives she had been away
from them.

"Are we going home now, Mommy?" Annie asked.
"I'm tired and hungry."

The coachman wondered the same. He didn't mind
all these extra fares from shop to shop, but he wondered what it was all about.

Elsa Jane had to make new plans. Driving out to
the orphanage, she had thought about the cleaning
the house would need. She had decided to hire help
and have it put to right as quickly as possible. But
now there was no money. What did she have? she
asked herself. Ashes in her mouth.

"No," she said aloud, "I at least have my children
back."

The coachman and children looked at her.

It was no use chiding herself about the money she had wasted on her own New Orleans wardrobe. She couldn't get that back any more than she would be able to get back her thirty thousand dollars. Still, she was not destitute—not yet, at least.

"Driver, when you picked me up at the dock, weren't they loading the *Southern Belle?*"

"Yes'um."

"Would we still be able to catch it?"

"Don't sail for an hour, mum."

"Then that shall be our destination."

He shrugged and clucked the horses into motion.

"Aren't we going home, Mommy?"

She pulled them each to her side and hugged them close. "Yes, we are going home, my darlings. Home to where your mother was born. Home to your grandfather's house."

"What's it like?" Charley inquired.

That was much easier to answer than 'what will it be like?' She could only pray. All she knew was that she had to put the children in some safe harbor and get quickly back to California. Two years of hard work and all of their future had been deftly stolen away.

10

ELSA JANE would always wonder why the immediate love that Calvin Bender showed Annie and Charley had never been shown to her. And they loved him as if he had always been a part of their lives. They took to the island-plantation with an ease and grace that made her wish to remain forever.

Calvin Bender was astute enough not to ask her plans. He would watch her in the fields as she became familiar with every available weapon on the plantation. He never questioned her motives. Their conversation always centered on the children. He knew he was going to lose her again, but was happy she had finally come to him.

She stayed a month, to make sure Annie and Charley were happy and felt secure.

"Just like that!"

She bit her lip. "It has to be that way. It was the same in the orphanage. No goodbyes, just a quick disappearance until the next time."

"Do you know when that will be?"

"Maybe never," she said honestly. "I have taught myself to handle weapons. The overland route, through Indian country, is my quickest way back."

"But you can't chance that alone with winter coming on!"

"Because I am a woman?" she scoffed. "Believe one thing, if nothing else about me, as a man I have learned not to be a fool. I'll go back to St. Louis, sell the house, and try to hook up with a wagon train."

"I could . . ." he stopped himself. "No, I know better than to impose myself. You know your abilities and strengths better than I. Tomorrow, I shall take the children to the other side of the island so that you can make your normal departure. And if it be normal for them, I shall just say goodnight now."

"Goodnight." She could still not bring herself to address him as father. She felt guilty. The children had automatically addressed him as grandfather from the first day.

Her guilt increased the next morning when she reached the landing. She was presented with a large parcel by one of the slaves.

"From Mass'ah Calbin, Missy." Only when she was within her cabin, and Bender's Landing had slipped away, did she dare read the attached card: "To add to your admirable strengths and abilities. With deepest respect, C.B."

It was the rifle she had coveted. She didn't look back. Her children were in the finest hands possible.

* * *

Returning to her male role was harder than she had anticipated. Her costume was in California, her house was a hovel that she could not sell or even give away, and there were no wagon trains heading west.

"Alright, girl, walk away from it all," she said to herself. "It's time for some hardening up."

Independence was two hundred miles away—the end of civilization. Her boots made blisters on her heels but she ignored them. The woolen trousers chaffed her thighs. She split cords of wood at a hundred farm houses for a meal. Her blisters cracked and burst, only to be replaced by new blisters. For days she purposely did not wash. Blackheads formed and turned into ugly red splotches. She let her hair mat and grow dull. She hated what she was doing to herself, but somehow she knew that God would give her the chance to look Daris Jamieson and Bishop Landry in the face once again.

"Of all the horse-puckey ass-brained things to let happen!"

The men made uneasy, shuffling marks in the dirt with their boots. On the edge of the water hole, E.J. straddled an old white horse.

"Alright, colonel," she said finally. "If you want to save any of your damn herd we've got to push them through the night. Maybe if we keep them moving they will piss and sweat that alkali water out of their systems."

Browning, overweight and drunk, shouted that E.J. was responsible and that three cows were already dead and four down and dying.

"Listen, ass-hole," Elsa Jane said tartly. "I can't be everywhere at once. When I left this morning to find fresh water I warned that worthless overseer of yours about this alkali water. Now mount up and move 'em out!"

Browning never mounted up; no horse could carry his three hundred pounds. He waddled to the first supply wagon and crawled up beside his brother-in-law.

Jeams Fischer was nearly as stout as the colonel and was supposed to be the overseer from the colonel's Missouri plantation who would act as cook on the trip. The only thing he oversaw was a corn liquor jug. The cooking was left to one of the slaves.

E.J. had turned to a massive black man by the name of Dayton to help her with the other slaves.

Dayton nodded brusquely at the order to move out. He met the embattled scout's eye with a knowing gleam of his own, and said, "He been too damn drunk tah tell us 'bout dis bad water, Mass'ah E.J."

"How many drank at the hole?"

"None I'm charge ob," replied a delighted boy of fifteen, pointing to where near a hundred cattle were grazing.

"No mine," another grinned.

"Still, let's move 'em all out."

They jumped to their horses as though born to them. To these young slaves, the last month and a half had been near like a holiday. E.J. was a very easy person to work for, and the fact eased some of their homesickness. They had all been with the Browning family since birth and were used to harsh treatment and broken promises, so they prayed the scout would stay with them on the new plantation until the colonel could bring their families and the rest of the Missouri plantation staff to join them. They were not aware that it was illegal for the colonel to take them to a nonslave state.

Elsa Jane had suspected as much from the very

first, but her personal motives for getting to California kept her from getting involved. She was just as happy that Browning and Fischer stayed drunk three-fourths of the time as it kept them out of her hair.

But she wasn't too happy about it right now. Throughout the day she had been elated to see the far horizon broken by a purple-black line—the Rockies! Soon they would be climbing into the Wind River basin where all of the water would be fresh and pure. Soon she could dump the group on Jim Bridger and head off for Sacramento alone. She figured she would be home for Christmas.

Then her elation turned sour. She had found fresh hoof marks—no more than an hour old and all unshod—around the next water hole. She cautiously rode back to the camp, looking over her shoulder all the way. A nervous twitching in her stomach warned her that, although she couldn't see them, Indians were following her.

Fortunately, the scouts in Independence had told her that Indians didn't attack at night, so the sick cows had turned out to be a blessing in disguise. She would not have to persuade the colonel that they should keep moving.

But nature was against them. No sooner had the orange and scarlet sunset faded than a massive bright moon climbed up out of the eastern horizon. On the plains, the moon seemed larger than the earth. It basked everything in a silvery glow. The snow-capped mountains suddenly looked like they were barely ten feet away. By the time they reached the new water hole, the moon was a disc of bright light over their heads.

It was incredible how quickly the cattle were dying. Over forty had been left behind to mark their trail.

"Camp here?" Browning bellowed from his seat.

Elsa Jane couldn't tell if it was a question or an order.

"No," she bellowed back and rode over to the wagon.

"Shit, E.J., my ass is near numb from sitting."

"Then walk awhile, Colonel."

"Hey, runt," Jeams Fischer growled, "I'm getting sick of your wise-ass mouth. The Colonel said camp and camp we will."

Elsa Jane ignored him. Her weathered face, lean, alert, quick-eyed, looked to where the foothills were rolling up the plains like mounting waves.

"Perhaps you'd like to camp with them," she said mockingly. "They've already got their fires going."

The night was so clear that they could easily see fifteen to twenty miles around them. The Indian camps were scattered along the top of the foothills. Their fires looked like hundreds of glowworms.

"That don't look too good for us," Colonel Browning said.

"We'll steer the cattle north and then west," Elsa Jane announced calmly. "By morning we should be into timber country ourselves and thus hidden."

"How long have you known of this?" Fischer demanded, fright edging his words.

"All day and night. I haven't seen any signs of a scouting party, but just in case, I want us ready by dawn."

"Ready?" Browning asked. "How ready?"

"Like we discussed before leaving, Browning. It's time to break out your rifles and arm all the men—not just the three of us."

Browning hesitated. "Fine. We'll do it at dawn."

"I said I want us ready by dawn. I'll let you know."

With their bellies full of water, the cattle were reluctant to move. The blacks did not need to be told to move the herd quietly; they too had seen the camp-fires.

In the next two hours another forty cattle lay dead or dying. Elsa Jane was not aware that the fresh water and moving around was pumping the poison straight to their hearts. Nor did she stop to consider that their bodies would leave a trail right to them.

By the time the eastern sky was pearly gray, they had reached the juncture of Horse Creek and the Platte. The alkali water had claimed at least a hundred head of cattle and two slaves. Elsa Jane could push them no farther. Men were falling asleep in the saddle and dropping to the ground. Every stomach growled from lack of food. No one had dared mention that supper had been forgotten. It had not mattered to Browning and Fischer. They had eaten the night through as the wagon rolled along.

Elsa Jane gave orders to Dayton and two of his men to set up camp. She stopped in midsentence and cocked her head. For a moment, the only sound was the flowing of Horse Creek. Then queer noises mingled with it: the clink of beads on a muscular chest; the low neigh of a horse; the hooting of a small owl back in the pines; the grumble of a frog by the waterside.

"Scouting party." Elsa Jane whispered. "No more than two."

The two Indians came quietly out of the dense forest into a clearing. They gazed down at the river and cattle in disbelief. Within seconds they had turned back into the woods.

Elsa Jane could see that one of the horses pulled along a travois loaded with rolled tepee and supplies. She didn't know if they were the vanguard of the camp or just an Indian couple traveling alone. She frankly didn't know enough about Indians to know how they traveled. But her calloused hands had held her rifle the whole time.

Sleep or no sleep, they had to be prepared for whatever the Indians decided to do. She repeated her orders to Dayton and walked over to where the colonel and his brother-in-law were sprawled upon the ground.

"Alright, I guess you saw them. Let's break out the arms and be prepared for them."

Browning said nothing. He looked up at the sky with his bellicose face and staring eyes. Fischer, moon-faced, simple, drunk-eyed, looked worried.

"Well?"

Browning nodded his head.

"All the arms there be is already broken out."

Elsa Jane looked around.

"I don't see no arms."

"Right," Fischer said. "You don't think we are so damn stupid as to put a weapon in a nigger's hands, do you?"

"This is no time to think like that. Get off your lard ass and break open that rifle and ammunition chest you showed me in Missouri."

Jeams Fischer chuckled. "Hell, that ole chest ain't been filled with nothing but corn liquor jugs."

Elsa Jane looked from face to face. She prayed it was a lie, but realized she was looking into the faces of stupidity.

"Three rifles and three revolvers," she mused. "How does that stack up against the campfires we saw last night?"

For a moment no one said a word. The two men looked at E.J. like it didn't matter. The morning birds cheeped in the surrounding trees.

It didn't take the blacks long to figure out the situation.

"Y'all mean we ain't got nothin' tah protect our arses?" Dayton asked.

"He lied to me."

"Same. Same," Old Moses said. "Same broken promises and lies."

Elsa Jane said nothing.

"E.J.'ll tell us what tah do," Dayton said loyally.

"Will he tell us how not to be scared?" asked the fifteen-year-old.

"Don't be scared, boy. We'll outnumber them."

"You ain't ever seen an Indian massacre; I seen one as a boy in Kantuckeye."

"Oh, my God," cried Elsa Jane, "this is getting us nowhere. With any luck, they'll only have bows and arrows. We'll make them come in close, so get clubs, shovel handles, knives, anything at all. Now move!"

Oddly enough, the raiding party came at them from the north. They were part of the Snake tribe of the Crow people. For days they had been pursuing an Arapaho brave who had stolen away their chief's daughter. They approached the camp with their arms raised in a sign of peace; they only sought information.

There was no sense to what followed. Browning and Fischer opened fire in panic. Their shots fell far short of the Indians. The Indians mistook it to be a warning signal and desperately tried to signal their intentions. No one understood them. The braves came closer.

If the Indians had stayed put, or if Browning had not fired his next shot, nothing would have happened. But the shot was fired and it pierced the heart of a Snake brave.

The war-party chief quickly pulled back his force

to determine the strength of the enemy. A squad of twenty-five split up and came charging in from two directions. The war chief counted the rifle and revolver shots coming from behind the three wagons.

The chief had learned from similar situations to distinguish between a rifle blast and a revolver pop. He also knew how long it took to reload a rifle.

He had lost only one brave when reloading began. He could not believe his ears. Perhaps, he thought, these pioneers are holding back their firepower for the full attack. But One-Who-Thinks-Carefully never assumed anything. He sent out another wave of twenty-five braves so he could recount.

This time he lost two braves, but the information he gathered was totally unbelievable. Three rifles and three pistols? Could that be possible?

Behind the wagons his braves had seen men with faces as black as a starless night. One-Who-Thinks-Carefully's face wrinkled. Was that possible or was it some form of war paint the white-men were using?

Beaver Paw, the medicine man, came riding to the chief's side.

"I have heard before of these men who have the hair like the buffalo. They are demons."

One-Who-Thinks-Carefully scoffed. "I have been given but a count of fifteen to twenty, Beaver Paw. The Buffalo Hairs are weaponless."

"Perhaps they are so powerful they do not need weapons."

The chief began swearing. "Then why aren't the fifty braves I have sent against them all dead?"

"Because they don't want the other fifty of us fleeing harmless."

"Bah! You make as much sense as an old woman."

"We should be on about our business of finding Pine Cone Woman."

"Beaver Paw," the chief growled, "you are blind. They have some two hundred cattle and forty mules. Our chief will be far more pleased with such a prize than the return of any woman-daughter. By now she has probably already slept with that Arapaho and we would have to kill her."

"We do not eat the flesh of their beasts," the medicine man persisted.

"No, but the Pawnee do and we shall need their help to avenge ourselves on the Arapaho. This time I send in fifty to make them waste their powder and see if arrows pierce black skins."

With twenty-five braves charging from both directions, the arrows did indeed pierce black skin, and white skin as well.

Dayton saw the arrow strike Colonel Browning's skull and throw him backwards. He was quick to jump down into Browning's spot and grab for the rifle.

"What the hell you think you're doing, nigger?" Fischer cried, snatching the weapon away.

"Ah knows how'ta use dat!" Dayton insisted.

"Like hell!"

Jeams Fischer threw the rifle out beyond the triangled wagons. It fell beneath the hooves of the circling pintos and was smashed to splinters.

Dayton went berserk. He grabbed Fischer and lifted the obese man over his head, and spun him around as some ancient and long forgotten tribal utterance escaped from deep in his throat, then tossed the screaming man out to the Indians. Fischer scrambled to his feet and tried to find an opening back into the triangle. The Indians laughed and chased after the terrified fat man. They slung their bows over their heads and pulled out their lances. Fischer was terrified. They poked and jabbed at him, forcing him to run farther and farther away from the wagons. He dropped his rifle and frantically tried to get his pistol out of its holster. One daring brave, wishing to gain coup, rode right up next to him, leaned over with his knife, and made a neat slice along his hairline. Blood began to trickle down into Fischer's eyes. He started to stumble.

Another brave grabbed the big man by the hair and held him up. The first brave turned around and charged back at a full gallop. Fischer's scalp was severed from his skull. The second brave waved it proudly in the air and howled.

Jeams Fischer took a half dozen more steps and stopped. His eyes rolled white, he clutched for his chest and opened his mouth to scream. No sound came. His heart failed before he bled to death. The seizure was so quick and so massive that his dead bulk stood upright for several moments before it crumbled.

The sight had been too much for many of the young blacks. They jumped the wagon tongues and tried to flee.

"Get back here!" Elsa Jane screamed after them. "We need every man-jack of you!"

But panic has no ears. They scattered in six directions. The Indians gave chase with maniacal war whoops and soon were adding the buffalo hair scalps to their belts.

"Take everything out of the wagons and pile it around the tongues and underneath," Elsa Jane shouted. "We'll make them climb over the tops. Dayton, put one man inside each wagon with the longest knives you can find. They can stab up through the canvas at them and we can club them as they topple down on our side."

The black men looked at her helplessly. They knew

it would be impossible for seven men to kill a hundred, but still they obeyed.

Elsa Jane bought time by using up every round of ammunition for her rifle. Her first few shots that morning had left her squeamish. These redmen were also God's creatures, but when it became a matter of survival, she shot to kill. Now as she fired, reloaded and fired again, she pretended that the wildly painted faces were like Daris Jamieson's.

Twenty-four remaining shots felled twenty-four Indians.

Elsa Jane set down the rifle and knew the end was near. She was thinking of her children when she became aware of the odd silence. The Indians had pulled back and were awaiting further orders from their chief.

One-Who-Thinks-Carefully was thinking.

"Have I made a mistake?" he mused. He had very few scalps to show for the thirty-three braves dead. Granted they had won many coup so far, but was there something supernatural about the men still within the wagons? He knew there was only one rifleman left, but that one never missed.

He raised his feathered war staff as a signal. He would personally lead the seventy-seven remaining braves in a direct frontal attack. He would pit his own powers against those of the rifleman.

"Here they come!"

The Indian's war screams were terrifying. Within moments they were leaping from their horses on to the curved supports of the wagon coverings. The men inside jabbed their knives into every sagging portion, but the Indians were coming across four and five at a time. They crammed down into the triangle. The black men fought fiercely with clubs and pitchforks. The Indians countered with hatchets and knives. The Indians did not fear death. They would be glorified in their next life for their bravery. The blacks were fighting for the miserable life they already had. Death was an ending for them.

"E.J.!" Dayton cried.

Elsa Jane spun just in time to see the Indian crouching for the attack. As he leaped, she grabbed up a pitchfork from the dead hands of Old Moses and braced the tongs so he landed on it. The hatchet fell from his hand. The five prongs went in through his lower abdomen and broke the skin of the lower spine. His was a death scream.

As Elsa Jane lifted the painted warrior, pitchfork and all, she was blindsided by another attacker. His hatchet ate into her neck and sliced under the shoulder blade down to her armpit. There was no pain, just numbness as she let the forked Indian fall.

Dayton ran to her rescue but the Indian was far too agile. The hatchet point entered Dayton's forehead between the eyes and cleaved his broad nose. Dayton, with the hatchet still sticking out of him, grasped the savage about the throat and used his last strength trying to choke him.

Elsa Jane tried to find a new weapon, but could not move her right hand or arm. Another Indian jumped on her back, clawing at her hair. They fell to the ground and rolled. She had only her weaponless left hand to defend herself as he tried to sever her scalp. She felt the pain as the knife sliced down from her right temple to her ear. The Indian moved to make a similar cut on the opposite side. Her hand closed on the only thing available. With a quick roll she brought her hand up and shot dirt directly into his eyes.

Momentarily blinded, he sat back, dropped the

knife and clawed at his eyes. In one continuous motion E.J. scooped up the knife and plunged it into his chest. She didn't wait to see the results, she just kept rolling toward the nearest wagon and crawled in among the piled crates and supply baskets.

Blood was coursing over her face and she had to keep her right eye shut. She had just enough vision out of her other eye to give her a new fright. The mayhem was over and the Indians were beginning to search the wagons for valuables.

Suddenly, a solitary war whoop sounded from the trees to the right and left. The Snake Indians froze.

The couple had made it back to the Arapaho camp. Their chief had been quick to react to the news of such a prize. Now the prize would be doubled. Arapaho Indians poured out of the trees *en masse,* two hundred strong.

The Snake Indians didn't wait for an order to vacate. They scrambled out of the triangle and fled. The Arapaho warriors flanked them and began to close their pincer movement on a low knoll of pine trees. No Snake Indian would ever again see home.

Elsa Jane feared she would have to live the nightmare over again. Lying beneath the wagon would not protect her when the Arapaho returned. Going back out into the center of the breastwork was little better. Her only chance was to get to the woods while the Arapaho were still busy with the Snakes.

When she got on the other side of the wagons, she was surprised to see how far the cattle had roamed. It would take the Indians some time to round them up. It was time she would use to her advantage.

She cursed her right arm, still unaware of the seriousness of the wound, and gently touched her scalp. She clawed up a clump of prairie grass and held it to her forehead until it matted with her sticky hair and clotted the blood.

The horses and mules were scattered too far for her to reach, so she stayed low to the ground and scrambled to where the nearest cattle stood. Using one as a shield, she grabbed it by the hide and urged it to move forward. Once in the middle of a small herd, she was able to walk crouched among them. She patiently drove them toward the trees.

It was a slow and tedious process, but she was getting nearer to the forest. She could hear the pounding of horses behind her. The Arapaho had started to round up the herd, and a half a dozen braves were bearing down on her. The cattle sensed the intruders and moved faster. The Indians tried to turn them. Elsa Jane could feel the ripple of panic charge through the beast she clung to, and knew that the cattle were fast becoming a danger.

They moved away from the woods. Elsa Jane crouched down, throwing her left arm over her head to shield it from the turf thrown up by the hooves. They started to stampede. A hoof hit her numb arm and threw her. She hit the dirt with her chin as a cow nearly trampled her.

The Indians began herding the cattle back toward the wagons. When their backs were turned, she crawled the rest of the way into the woods.

The texture beneath her hands began to change. The prairie dirt was covered with pine needles, and the massive trees shaded her from the heat. Still, she did not stop. She struggled on until she was well within the forest and engulfed in its soothing silence.

Her rest was brief. A branch cracked and a face appeared among the trees. She grabbed up a dead tree limb and swung it feebly against the arm that was reaching for her. It was ripped from her fingers.

The man whispered harshly, but she could not understand the small clear sound. He grasped her right arm and twisted her down. Pain exploded so fiercely that she thought her whole arm had been torn away.

The blackness of unconsciousness washed over her as she struck the ground. She was aware enough to know, however, that the man was walking beside her, three steps down the length of her body. She felt sick. She was sure she was about to die.

11

SHE BEGAN to awaken. There was the sound of a horse neighing, the bark of a dog and the smell of smoke from a fire. Plantation noises, she immediately thought. Her body felt torn, sore and exhausted. She couldn't remember why. She struggled to open her eyes and looked up at a bower of pine boughs over her head. She struggled to rise, but got no higher than her left elbow. Her right arm was strapped to her side.

Outside the lean-to, she could now see the playful dog nipping at a tethered horse. A giant man sat before a fire, with his back to her. He was wrapped in a blanket and turned a spit with a roasting rabbit.

Now she remembered how terrified she had been, thinking the Indian was going to kill her. She couldn't help but wonder why he had not.

"Hello," she called tentatively, wondering if he spoke English.

The man tossed the blanket aside and rose. In buckskins and fur leggings he seemed even taller than his already towering six feet four inches.

"Well, lass," he said, "you've had me bloody scared."

Elsa Jane gasped. This was hardly an Indian. He was a golden Viking. Masses of wavy hair curled down to his wide shoulders. His skin was clear and creamy, his forehead high and his eyebrows such light blond that they were nearly invisible; but not so the moustache. It drooped down either side of his wide, grinning mouth and was several shades darker than his hair and eyebrows.

He came toward her, his eyes twinkling in an amused way. She had never seen eyes of such light, vivid blue. They were like clear depthless pools.

"Who are you?"

His laugh was like booming thunder. "My dear child, that question could be mine. For the moment let us say that my *nom de plume* is Mountain Charley."

"E.J. Forest." She used her male voice.

This brought forth a new burst of laughter. He squatted down so that she would not strain herself looking up.

"Well, E.J. Forest, as you took a nice slice from a hatchet from neck and shoulder, it was put upon me to learn certain secrets of your anatomy while dressing the wound."

For the first time she realized that she was covered only with a bear skin. She flushed. There was a moment of *déjà vu*.

"Thank you," she said softly.

"Would have done more, lass, but saw no sense in giving them my scalp as well. Saw it all from the timbers. Quite a bloody good showing your group put up for a while. Never thought I'd see a body come from it alive, however."

"What are you?" she couldn't help but ask.

Again Mountain Charley roared. "Again the question could be mine. However, I am English, born and bred."

She giggled slightly. "You look more like a Swede I once met in the California mining camps. I thought he was the biggest man I had ever met."

"Well, lass, Norse blood is in many English veins, either by ancient rape or design. But chit-chat is not important at the moment. A section of that roasting hare seems more in order."

Elsa Jane was ravenous. While she was eating, he described her wounds and how he had been dressing and caring for them.

"Honey?"

"My father's pastime is the raising of bees. Honey to him is the Balm of Gilead. At least it will keep you from having too nasty a scar from temple to ear. They came near getting your scalp, my girl. Very clever of you to pose as a lad. They would have carried you off for unmentionable things."

She was already feeling very friendly toward this kind man.

"It's almost seven years I've been posing as such, Charley."

"To be sure." He did not seem shocked. He pointed at her fur-covered breasts with a long forefinger. "That would then account for the weird strappings I found, the bands and the very nasty scar on your thigh."

"Yes," she sighed, "I guess my body is like the written pages of a book."

"I didn't mean to pry. The English are not normally

inquisitive by nature. Must be my Norse blood that makes me lust for every scrap of knowledge that falls in my wake."

"Well, you certainly don't sound like the mountain men I have come across."

"My little masquerade, E.J." He stopped. "Lord, that sounds so stuffy and formal, like I was addressing a bank clerk. We shall have to devise something more appropriate."

"E.J. will do fine. I must be on my way to California as soon as possible."

"I say, you do have bloody nerve. But it will be a couple of weeks before that wound really starts to knit and perhaps months before the tendons under the armpit are ready to give you movement. To say nothing of transportation for that thousand-mile journey."

"How do you know so much, Charley?"

"Because I am a student of everything," he answered with a sigh, "and master of nothing. My father wished me to go into medicine, for we had no such in the family, but I was a miserable failure. That was when I was a twenty-year-old twig. Growing into a branch over the next twenty, I have dabbled as a naturalist, mineralogist, historian, explorer and escapee."

"Escapee? Does that mean that you were also a criminal?"

"Interesting question," he mused. "My father, while he was alive, would have considered that a most apt description. Never got along with the old boy. My younger brother Frederick was more to his liking. Puffy as a Yorkshire pudding. Beastly dull character and sly. Parades around London as though I were dead and sends me secret stipends to keep me away from home."

"Parades? Stipends? I'm afraid I don't understand any of this."

Charles Henry Humrick grinned until his even teeth gleamed white and his blue eyes twinkled.

"It's odd, my lass, that in the five years I have been upon North American soil, I have gone out of my way to make sure no one understood. But here we are, with no one to hear but a horse, a pack mule and a mangy old dog, and I have no qualms about making you understand. In Jolly Ole England the tale would be a common one, I assure you. The ne'er-do-well son who would rather be free of pomp and circumstance and untitled. That was fine until the gout killed father. The Duke thought that life meant overindulging in everything; food, drink and a string of women so infamous that it kept my sensitive mother in seclusion and sent her to an early grave. Which brings us to dear, simpering Freddy-boy, who will more than likely die of the gout, as well. He covets the title, the land, and the customary seat in the House of Lords. Bully for Freddy-boy. Let him pretend I am dead and be the Duke of Plover, for I wish it not!"

When there was no response he looked down to see she had fallen back to sleep.

"Ah, well, time enough to gain your tale, lass."

When she next awoke, he and the dog were gone, so she lulled herself back to sleep.

Hunger woke her a third time. She was not aware that sixteen hours had elapsed.

The man was again squatting by the fire. He was dropping white-hot rocks from the fire into a bark kettle. The water within hissed as it boiled. It gave off a most enticing aroma.

"What is that?"

"Aha! Back among the living again, are we? Well,

we have here a plump partridge hen, some roots that the Indians think are delicious, but that I find bland, and some pine nuts to give it a touch of flavor. I think it will make a very nice broth for your weak little tummy. Oh, if you care to dress for dinner, I've washed your clothing in the stream and the sun has dried them. Jolly good weather for mid-December, eh wot?"

"Can't be!"

"Look at that notched pole. I am a most methodical man. Fourteen notches."

Elsa Jane didn't answer. Being alive and late, she decided, was better than it could have been. She reached out and pulled her clothes to her. She noticed that her right arm was no longer strapped down and that she was regaining a bit of movement. As the man was aware of her sex, she let her breasts hang free under the shirt.

The broth was exactly what she needed. A little later in the evening, she was able to pick at some white meat of the hen. Between the two meals, she rested in the sun and told bits and pieces of her own story.

"I have buffalo jerky, if you are still hungry."

"I'm fine."

He was silent for a long time. She shyly studied him. She couldn't help but wonder why he lived such a lonely life. He was handsome enough to have any woman in the world. There was so much strength in his jutting lantern-jaw, the finely molded nose and square cheeks. Lying on his side by the fire, the buckskin became taut on his muscular legs. His legs were so long that Elsa Jane knew she would only come midway up his flaring chest.

"I hope I am not detaining you."

He shrugged. "I was just off to witness one of your Yankee phenomenon."

"Which one?"

"The one at Pike's Peak."

"Again, I don't understand."

He sat up. "That could be true, because you were on a rather slow northern route, with the cattle and all. But the rumors did reach all the way into Canada. I came down out of pure interest. It seems that early this fall some Cherokee Indians and two white men found gold near this Pike's Peak. I was under the impression that there was quite a stampede on for the place."

"And I've kept you from being one of the first to get there. I'm sorry."

"Nonsense," he chuckled. "I was not interested in the gold they would find, but the gold they might not find."

"Must you always talk in riddles?"

"All right," he grinned, "common sense. These mountains are quite different from those you saw in California. This ancient volcanic chain was probably here billions of years before California was spewed from the ocean. Once they have scratched the surface, they will find the gold harder to come by, because it will be harder rock. I have been testing my theory all the way down from Canada. I shall continue to do so after I make a decision about you."

"See, I *am* a problem for you. Where would be the nearest place that I could purchase a horse and supplies? I still have some money left in my belt."

Again he shrugged. "My maps of the region are rather primitive. I would venture a guess that this new mining region might be the closest and, if I might be permitted to give a bit of sage advice, I would recommend you travel south and pick up the Santa Fe Trail at Bent's Fort. From there you could go by stage to Tucson and San Diego."

"I will think on it."

She was impressed by the man's wealth of knowledge.

She had considered this country just a great, vast wilderness. He viewed it as a fascinating mistress with changeable moods and manners. He knew the Indian tribes, where they lived and their customs. He was a mountain man—a wanderer who did not covet their land or women. He was accepted among them as such.

They traveled slowly, letting her mend and giving her exercise to rebuild her strength.

Elsa Jane couldn't go more than half a dozen steps without looking up to catch him watching her. Then he would avert his eyes and look across the foothills at the mountains that towered ten to fourteen thousand feet above them. Then he would look back at her again.

It was worry, but not for her health. He had always been a sensible man when it came to women. As a schoolboy at Eton and Harrow—and even later at Oxford—it had taken a great deal to stir his lustful blood. For a long time he had thought this was a very serious problem, taking into consideration the actions of his father. He finally learned that most schoolboys and college men were a great deal more talk than action. He relaxed and formed a lifestyle that was suitable to his temperament. He knew that someday a woman would suddenly be there to full-fill him.

He feared that such was now coming to pass.

"I was wondering . . ." he said.

"Yes?"

"That stream," he said flatly.

"What about it?"

"I would love to explore it up aways. It's not on this map I got from that old mountain man at the Crow camp."

"Then do so."

"Will you come?"

She nodded. She was contented for the first time in many months. Her children were safe with Calvin Bender. No one really expected her back in California until spring or summer, and her obligation to Colonel Browning had been abruptly cancelled by the Indians. She didn't have to think for anybody, not even for herself. She was quite happy.

"I will follow," she answered.

It was the first of many rivers they explored—rivers that would later bear such names as Cache de Poudre, Thompson, North and South St. Vrain.

Charles, Duke of Plover acted as though a soothing grace had entered his life. He would begin a discussion on geography and it would dissolve into a description of an interesting segment from his life. Elsa Jane also told stories and he absorbed them like a thirsty sponge. They felt these moments were like precious gifts.

"That would be the mountain that was explored by Major Stephen A. Long. He's right about it being over fourteen thousand feet. The next great giant in this range will be this Pike's Peak. I would, therefore, guess that the rumored Cherry Creek would be no more than a day's travel."

He began to sing a tune from his past. Elsa Jane drifting with the slow melody, paid no attention to the murmuring words. She walked with an easy gait, conscious of Charley's nearness, yet keeping sight of anything that would give them something to talk about.

As he continued to sing, she suddenly became aware of the words.

Look down, look down, that Lonesome Road,
Hang down your head and sigh.
The best of friends must part some day
And why not you and I?

She turned her head and looked up at Charley's handsome face. He seemed lost in the words.

"What a horrid song!" cried Elsa Jane.

"I wasn't aware," he said dully. "I say, look there, lass. What a charming little lake. Mild winter for it not to be fully frozen. How would you like to have a nice trout for dinner?"

She nodded and followed him down to the water's edge. She took the pack off the mule, found a spot under some bare cottonwoods for the bedrolls and began gathering wood for a fire.

Charley unsaddled the horse, shackled it and the mule and gathered stones for the fire circle. Soon the flames crackled and gave off warmth.

Elsa Jane stared at the yellow tongues.

"Charley—" she said.

Charley was preparing his fishing line. Beneath a mossy rock he had found some slugs for bait. He wrapped the line around a stick and came to her.

"*You* don't think that's a horrid song, do you?" she said. "You think it's true."

"It was true for my mother."

Elsa Jane kicked the dirt impatiently. "I'm healed now. I have the full use of my arm back. Is that why you said the mining camp is probably a day away? Is that why you were singing that mournful song?"

"Lass—" he said as he took a step toward her. "It has been jolly."

"But it's true, isn't it?" she persisted. "Have you given any more thought about coming on to California with me?"

He shrugged his broad shoulders and walked to the edge of lake.

"Look, lass, no man has been happier than I. We've been our own Adam and Eve in a very special Garden of Eden—prior to the apple incident, of course. I can learn so very little back in civilization . . ."

"Then why did you? . . . Her voice thickened and she turned back to the fire.

He sighed. "I allowed myself a moment of beautiful delusion—rare for me."

"Without meaning it."

"Without meaning it could go on forever."

"Forever in California?"

In the moment before he answered she felt what he could say wrap around her heart. It had been her dream and not his. She had felt that if she could keep him with her, something would automatically grow out of it, as had happened with Peter. The words of the song began a measured beating in her head. "The best of friends must part some day and why not you and I." That was all that they were— the best of friends—no more and no less.

"I'm going to catch us a fish now."

She didn't turn around. The question had gone unanswered. It was unanswerable. They couldn't travel two roads at once. Her world became silence.

Suddenly, there was a sound like a rifle shot. Then there was Charley's cursing cry.

She spun around just in time to see him disappear below the ice.

"Charley!" she screamed and raced to the edge of the lake. Cobweb cracks were creeping out from the hole his bulk had created. She saw his hand claw out of the water and grasp at the ice shelf. Hatless, his soggy golden head emerged.

"Don't come out!" he shouted, then the ice he held cracked away and he disappeared again.

He came to the surface again, gasping. "It won't support me, lass."

Elsa Jane shivered with fear. She knew the numbing effect such water had.

She dashed away and looked for something long enough to reach him in time. She remembered seeing a felled tree. It was long enough, but impossible for her to drag alone.

She quickly put the pack back on the mule, secured a rope to each of its sides and unshackled the beast. The mule shied, sensing her panic, and tried to get away.

"Alright, jackass!" she cried, running to its head. "Mules I know about!"

She swatted it smartly on either side of its head and grasped the lead rope tightly. She pulled its head sharp to the right and it followed.

In less than a minute she had the mule in place and had tied the trailing rope to the tree trunk. She whacked the mule on the rump and it jerked forward, brayed and stopped. Elsa Jane immediately saw the problem. Many of the under branches and much of the root structure were held by the frozen ground.

It would be time-consuming to free it, but there was no other choice. It seemed to take her forever to go back for Charley's double-bladed ax, but it was only seconds. She slashed at the root ends and then the larger branches on each side. She went to the front of the log and called back to the mule.

"Alright you brown-eyed beautiful half-breed—Yee-haw!"

She set her shoulders under the front of the log,

braced her legs and began to straighten. The log
came up slowly. It was ten times heavier than normal
with the mud and ice. She gritted her teeth and lifted.
She could feel the mule straining forward. It moved
a quarter inch—half an inch—and then a jolting
foot. The mule gave a jerk to free the roots and Elsa
Jane fell sprawling into the log hole.

"Beautiful, baby!" she cried, scrambling up. She
unhitched the mule and trotted him back around to
the front of the log. Rehitched, she hit its rump again
and ran to gather up the lead rope. She kept running, forcing the beast to pull the log faster and faster.
The downhill slope to the lake helped them gather
momentum.

"Over here!" Charley shouted. "I'm over here!"

She didn't waste her breath answering but jerked
the mule's head to the left. As he turned, the rope
went taut and nearly pulled him backward. Elsa Jane
pulled on the lead rope to keep him at a trot. The
log cracked and bark chips flew as it rolled down
onto the ice. It skated along, coming nearly abreast
of Elsa Jane and the mule. Still, she did not lessen
her urging.

She could hear the ice cracking and breaking under the log's weight. She jerked the beast back around
up shore and pulled him to a halt. The log rolled
right to the hole Charley had made. Its roots nearly
covered him over.

"Hang on!" she shouted. She whacked the mule's
hide until her hand stung. The log caught on the
broken ice and jammed. Elsa Jane pulled along with
the mule.

She was concentrating so hard on pulling the log
out of the water that she didn't see Charley scramble
over the roots and pull himself through the wet tangle of dead branches.

"I'm ashore! Ashore!" he wailed as he sped by her to the fire.

Exhausted, Elsa Jane sank down beside the mule and lovingly wrapped her arms about its hind leg. It twitched at such unusual behavior but didn't kick.

"I'm not as healed as I thought I was," she said to the beast, "but you are such a working beauty. How about you going to California with me?"

With no show of modesty, Charley began to strip away his sodden buckskins. The water had plastered them to his skin and already he could feel ice crystals forming in the pounded deer hide.

Elsa Jane pulled herself up and untied the tow rope. The mule followed her along like a pet dog as she stumbled up and threw more wood on the fire. She shackled the mule and left for more firewood. They would need plenty now.

Charley was wrapped in a buffalo robe. He had thrown his dripping clothing over the lower branches of the cottonwood, and his teeth were chattering so that he couldn't talk.

Elsa Jane built a second fire beneath his clothes. She feared they would not dry before morning.

From the supply pack she took the blackened coffee pot, filled it with water, broke several lengths of jerky into it and put it on the fire to boil.

The second fire sputtered and spurted smoke from the dripping buckskins. Night was beginning to lay black against the skyline.

"Tit," he chattered, "for tat."

"We'll have to keep that fire going all night to dry your things."

"No hurry," he said uncomfortably. "A day or two more won't matter."

Suddenly, a day or two did matter to Elsa Jane.

Her legs and arms began to tremble from the exertion of moving the log. Her head throbbed. It was hard to keep her eyes open.

"I need to rest for a spell," she said dully. "Wake me in an hour or so and I will relieve you."

"Right you are, lass."

Lass. It seemed ironic that he should call her lass. She crawled into her bedroll and was soon asleep.

Cold. She was so terribly cold. The black waters of the Mississippi were freezing her. There were so many to save—and herself. She cried out to them, pleading and begging them not to give up, but they seemed deaf. Why won't they listen to me, she sobbed. Why?

Suddenly hands were lifting her and cradling her like a baby. She was safe but couldn't stop sobbing. Peter had saved her. Peter now held her and comforted her. Peter would soothe away her fears.

No! Peter was not a part of this nightmare! Peter belonged to another nightmare. Peter was . . .

The black truth receded before being uttered. A hand stroked her head gently. Her cheek lay upon the matting of fine, soft chest hair.

"It's alright, lass. Just a wee dream."

"No, no . . ." she whispered. "Peter isn't dead."

"You told me such was true, lass."

His powerful hands continued to soothe. "Well . . ." he said. "Well . . ." His breath came like smoke in the chill air. "I'm not your Peter, lass, but he is surely a ghost that stands between us."

She looked up at him and smiled a little. His big comforting presence warmed her through. How different he actually was from Peter, she thought vaguely. "Is he really a ghost," she asked, "between us?"

"The questions'll wait, lass," he answered quietly. "I've the fires roaring high and the robe about us both. Warm yourself and sleep."

"Thank you," she murmured. It was warm and comforting in his arms. She snuggled closer and put a hand on his chest. She sighed. The hair on his chest was like that of a newborn kitten, soft and downy, with warm flesh beneath. With Peter she would have felt self-conscious in such a position, but Charley made her feel weightless and giddy.

"Mind you don't start getting strange notions . . ." she said with faint humor. "Oh, I forgot, you're celibate. Did I get the word right?"

Charley dropped his chin onto the top of her head. "Right and wrong. I used that as an example of how I was around the Indian women and those who dress like men."

Elsa Jane cursed him softly, but Charley was happy —happier than ever before in his life. He had thought of holding her all these weeks. His happiness faded only when he thought of Peter.

During Elsa Jane's fevered period she had thrashed about and called for Peter. At that time he had feared that Peter was back among the wagon corpses. But he had come to learn the story of Peter Forest, and Annie and Charles Peter. They were ghosts, living and dead, who consumed every ounce of love that Elsa Jane possessed. There was none left for him. But at last now he had hope. It would be a long time before Peter was fully replaced. And where should they go? California? He quailed at the thought, for in California Elsa Jane would want to run her mule-freight business. He wanted her to be a lady— his lady—his duchess. His duchess? It could be done properly and that would certainly give Freddy-boy reason to fight for the title he had ignobly claimed for five years.

If she'll have me, he thought, we'll face them all down. How marvelous! He wouldn't mind such a life with her as his helpmate. He imagined her dressed in royal-blue velvet and lace, a decent dress for a duchess, standing in the gilt and rosewood hall of Humrick Manor, waiting to greet his father's distant cousin, Queen Victoria. Elsa Jane would be smiling as she was now; gently, graciously, genuinely.

He wrapped an arm over her shoulder and slowly unbuttoned her shirt.

Elsa Jane didn't move. She had waited seven years for this moment and she had known for weeks that this was the right man.

"Ah, my duchess . . ." he sighed, "my dream is to take you home, where you belong."

"And mine to go . . ." she whispered and rose.

Oddly, as she removed the rest of her clothing, a name for "home" did not enter her brain. Wherever Charles Henry Humrick put down his bedroll would be home for her.

She crawled beneath the buffalo robe and nestled down beside him, feeling his nudity against her own. She was startled for a moment when she realized how big he was. Then she calmed. She found his lips with her own. They were soft and sensuous. She kissed them hungrily, as if they were the food of her soul.

He accepted her tutelage as an awakening from hibernation. He responded slowly, gratefully, with love in his heart.

A dozen times in his forty years he had been with a woman with emotion, but Elsa Jane was fire and brimstone, fleecy clouds and singing angels. She had honey lips, firm breasts—and hesitation!

His own ghost, and not that of Peter Forest, rose between them. His fear soared more quickly than his physical arousal. He was going to lose her just as surely as he had the others, he thought. He was just too much man for any woman. He feared her next words, just as he had feared them before. They had always made him flee in utter embarrassment and curse anything sexual.

"Gently," she murmured.

"I . . . I . . ."

"Gently," she repeated cooingly, pulling him slowly down. "We've all the time in the world."

But his fear did not diminish. He could feel her muscles tighten. He could not hurt her, he dared not, but her arms were like vises about his neck that would not release him. Against his ear he could hear her harsh breathing. He knew that momentarily it would erupt into a painful scream.

She did not scream, although she felt as if she was being cleaved in two. She pushed the pain from her mind and concentrated on a single thought. "Do this for love. Do this for the love of this man. You have gone through much worse than this to make yourself a man. You can go through this to make yourself a woman again."

They had no way of telling when their combined emotions eased the tensions. It was the nucleus of a rebirth for each.

The apple fell from the tree in Eden. ⌇

12

THE SIGN saying "Pike's Peak or bust" had been changed to "Pike's Peak Bust-ed."

"Lord," E.J. gasped. "Nothing like this in California."

The camp was exceedingly primitive. Tents had been flung up willy-nilly along with a number of crude cabins on either side of the frozen creek. Some of the cabins could be distinguished by their smell. They were rum shops and cheap saloons.

"This way," Charley said as he spotted the skeleton frame of a two-storied building. Oddly, the unwalled building already displayed a freshly painted sign over its canopied front.

"I gather that *Wootton's General Store* is doing business in that hovel for the present."

"Present," Elsa Jane scoffed. "In our camps a one-storey house, fourteen by twenty feet, with eight feet of shed for a kitchen, would be like my original office and stable. Here it's got to be a palace."

Charley chuckled. "My dear duchess, you would make anything connected with California sound better. See to the animals, would you? And I shall see to the news and some provisions."

Mountain Charley was accepted for exactly what he looked like—a true mountain man. Traders were far more apt to be friendly with that breed of man than with the pioneer miners. Richens Lacy ("Uncle Dick") Wootton was no exception.

"All the way down from Canady, eh? Accident or design?"

Charley smiled.

"I'm not depending on gold from the ground to pay for my supplies, if that's what you mean."

The squat, bow-legged man chuckled dryly. His face looked like a dried-up pansy.

"Accident on my part, if the truth be known. Let me fill you a tin while you think up a list."

Charles Humrick knew exactly what the man meant; he had traded with many such men in the north. Tales had to be swapped before business was conducted. It was the social custom and couldn't be denied.

Wootton tapped one of the barrels at the end of the counter and filled two tin cups.

Charley nearly choked on his first sip.

"Easy on," Uncle Dick warned. "That's Taos Lightning, the rawest distillation the Mexicans ever came up with. That were my accident. I was bringing three barrels of it and a wagonload of supplies to trade with the Arapaho. Hell, didn't even know about this gold strike—or nonstrike as it's proving. Stumbled into this camp and a clamorous bunch of idiots.

T'were Christmas Eve and they were hard pressed. Sold everything I had in an hour and turned right back for Taos. Could have made a greater profit from the Injuns, but they won't be here forever. By the time I got back with two wagons they was calling the place Auraria and they still had no such thing as a store or anything like one. The four Mexes with me threw up this cabin almost overnight and I didn't even have to bother with counters or shelves."

"Hardly necessary with the new building going up next door."

"That's for Mrs. Wootton, man. Fine woman she, but demanding some roots out of her hubby. Been trapping and trading all these years, mainly for others—Colonel Bent and Jimmy Bridger. Yep, I weren't back a week, and in rolls two wagons of lumber and Mexican carpenters sent by my wife. She ain't very often wrong, but this worries me."

"Why is that?" Charley's head was beginning to spin after just a few sips of the raw, rank brew.

"Ain't no mining at all been done along Cherry Creek since fall. The gold hunters are drinking and gambling away their time until spring."

"And then?"

"Off to the mountains, I reckon."

"They're not in the mountains now?"

"You daft? Only men like yourself and trappers know how to handle a blizzard when it sweeps down without warning and buries the pines under forty or fifty feet of snow. These are mostly farmers and dreamers and folk down on their luck. Just ask me. That whole corner of the cabin is loaded with bartered goods so they can get a little flour, salt or sugar. More come each day and just as many start heading back. How's winter been in the north?"

"Same as here. Mostly mild."

"Then it's bound to come soon. What will you be having?"

The talking time was over. Charley had a long list, but Uncle Dick Wootton's stocks were very low.

"My woman is bringing more supplies and lumber within two weeks, if you're staying around."

Charley slowly took gold coins from his money belt. He had an idea but would have to confer with Elsa Jane.

"I might be doing just that."

Wootton looked at the coins. His eyes grew round and his lips puckered as he whistled admiration.

"Gold of the realm."

"It's quite good in Canada—and every other trading post along the way."

Wootton bit a coin with his yellowed teeth. "Good here, too. This is the manner of gold I like best."

"Then I've a bargain to strike with you, Trader Wootton. I've a wee bit of exploring to do hereabouts. Give me a chit for my change and I'll take it in supplies on my return. I shall require enough to get me to Santa Fe."

"You alone?"

"I've a companion."

Wootton thrust out his thin, parched hand.

"I'm your supplier," he agreed, "Mr.—?"

"Make the chit out to Charles Humrick."

Wootton helped Charley carry his supplies out to the pack mule. He did not think it odd that Mountain Charley did not introduce him to his traveling companion. People passed so quickly in and out of Auraria that introductions never mattered.

However, Richens Lacy Wootton was a curious man. He was even more curious because he had seen the size of the man's money belt and had been paid with British crowns. He was also curious about Charley's companion. He was a fair young man, about half the age of the mountain man. But what really made him curious was the pack mule. There were no traps or trap lines and there was only one rifle between them. Mountain men were trappers and hunters by trade.

He watched them weave their way down the street, dodging horses, cows, pigs and mud holes. Then he suddenly realized that the mountain man and his son had only one horse. This made no sense to Wootton as the man had ample finances to purchase another horse and he would have arranged it.

He was fussing over the matter when an old friend arrived.

"Let me draw you a tin, Patch Eye, 'fore we look at your pelts."

Patch Eye Wilson accepted eagerly. He was not a favorite of many of the traders as his pelts were always inferior. Ever since losing his eye to a grizzly bear his hunting sight had not been too good.

Wootton cheerfully relaxed. In fact, he spent ten minutes recalling boon companions they had in common, mainly those in the northern trading areas. Then he got down to business.

"Got me a new customer. Charles Humrick by name. Ever run across him? Calls himself Mountain Charley."

"Big blond monster?"

"That's him."

"Seen him a couple times in the Canadian Rockies. Strange one."

"How's that?"

"More an explorer than hunter. Gentleman talker, too. But that stands to reason."

"What stands to reason?"

"Educated. Always buying information for the maps

he draws. But he ain't no fool, Wootton. He goes off to see if the information is correct. Ain't ever heard of anyone lying to him more than once."

"Explorer?" Wooton asked. Thinking of the maps and British coin, he wondered if perhaps the British were secretly interested in this territory.

"Man knows a hell of a lot, I tell you. Only time I saw him right angry was at Moose Jaw. Must be five years ago, when I still had both eyes. Mail packet had come over from Winnipeg. Got roaring drunk when he heard his old man had died in England. Seems his old man was a duke or something, but he didn't go back."

"Well, let's look at your pelts, Patch Eye," Wootton said, quickly changing the subject.

He overpaid the man for the beaver pelts, but rubbed his thin fingers together as though he had made the best from the bargain.

"Ah, Charles Humrick," he said aloud to no one, "I must find a way to keep your money belt in Auraria. I've fifty-five years experience that I could sell."

"I didn't get you a horse, Duchess."

They were far enough away from the camp that she felt she could reach out and take his hand without causing scandal. "So I noticed."

"It was by design, lass."

She giggled. "I like Duchess better."

His face was suddenly as black as a thundercloud.

"I've a favor to ask," he said sharply.

"Name it," she answered quietly.

"It has to do with not getting the horse. I've learned that the gold-hunters are not prospecting because of the winter. I think I could put my theory to its truest test here. Grant me one more side trip before we head south."

"Granted," she said quickly. It was the first indication that he would go with her beyond the mining camp.

The thundercloud was gone now, and a happy grin took its place.

"We only have enough supplies for ten to twelve days. Then we shall return to Wootton and lay out our future plans."

By his manner she knew he had already made his plans. They were so alike. Both had learned to keep their thoughts and secrets to themselves. As neither was used to sharing, she understood his silence and refrained from probing.

She would have followed him to the ends of the earth, anyway. Their one night of love had been fearful yet fulfilling. He had reached harp strings so deep in her soul that not even Peter Forest had been able to reach them. Just to be with the man, to touch his hand, was gratifying.

They explored unnamed rivers and streams with enthusiasm and trust. Charley made marks and notations on his maps. The area was fascinating for him. He was like an expectant child. Each rock turned, each mountain crest followed, was like an uncovered mystery.

Unfortunately, his excitement produced a deficiency. Elsa Jane shared in his daily adventures but not in his nightly bedroll. It was not that he loved her any the less. It was simply that the pangs of desire were absent when he worked.

Elsa Jane was angry. Night after night she ached for him, but she remained silent. Her knowledge was such that she feared a rebuff if she tried to be the aggressor, and deep inside she was still woman enough to be squeamish about premarital dalliance.

She was aghast at her own thoughts. She suddenly feared that marriage was the farthest thing from Charles Humrick's mind. He had spent forty years running from it. She'd have to be mad to think she could change all of that. For one night she had been like what she had always hated—just one of Sally's girls.

The bad weather didn't help her mood. The snows had come with treacherous fury. Elsa Jane and Charley would go to sleep under a blanket of stars and awaken under a blanket of snow. Each day it changed. One day it would be a fleecy powder lacing the pine boughs. A day later the snow would be so laden with moisture that in less than an hour they would be sodden.

Then the wind came, like a thousand banshees let loose from hell. It drove the surface snow into new blizzards, drifting it dangerously over gullies and making them appear flat when they were often ten to twenty feet deep.

Several times they heard the ominous roar of a mountainside avalanche and would later see its devastating aftermath. They were only tiny creatures against such forces of nature.

"We'll camp on that ridge," Charley called. "Tomorrow I think it best that we start back. The supplies are low and the storms have chased all the game down to the lower elevations."

Elsa Jane was tired and hungry. She had been tired and hungry before, but never like this. For the past few days everything had become so futile. The storms had taught them nothing but new forms of cold and misery.

"How far back?" she asked dully.

"Only about thirty miles."

Only, she thought miserably. She suddenly heard the yapping of a dog. He was plowing down the ridge toward them, his tail wagging with excitement. Having gotten their attention, he turned and started back up through the trees.

Charley silently motioned for Elsa Jane to take the reins. He pulled out the rifle. The dog had warned him that there was some form of game ahead. He took off after it and left Elsa Jane to tug the horse and mule along.

Charley's face was aglow by the time Elsa Jane caught up to him. The dog had made an unusual discovery. They gazed together down into the clearing.

The natural hot springs bubbled out of the rock facing and formed a pool. Like a fairytale scene, a foggy veil shielded the area against the cold upper air. The warm vapors melted the snow and the grass was a brilliant green.

But the real beauty of the sylvan scene were the hundred-odd mountain sheep that nibbled at the dewy grass and posed majestically among the rocks. As though frozen in place, a ram with great curled horns stood protectively over a group of ewes and lambs.

Charley raised the rifle and aimed.

"What are you doing?" Elsa Jane gasped.

"Fresh meat."

She felt suddenly sick and turned away. She had never been with him when he had been hunting and had not seen the rabbits, partridges and ducks alive. But these were some of the most beautiful, graceful creatures she had ever seen.

The blast went straight to the depths of her soul.

She could hear the frantic clamor of the cloven hooves as the sheep raced up the rock formation, but she could not look.

Only after Charley and the dog had scrambled down into the clearing could she rise and lead the horse and mule down. She tethered the animals and did the chores expected of her. She shuddered as she gathered rocks and wood for the fire. It was food and survival, she told herself. It would be a needed change from their ration of jerky and beans.

She took the coffeepot to the pool for water. To her utter amazement it was as warm as bath water. She cupped her hands and sipped some.

"Ugh!" she growled, spitting it out.

Somewhere behind her Charley laughed. "It's mineral water, Duchess. We'd best stay with melted snow for drinking or that will clean us out in a most uncomfortable way."

Elsa Jane poured the coffeepot water back into the pool, running the stream water over her other hand. It was so delightfully warm—the warmest thing she had felt in days. She washed her face with it.

"Oh, heaven!" she said sighing. "I can feel it cut right through the grime."

It gave her a sudden inspiration. She raced to the far end of the clearing to scoop snow into the pot and brought it back to the campsite. For once the flint and steel sparked instantly for her and the fire started like magic. She could hear Charley axing but she put it out of her mind.

Mindlessly, she left her clothing and boots lying in a heap. She stretched and enjoyed the rare luxury of being nude.

"Ten days?" she chuckled. "I haven't been out of those clothes in two weeks." Then she giggled. "And

I know that for a fact because of the master's methodical way of keeping track of time."

She shivered half delighted and half cold. She ran
to the pool's edge on her toes and stood there drinking
in the scene before her. It just had to be a dream.
Nothing could be so beautiful.

She moved forward into the pool and was amazed
to find that the water now seemed icy. She shivered
again but moved forward. The rock shelf dropped
sharply and she was suddenly up to her neck in
water. The water then became as warm upon her
body as it had been upon her hands and face. She
took a deep breath, ducked her head under the surface and stayed a moment. When she came up the
air felt icy on her face. She ducked again and came
up splashing ecstatically.

"Swim on out," Charley called.

"Can't swim!"

"Then splash around until I can teach you."

She crawled back up on the shelf and squatted
down until the water covered her neck again. Her
arms floated to the surface. She moved farther back
to see if her legs would do the same.

"Hey! I float!" she giggled.

"Pretty much so. They tell me that there is a huge
lake on the other side of the mountains that is so
salty you can't do anything but float."

She bounced about on her rump as she watched
him. He had hacked out a spit from green branches
and the lamb was roasting. So were her clothes. He
had pushed other branches into the gravely sand and
had hung her clothes upwind of the fire. Other
branches were ready to accept his own.

Before, modesty would have kept her from watching him strip. Now, she rolled over on her belly,
using her fingertips to help hold her up. It gave her

a vicarious thrill to watch him disrobe and hang up the buckskins. He wore no undergarments beneath his attire.

She watched him with fascination. The man in the dark beside her was quite different from the man in daylight striding toward the pool.

He was a Viking. His neck was as thick as a sapling. His shoulders were like craggy shelves protecting the muscle-rounded breasts. It seemed near impossible that such a massive torso could be supported by such a thin waist and flat belly. He had long firm thighs and legs. Nowhere on his golden body, covered by almost invisible hair, was there an ounce of fat.

He ran like a child, leaped high into the air, grabbed his knees to his chest and crashed into the water a few feet away from Elsa Jane. A geyser of water shot into the air and came crashing back down on her.

Then, abruptly, he was on his belly and swimming across the pool. His powerful arms knifed through the warm water with fierce strokes. His stiff legs and flapping feet churned up a wake. Just before he reached the bubbling springs, he dove beneath the surface and swam towards her.

She watched in awe. It never ceased to amaze her how accomplished this man was.

"Why didn't you swim like that when you fell through the ice?" she joshed.

"Worst thing in the world, Duchess. That called for calmness and staying afloat. Anyone can stay afloat, in any type of water, if they stay calm. The body is buoyant, you see. Lie on your back and I'll show you."

His strong hands beneath her shoulder blades and waist were reassuring. He rolled her over and supported her just below the breasts and stomach. Around and around the shallow water he guided her, forcing her to kick her feet properly and showing her how to move her head and arms. Still he held her until he knew she was not afraid.

Then, from what seemed a long way off, she heard him laugh. Panic gripped her. She was alone and half-way across the pool.

"Relax!" he called. "And just swim back to me as you swam out there."

It seemed to take forever to swim back, but at last he held her by the hands and pulled her up out of the water.

"Now you are a swimmer," he said grinning. "Do you have a reward for the teacher?"

Elsa Jane had waited two weeks for just such an opening. She locked her hands behind his neck and pulled his head down until their lips met. He returned the kiss as though surprised. She did not relent. Then his became the more passionate of the two mouths. Slowly they sank into the warm shallow water. Their desire had been unspoken but mutual. This time there was no fear or hesitation. They molded together and made love as if they had been inseparable for many years.

They rolled from the water and lay waiting for the sun to replace the water's warmth. There was no need for talk; it would have ruined the magic moment. After a time Charley rose to turn the spit.

Elsa Jane suddenly felt ravenously hungry. She glanced up at Charley. Still nude, he showed no embarrassment as he cut off some of the already done ribs.

"Look at us," she cried, running to him on tiptoe. "We're acting like it was really summer."

He shrugged. "Clothes aren't dry yet. Want to share

the buffalo robe while we nibble on these? They sure smell good."

"Yes, and they do smell marvelous."

"I was afraid I would have to eat them alone."

Elsa Jane laughed and got the robe. As they ate she shared her views about hunting and eating.

"I thought we would eat some of the chops and smoke the rest," he answered.

She didn't comment. She was getting to know the man quite well and knew that such a statement had a motive behind it.

After they had eaten, and were again in warm, dry clothing, Charley glanced across at Elsa Jane and winked surreptitiously.

"Well, what about the smoked lamb?"

She winked back playfully. "What about it?"

"Shouldn't it give us ample food supply if we cross over that next ridge and go back by way of the south fork of this creek?"

"It should, but how do you know there is a south fork?"

"Has to be," he grinned sheepishly. "The formation of the mountains tell me it has to have a watershed equal to this side."

Elsa Jane looked at him, the shadow of a smile touching her lips. The man never ceased to amaze her. "Well, one way back is just as good as another, I suppose."

She rumpled his hair fondly and froze. She had felt his body stiffen at her touch.

"Is something the matter?"

He had a cold empty feeling in the pit of his stomach. After their first time being together he had felt so guilty. Today had been so carefree and light-hearted that the feeling had not returned until this moment of her touch.

"The matter? Well . . . I . . ."

"It's alright," she said pouting. "I think I understand."

Charley raised his eyes questioningly.

"Charles Humrick, you forget that I have lived in a man's world for these seven years. I am not naive. Let's forget today and the other time as though they had never happened. No strings. No obligations."

He took a deep breath and cleared his throat. "Well now, I'll tell you, Duchess . . . you see . . ." He glanced at Elsa Jane beseechingly, wondering why she was making this so difficult for him. A sudden gleam came into his eyes. "Well, it's like this, Duchess. I can't erase it from my memory, but I can't live with it, either. I'm . . . I'm making a fallen woman of you."

Elsa Jane was silent for so long Charley exploded. "I don't have the right to say what is in my heart until I can be sure I can do the right thing. I've got a full money belt, but not enough to get us from California to England."

"England?"

"As my wife and duchess!"

"What of my business? What of my children?" she asked in alarm.

Charley reached out and put a hand on her arm. "Now now, Duchess. Don't you think that I haven't thought that all out?"

She refused to be placated. "Perhaps, but without consulting me on the matter."

Charley shifted uncomfortably. "Well, lass, I'm not one for spouting off my dreams until I know they can become a reality. So far this little side trip has not lived up to my expectations. What have we really found?"

Elsa Jane swallowed. "What were you really looking for?"

"A foolish notion, I suppose. Bitten by the gold fever. I thought I could find it when other men have not. Then we could go home with you as a real duchess and not have to fight Freddy-boy for my heir's right."

E.J. chewed her lip in an agony of indecision. "Is that all very important to you?" she finally asked.

He shook his head. "Never was before I met you, Duchess. That's why I feel guilty. I've taken you out of wed-lock. Oh hell, don't say it. My father did the same countless times and that's what gave you birth. But we are different. I love you so desperately, but I want to make sure that I can be the proper provider for you and your children—our children, if you will."

"I love you just as deeply," she answered.

He put a hand on her arm again. "Duchess, I have no intention of taking you again until we are joined by the Church of England."

Elsa Jane stared blankly at him. It sounded so far away. But wasn't this her dream as well—to have him as a husband? It was just the shock of other things she had never taken into consideration. Duchess? He was just Mountain Charley to her, and not the Duke of Plover. England? She wasn't even sure she knew where England was.

She took a deep breath and smiled bravely. "Well, I think perhaps we'd best take things a step at a time. I've no objections to going back by way of your south fork."

Charley's eyes brightened. "Perhaps that will change our luck."

She smiled wryly to herself. That's what the Mississippi rivermen used to say about going ashore and finding a little black girl. She decided that was one crude joke from her past that she would not share with the man. Nor would she share a new worry that he had implanted in her mind. Duchess? She had almost forgotten how to be a lady, let alone a duchess. Duchess? What in hell was a duchess, anyway? ✑

13

EASTWARD out of Eden. The original Eve must have felt just as lost and forlorn leaving her garden spot, and a portion of herself behind. The love Elsa Jane felt for Charley was not diminished, but a barrier had come up, just as before. She knew she should have been singing his praises to the sky for respecting her womanhood. Had she seen too much of the seamy side of life in seven years to not really care? She loved him and wanted him, and that was all that mattered.

Mountain Charley wiped a sleeve across his perspiring forehead and sighed. They had been on the south fork since dawn without seeing a bare patch of ground. The creek water was so clear that the ice was like a thick plate of glass. The sun was high but the air was still cold. They rounded a corner and

came onto a gravel bar that was protected by a large
shelf overhang.

"Good place to rest."

Elsa Jane didn't need encouragement. She leaned
across the mule and rested her head on its neck.
Despite the snow, their downhill pace had been rapid.
Charley calculated that they had covered a remarkable ten to fifteen miles.

Now he studied the rock shelf with great curiosity.
"It must have been carved out by a great flood at
one time."

Elsa Jane laughed drily. "From that little stream?"

"Don't let its present size fool you. It probably
roars in the spring when all that snow begins to melt."

He squatted and tried to loosen a few of the gravel
pebbles. They were frozen solid.

"Looks promising, but I'd probably break the ax
getting a sample."

"Then why don't you build a fire and thaw it out?"

Charley drew his eyebrows together and squinted
at her shrewdly. "I think a pot of hot coffee might
do us some good, as well. It's the last of it, but we'll
be back to Wootton's by tomorrow."

"Might as well eat something while we are
stopped."

She untied the canvas sack that held their cooking
and eating gear while Charley crossed the ice-covered
river to search for wood. She filled the coffeepot with
snow and looked around for some kindling. She recalled seeing a felled tree just before they rounded
the corner of the shelf.

It had been dead for some time and the smaller
branches broke off easily. When she had a good arm-
load she thought she heard Charley behind her.

"Here's a goodly supply," she said, turning.

Ten feet away, perched on the lower rocks of the

shelf, was a mountain lion. His yellow eyes studied her.

Of all times for the dog to be off with Charley, she oddly thought.

The great golden beast opened its mouth and yawned. It was immediately apparent to her that the lion had never before seen a human being. She slowly turned and walked carefully back down to the stream before looking back. The lion had noiselessly climbed higher, but Charley often had warned her of their great leaping ability. She crossed the river and made a wide circle that would bring her back to the camp ahead of the animal. She moved as silently as the cat. Every sense was alert. When she came out of the trees and looked across the river she could see that the horse and mule were nervous. She cursed herself for not having shackled them. Then she looked up. The lion was perched right on the lip of the shelf, its mouth oddly agape.

Elsa Jane swallowed and unconsciously moved back a step. My God, it's grinning at me, she thought. Then she realized it was leering in anticipation of a horse and mule lunch.

"Damn, where's Charley with the rifle?" she muttered.

Within seconds she realized that Charley would not have taken the rifle to go for wood. It was still in the saddle sheath.

She felt her heart hammering. The beast suddenly snarled, sensing her presence, and leaped from the ledge.

Elsa Jane screeched a warning but it was too late. The lion had landed on the pack and was biting and clawing at the mule's neck. The mule automatically kicked backwards, then in its panic, reared high into the air, made a twisting turn and crashed to the ground. The lion was not shaken free, but it could not reach the mule's throat.

Elsa Jane leaped forward, slid across the ice and screamed to the horse to remain calm. Instead, it charged past her and she was barely able to grab at the trailing reins. The jolt of trying to stop it nearly tore her arms loose and the horse dragged her as she worked her hands up the reins to the bit. She held the horse's head down with one hand while slipping her free arm out of her jacket sleeve. Then she quickly reversed the process and threw the jacket over the horse's head and eyes, tying the sleeves together under its jowls. Its neighs were nearly as fearful as the braying of the mule, but it was now motionless in its fright.

She pulled the rifle out of the sheath and drew a straight sight along the blue-black barrel. The rifle slammed hard. The lion growled as it leaped and twisted high in the air. It was not dead. The instant she had fired, the lion, sensing danger, had spun toward her. The soft-nosed bullet that had aimed at the heart had struck at the base of the neck ripping through the jugular and shattering the backbone. It tore a great gaping hole in the animal's flesh.

Still, it was on its feet and snarling in her direction. There was no time to reload. Only time, she thought, to reverse the rifle and use it as a club.

They eyed each other, each expecting the other to make the first move. Then everything seemed to happen at once. The dog came yapping across the creek and Charley bounded from the trees. The lion stood still. The mule leaped to its feet, its frantic heart pumping great streams of blood out of its ragged neck. It staggered once and then ran wildly across the stream, hurdling fallen logs and smashing branches in its way.

No one had time to stop the mule. Sensibly, Elsa took a firm grip on the reins of the horse. The old dog darted around the lion's head, yapping and gnashing its teeth. The distraction gave Charley an opportunity to creep up behind the beast and plunge his skinning-knife into its heart.

The lion was barely down on the gravel before Charley was up and running, with the dog following. Charley hadn't a hope of catching the mule alive, but they couldn't afford to lose the pack and all their supplies.

Elsa Jane bit her lip and trembled. Her head felt fuzzy and her eyes and throat ached. She shackled the horse, took back her jacket, and walked across the ice to where she'd dropped her bundle of branches. She couldn't even remember having dropped them. Her movements were slow, as if only her torso was alive. She came back and got the flint and steel case from the saddle bag. It took a couple of dozen strikings before a spark caught on a piece of furry bark. Slowly, she gently blew the spark into a flame and added little twigs until it was a blaze.

Once, from far off, she heard Charley calling for the mule. She stopped and listened but the call was from very far away and it wasn't repeated.

She went to find where Charley might have dropped his load of wood. It wasn't far and it was neatly stacked. He had obviously carefully and silently put them down so as not to startle the lion.

Elsa Jane put the logs down just as carefully and silently by her little fire. And just as carefully and silently she crisscrossed some of them log cabin style around the fire and set the coffeepot on top. She acted as if she were afraid she might awaken the lion.

When she looked up, it was well past noon and

great gray clouds were piling like shadowed snow-drifts against the wall of the mountains. The sun was dull and the air grew cold.

She sighed as if she had been holding her breath since having first seen the lion.

"Silly," she muttered. "You've had many worse frights in life. Why act like a goose over this?"

There was no answer. She had never been afraid of animals before, or they of her.

"Duchess," Charley advised when she revealed that she had been terrified, "lions, bobcats and bears are the natural predators in these parts. Even mountain men give them a wide berth. I'm proud of the way you handled the whole matter."

"Sure. I lost the mule for us."

"Put another way, you could say that you saved the horse and yourself."

"Which do you wish for supper, me or the horse?"

He said gently, "Some choice. Well, there is always the lion."

"Ugh!"

She couldn't even stand to smell it cooking and after one bite, Charley also threw it away. It was simply too gamey and tough.

"With the bedrolls gone we'll have to keep the fire up all night. Where's the ax?"

Their bad luck continued. They searched and searched, but could not find the ax anywhere near the spot where Charley had put down his load of wood. They poked about the snowdrifts but to no avail.

Elsa Jane and Charley rolled the log she had found earlier down onto the ice, skated it around the corner and pulled it up onto the gravel bar.

"At home we would deem this quite a yule log."

"Now you are being silly. You aren't going to burn the whole thing at once."

"Of course. It will make a glorious fire."

It was actually four fires until they joined and burned together. It was warming to the front, if not to the back. Charley put his arms around her and held her tightly, rubbing her back to soothe and warm her. At last she slept, but he sat wide-eyed and deeply troubled. The coming storm looked bad. All of the supplies, including the extra rifle ammunition, were somewhere with the mule. He felt terribly sorry for the beast, but he had followed the blood trail until he and the dog were nearly exhausted. He was never going to catch up with it, dead or alive.

The fire started to die. Charley laid Elsa Jane gently on her side and went to turn it and expose fresh wood. It rolled too far. He took a stick and scraped the embers back under the log.

In the illumination, he noticed that the stick had scraped the sandy gravel along with the embers. He squatted and dug at the surface with his fingers. It was warm and it loosened easily. He took out his belt-knife and dug deeper. It had thawed as deep as two inches. He moved along the length where the burning log had lain and dug up several fair sized piles of soil. He ran his fingers through the earth, distinguishing the difference between the various rocks that had been pulverized by the creek.

His mouth grew dry. The grains were heavy with quartz particles. Now he, too, began to curse the lion. All his panning equipment was on the mule. Desperately, he looked around. The coffee pot would supply him with the water that he needed and a tin plate would have to suffice for cleaning.

For an hour he sat cross-legged, pouring a half

cup of gravel in the plate, adding water, swishing it around and then gently pouring off the water and gravel. Each time he swallowed harder. He continued until the plate contained a quarter-ounce of gold dust.

The tears welled up in his eyes. His theory was correct. Suddenly, he flung himself up and grabbed the rifle. He rushed to the creek edge and battered the ice with the butt of the gun.

Elsa Jane awoke with a start. "Charley, have you gone mad?"

"Stark raving," he roared. "Come help me, Duchess! We've done it! Bring the coffeepot for water."

"Gold?" she whispered.

"Look in your plate!"

Joy hit her as she looked. She had seen gold dust in California, but it had never been hers. She poured the drying granules into a tin cup and then took the coffeepot to Charley.

Like two children on a beach, they giggled and laughed and played on the gravel bar. But it was serious play. They dug and panned until the belt-knife was worn out. They switched to the skinning-knife. They had to keep turning the log and securing more pots of water, but that was all part of the game.

"Prize! Prize!" she chortled. "This is the biggest prize yet!"

The nugget was no larger than a pea but it looked enormous next to the dust particles in the bottom of the plate.

Charley took a deep breath. "That puts us over an ounce, Duchess. Enough to lay claim. Let's cover over what we have done and get out of here."

But Elsa Jane had been struck by gold-fever. "But there is more! More!"

"And it will wait for us until spring."

She saw the wisdom of his words, but wanted to rebel. Spring was three to four months away.

"What until then?"

Charley hesitated. He too had the fever. He could almost feel the gold around him, and he wanted it for her.

"Why don't we talk about it when we are not so tired and hungry? It's the practical thing to do."

"Damn you for always being so practical about everything. Haven't you ever done one impractical thing in your life?"

"Yes," he answered grinning. "I fell in love with you."

"Go to hell!" she shouted, but softened. "What shall I do?"

They filled up the hole, rolled the charred log to the center of the creek so that the spring thaw would carry it downstream, and scraped the charcoal remnants back over the hole so that it would look as if only a normal campfire had been built.

Charley hauled the mountain lion by the tale over the ice to the opposite side of the stream and left it among the trees. He started away and turned back. Smiling, he carved a heart with their initials into the white bark of an aspen. He thought it a wry joke for any stranger who might happen along to see such sentiment in the wilds of the Kansas Territory.

No more than a mile upstream George Jackson, cousin of Kit Carson, sat shivering with his rifle at the ready. On January 7, 1895 he had found gold a mile above his present camp and had been looking for more. He had heard the echos of the rifle when the lion was shot, and had been on the lookout ever since. Like Charley, he knew he could do little about the gold until spring, but George Jackson was ready to kill to keep the secret quiet. He had waited around the area for a week just to make sure that no one else found it.

Another, more plentiful strike, unknown to either of these camps, had been made that day over the high ridge on the North Fork. It was made, in fact, in a narrow side gulch which Charley had decided against exploring. The gulch would bear John H. Gregory's name, as he had been cunning enough to climb the ridge and return to the plains via the South Fork of what he called Clear Creek.

The Woottons had spent a busy few weeks in the mountains. The new general store was all Alice Wootton had demanded that it be. If Uncle Dick were to establish no further business, this seemingly endless influx of gold starved people would still insure his being a wealthy man. But Wootton used it only as a means to greater goals. Cleverly, he recognized the dishevelled Charley and sought to turn his knowledge to his own advantage. When Charley inquired about the availability of double lodgings within the inn itself, Wootton replied that a small single room was all he could offer.

"There are two of us," Charley interrupted.

Alice Wootton glared at her husband. Uncle Dick had already taken this point into consideration.

"I thought your companion might be able to stay in the cabin next door."

"They both could," Alice nearly shouted.

"No! Excuse me, sir, but I am not normally a busy-body. Still, your coin made me curious enough to question an old mountain man who knew you in Moose Jaw. Of course, your manners and accent are most unusual for these parts, as well. I've not even told your secret to my wife."

Much good that'll do, Charley thought grimly. The woman would hound the information out of him now. Then he brightened. Perhaps it was time to reverse his roles. Who would ever question an English nobleman, with a fat money belt, of being a gold seeker?

"Secret?" he said, on a quizzical note. "Charles Humrick has no secrets to hide. I am just a simple historian and explorer."

Wootton winked. "Except I know about the death of your father, sir, We've a man in camp with the Smith party by the name of Jack Jones. As his accent was near to your own I loosened his tongue with a few tins of the lightning. Of course, I didn't mention any names, but he told me how these titles work and how one should be addressed."

Interesting, Charley thought. He was aware of "Jack Jones" and had purposely avoided the man. He had known him in his youth as William McGaa, son of a Lord Mayor of London. His education was for the Church, but McGaa disqualified himself with his passionate devotion to whiskey. The last Charley had heard of him, he had been living with an Arapaho squaw. Once McGaa recognized him, no one would dare question his credentials. Charley felt like laughing at such luck.

"My title means nothing while I am travelling in the colonies," Charley purposely said with a stuffy air. "Now as to the lodgings."

"The room upstairs and the cabin for . . ."

Charley held up his hand. If he was going to play this new role, he would have to play it to the hilt.

"Perhaps my other secret has been well kept, Mr. Wootton. For safety reasons my companion has been forced to travel with me incognito. We shall share the room."

"But . . . but . . ." Alice started to protest.

Charley had anticipated just such a reaction and was ready to pounce.

"Dear woman," he said grandly, "you should be the first to realize the rigors of western travel on a woman. Lady Elsa Jane is tired, greatly disheveled, and distraught over losing all of her possessions with the mule. A bath, bed and meal are her immediate needs. Proper clothing I shall see to at a later time."

"Oh my!" Wootton gasped. "No wonder I took her to be a young lad. Mother, Elizabeth Byers has not used the tub, as yet, this morning. Lady . . . Mrs. Humrick shall have first crack at the water I have already poured. Poor woman! Get her off the horse and inside, sir."

Charley took Elsa Jane up by the outside staircase. In the hallway they met a younger version of Uncle Dick toting a pail of steaming hot water.

"Paw says your room is the door at the end of the hall. The room with the bathtub is that door. Here's a fresh bucket. Maw says she'd like to see you as soon as possible, sir."

The young boy opened yet another door and vanished down a narrow stairwell.

Charley picked up the hot water bucket and entered the room. It smelled of freshly cut lumber and fresh water. A copper bathtub sat in the center of the floor; on a three-legged stool was a pile of towels.

Elsa Jane was so weary and hungry that she simply looked at it and sighed.

"I expect that she wishes to see me about the charges," he said. "You go right ahead and bathe."

Alice Wootton was in a state of agitation. She didn't ordinarily care about social strata, but a Duke and Duchess staying under her roof—that was different. All the inherent snobbishness of her English ancestry bubbled to the surface.

"Ah, sir, there you are. I've been giving your dear wife my every thought. Come with me."

Charley silently followed her out of the store and into the original cabin. The room was packed with other peoples' treasures.

"We can't let people starve," she said by way of explanation. "Someday it shall be worth something to someone. However, that seatrunk may be worth something to your wife right now. It's sad, to be sure. A young doctor, John L. Merrick, by name, brought his young bride all the way from Georgia. Poor dear passed on at Bent's Fort. Dr. Merrick traded her trunk for supplies to get him up to Fort Laramie. I'm not sure if the clothes will fit, but you feel free to take a peek."

The trunk was full of women's clothing, but Charley pulled out only a single dress.

"How much for the whole trunk, Mrs. Wootton?"

Alice was flustered. She wasn't sure of the protocol for doing business with a duke.

"My husband will handle that, sir."

Charley smiled to himself. She no longer sounded like the forceful woman who had seen to the building of the new store. He started to lift the trunk.

"Oh, no sir," she gasped. "I've sons who will see to that. They are already putting things in your room. I'm afraid, however, that bedrolls will have to suffice as real beds."

"They will be most adequate, ma'am."

"And," she blushed, "I've taken the liberty to have our Mexican cook prepare a small bite. Nathan will bring up the trays when they are ready."

"You are most kind." He took her hand and raised it to his lips in the European fashion.

Alice Wootton tittered like a young girl. She could hardly wait to give Elizabeth Byers the news. The editor's wife thought she was the "social center" of a still society-barren town, but Alice Wootton now felt equal.

Charley could still hear Elsa Jane splashing in Elizabeth Byers' tub as he and two of the Wootton boys passed the closed door. The room was exactly as Uncle Dick had warned—incomplete. Bedrolls had been placed on the wooden floor. Crude wooden benches sat on either side of a badly scarred table, and wooden pegs on a wall served as the wardrobe. A pot-bellied stove roared in a corner, but gave forth little heat. Muslin was all that covered the single window.

The price for such a hovel was staggering, even though Uncle Dick had thrown in the trunk of clothing for nothing, and Alice was quick to add that bathing rights would be included in the eighty-five dollars per month.

Charley had astonished them both by paying in advance for the first five months of the year. He then realized his own weariness and excused himself.

He stretched out on a bedroll and tried to relax, but relaxation wouldn't come. He was worried about Elsa Jane's reaction to the sham. He wondered if he could keep her there until spring, or longer.

Finally he drifted off into a troubled slumber. Hours later he was dimly aware of soft lips touching his own and a delicate scent pervading his nostrils. He fought through heavy layers of sleep and forced his eyes open. Elsa Jane squatted beside the bedroll, smiling down at him.

He yawned. "Did you sleep?"

"I've been too excited. When that boy Nathan came to tell me another lady was waiting for the tub, I learned about the trunk. It's unbelievable. It has everything a woman would require; everything! Hair

brushes, pins, petticoats—even some vials of perfume
—everything. I've hung it all up on pegs. What do
you think of the fit?"

She rose and spun around. She wore a dress of
emerald green velvet that enhanced the light, bright
green of her eyes. She was lovelier than any woman
Charley had ever imagined. Her cheeks were flushed
and rosy and her eyes danced. Her lips were touched
with pink rouge, soft and alluring, and she blew him
a kiss as she turned.

"Blimey!" he exploded. "Are you the same lass?"

"Hardly," she giggled. "Nathan calls me Mrs. Humrick. His idea or yours?"

"Mine," he grinned, "all mine. I did have to protect
your reputation and . . ."

"You talk entirely too much. Shut up now, and go
take your bath. Mr. Wootton has sent up some new
clothing that he thinks might fit you."

"And which he will put a dear price upon. The
rascal seems to know the weight of my money belt
better than I. Your attire was given for free, but we
shall pay for it sooner or later."

"Then eat twice as much."

He rose, looked toward the table and saw the two
empty plates. "What happened? I'm famished."

"I ate them both," she grinned. "You were sleeping
so soundly, and besides, we are invited for dinner—
your lordship."

"Oh, oh! I'd best explain."

"I think Nathan has done it for you." She imitated
the sixteen year old youth. "My Maw," she mimicked,
"Mrs. Humrick, wishes for you and his lordship to
have supper with us all."

"Wootton already had most of it figured out, Duchess. It seemed best to just go along with it."

She frowned. "But how do I go along with it?"

"In your normally sweet and natural way. Now, I'd best bathe."

Elsa Jane giggled. "We are not at the hot springs, your lordship."

"Ah, civilization," he kidded, looking down at his nudity, "does have its disadvantages."

Alice Wootton was not about to miss a golden opportunity for having a dinner party. She invited the Byers and General Larimer and his son, and informed them all of Charley's position as Duke.

Bill Byers acted like a cub reporter on his first assignment, and General Larimer acted like he was interrogating an alien spy.

Charley took it all in stride with humor and good grace. He felt comfortable and happy in his common twill trousers and cotton shirt, although he looked more like a god to Elizabeth Byers. Her husband was an attractive man, but the duke was unforgettable. Elsa Jane had brushed his hair until it shone like spun gold, and clipped his mustache back to his upper lip.

For the most part, Elsa Jane was quiet and demure, answering any questions directed her way in a soft and lilting voice. She seemed regal. Elizabeth was enthralled with her gown, and Alice cunningly kept it's origin a secret. Knowing some of the hardships Elsa Jane had endured with her husband, Alice admired and respected her immediately.

To the men, Elsa Jane was one of the most enchantingly beautiful creatures they had ever seen. She had brushed and pinned her hair all to one side, hiding the pencil-line scar from forehead to ear lobe. In the trunk she had found a jar of cream and had rubbed it into her skin, giving it a soft, translucent glow. She applied a dab of the rouge cake to her cheekbones and lips, highlighting their natural color. The gown was slightly too tight, but accented her slender figure exquisitely.

Nathan Wootton wasn't enchanted, he was awed. He waited on her so exclusively it came close to being embarrassing. And, as Charley naturally referred to her as "Duchess," Nathan did also, thinking it was the proper form of address. Soon the title rolled off of everyone's lips quite naturally.

Charley chuckled to himself but did not correct them. Despite Byers and Larimer, the dinner party did please him. The room was primitive, but Alice had brought out a lace tablecloth, silver candlesticks and a most attractive set of china. It showed respect and he appreciated it.

"Did you enjoy it?"

"It was alright. I like Alice Wootton, but Mrs. Byers reminds me of a nun; stiff and formal. Button me down."

Charley worked at the buttons. "And the men?"

"Nathan is just too funny for words," she answered. Then she frowned. "I think that General Larimer would sell his mother if it would benefit him."

"Agreed. He's a man to watch. Byers just wants a good news story. There you go."

The gown dropped to her slim ankles. One by one she let the other garments fall and made the two bedrolls into one.

"What's this?"

"My price for becoming the Duchess of Plover."

Charley put his arms up to her and she nestled into them.

Long afterwards, while she slept at his side, he worried anew—not if he could keep her there until spring, but whether he could keep up with her fire and spirit until then. She had been all woman; even wanton.

"Blimey!" he murmured. "What a duchess!"

14

"IMAGINE, not having to lift a finger to care for her husband. Leaves it all to Alice Wootton and that poor Mexican cook. What's she doing here, anyway?"

They never thought to ask Charles Humrick. However, as they very rarely saw him, they began to wonder about him too.

Uncle Dick had found paper and pens for Charley to redraw his maps. The work kept him busy during the day, despite numerous interruptions from Bill Byers and General Larimer. Larimer was the worst offender.

"As one gentleman to another, sir, I ask for your help in speaking out against this dissolute, licentious and uncivilized life around us. I've counted among the cabins and tents thirty-one saloons, and not a single church, school, hospital, library or bank."

"Your point is well taken, General, but my voice would be for naught. I am not a citizen of this country, but only a visitor."

Larimer decided that that was no excuse at all. There had to be a decent place for men such as himself and the duke. That night he slipped quietly across the dry bed of Cherry Creek and staked out a rival townsite. His son, Will, joined him at dawn, and together they hastily began building a cabin, for no claim would be recognized without one.

Throughout the day the General marched back and forth, talking to the leaders of the Leavenworth, Oskaloosa and Lecompton parties. They were "dries" like himself and as such, he granted them building rights within the new townsite limits.

Again he approached Charley.

"I am not a resident, sir. I shall be gone from here by April or May."

By the middle of February, the cottonwood grove rang with the busy sounds of ax and saw and hammer.

The General and his friends had formed a town company of their own and they debated long and earnestly about the best name for the still nebulous city.

It was Larimer's town and he insisted on having the final say. As he had high hopes of gaining favors from the man, he named it Denver City in honor of the governor.

The people of Auraria laughed at him, and when they learned that Governor Denver had resigned the month before, he lost most of his credibility. Some of his townspeople moved back across the creek.

However, the mistake did nothing more than make General Larimer even more stubborn. He seized the abandoned tracts and hired men to finish cabins on twenty choice lots in Denver City. He rented them as quickly as they were finished. People had continued to filter into Auraria, but those who had been daring enough to bring their families crossed the creek to Denver City.

"Sir," he said once again approaching Charley, "I envisage the necessity of still another townsite. Yesterday at dawn, my son and I forded the icy waters of the Platte and clambered up the bluffs on the far side. It is grand and I have staked out what I shall call the City of Highlands. I beseech you to take a tract for a hundred dollars. An investment, if nothing more."

To be free of the man, Charley agreed. Then he had a second thought. "I am still an alien, sir, but my wife is native-born. To make it most legal, put the land in her maiden name, Elsa Jane Forest."

Larimer was elated. He could now boast that the Duchess of Plover was one of his landholders. He then devised another scheme to steal some of the Wootton business.

"Will, I dare not trust my thoughts to paper, lest they fall into the wrong hands. I am sending you back to your brother John at Leavenworth. Exhort him, in my name, to expand his land and banking business to include a wholesale and retail grocery, with iron, nails, picks, shovels and axes on the side. All the world and the rest of mankind will be fitting out there by spring. Then, quickly lad, sell everything I own in that region and turn it into like goods. Once returned, the residents of Denver City will not be obligated to cross the creek and do business with the likes of that drunken Wootton."

Charley and Elsa Jane had also been listening to

the reports of gold fever. Excited, reckless gold-hunters by the tens of thousands were beginning to fill up the Missouri River towns.

"It's madness," Wootton said to Charley. "The South Platte diggings have yet to produce one thousand dollars of dust. It will be hardship and death if such a great human flood descends upon us. I'm hard pressed to bring in enough supplies for the four to five thousand already here. Bent is already gouging me at thirty dollars per thousand pounds on poor grade Mexican flour, and traded goods already reach the rafters of the cabin."

Charley was well aware of these problems. Elsa Jane had used many of the articles to transform their large room into something livable. And there were many more articles in the cabin that Charley coveted. He wanted to re-equip himself for a return to the mountains, but had not thought of a way to do it without arousing suspicion.

With the coming of April, the relationship between Charley and Elsa Jane had become increasingly strained. The cottonwoods were budding, but the mountains were still blanketed in snow. They could not leave.

"What shall I do?" he muttered to himself as he worked on his maps.

Elsa Jane turned.

"Do? I think you should stop carping on the matter and take Uncle Dick into your confidence. You've made out that list a hundred times. Without him, how are you going to get a wagon, mules, tent and on and on and on?"

"I was speaking about us," he answered despondently.

"There is nothing to speak about," she stated calmly. "When you are ready to return to the mountains, I shall be ready to go with you."

"You mean it?" Charley asked happily. "When did you decide this?"

"What was there to decide?" she answered. "Oh, my darling, go and talk with Uncle Dick. You look so foolish with your mouth hanging open."

Wootton's also dropped open. He scanned the list of provisions, tools and teams. Everything that Charles Humrick desired, except for the wagon and team, could be gotten out of the traded goods cabin and no one would be the wiser.

"How do you know my goods better than I?"

"The Duchess. She would keep track of it every time Mrs. Wootton would take her to the cabin to purchase something for our room. You can understand my secrecy on this matter."

"Quite. Remarkable woman. Does she intend going with you?"

"Of course," Charles answered. "Her true abilities and accomplishments would stagger you."

During the next month Elsa Jane worked daily in the cabin. She sorted through the traded items, cleaned and mended items that she and Charley would require, and threw the rest into boxes for future sale. With Alice's help, she fashioned male work clothes for herself. She greased and regreased her old boots until they were nearly waterproof.

As she worked she described many of the items she had used in the California fields. Charley transformed her memories to paper designs and the Wootton boys turned them into wooden realities.

There were no longer guests at dinner. The evening meal was a time for planning. The Woottons were excited but did not ask for any share in the area. If Charles Humrick was anywhere near correct in his calculations, they would be busy gathering the gold from the miners in exchange for supplies.

Uncle Dick pounded and pounded on Charley's door. His hand was trembling when Charley finally answered.

"Quickly dress for travel," he stammered. "The secret is no longer a secret, I fear."

Charley paled. "How?"

"I've just spent a most uncomfortable hour with an old drunken customer and his new partner."

"At this hour?"

"They also wish secrecy, it would seem. They paid me double and I played dumb, but it didn't stop me from listening. Gregory seems to have made a strike in the same region you described. For a grubstake he has sold this Wilkes Defrees and his party equal shares in his discovery. They are leaving camp tonight without anyone knowing of it."

"But I will never get the wagon through the snow," Charley insisted.

"Granted, so I took the liberty of arousing my family before you. My boys are putting what provisions and tools you will need immediately on mule packs. One of them can bring the rest and the wagon when you deem it passable. My wife is preparing some hot food for your departure. Please hurry, the sun will be up in a couple of hours."

"Fine," Charley agreed. "My wife can wait and come up with the wagon later in the spring."

"But I am already dressed to go," Elsa Jane stated, stepping to his side. "I'll go help Alice with the food."

Charley knew there was no use arguing with her.

All her gentle feminine qualities seemed to vanish when she was dressed to work.

Wootton gasped as she stepped into the candle-light. Her hair was pulled back from her face, knotted at the top and covered with a slouch hat. The jagged, fine-line purple scar oddly transformed her face, making it harsh. The boots, coveralls and heavy woolen shirt were straight and plain. As she walked down the hall her stride was firm and assured. She felt comfortable for the first time in months.

Neither felt much comfort for the first few hours out of the camp. They had to follow in the tracks left by the Gregory party. It was also disturbing to know that it was a party of eight men and mules.

Elsa Jane was glad that Wootton had insisted that they go more heavily armed than they had first planned. She had seen some of the reactions men had at the mere thought of gold. They relaxed when the tracks of the Gregory party veered off into the North Fork of the creek.

The South Fork had changed dramatically. The creek was nearly thawed, and rolled back and forth. They floundered through snow deeper than any they had ever seen. Nothing was the same and Charley began to fret that his memory was wrong.

"We made it down in a day," he fussed. "Why is it taking us three days to get back up? We've gone too far, Duchess."

"No, look! There's the charred log."

A mile further they found the rock overhang, but the gravel bar was under six inches of spring water.

"No campsite here," he moaned.

"Try your luck anyway, darling. I'll take the mules on upstream to locate a spot."

"Watch out for mountain lions," he said gruffly.

"I've had my rifle at the ready for the last hour," she called back.

With the proper tools, it didn't take Charley long to scoop up the gravel, wash it out in the stream, and find as much gold as they had earlier. However, he now realized that it was probably "float" gold that had washed down from the veins of the mountains.

Elsa Jane had found a perfect campsite at the mouth of a little gulch. The clearing was wide and deep, with easy access to the water and ample firewood. By the time the four mules were shackled and their packs removed, Charley had joined her.

"Fire or tent first?" she asked.

"Bring your shovel and come with me," he commanded as he led the way up the narrow timbered gulch.

Elsa Jane smiled to herself. She had seen that look before.

"Try there," he demanded, as though she were a servant.

She understood and tried. She knew it was best to let him burn this out of his system quickly. With considerable difficulty, she was able to get a few shovelsful of gravel out of the still nearly frozen bed. Charley put them in his pan and started back to the creek.

"Well, try there and there while I am gone," he yelled.

Elsa Jane sighed. She prayed he would find something before she exploded.

The more she worked, the softer the ground seemed to become. She never gave a thought to the fact that she was regaining her strength.

Charley became more and more excited with each

panful he washed. He was so preoccupied that he
didn't bother to comment on his finds.

"Oh, Duchess!" he shouted. "Come and see!"

It was four times the amount they had gathered in
before, with some of the nuggets being as large as
thumb nails. He grabbed her hands and danced her
around but she flinched.

"What is it?"

He opened her hands and stared at the palms.
Even Elsa Jane was unaware that she had worked
up some very ugly blisters. Charley pressed them
gently to his cheeks.

"Oh, my poor darling. How unthinking of me."

"They will heal over," she soothed. "They have
many times before."

The blisters were worth it, she thought. He was
finally calm and rational.

There was no calm in the Gregory camp. The first
gold nugget started the dispute that led the partners
to split and file eight different claims. Green Russell,
who had found the first gold on the South Platte,
struck it rich in a side gulch three miles below the
Gregory diggings.

George Jackson, who had sat watch throughout the
night with rifle at the ready, returned with the Chicago men and their money. The Chicago Mining
Company wagons by-passed Auraria and Denver City,
but did not go unnoticed. There had to be a reason
for such a large group to head up into the mountains and rumors ran rampant in the two townsites.
Men began to leave quietly during the night and
when the Gregory and Russell strikes became known
there was a stampede of fortune hunters to the mountains.

Within a week, nine hundred miners were working in Russell and Gregory Gulches, panning more than thirty-five thousand dollars worth of dust a week—a better initial average than the best of the Californian and Australian fields.

Dangerously overcrowded one day, Denver City and Auraria were deserted almost overnight.

"We'd best be taking up their wagon, Paw."

"We'll all go," Wootton chortled. "Lock up the store."

"What about Mr. Byers and his newspaper in the back?"

"He left yesterday, right behind General Larimer and his son."

Alice Wootton was more rational. "You take but two of the boys, husband," she said. "Sam and Nathan. I'll take the other two down to Bent's Fort to get new supplies."

"Woman, this is going to become merely a way-station on the road to the mines. It will fall to ruins as the pilgrims sweep on."

She glared at him until he was silent. Finally, he departed with the boys.

In the South Fork, the Chicago Mining Company was becoming quite profitable. Charley and Elsa Jane did not fare as well.

"Jackson claims to be taking a couple thousand out every three days."

"Jackson is the damnedest liar in the mountains," Wootton said scowling.

"Perhaps. We are making only fifty to one hundred dollars a day."

Uncle Dick and Nathan stayed but a week.

"My friends," Wootton admitted sheepishly, "I am not much inclined to undergo the bone-wearying antics of this get-rich-quick scheme. The good Lord never gave anyone anything for nothing. By comparison, I can earn just as much as a merchant and look forward to a longer life."

The mining company took it upon themselves to call the stream Chicago Creek. By the end of May the creek was running full—full of pollution. It was so muddy that Elsa Jane had to let water stand in buckets overnight to settle for drinking and cooking.

One day, while Elsa Jane was boiling water over several fires, Charley approached with a stranger. The rangy bald-headed man with an enormous walrus mustache eyed her labors suspiciously.

"This is H.A.W. Tabor. He saw our stake claim on the gravel bar and wants to know if it is for sale."

"What I wish to know first," Tabor muttered, "is if this boiling water is part of the process? I'm man enough to admit that I am a tenderfoot."

"Yes," Charley said, "I'm curious about the water myself."

"It has nothing to do with the gold," Elsa Jane answered. "When the snow waters were running heavy the bedrock purified the water. Now it's beginning to drop and all manner of animals, man included, are using it upstream. Drink it unboiled and it brings on mountain fever."

"Do tell." Tabor was impressed. "A bit of information that will be helpful to my wife."

"Your wife is with you?"

"Downstream a piece. Set her up in business at Payne's Bar."

"Business?"

"Augusta is a strong-willed woman, young man. Made me cart along her cows, chickens and ovens. Right fine baker of bread and pies, if I do say so myself."

Charley saw the gleam flash in Elsa Jane's eyes. They hadn't had a fresh egg or an ounce of milk in over a month.

"Mr. Tabor," he said slowly, "I can't vouch for the gravel bar, but I would be willing to trade it for some eggs and milk."

"I would be agreeable," Tabor said simply, "but would Augusta? She thinks this is just another of my tom-fool notions."

Elsa Jane rode the mule up to the seven-by-nine foot, tent-roofed cabin. Mr. Tabor's wife was so buxom that Elsa Jane feared she would topple forward when she walked. She wore her mousey brown hair in a tight bun and squinted through pince-nez glasses.

Elsa Jane sniffed. "That is heavenly. Mr. Tabor said you were a good baker."

"Did he now?" Augusta snapped. "And where would you have been seeing him, young man?"

"About four miles up the creek."

Augusta scowled. "Indeed? Three long weary weeks I've held this fort alone and he was that close. I've a sick child in the tent, a tent which I made with my own hands, and a sick miner lying in that wagon. Yesterday another miner came to me with a gunshot wound through his hand. I am all things to all people but my husband."

"Are the child and miner still taking water?"

"Naturally," she snapped. "They would be burning with fever otherwise."

"It's the water that is keeping them sick with mountain fever, Mrs. Tabor. Boil it before you give it to them."

Augusta softened. "I'll see to it. Now, why did Mr. Tabor send you? If it is for more provisions, you can turn right back around and tell him that what I have left is for resale."

"He did not send me, Mrs. Tabor. I've brought a covered bucket for milk and a basket with straw to carry eggs."

A pained expression crossed her face. "Is it a cash sale? Every beggar going to seek gold seems to find their way to my doorstep. How does a body say no to such misery?" she asked sighing. "Mr. Tabor expected to arrive here and see them backing up carts and filling them with gold by the shovelful."

Elsa Jane didn't have the heart to tell her the truth about the trade. She too had tasted the isolated and lonely life when Peter was gone on the river. Here was a woman who had mastered her own talents to enable her to support her family and keep it together through long periods of discouragement and defeat.

"It's a cash sale," Elsa Jane said, taking out a bag of gold dust. She had brought the gold, having convinced Charley that it would be to their benefit to try and purchase a cow and some chickens from the Tabors. However, there were only four cows and a dozen chickens. She never mentioned her plan.

Besides, after four months of close association with Alice Wootton, she missed having the company of another woman. For the time being Elsa Jane would not expose her masquerade, but it was comforting to know that another woman was so close at hand.

H.A.W. Tabor worked the gravel bar for a week, taking an average of four dollars a day from the sand, and moved on. Gold would continue to elude the man who was destined to become the "Silver King."

Gold was beginning to elude everyone on Chicago Creek. From Jackson's diggings on down, the creek took on an air of premature decay as miners began to desert it for the richer diggings in Russell and Gregory gulches.

Charley was depressed so without consulting him, Elsa Jane began to break camp and load the wagon.

"Duchess?" he whispered. "Are you giving up?"

"*We* are giving up. Oh, not for good, but on this claim. Charley, except for fragments, we are not finding the proof of your theory. The "blossom rock" is just not here. And, because it is not here, you blame yourself and change yourself. Don't let this place hurt you, Charley. Don't let the meanness and ugliness of not finding it get to you. I don't mind working right alongside you as a wife, but of late you have been treating me like an Augusta Tabor—out of sight and out of mind until needed."

He straightened up, towering above her. "I'll help you pack up."

Charley had only heard of Augusta Tabor. The woman frankly made him cringe. She was too much like his dead mother; a lonely shell that cries out for her husband's love but does not find it. He could not imagine how Elsa Jane had struck up such a warm friendship with such a cold, impersonal creature, and was amazed when she tried to encourage the woman to relocate at the North Fork.

"What was that all about?"

"Darling," Elsa Jane laughed, "Mrs. Tabor looks on me as a son. She doesn't know the truth. But never having had a mother I rather enjoy the way she caters to me. She's a lot like the blossom rock you seek. Hard white quartz on the outside, but streaked and seamed with the rich orange-brown of real gold. She's pure."

A few hours later they entered the land of sickness and poverty. Gregory's Gulch was black with prospectors and fortune hunters. Chicago Creek seemed like a wilderness in comparison. As they rode through, their four-mule wagon brought ridicule and warnings.

"You'll be eatin' those critters when you learn hay is one hundred dollars a ton."

"If you can afford them, mister, you don't need the gold."

"Go back! Too many here already. No claims left!"

For five miles they were abused and threatened.

"Too many already is correct," Charley moaned.

On both sides of the creek there was hardly an inch that was not covered by cabins, tents, wagons or the crudest kind of shelters. Hammocks were strung from trees three and four deep.

"Picks sharpened! Picks sharpened!" the blacksmith called out. "Just fifty cents a point."

His voice was nearly drowned out by a fat Mexican on the back of a wagon. "Señor, the finest Taos flour at only forty-four dollars a hundred pounds." The flour was gritty, and full of chaff and dirt.

There was a crude sign in front of one of the tents "Beefe! Fresh Beefe—one dollar a pounde!" The meat was ill-fed and well-whipped oxen just in from a fifty day journey from across the Plains.

Elsa Jane giggled. "Wait until Augusta Tabor sees this. She's not the only white woman for twelve miles around."

Charley looked and quickly averted his eyes. A bare-breasted woman stood behind a plank bar selling bad whiskey for fifty cents a glass.

Charley kept his eyes on the creek and the sluices. His face was calm and composed. He had noticed that the miners were not only running bedrock gravel through the riffle frames but broken blossom rock.

The pools of quicksilver were catching and holding only the heavy gold sinking to the bottom, and the blossom rock was being ignored.

"It needs to be crushed," he muttered.

"What?"

"Later."

Elsa Jane feared there would be no later as they moved deeper into the hopeless confusion of men and beasts. The road was steep and veered away from the creek. They had to slow considerably behind a lumber wagon. The driver gave the oxen their heads and came to the back of the wagon to push.

"What's up ahead?" Charley called.

"New buildings for snobs and whores," the man called back.

"Good," Charley chuckled.

"What's so good about that?"

"They won't be laying out claims this far up the mountain."

For the next quarter of a mile the road twisted and turned. When it finally leveled, Charley was able to urge his mules onto the meadow siding and around the lumber wagon. Ahead, a dozen buildings were in various stages of construction. Again there were hand painted signs. "Central City needs carpenters! $4 a day, with room & board. Miners only pay $1 and nothing!"

"Central to what?" Elsa Jane murmured. There was nothing ahead, or to either side, but towering mountains.

Charley again urged the mules onto the meadowland and made his own track to a distant ravine. There was no sign that any had come this way before. The wagon jostled so badly that Elsa Jane walked. Within twenty feet she was panting for breath. She would not have believed that they had steadily climbed nearly three thousand feet since leaving Augusta Tabor.

Charley brought the wagon to a clearing within an aspen grove and jumped down.

"I'm going to take a pick and shovel and inspect this mountainside. How about some lunch?"

"When I catch my breath."

Elsa Jane took off her slouch hat and let the July sun warm her face. Everything smelled so clean. She looked down at the construction site and at the haze further down in the valley left from thousands of campfires.

Charley came up behind her and kissed the back of her neck. As he did so, his mustache tickled her, and she laughed aloud. He dropped something heavy into her lap.

"Duchess," he roared, "it's here! No more than a hundred yards up the hillside. Oh God! Darling, the surface vein is so soft and decomposed that I was able to pick and shovel down several feet in this little time."

Elsa Jane grinned and then frowned.

"But we have no sluice water up here."

"For the moment I'm glad of that. First, we are going to stake out a claim and start a cabin and corral. What mining we do will be masked by the trees. When we are ready we will have the mules to take our crushed ore down to the creek. But there is plenty of time, my darling. They are not yet aware that it is the mountains that hold the real gold."

Another man, racing across the Plains at that very moment, possessed the same mineral knowledge as Charles Humrick.

Horace Greeley had tutored himself in geology. For his *New York Tribune,* he was coming to prove that this *Pike's Peak or Bust* stampede was just as big a hoax as the California Gold Rush had been.

Two weeks later, precariously mounted on a mule, he had become a curious sight to the miners. Covered by plaster and bandages from a stagecoach accident, Greeley began to poke and snoop about as though he were on the streets of New York.

His paper-thin ego was badly bruised when he had to continually introduce himself.

"Jackasses!" he carped to Henry Villard of Cincinnati's *Commercial Enquirer.* "Everyone is illiterate outside of New York—and possibly Cincinnati!"

But Greeley was frankly impressed, until he looked more closely at the sluices. He tried to explain to the miners about the blossom rock, but the miners would not take heed of his words.

"Take me to a digging," he bellowed, "and I shall prove my point!"

There was nothing the miners liked better than to prove that a tenderfoot was nothing more than a city slicker. Two miners raced ahead to what was considered a dry digging. They loaded an old shotgun with dust and fine nuggets and fired it into the gravel.

The pear-shaped man picked and shovelled until the sweat was peeling back his plasters. Then he filled his pan and went to the creek to wash it.

"Gentlemen," he exclaimed, "my point, exactly. News of your rich discovery shall go forth all over the world, or at least as far as my newspaper can carry it."

Villard saw the miners snickering behind Greeley's back. He suspected that they had "salted" the mine, but felt the arrogant little pipsqueak deserved a comeuppance, and said nothing.

Greeley filed his report with the *Rocky Mountain News,* and it was reprinted eastward until reaching his *Tribune.*

The miners stopped laughing when hundreds of new seekers began to pour in on them daily. But this new breed took to the mountainsides.

Gulch gold lost its allure as the rich "burnt" quartz was found. Soon, it was down the slopes by the ton, carried in rawhide sacks on the miners' backs.

The fortune hunters were quick to react to this new development. They moved their campsites right to the creek edge, took over the abandoned sluices and demanded a percentage for water rights. Many a muffled shot rang out during the night, but there was no one to investigate who or what might have been shot. Most men were alone, and no one missed the missing.

By August ten thousand fortune hunters covered the ravine and mountainsides. The building boom in Central City was monumental. The madams each wanted the finest "house" erected and were willing to pay good carpenters ten dollars a day plus "privileges." John Gregory sold his original claims for twenty-one thousand dollars and began prospecting the mountains for others at two hundred dollars a day.

If there was to be a last laugh, it probably belonged to Greeley. The miners, still chuckling over their hoax, asked him for a suitable name for their campsite.

"Black Hole," Greeley had muttered.

The miners had not fully understood him and called the area Black Hawk. Greeley's version was more correct.

As the green mountains turned into bleak brown hogbacks, denuded of pines and scarred with slag dumps and tunnel shafts, a panic grew in Central City.

Elsa Jane sat quietly as two men talked to Charley. Both had been by the *Duchess Mine* before. Each had a similar claim directly across the valley. Elsa Jane especially liked the English gentleman, W.H. Stanley. He was home folk and could animate Charley with his tales. But W.A. Clark was far more somber and a bit of a worry wart.

Charley would listen to their argument a moment, then pull the granite rock up to the tree limb and let it fall. When the quartz was crushed he hauled the granite back up a few feet, tied it off on the tree trunk and let Elsa Jane brush away the crushed particles.

"Humrick, we beg you to be sensible. Look at what is happening to Black Hawk without proper laws. It was hastily and recklessly exploited and is near exhaustion. They almost have Clear Creek down to a trickle. Once they hit the hard quartz they will give up and look in our direction."

"Ten thousand strong," Clark added ominously.

"I'll consider it," Charley answered drily and returned to his work.

"Will we go to their meeting?" Elsa Jane asked later.

"If they would put in the same amount of work on their claims, Duchess, as they do running around, they might accomplish something. They sit here watching me stamp the quartz to powder, primitive as my system is, and still go back to their sledgehammers. Water? Can they not dig a well as we have done and have their mules turn and turn to pump it out? Oh, I'm sorry. They just madden me so. Good men, sure, but just not suited to this manner of life."

Charles Humrick was correct. W.A. Clark would leave the area still a poor man to wander in the southwestern deserts until he stumbled onto a different type of mining operation. He then became the Anaconda copper king. W.H. Stanley continued to be nothing more than an adventurer and explorer, but one day he would search Africa for Dr. Livingston.

"Well," Charley sighed, "I guess that I best go."

"Good. I'll walk down with you this evening. I'd love to see how Augusta is doing with her bakery."

She knew immediately that she should not have said anything. Charley was still angry about her loaning the Tabors five hundred dollars of their gold without consulting him. He hadn't balked when she wanted to send money back to her children via the Pike's Peak stage, but he resented supporting a deadbeat like H.A.W. Tabor in any way. Twice he had tried to hire the man to work for him, but Tabor still had the gold fever in his veins.

"Do as you wish," he said sourly. "The rain last night put enough water into the cistern for me to sluice for a while."

That was their greatest secret. For the time being, they did not need to rely upon the creek to wash the quartz. They had ample rain water and well water, and behind the loose rock in the stone fireplace rested nearly ten thousand dollars in gold dust and nuggets.

They ate an early supper without speaking, and walked down into Central City. Elsa Jane was rather excited. There had been no reason for her to come down among the new buildings since their arrival. Every three weeks, Augusta trudged up the mountain with freshly baked bread and supplies from Wootton's General Store, a branch run by the Wootton's dour son Samuel.

At seven, the alpine glow basked the town in rosy light. Real darkness would not fall until nearly ten.

Elsa Jane suddenly understood why men were worried. The buildings were pretentious and permanent. The one main street already possessed something Denver City did not—a board sidewalk. Above the main street, perched high on stilts along the mountainside, were homes sporting wide porches and gingerbread decorations. It was quite a different world from Black Hawk.

Russell Green had even used some of his mining profits to build a theater. There hadn't been any performance, but the citizens used it for their town meetings.

"*Jeee-sus*! I can't believe my eyes. E.J., we thought you were dead!"

Elsa Jane knew who it was without turning.

"Hello, Sally," she said quietly.

"Hello Sally," she mimicked. "Is that all you have to say to an old friend? And who is this hunk? Lord, my girls would pay him!"

Elsa Jane was speechless.

Charley stepped to her side and looked at the woman. She's everything that Elsa Jane described her as, he thought, and then some. He put out his large hand and Sally caught it in her own, cooing with delight.

"I'm Charles Humrick. E.J. has told me all about you."

"You . . . you're the recluse of the *Duchess Mine*?"

"Hardly a recluse," he answered serenely. "We just work very hard at our claim."

"We?" Sally smiled wickedly.

"E.J. and I."

Sally Kallenbrough looked again at E.J. She's so changed, she thought, the character of her face . . . I wonder if she is a man or woman to this English nobleman. Except for the fright in her eyes at seeing me, she seems most happy and serene. I never thought to see her again. I never loved anyone in my whole damn life as much as I loved her, and she most likely doesn't even know that she is somewhat responsible for my being in this place.

"Well, Mr. Humrick, for I don't know how else to address you, thank you for coming to our meeting."

"Our?"

She waved her hands in an exaggerated gesture at the overdressed women who had begun to gather about.

"My competitors and I are the ones who pushed for this meeting. We each have quite a large investment in this town and do not want to see it pulled down to the depths of Black Hawk. May I present Molly b'Damn, Em' Straight-Edge and Peg-Leg Annie. The others are some of our girls. Ladies, Charles Humrick and—"

She didn't know how to introduce E.J. and Charley didn't offer.

The formalities were dropped when there was the discharge of a firearm at the far end of the street. Several hundred down creek miners were marching on Central City with pine torches ablaze, all united and ready to have their say at the meeting.

"Radicals!" Sally scoffed. "Wouldn't have a one of them as a customer. Ladies, inside!"

"Get to the bakery," Charley hissed. "I don't like the looks of this."

The miners didn't frighten Elsa Jane as much as Parasol Sally frightened her. She had told Charley everything about Sally and the trip to California, but she had never been able to disclose the intimate nature of their relationship. Elsa Jane knew how vengeful Sally could be.

Augusta was setting dough for the next morning's

bake. Elsa Jane muttered a greeting and slumped into a chair next to the large wooden table. Her slim body expressed pure despair. Without comment Augusta dusted the flour from her hands and gently put an arm around her shoulders.

"Trouble, child?" she said.

Elsa Jane looked up, startled. It was the first time Augusta had ever touched her. It was a mother's touch.

"It could be. Charley and I just ran into someone I knew in California. Frankly, one of the madams in town."

"What is to fear? Does she know you are a woman?"

"You know?" Elsa Jane gasped. "How could you have known?"

Augusta laughed. "Child, to keep Mr. Tabor's irons in the fire, I've had to take in boarders—male boarders. Don't you think I've come to know everything there is to know about men, all manner of men? Oh, you are successful with your disguise, I will be the first to admit. But to another woman, once you have shown your friendly side, the mask is just a very thin veneer. Now, why don't you tell me why you are so troubled? Woman to woman."

"My!" Augusta said an hour later. "You've given me quite a different picture of those types of women."

"The question is, What am I going to do now?" Elsa Jane said.

"See her," she said quietly.

"See her?"

"Yes, see her. Put your cards right on the table."

"But she's vengeful," Elsa Jane protested. "She's hateful and cruel and spiteful and . . ." She stopped when she noticed Augusta's face.

"How odd," Augusta said sadly, "to hear those

words used against another. They are Mr. Tabor's
favorite retorts when things do not seem to be going in his favor."

"Oh, no! Then why do you stay with him?"

"It would be too simple to just say that I love him.
He is not always greedy and selfish, you know. He's
a dreamer. A man who dreams too much gets frus-
trated and needs someone to lash out at when those
dreams go sour. You could not be a part of this
Sally's dreams and she had to lash out at you. Do
you see me caving in because of my tongue-lashings
from Horace? You can't cave in, either."

"I'm beginning to think I don't even know you."

"Child, they call us the weaker vessel because they
don't want to admit how much they really rely upon
us. We all, as women, must wear many masks—and
not just outer clothing as you have done.

"I recall, as a child, hearing my grandmother talk
of the hardships when we were still colonies. Lord,
they came from a civilization and just duplicated it.
They would have cringed at having to go through
this westward movement. I question whether they
would have endured. We will never be remembered
for what we have done, but we know that we are
the backbone of what it is all about."

"And Sally?"

"I never thought I would hear myself saying this,
but her backbone serves a purpose in our strange
new world as well."

15

ELSA JANE avoided the theater. The street was packed with shouting men who could not find room inside.

She climbed a well-worn path to a pink gothic structure with a sign that read "Parasol Sally's Pleasure Palace." Every window was brightly illuminated and tinny piano music cascaded down the hill.

She felt a little foolish knocking on the front door. Exactly what was it that Augusta wanted her to confront Sally with?

The door flew open and Elsa Jane's jaw dropped.

The woman who answered was in men's clothing, and sported a brace of revolvers. Her clothing made her look like she was built out of a busted bale of hay.

"Screw off, kid! Place don't open till the meeting's over."

Elsa Jane realized they were near the same age. "I'm not a kid, and I'll just wait for Sally."

"Bull crap!" Martha Jane Cannary growled, putting a hand on each pistol butt.

Elsa Jane eyed her coldly. "I said I'd wait!"

A familiar laugh echoed from the back parlor. "Let E.J. come on in, Calamity."

Calamity Jane hesitated but stepped aside. The affectionate but eccentric harlot felt a certain affinity to protect her more sociable sisters, but E.J., in her opinion, wasn't worth brawling over. She liked real men who could brawl, curse, booze and roister right along with her. E.J. was too soft, pretty and pouchless between the legs.

Sally came from the parlor in a cloud of chiffon. She had a bemused smile on her face.

"Looking for someone, E.J.?"

"You."

"Oh!" It was not the answer Sally had expected. She thought E.J. was keeping close tabs on Charles Humrick.

"Oh," she repeated, "you two haven't met. Calamity Jane Cannary, this is E.J. Forest. Now here, E.J., is a woman who is not afraid to hide her talents. Bullwhacker, wagon-train boss, Indian scout and Pony Express rider."

It was meant as an insult, but Elsa Jane ignored it. "I want to talk to you."

"But of course," Sally simpered. "Come and join the ladies. Since we were rudely asked to depart the meeting, we have been sitting around awaiting the results."

"Alone."

Sally shrugged and pointed toward the ornately carved staircase. Elsa Jane followed her up the heavily carpeted steps and turned at the landing. Sally waved toward a door down the hallway. As they turned, Elsa Jane couldn't help but notice the look on Calamity Jane's face below.

Calamity just could not figure out how some women could desire youthful boys when there were so many he-men about. Some, like Wild Bill Hickok, she couldn't even bring herself to charge.

Elsa Jane laughed as they entered Sally's private bedroom. The room was cluttered with white polar bear rugs, delicate brocaded furniture, crystal chandeliers set in gold scrollwork and gilt-framed mirrors. The bed was large enough to sleep six at once. The fireplace was marble fronted, with an oil painting of a much younger Sally with exaggerated breasts in nothing more than a gossamer wrap.

"Well, that at least is a cheery note."

"I was just thinking that you finally got the bedroom that you always described to me—right down to the inlaid rosewood and cedar wardrobe closet."

"Thank you for remembering," Sally said with genuine pleasure. They sat in the two Queen Anne chairs in front of the fireplace. There was a moment of embarrassed silence.

"So now we are alone."

"Yes. Suddenly I am curious about what you said on the street. Why would you consider me dead?"

Sally blinked. "The shipwreck off Peru. The *Sacramento Bee* said all hands were lost. Eleanore was crushed."

"Poor Madame Moustache. How could you have known that I off-loaded at Panama and went overland to another vessel?"

"Oh," Sally gasped, "your business! They also thought that you were dead and so it was sold and

I'm not really sure what happened to that man running it for you. We were not on speaking terms, as you will recall."

"If you don't mind, I would rather not recall. Funny, I was cheated out of the money I had saved from that business and now the whole business is gone. No need to return to California at all."

"Poor lamb," Sally soothed, and then caught herself. "I'm sorry. I didn't mean to sound overly affectionate."

"It's alright," Elsa Jane said gently, "I understand . . . now. You wanted something from me that I was not able to give, and so we lashed out at each other."

There was a light rap at the door and Molly b'Damn stuck her head in.

"Meeting's over, Sal. The Hawkers are going down the hill as though they won something. Shall I keep you posted?"

"No, Molly, come in. There is someone here I personally want you to meet. This is my old friend E.J. Forest."

Molly had earned her name by constantly declaring that "she'd b'damned if anyone dared call her a whore." She was a ravishing beauty, with as many hair-dos as Sally possessed parasols. Although she was well into her fifties, her face gave no evidence of dissipation and her clothing gave no hint of her profession. She entered the room with an air of refinement and culture.

"I surmised as much on the street. Ah, the infamous Elsa Jane returned from the grave, but far fairer than described."

"You know my real name?" Elsa Jane gasped.

"Know?" she laughed lightly. "If the truth be known the tears shed over the news of your passing ruined one of my best velvet gowns."

"Hush, you old hussy!" Sally hissed.

"That is a most cruel cut but laughable. I'll match you customer for customer any day of the week." Then she sobered. "But this is being most remiss of us. E.J. is probably worried over her man."

"Worried? Why?" Elsa Jane cried.

"He was disallowed to speak while we were still present. The radical group considered him a "furriner" and shouted him down."

"Did he leave? Where did he go?"

"Easy," Molly soothed in her gentle voice. "As far as I know he went nowhere, because they kicked our pink little butts out right thereafter."

Elsa Jane rose. "I think I'd best get back to the camp."

"Wait!" Sally nearly shrieked. When Elsa Jane looked at her, she said calmly, "Thank you for coming, E.J. We haven't really said anything, but thank you, anyway."

"Are words necessary?" Molly asked. "Friends may differ from time to time, but the anvil upon which that friendship was first hammered out is eternal."

E.J. and Sally looked at each other searchingly.

"I love him," Elsa Jane whispered, without knowing why those were the only words she could muster.

"And he you," Sally was quick to add. "That's obvious, even to an old whore like me."

"But I can't continue. He calls me Duchess and some in Denver City think I am his wife and duchess. Here, yes, we can work together and love and be man and wife. But I can hardly return to England and be his real duchess."

"Real?" Molly scoffed. "Oh, that is priceless. I once knew a Russian grand duke in Sitka . . . but that is beside the point. Birth only gives some people a higher rung on the ladder to nobility. Most should be shoved off, if the truth be known. But they are only people, and mostly lazy ones to boot. If he loves you, that's all that matters."

"And we are here if you should ever need us," Sally soothed.

Charley was quiet when she returned. There was a chill and he had started a fire in the fireplace.

"How did the meeting go?"

He shrugged. "Too many long speeches."

Elsa Jane made him a cup of strong tea. It was a luxury but she had learned that it relaxed him and made him communicative.

"Amazing," he muttered, "the stories that were related of the petty warfare that has been instigated in other mining areas and constantly kept up by the jealousy and egotism which prevails among the gold-hunters. An odd breed. One moment they are treating the prostitutes with idolatry and the next kicking them out."

"Was anything really accomplished?"

"Perhaps too much," he sighed. "Perhaps too little. A mining district was formed with a president, sheriff and recorder of claims to execute the ordinances."

"Sounds reasonable."

"Yes, except they were bullied into making everything from here down to Payne's Bar, which they now call Idaho Springs, the district. That then gave them the power of the vote. They jumped on monopolization as though we who were here first were some form of evil beings. No miner will be allowed to hold more than one claim by right of discovery."

"Then we are safe."

He laughed drily. "The recorder and a jury of three disinterested miners are to draw up the limits of a creek claim, gulch claim and mountain claim.

When I left they were still trying to find the three disinterested miners. That was the 'too little' aspect. They should have hammered it out then and there." He was silent for a long moment. "I'll begin in the morning drawing up a map of the claim. Would you mind taking it to town when ready?"

"Not at all.'"

Elsa Jane did not ask why he wanted her to take it.

There was little logic in the claim's decrees. Augusta Tabor was granted one hundred and sixty acres for her cows and chickens. She filed her claim, kept only five acres of grazing pasture and sold the rest for four dollars an acre. The sale cleared her debt to Elsa Jane and left her a little working capital. The madams of Central City were granted building claims for structures with forty foot fronts and one hundred foot depths.

The jury sided with the little miners on the real issue. Claims could be no more than one hundred feet by fifty feet. It was slightly different for the gulch and placer areas.

This was an agreeable limit for the masses in Black Hawk, but the original sites in Central City covered far greater portions of ground. The disputes began and until they were settled by a vote of the miners, the claim could be worked but no profit could be taken.

Charles Humrick did dispute, but kept working with a quirky grin on his face. Elsa Jane was troubled. She began to go to town, rather than have Augusta bring supplies to her.

"The talk against your claim and Stanley's ain't good, child. I hear a lot since I started putting out tins of coffee to go with the miners' morning rolls. They don't like the size of the claims, first, and really carp that they are in the hands of foreigners."

She heard the same from Sally.

"There is nothing a man likes to do more when he is with one of my girls than brag and talk. Honey, they seem to think that you and your Charley are sitting on the only real gold mine around these parts. They are jealous and that makes men ugly and mean. I'd sleep with a rifle by my side, if I were you."

Charley scoffed at the rumors. He just kept smiling.

"Damn it!" she roared. "Is that all you can do—smile?"

"Stanley sold out while you were in town today."

"I hardly find that anything to smile about. It leaves us all alone."

"I find it most amusing. His surface quartz is all but gone. The new owner will be able to go but another foot or so and then find the hard quartz. Our surface veins pinched out a week ago."

"Then the piles we have yet to smash are it?"

He grinned broadly. "No, but that's where we will have them on this claim. The hard quartz holds the real gold—underground. Summer is nearly gone and winter is coming. That will slow things down. But, in the meantime, we are going to show that we are not greedy, Duchess. We will withdraw our dispute and refile our claims."

"Claims?"

"Ah, Stanley reminded me of something I overlooked. The minutes of the claim meeting state that 'no miner, except the original discoverer of a field, who is allowed two of each, can hold by right of discovery more than one claim.' We will keep the *Duchess Mine* claim, of course. I've selected our second best spot that should go deep into the mountain. You file tomorrow and I'll work on it the next ten days to establish title."

Elsa Jane breathed a sigh of total relief.

The recorder was more than happy to retire the dispute case and file the two claims.

"English bastard is up to something, I tell you."

"Only an idiot would turn back disputed claim land, unless it's good for nothing."

"That's it! The dirty limey wants us to think that so it will go unclaimed. Bet the skinflint don't pay his helper no more than we get."

"Horse pukey! That young man is a regular at Parasol Sally's. Seen him going up her trail many's the time, and you know none of us can afford her girls. No, he's either getting good wages or hefty 'keep your mouth shut' money."

"I'd say the latter. Anybody ever see the ole duke or his helper cart anything into the new bank? I ain't and I carry Gregory's bags up daily. He don't want anyone knowing what he's taking out of the ground, because it's probably so much."

"Yah, and he's probably stashing it all away to cart back to England."

"Is that legal?"

"Not in my book, it sure ain't."

"Bet he's got tens of thousands notched away."

"Bet there's tens of thousands notched in the land he gave back."

A tall, slim figure silently listened to the gossip. He, like thousands of other souls, desired the gold, except he was slightly different. He didn't want to work for it.

The stampede for undisputed land was both comical and devastating. Men fought in hand-to-hand combat for mere inches. In a matter of three days, the entire mountaintop above the two *Duchess* claims was denuded of trees and stumps. Sam Wootton, a true product of his mother, was quick to act on this god-send. As a favor to the would-be miners, he hauled the felled trees down the mountain to his fledgling lumber mill. He knew Charles Humrick well enough to know that the methodical man would give nothing of value away.

In those last days of August, a few men did find a few small pockets of decomposed quartz. Most found what they had been finding throughout the summer; nothing.

The vandalism they started at first was petty— overturning the outhouse, breaking pick and shovel handles, and shoveling the diggings back in the holes. The sheriff wouldn't come. He was too busy working his own claim.

"This time he will have to come," Elsa Jane said hotly.

Charley was also angry, but advised caution. "It was only my homemade pulley they smashed, Duchess."

"Only?" she exploded. "Does anyone else have another like it? Sometimes, Charley, you make me so mad I could spit."

That night twenty sacks of unpulverized quartz were stolen.

Tom Watson scratched his scraggly beard. As a lawman, he was very unsure of himself.

"I see it's gone, Mr. Humrick, or what you claim is gone. But do I call it grand larceny or petty larceny? How much gold you figure you get out of a sack of ore?"

"That's none of your business!" Elsa Jane snapped.

"Sonny, I'm talking with your boss."

"E.J. has a good point, Watson. Why should I reveal what no one else shall? I'll just protect my property from now on."

"Now look, Humrick," he said darkly, "the law is the law. If you shoot or threaten to shoot or use any deadly weapon I'll see that you are lashed and banished from this district."

"Then, Watson," Charley said so coldly that the man took a step backward, "I'll make sure that I kill the damn thief so you'll get the pleasure of hanging me."

"Humrick," he said, his voice quaking, "you'd best know that you are not liked around here, but that does not give you the right to take the law into your own hands."

During the night E.J. and Charley listened to the distant, dull thud of axes eating into the trees. In almost a single movement Charley grabbed his rifle, sprang from the bed and dashed into the yard.

Just as he raised the rifle, there was noise like a thousand thunder claps. Water from the cistern came cascading down the mountainside. Charley screamed to Elsa Jane and wrapped himself around the nearest tree. He knew the crashing wave would pass in a moment, but it's force nearly loosened his grip and washed him away.

The aftermath was devastating. The cabin still stood, but the corral and mules were buried under the tons of washed away slag heaps and the piles of yet unpulverized ore. In disbelief, he watched the wall of water veer away from Central City and wash down the gulley to Black Hawk. There the creek bed would absorb it without further tragedy.

But the stage was set, Elsa Jane knew, for real hardship.

"The utter asshole!" Sally fumed, taking the leather pouch from Elsa Jane and putting it in her safe. "Watson is letting it be known all over the district that he thinks Charley axed his own cistern."

"I'm frightened, Sally, and you know I don't frighten easily."

"At least the gold is safe."

"Until Charley finds out what I've done."

"He doesn't know?"

"He was the last I wanted to know. He would have demanded that we keep it close and protect it ourselves. I don't even know if we can protect ourselves any longer. I greatly wish that God had never created gold."

"Honey, first wish that he had not created greed and envy."

"It's late. I've got to get back. Thank you, Sally."

In Black Hawk, men were planning new ways to make the duke give up and depart. Some plans were too complex and others too simple, so they argued. A few cabins away other men plotted more deviously.

Neither party had a chance to act. A blizzard swooped down the front range out of Canada and was forced westward. It rose to climb over the Rockies but was too laden with moisture. For hours the warm ground melted and absorbed it, but then it began to stick, flake upon flake, until everything was white. The inches grew to a foot—and then two and three—and still the snow fell. By dawn nothing moved nor was there any visibility.

"Magnificent!" Charley shouted. "God has wrought what the sheriff could not. This will bring fear and a standstill."

"And rest for you?"

"We have seen winter storms before, Duchess," he grinned. "There are certain chores that I can do while they sit upon their hindsides. For the first time in weeks I feel free and alive and without dependence."

"That is for sure," Elsa Jane laughed. "For the first time in a long time, you leave me confused. Dependence on what?"

"That is the painful question that has been getting me down and yet oddly amusing me. The sheriff and the district rules became little more than a rebirth of my father for me. I was dependent upon them and they grated against my ever-present desire for individuality. In my early years my father made me too dependent on him and his wealth. He stifled any independent bent, as though it would run him competition. I am reliving that nightmare. Before, I ran away to find my own individuality. This time they can run. Our cabin is snug and warm. We have peace and contentment in the knowledge that we can survive and outlast the winter. I have been thinking of various ways to cut into the hard quartz. To bring them about I shall need a workshop."

Elsa Jane couldn't help but laugh, she felt so lighthearted. It was the first time in months that Charley had said as much at once.

"And do you intend starting such a project on a day such as this?"

He smiled a gentle, sad smile.

"Something a little more mundane, my darling. We require water from the well if I am going to have a smashing cup of morning tea."

Elsa Jane scrambled out of bed and dressed.

"I think flapjacks, eggs and bacon would go right nicely with the tea."

For a long time she could hear him shovelling a path out to the well. He whisled and her heart was gladdened. She was frying the thick bacon slabs when the door opened.

"As long as you are dressed," she said, without turning. "I'll need more wood for the fire."

He grunted and came up behind her. She thought he was going to wrap his strong arms around her and was going to complain about letting the bacon burn when she saw they were not his hands in front of her face. She opened her mouth to scream but a gag was quickly pulled between her teeth and tied at the nape of her neck. Her arms were roughly forced behind her back and lashed with rawhide. She began to kick. It took two men to wrestle her to the dirt floor and tie her legs with more rawhide. A flat palm smacked soundly against the side of her head and she lost consciousness.

When her senses cleared, she was tied to the bed. She shivered. The door was open and the draught was cold. She raised her head and looked out, but there was no one there.

When a figure finally appeared in the open threshold, she quickly closed her eyes.

"Let's find it before the worker wakes up!"

She heard several sets of booted feet tramp into the house and heard the door slam.

As they began to rip and tear the cabin apart, Elsa Jane took a cautious peek. She could not recall having ever seen any of the four men before. Heavily bearded and wearing dirty clothes, they looked no different than thousands of other miners.

"Ain't nothin' here!"

"Shut up! The boss said they ain't ever taken anything to the bank, so it's got to be here."

Elsa Jane's frown tightened. They were being robbed and it had been planned. Fortunately, they didn't seem prone to murder. She shivered. Was Charley bound and gagged out in a snowdrift?

She looked again and saw the four men searching

everything a second time. They stomped on the dirt floor to see if any section sounded hollow, felt every fieldstone in the fireplace and pounded on the log walls to find any secret cache.

Elsa Jane measured each man through her half-open eyes. They were all great-thewed men, bulky with wide shoulders—probably the result of heavy work in the diggings. There was not a one who did not have to squeeze through the cabin door sideways.

"Get picks!" one shouted hoarsely, but another touched his arm.

"No, no noise, remember! No one is to know that we have been here. Let's wipe out our tracks with pine boughs and go see what the boss has to say."

"No!" the other three men shouted in unison.

But the man scowled and shook his shaggy head.

"It's not here, men," he said, "and I begin to question if it ever was—so who do we blame for that? The bastard sends us up to do the dirty work; and *why?* I begin to ask. Do you want the sheriff lashing your back for nothing?"

"Hell, no!"

When they left, Elsa Jane strained to free her hands, but it was useless. Then she strained to see if she could hear Charley, but heard only the muted silence of the snow covered area.

By late afternoon, the fire had died. She hoped Augusta would expect her in town and grow suspicious when she didn't arrive. However, she knew it was unlikely. No one would worry about someone not being out in a snowstorm.

When evening came, Elsa Jane was suddenly horribly afraid. She feared only for Charley. She might be able to survive the freezing nights within the cabin, but could Charley survive outside?

She gnawed on the gag until the corners of her

mouth were raw and bleeding, and the inside of her throat was too dry to swallow. She wiggled her body back and forth until the bedroll blankets were to each side and she was nestled down in the straw. It gave her a sense of warmth.

Fear crawled agonizingly up her spine each time she thought of Charley. Tears stung her eyelids and she scolded herself. She cursed the men for their laggard return with their so-called boss. Perhaps he was a man who would listen to reason.

Her head ached dully until she finally fell into a fitful sleep.

Was it daylight or was she just dreaming when she woke? She was aware of being hungry and of an odd dizzy feeling in her head. Consciousness slowly left again. Numbness started creeping up from her toes and from her fingers out along her arms.

Again she became aware of light streaming in the window. She was not aware, however, that it was the third morning since the attack.

At long last she heard the cabin door creak open. Through her swollen eyes she recognized the man entering the cabin. She felt the rawhide bonds being loosened from the bed. She was pulled upright and swung about so that her feet dangled over the side.

She was still nearly unconscious when the gag was removed. Her tongue was so swollen that she could only work her jaw up and down to create a bit of moisture.

"Alright, working boy," a voice whispered, "now we will learn where your boss stashes his gold."

The man stepped in front of her and Elsa Jane slowly raised her head. She could see the shock in Daris Jamieson's face as they recognized each other. He opened his mouth, but for the life of him he could not speak.

"Hurry!" the guard by the door croaked. "You said the workman would probably be dead by now, too."

"Probably," Jamieson whispered, "probably . . ."

"Well, I'm not," Elsa Jane said clearly, surprised at the strength of her own voice.

Jamieson glowered, as though warning her to shut up.

"Look," he said softly, "we mean you no harm. Just tell us where the gold is hidden."

"Where is Charles Humrick?"

One of the men rushed forward. He held Charley's money belt.

"Look, man, we know he had more than what was in this. Don't be stubborn like he was. Tell us!"

"Was?" she wheezed.

"A figure of speech," Jamieson said uneasily. "We'll release him as soon as we have the gold."

Despite all she knew and hated about Daris Jamieson, he seemed to be going to great lengths to protect her. Still, to trust the man galled her.

"There is no gold," she said softly.

Jamieson's laugh was mean and ugly.

"I'm not lying," she said morosely. "Dislodge those two flat stones at the base of the fireplace and see for yourself."

They were quick to do as she directed. Finding it empty, spots of rage appeared on Jamieson's cheeks.

"Where . . . where is it?" he asked gruffly.

"Banked."

"No!" Jamieson roared. "It's a lie!"

"Well it sure as hell ain't here!" one of the men exploded.

Jamieson thought for a moment, glaring at E.J.

"All right," he snapped. "You are going to go and get the gold for us."

"I only work for the man," she said, smiling wickedly. Jamieson would be the first to believe such a statement, and it would force him, she thought, to bring the duke out of hiding.

"It's going to be a long cold winter, men," he said oddly. "People are leaving by the wagon-load. I suggest we melt in among them and do the same."

"But boss," one of the men asked, "What about the gold?"

"That's exactly what I'm now thinking about. Look at that hole. It wouldn't hold but a few thousand. I think the rumors about this Englishman are correct. He is sitting on millions, but it's still in the ground. Is that right, workman?"

Elsa Jane saw no reason to lie. "Right."

"That ain't going to do us no damn good!"

"Calm down," Jamieson soothed. "It could make us millionaires come spring."

"You're daft! We don't have the claim on these diggings."

"Perhaps we don't now. But if the claimer and his worker don't happen to return in the spring, as many won't, then we will be here first to take over the deserted property."

"But, boss, that would mean we would have to . . ."

Jamieson silenced him. "No it don't! Our original plan will still work. From what we have learned, they are not liked and have no friends. You can tell by the snow that no one has been up here in three days. Gag the workman again. Nature will take its course by spring."

Jamieson crossed over to Elsa Jane and looked down at her. She glared at him with hatred in her eyes but did not protest when one of his men replaced the gag. She was stunned to have learned that she had been bound for three days, but elated that

Jamieson had not changed much. His actions were still based on rumors and half-truths.

"But boss," the man protested again, "why can't we stay in the area for the winter, as well?"

"Harrison, I've told you before that Parasol Sally knows me from the past. There will be no trouble if she learns nothing about my having been here. Spring will be different. We will get back and be established before she returns with her girls."

Harrison chuckled. "Then she won't be able to deny us her soiled doves. Shall we tie the workman to the bed again?"

"No," Jamieson answered casually, "we'll just bar the door from the outside. That will keep her in and others out. Let's go."

Elsa Jane noticed two things. None of the men had reacted when Jamieson referred to her in the female gender, and Jamieson had a gimpy arm from her gunshot wound. She vowed he would have far worse come spring. After three days of being absent, it would not be long before Augusta would come to check on their snowbound condition. Their? She still held out hope that they had Charley bound and gagged somewhere he could survive. And now she had every reason in the world to survive. Jamieson had taken too much from her in the past and she would not let him take her future as well. As long as she had been with Charles Humrick she had not even thought of Daris Jamieson. Now she would. ⋐§

16

ELSA JANE looked out of the window at the bleak sky. Several times she had tried to rise off the bed, but her feet were bound so tightly that she stumbled and fell back.

She was beyond being cold. Her anger kept her warm and the hope of rescue kept her from thinking about her hunger.

Outside, the early September snow came steadily down. There had been no sound for a long time. Suddenly there was a crunch of boots in the snow. Elsa Jane held her breath and strained to listen. No, she had not been mistaken. But what were they doing? she wondered. She listened more carefully and decided they were circling the cabin to see if anyone was about.

She recalled what Jamieson had said about barring

the outside of the door. That and the lack of smoke from the chimney would indicate that the cabin was deserted.

Augusta Tabor would at least peek in the window, so this had to be someone else. She couldn't let them get away, so she flung her legs back up onto the bed and jacknifed her knees. Again and again she pounded her feet against the footboard.

Finally, a head appeared at the window, shielding it's eyes to peer inside. It was pressed so close that she couldn't make out any features. She stopped kicking and breathed a sigh of relief.

However, seconds later there was still no sound of the door being unbarred. Within moments she knew the horrendous error that she had made. Daris Jamieson had protected her for a single reason; he was not going to wait for natural causes to kill her. He was going to burn the cabin down around her and destroy all evidence that she had ever been a captive.

Within forty seconds of smelling the smoke, Elsa Jane rolled off the bed and caterpillared her body to the center of the cabin. By then, the kerosene-soaked logs on all sides of the cabin were roaring with insensate frenzy.

Daris Jamieson watched until the great livid tongues licked at the pine bough covered roof. He had feared that the deeply packed snow might put out the fire, but the under boughs were tinder dry. They ignited with a sudden, excruciating whooooom! The intense heat caused the snow to steam and sent it avalanching off the peaked cabin roof. The wall fires were such that the cascading snow was quickly melted and puddled.

Convinced that the fire would be all-consuming, Jamieson turned to depart. He stopped short. Up from the draw came the musical tinkle of sleigh bells.

He knew who it was. Coming back up from Black Hawk, he had seen the sleigh and the woman in front of Tabor's Bakery. Daris Jamieson surmised that Sally Kallenbrough was coming up to see the duke.

"Too bad, you old whore," he murmured. "You're going to find nothing but a flaming inferno."

He slipped into the aspen grove and stumbled down the gulley toward the creek. He had but one regret. When he had gone back to the well to find the unconscious and bound body of Charles Humrick, he had only found a snowy covered trench that led up to the forest. He assumed that some large beast had hauled away the body for a royal feast. Unfortunately, it would have been so much more logical for the charred bones of two bodies to have been found among the ashes.

At the time he had laughed to himself. Now he was not laughing. The arrival of Parasol Sally could alter everything.

Throughout the summer, Black Hawk and the other gulch communities had experienced many cabin fires, with many of them resulting in deaths. No one had paid them any heed and Jamieson had hoped this would be true now, especially as there were heavy snow drifts.

But could he now afford to cheat his four partners, and keep faith with his fifth and only silent partner?

It had taken every card trick that he knew to get Murton Mullholland in debt to him. The claims recorder was an incurable gambler and would play in the Black Hawk saloons hoping no one in Central City would find out. Any vice was permissable in Black Hawk—but a bad gambling debt was not tolerated.

It had taken him less than thirty seconds to agree

to Daris Jamieson's plan. No one would ever know that he let the gambler trace Charles Humrick's signature out of the claim records. He did not even want to know why the man wanted it. He was free of debt, and that was all that mattered.

Jamieson paused and looked back. The white smoke blended well with the bleak sky and snow. No one would even be aware of the fire until Sally reported it, and that would take time.

"Yes," he mused aloud, "I think it best that I stay around for another day and have a friendly game of poker with Mullholland tonight."

Sally frantically whipped the horses' rumps, but they floundered in the deep snow. Had she not owned the sleigh, she never would have let Augusta Tabor talk her into this madness. In town the sleigh was a lark because the streets were packed down by horses and trampling feet. Here she could not even tell if she were still on Charley's mule path.

"Damn!" she cried, still a hundred yards from the cabin. The two horses refused to haul the light sleigh another inch. She scrambled down into the snow and tried to walk, but her great, bearskin coat was just too much bulk to drag along. She shed it and left it lying where it fell.

There was a thunderous roar and a blinding flash. She looked up to see the giant pine next to the cabin ignite like a lucifer match.

Calling to Elsa Jane and Charley in a shrill voice, she fought her way over the yards, while hot sparks popped and hissed as they hit the snow.

The air in the cabin was choked with dust and smoke, and so hot it seared Elsa Jane's nostrils when she tried to breathe. Her clothing was full of holes

where hot sparks had fallen on her from the roof.
She dared not look up as it was only a matter of
time before the flat boards holding the bough covering would be eaten through and the heavy timber
rafters would come crashing down on her. She knew
she was facing a cruel death, as she had seen and
heard the people who had burned in the river collision.

What Sally saw was equally terrible. Not only was
the door barred, but a log had been wedged under
the bar. It confused her. Charley and Elsa Jane would
not leave the area without their gold. She called
their names as she tried to dislodge the log.

Above the roar of the fire, Elsa Jane heard her
screams. She put all thoughts of death out of her
mind and caterpillared to the door. She used her
feet to signal that she was within.

"Oh, my God!" Sally cried. "They are in there and
I can't budge this bastard."

She frantically ran to the tool shed. She found a
sledgehammer and several long iron rods that Charley had used to break through the heavy quartz. The
sledgehammer was far too heavy for her to lift, so
she hauled back one of the tapping rods. She remembered when her husband had moved a log or broken
wagon axle by levering it. Memory helped her judge
the right spot to place the rod. She was not aware,
however, that four bulky men had taken turns jumping upon the log to secure it into the wooden bar
and into the ground.

She pried until she thought the blood vessels in
her arms would burst. The heaviest work she had
done in years was lift a bourbon glass.

Black spots spun before her eyes and her back
screamed with pain. The log moved a fraction of an

inch to the left. She reset the bar at a higher point and started over. The melting snow made the ground muddy and she slipped repeatedly.

Then she froze in disbelieving terror. The entire roof caved inward, sending up a great cloud of smoke and sparks. Within the flaming walls was an explosion and the insistent crackling of a thousand new little fires igniting the furniture and the interior surface of the logs.

Without conscious volition, Sally turned and put her back under the prying rod. She strained and forced it upward until she could feel the blood trickle down her back. The rod had eaten through her clothing and into her flesh. She gritted her teeth until she could feel bits of enamel chip away.

With a scream of its own, the log suddenly slammed away from the bar and brought Sally tumbling along with it into the snow and mud.

She twisted as she fell and landed on her arm. She didn't acknowledge the pain of her broken wrist, as she pushed the bar across the door.

The inside of the door was already aflame when she threw it open, and beyond was a holocaust. Caught between two burning rafters, she saw a human torch rolling back and forth. Elsa Jane's hair and eyebrows had been singed away and her face was so blackened Sally didn't know who she was.

Disregarding her own safety and the pain of the bone sticking through the skin on her hand, Sally plowed right into the flames and climbed over the burning timbers. The flames ate at the hem of her gown and she beat them out with her hands.

In later weeks Elsa Jane remembered the vision of a woman trying to get her to her feet while she was still aflame. In the vision the woman was crying, tears making streaks down her sooty face.

Sally was crying because she could not loosen the bonds and dared not try to find a knife within the inferno. She tugged and pulled and half carried Elsa Jane over the timbers and out through the door. They collapsed into a snow drift and Sally scooped up great armloads of the fleecy powder and dumped them on Elsa Jane. Her charred clothes hissed and steamed until the last embers were smothered out.

Sally was now aware that she had brought out Elsa Jane, but that was all she was aware of for the moment. Besides her broken wrist, her hands were badly burned, but she did not feel them.

Elsa Jane was beyond feeling. Even before being hauled from the cabin she had lapsed into a coma.

"Halloooo!"

Sally turned to see a man pulling the horses and sleigh toward them. She didn't have the energy to call back.

Murton Mullholland had seen the flash of light when the pine tree exploded. He had no great love for the duke or his worker, but he feared one thing more than anything else in life.

Twice, as a trapper, he had nearly been consumed in forest fires. Despite the heavy snow, he wanted to make sure that this fire did not spread down to Central City. He had a very lucrative swindle going for himself, and he didn't want to risk losing it to a fire.

"God!" was all he could say when he came upon Sally and the blackened figure under the snow.

"Help me get her into the sleigh," Sally was able to gasp.

Unlike Jamieson's henchmen, Mullholland picked up the reference.

"Her? Who?"

Sally didn't feel like beating about the bush or

mincing words. She needed to save Elsa Jane's life, and, like Madame Moustache, she always measured every man's weakness to her own advantage.

"Mullholland, you now have the run of my house for your silence. *She* is Humrick's wife."

"The workman?" he stammered. "But where is . . . is . . ."

"Fool!" she snapped, glancing at the cabin and the walls ready to collapse. "Give me your belt knife."

"Knife?" he asked foolishly.

"Look at her mouth, jackass! Her hands and feet are bound and the door was barred and wedged from the outside. Knife!"

He studied the hand she extended, his brow furrowed into a frown.

"I'll do it. You're hurt."

Sally looked at her wrist as though it belonged to someone else. She shrugged and helped scoop the snow away from Elsa Jane in order to roll her over.

Mullholland slashed through the bonds and then wished he had left them intact. Elsa Jane's arms and legs were so limp that they continually got in his way as he lifted her onto the sleigh.

"Where's my coat?"

"I picked it up and put it in the sleigh. You'd better wrap up in it."

"Hell, man, put it around her. I can bundle up in the lap robe."

He did as directed, turned the horses about by the head and got in to take the reins.

His fear of a forest fire was calmed, but had been replaced by a new fear. If the duke had perished in the flames, it was murder.

"Who could have done this?" he thought aloud.

"You will be the first to know." Sally said coldly.

"What?"

"It stands to reason that someone went to a lot of trouble to get rid of them and with only one motive that I can see. As soon as news of the fire gets around someone is going to try and get their claim."

"Then isn't this something for Tom to be handling?"

Sally thought a moment. "Murton, let's not get into a discussion on that man's lack of ability. Let's just play our cards close for a while. We have a patient to see after first."

"Two patients," he said with genuine concern.

Sally's problem with her wrist and hands did not keep her from staying in control. While her girls were making E.J. comfortable, Molly b'Damn brought her medical kit.

Molly stood by the bed, trembling with fury. She had come to like and respect Elsa Jane.

"The cloth is charred right to the skin. We would probably kill her if we tried to rip it apart."

"Miss Molly," Sharon Whitaker said hesitantly, "same happened to my baby brother once. Our nigger mammy covered Tommy with honey and it helped lift the cloth away."

Almost mysteriously her words made their way into Elsa Jane's unconsciousness. For a brief moment she was lucid enough to murmur: "Yes, honey!"

The soiled doves scoured the town for pots of honey.

The largest supplies belonged to Augusta Tabor and Samuel Wootton, and once the reason for it was known, Sam stripped his shelves of every kind of honey and bundled up for a trip down to the Plains to get more from his father's store.

"What?" Horace Tabor roared. "All of it . . ."

"Hush," Augusta said quietly. "It is needed for E.J."

"I forbid it! Without honey you will not be able to do half of your baking."

"Go to hell," she sneered. "Without E.J. there would have been no baking in the first place."

It was a messy process but it worked. Within twenty-four hours the honey had loosened the charred cloth from Elsa Jane's badly burned skin. The women then placed her on oiled silk sheets and covered her with more honey sent up by Alice and Uncle Dick.

Every moment of the day or night one of the girls or Molly b'Damn sat beside the bed. Sally, her hands bandaged like oversized mittens, floated in and out—she had many matters of her own to see to.

"Nothing?"

Coal Oil George shook his head and scratched at his scraggly beard in bewilderment. The old prospector looked as though he had been through a fire himself.

"Miss Sal, I raked and shovelled over the whole burnt out area. I should know human bones when I sees 'em 'n I see'd none. Did find somethin', though."

"What?"

"That dog of their'n. Throwed to the bottom of the well with its throat slit. Mean and ugly, I say."

"Thanks anyway, George. Go to the kitchen and have cook get you something to eat."

Calamity Jane rose from a horsehair chair and stretched.

"Wish I could help, Sal, but I ain't much on nursing."

Sally thought a moment. "I think you could help, Jane. You know a lot of men who know how to keep their mouths shut. Could you get some men to search out that whole area for the duke?"

"Get? Hell's fire, I'll lead them!"

※ ※ ※

Daris Jamieson finally showed up in Murton Mullholland's dusty office.

"Haven't seen you down playing cards, Murt."

"I've been busy," he answered simply.

"Busy? Ain't much of a time of year for people to be filing claims. Murt, people aren't trying to lay claims to the Duchess mines already, are they?"

"What do you know about that?"

"Just what the rumor mill is churning out. Did they both really die in the fire?"

Mullholland knew there was no such rumor floating around and his suspicions mounted.

"What's your interest in it, Jamieson?"

Jamieson took a piece of paper from his pocket, his face furrowing into a mock frown.

"Got myself a pretty stiff gambling debt against Humrick, Murt. All signed legal like. Seems to me I should have first crack at that claim to cover my debt."

Mullholland was not as big a fool as Jamieson believed. He knew damn well where the signature had come from and he knew that Jamieson knew that he knew.

"That's not for me to decide, Jamieson."

Jamieson leaned across the desk.

"You had better decide," he said coldly, "if you want me to keep my mouth shut about other matters."

"It's still not for me to decide," he repeated.

Murton knew that Jamieson was going to have to change his tactics.

"It's not that I was going to cut you out, Murton. The paper says the duke owed me twenty thousand dollars. We both know what those claims should be worth. You file for me and twenty percent of it is yours."

Mullholland sat back as though contemplating the offer.

"Most intriguing offer. Most intriguing, but out of the question at this time. You had best wait to see if the survivor does survive."

Jamieson's face twisted in disbelief. "Which one?" he asked stupidly.

Murton had promised Sally silence on the matter, but the temptation to have one-upmanship on the gambler was too strong. The question also gave him all the knowledge that he needed to connect Jamieson with the fire.

"Humrick's wife," he answered. "The duchess that the mines were named after."

"They got her up at Parasol Sally's," he said slowly. "Bad off, but has murmured some. In time she should be able to name names."

Jamieson's fearful gaze rested briefly on Mullholland. He rose so quickly he nearly toppled the chair.

"I'll hold on to the note," he said in a high, thin voice. "I have some business that will keep me away from the district for a while, but I'll be in touch."

Mullholland seriously doubted that he would ever see the gambler again, or that the badly burned woman could survive long enough to give names. He was glad to see the man leave.

He was not aware of the real fears Jamieson had. Twice Jamieson had left Elsa Jane for dead, but she refused to die. Wife? That was the greatest blow of all. It had all been in vain if she survived and could take over the mines. However, he didn't want to stay around to see if she lived or died, and didn't know that her hatred for him would help her live.

Fighting up from the depths of her darkness, an image loomed before her. Hands shielded a dark face peering in through a little square of glass. Elsa Jane fought and fought to give the dark blur some recognizable features. Slowly it cleared. There were eyebrows, eyes, a nose and a leering mouth. The mouth had leered at her too many times. She would not die and let him get away with murder a second time.

"Jamieson," she murmured.

Sally and Molly spun toward the bed.

"Saints be praised! She's coming out of it."

"Jamieson," she murmured again and dropped back into unconsciousness.

Sally might have put it all down to the sub-conscious dwelling on memory, had she not possessed a fairly accurate grapevine. She had been aware of Daris Jamieson's presence in Black Hawk, but had kept silent as long as he stayed away from Central City and Parasol Sally's Pleasure Palace.

She sent one of her girls for Tom Watson and sat down. Five minutes later her bell was ringing madly.

The sheriff had been on his way to see her, dragging the recorder along. Watson was incensed.

"Why has this been kept from me?" he demanded.

"Possibly because you are never around," she said sweetly. "Come into the breakfast room so we can talk privately. The patient is coming around, Murton."

"Well, that's one bit of good news."

"Said anything?" the sheriff growled.

"A name. Sit down, gentlemen. Harriet, bring coffee for three," she called to the kitchen. "A name you should know, Murton. Haven't you gambled some with Daris Jamieson?"

Mullholland slumped in his chair. "Some."

"Well, the man is known to the patient and I from the past. Pick him up, Tom, and you will have your murderer."

Tom opened his mouth and shut it.

Coal Oil George, who loved to cadge food from the cook, came in with the tray of coffee cups. When no one spoke, he left, but once back in the kitchen he kept an ear pressed to the swinging door.

"Don't go off half-cocked, Sal," Watson warned. "There has been an attempt, but no murder."

"How can you say that?"

"From what I gathered from Calamity and not from you. Ain't no body yet, so it ain't no murder. Frankly, how do we know Humrick didn't do the thing himself and vanish? Weren't no gold found in the ashes, from what I hear. I still think he did all those other crazy things."

"Don't be a fool!"

The sheriff rose. "Lookee here, Sal. I don't try and run your whorehouse, so you stop playing lawman." He stomped out without even tasting his coffee.

"Blind bastard!" Sally muttered. "You don't look so good, Murt. Did I strike a nerve mentioning Jamieson?"

She had, but he would never admit it. "It's something else, Sal. When you warned me that I would be the first to know, I went and looked back over Humrick's claims. There's no mention of a wife. Both are just in the name of Charles Humrick."

"So?"

"So everything. Can't do a damn thing about it until he shows up or she can prove that she is his wife. In the meantime someone may get the idea to jump it as being deserted."

"Folderol! The word seems to be spreading about E.J. Only a worthless bastard would think to deprive her after what she has been through. Besides, no one will even think on the subject until spring."

Coal Oil George was already thinking on it. He had never been anything but a worthless bastard, so being called such would not hurt his feelings. He knew the mines quite well, and his needs were simple. The tool shed would suffice for a roof over his head. He could keep a low profile by not letting smoke be seen coming from the shed. It was not his intention to really jump the claim. He would just secretly work it throughout the winter and gain a grubstake for spring.

As the weeks of recovery slipped by for Elsa Jane, another type of death was taking place. The healthy and hearty stayed in Central City and Black Hawk to protect their claims and businesses. But thousands feared the freezing creek and the long winter months and fled back to their former homes. By the first of October the twelve thousand dwellers had dwindled to a little over two thousand. Gregory Point, Mountain City, Nevadaville, Missouri City, Springfield City and Bortonburgh could count their populations on two hands. The long slow processes of ruin and decay had begun.

"What in the hell is that for?"

The heavyset Irish woman had a soft spot in her heart for Coal Oil George. He no longer came each day to cadge food, so she tucked it away for his infrequent arrivals. Lately he had been giving her a few grains of gold dust for her kindness. She was well aware of the source.

And Harriet Groton, not being one who could keep anything from Sally Kallenbrough, blabbed it all.

"Treachery, right under my nose," Sally screamed

at Murton Mullholland a half hour later. "Were you aware of this?"

"Yes," he sheepishly admitted. "I passed the word on to Watson, but he will do nothing. He says it is legal until Humrick comes back to dispute it. He still thinks E.J. is nothing more than a workman."

"Fine. Leave it at that, and I'll handle Coal Oil George in a manner that will make him think twice. He's been cut off from getting one more scrap out of my kitchen and I'll blast the bastard if he sets a single foot on the path up to my door."

She repeated the story to Elsa Jane's next two visitors. Sam Wootton knew exactly how his mother and father would have handled the situation—the old prospector would be denied any purchase out of his general store.

Augusta Tabor heartily agreed. She had even more reason not to sell to the old man, but she would not tell Sally. Her husband had fumed about her giving away their supply of honey, and raged when she went to check on E.J. He was not about to have his reputation sullied by his wife entering a house of prostitutes.

Augusta had enjoyed her visit and had found her meeting with Molly b'Damn most rewarding. The house and furnishings were exactly what Augusta had always dreamed of, and Molly's culture and breeding reminded her of what she missed most of her former life.

The battle raged anew each time she departed for a visit to the patient, but Augusta was learning to lash back at her husband.

"Haw! Aren't those your initials? H.A.W. Haw! When you start being the bread-winner again, Mr. Horace Tabor, I will deem it time to seek your counsel again."

When she returned, a mule, the provision larder, the tin cash box and her husband had vanished. Without letting anyone know, she eked out what bakery goods she could until the flour bin was bare. Quietly, cow by cow, chicken by chicken were all sold to the butcher. Not even Sally or Molly knew of her plight.

The honey applications were finally changed to creams and salves. Elsa Jane felt like her skin would burst if she moved. She tried to smile when visitors were about, but never when she was alone. It was then that she looked into the hand mirror and studied her new face.

The scalp scar had vanished, as had most of her hair. It had come back but it seemed to refuse to grow. Her facial skin looked as if she had aged a decade. Fortunately, the tautness gave her a regal, haughty beauty.

Her vocal chords had been seared and she was left with a husky, sensuous quality to her speech. Her tear ducts seemed to have dried out.

No one mentioned Charles Humrick and she knew why. He had departed from her life just as mysteriously as he had entered it. That seemed to be her fate; Peter, Melanie, a mother she had never known, Spider, Raymond Spurlock, Mother Catherine; to say nothing of the many lost friends on the *River Queen* and the wagon train—and now her Charley. They were her ghosts, who could no longer speak or feel or love.

By October she was on her feet again, but to her amazement she had to learn to walk just as if she were a baby.

In November, Russell Green finally induced a theatrical company to come play in his theater. Sally persuaded them to give a private performance for the patient. Elsa Jane was intrigued more by the leading man than the play.

"It's remarkable," she enthused. "One moment you are a swashbuckling gentleman and the next an ugly pirate. However do you bring it about?"

"Nose putty, ma'am. It can be made into almost anything and blends right in with the skin."

"Fascinating."

"Fascinating?" Sally asked later, getting her ready for bed. "You got something brewing in that clever head of yours?"

"I think so," she said simply.

"Don't you need more time?"

"I don't think so. Everyone drops bits and pieces that they don't think I'll fit together. I've still got obligations, Sally. Until spring I've got to put the gold to work for me. This is not the place."

"Where is?"

"Where all of the rest of last summer's gold is being spent. I must have about eighteen thousand dollars tucked away, right?"

"Hell, E.J., look at you. With that new face you can't very well go back into the mule driving business."

"Have you noticed Augusta lately?" she asked, pretending to change the subject.

"Who hasn't! Haggard as a pea-hen since walrus face skedaddled with . . ." Sally stopped short.

Elsa Jane laughed. "I know. It's hard to keep any secrets in this town with Calamity around. I worry about Augusta and I also worry about Coal Oil George."

Sally exploded. "Worry about him! Hell, E.J., he's the old goat trying to steal your claim. Worthless bastard!"

Elsa Jane grinned. "Then why have you been sneaking up there the last few nights with tins of hot soup?"

Sally blushed scarlet. "Why . . . why, that's just because . . ."

"Because he's downright sick of near starvation and a bad cold? You are a caution, to be sure. You and Calamity, both soft as putty on the inside. But if I can't have the claims, then I'd rather he have them than Jamieson."

"How do you know you can't have them?"

"Bits and pieces, again. We were never married, you know. How can I claim anything? I might not even have a right to the gold that you are holding."

"Horsefeathers! Who is going to try and claim it?"

"The district, perhaps. They could claim it was taken out during the time the diggings were under dispute."

"Let them try!"

Elsa Jane sighed. "That's what I wish to avoid, away from here. Do you think Augusta is about ready to start a new bakery away from here?"

"Without a hint of charity?"

"Without a single hint."

"I'll see to it," Sally said quietly. Then, after a long pause. "You do have one thing going for you, away from here. Down below they only really know you as the duchess."

Elsa Jane scoffed. "The duchess of what?"

Sally shrugged, "The Duchess of Denver, for all intents and purposes."   ❧

17

FOR EIGHTEEN months Elsa Jane had silently chuckled over the title Sally had given her. For those who were not privy to the truth, she was accepted as a most gracious hostess awaiting her exploring husband to return from a long trip. Those like the Woottons and Byers shared her grief.

For the remaining winter months of 1860 Elsa Jane had purposely kept a very low profile. Charles Henry Humrick had left her with a very valuable asset—a methodical approach to everything. To stand clear of the twin city rivalry, she quietly shared a small house with Augusta and her child, while she fully recovered and Augusta established a new bakery.

In April two events greatly pleased her and a third gave her a chuckle.

Larimer and Wootton buried the hatchet and the

towns were consolidated as Denver. This precluded the need for the City of Highland, which still did not possess a single dwelling, and it became known as Brown's Bluff. Here, at least, she possesed a title to land that bore her name. It was an anchor for the future.

The day after the election the second event took place.

"I do declare," Augusta gasped. "The Woottons must be moving to this side."

Uucle Dick was proudly leading three heavily laden freight wagons up Larimer street. Augusta frowned as he motioned the wagons over toward the clapboard bakery. A tall, dust laden man rode up and dismounted near Wootton. One look made Augusta bellow toward the living quarters.

"I think you'd best come on the run, Elsa Jane!"

Elsa Jane ran out to the street.

"Father! Father! Oh, land sakes, what a shocking surprise!"

They embraced and kissed as though it had been common for them to do so over the past twenty-six years.

"How did you know?" she laughed, introducing Augusta to Calvin Bender.

"Know? It's just a handsome male version of your own face, child. If I wasn't already married I'd set my cap for him. Now, isn't it lucky it's our stew for lunch day. Will you be staying for a plate, Uncle Dick?"

After the dishes were done, Calvin took Elsa Jane to inspect the wagons.

"All of the things you ordered from New Orleans are crated on the first wagon, Elsa Jane. Your letter suggested need for the rest, so I wrote to Wootton and his wife for their advice."

It was a stunning surprise. There were enough household furnishings for a mansion.

"It's fantastic," she gasped, "but did they also advise you that I have no home in which to store all of this?"

Calvin's eyes glistened. "Said he had a place. Hey, Wootton, how far to the unloading place?"

Uncle Dick was getting the teamsters back on the wagons. "Just up on Champa Street."

Elsa Jane looked from one to the other. "There are no warehouses up on Champa."

Wootton shuffled his feet.

"Didn't say there was."

Augusta came out of the bakery.

"Hush, you ole coot. Just take her along and show her."

"Augusta," Elsa Jane asked suspiciously, "what is going on here?"

"Why, how should I know?" she answered primly.

But nearly everyone in Denver City had come to know about the project. Calvin Bender's letter asking whether his daughter really intended to stay in Denver had prompted Alice Wootton to look through some of the duke's personal papers.

Charles Humrick had designed the house, and although it was not on quite the lavish scale that he had envisioned, the two-story brick Georgian edifice was the first of its kind in the town.

Elsa Jane was overwhelmed.

"Probably the only secret ever kept in this town," Uncle Dick chortled, "especially with Bedelia Porter involved."

"Bedelia? Is that why she has been having those little gossip sessions with Augusta?"

Before he could reply, Bedelia Porter stalked out of the new kitchen.

"Gossip sessions, my foot! A body needed to know

some of your personal desires without asking you direct."

She was a plump woman with graying brown hair and small bright eyes covered by gold-rimmed spectacles. She was an inveterate gossip and shameless busybody, but would work from dawn to dusk at any chores available in town, although they were usually few and far between. She was a woman of many talents and had been thankful for a month of cleaning up after the workmen, waxing the hardwood floors and hand stitching the yards and yards of drapery materials.

Elsa Jane embraced her and kissed her on the cheek.

"So far I am pleased and awed by everything I see."

Bedelia was never one to hesitate or hide her candle under a bushel.

"I'm available for the moving in and arranging, if you have need."

Elsa Jane sighed in relief. A house had been in the plans she had intimated to her father, and a business to support such a house. She had the business mapped out and had been waiting for this shipment from New Orleans. But the house? Everything was happening so fast and she had to calculate the expenditures.

"I have need."

Thereafter, it was never discussed. Bedelia automatically became the full time cook and housekeeper for the duchess.

The third event, which had amused her, came about on the next day. Elsa Jane, Calvin and Bedelia were busy polishing and arranging the furniture when Augusta came bounding in with two visitors from the mountain.

Sally and Molly b'Damn looked as though they had just stepped off a boat from Europe. Elsa Jane was casual with the introductions and Calvin was his gracious self. Bedelia gaped. She had never expected to see "ladies" in the company of the prim and proper Augusta Tabor.

Sally pulled the kerchief from Elsa Jane's head. She rumpled the fine hair that was no more than an inch long. "Damn, it still isn't growing."

Elsa Jane laughed dully. She had been so embarrassed that she would not allow herself to be seen without a kerchief tied about her skull.

"It no longer matters. My father brought me six wigs from New Orleans."

Molly beamed. "Now that is right up my alley. E.J., may I have the honor of styling them for you?"

"I can't think of anyone better suited."

Calvin Bender had to agree. Not even in Paris had he seen a woman with such gorgeous hair.

His ego was greatly uplifted with their assessment of his choice of furniture.

"It certainly is regal enough for a Duchess," Molly enthused, "and yet not overly lavish for Denver."

Sally frowned. "Speaking of the duchess, E.J., I best just blurt out one of the reasons we came down. Watson is going to let Coal Oil George jump the claim and file on both of them."

Molly looked at Sally with impatience.

Elsa Jane took a breath. "Any sign of Jamieson?"

"What has he to do with it?" Calvin asked angrily before Sally could answer.

Elsa Jane brushed a hand across her forehead impatiently. "Everything, just everything. But please, I'll tell you that quietly later on."

"No," Sally answered sharply, ignoring the interruption.

"Good. Then there is nothing to worry about."

"Nothing to worry about?" Sally demanded righteously. "Are you just going to let that old walrus steal the mines away from you?"

"I meant good for George's sake that they haven't come back this spring and tried to kill him as well. I don't think that they will. At least, I know of one that won't. In quietly searching about for a business I've run across the one named Harrison. Ironically, it's Charley Harrison. He now runs the Criterion Saloon. I have a certain person that I have hired to keep an eye on him and see if the others do show up."

"That still doesn't answer me on Coal Oil George," Sally said stubbornly.

"Oh, Sal, he's a sick old man. If my Charley couldn't get the hard quartz out of that ground with a pick and shovel, how will he? I've also quietly gone a step further. I've written the territorial governor to have the claims put under dispute and Charley's disappearance investigated. In the meantime I look upon Coal Oil George as the best caretaker I could have to keep it out of the clutches of others. I've asked Sam Wootton to see that he gets supplies and charges it to me."

Sally set her mouth angrily. "That may just be throwing good money after bad."

"Perhaps, but I am not going to fret over it. The way Watson and Mullholland operate, it could take a year or two to bring it to a conclusion."

"And you are willing to wait that long?"

It was that question which amused Elsa Jane. It reminded her of something Charles Humrick had given her that no one could ever steal away. She had learned patience. God had once again snatched her back from the grips of death. She had all the time in the world.

"I like them," Calvin said after the women had left.
"They are good friends."

"If you don't mind," he said slowly, "I would
rather not hear about Jamieson. I might make a slip
in front of the children and they only think you were
in a fire."

Elsa Jane nodded.

"I wish you had been able to bring them along."
Then she laughed. "I hope they are doing better at
Saint Rosa Lima than I did."

"Outstanding students, both," he said. "Oh, I suppose I could have brought them along, but I needed
to see you alone to ask a favor."

"Favor? It sounds important."

"Most important, as I see it, Elsa Jane. Year by
year the threat of war has grown stronger. The election of Lincoln will bring us to it, I fear. Without
slave labor, the plantation life cannot survive. My
way of life cannot survive. Oh, it is not just going to
vanish overnight, but the south is not industrial
enough to win any manner of war. But that is only the
backdrop to the favor that I seek. In your last letter
to Annie you implied that you would like to have the
children back with you by this summer. May I ask a
postponement? This may be the last year, for many
years, that I get to go to Europe. I also think, at
fourteen and thirteen, it is a marvelous age for them to
accompany me for their education."

Elsa Jane smiled wanly. It would mean another
year before she would see them. Fourteen and thirteen? How little they had seen each other in ten
years. Patience. Yes, even in this she would be
patient.

"How can I possibly say no to such a grand opportunity for them, Father?"

"Easily," he said, "by just going along with us."

She looked at him closely. She suspected that her joining them would have greatly pleased him, and it was a temptation.

"Thank you, but I have so much to accomplish here," she murmured gratefully.

Calvin Bender understood.

Mountain Charley and Old Phil were curious friends around the Mountain Boy's Saloon. Mountain Charley claimed his fuzzy short hair was the result of a scalping. He said his oddly shaped nose was from a brawl with Calamity Jane (which she would verify if any man dares ask her), and that his limp was from taking a slug in the thigh from a riverboat gambler.

No one dared try any funny business in Mountain Charley's saloon, as Old Phil was a filthy monster and was trailed by a large mangy dog almost as dangerous as his master. A fugitive from justice, Old Phil proudly boasted of several brutal murders in Philadelphia.

Saturday night was always rowdy in each and every one of the fifty-odd Denver and Auraria saloons. Saturday night was also the night that Mountain Charley would fill Old Phil's money belt for a drinking bout.

However, in April there was hardly elbow room in any establishment for drinking. Josh McNassar was going to officially open his racetrack. The four horse race caused more excitement and betting than the town had ever seen.

Mountain Charley did not allow gambling in his saloon, but for this occasion he let his rules bend a little.

"Charley," the old man wheezed, "I've got a good thing going on Mel Drummond's horse if I just had a fifty bet."

Charley's green eyes narrowed angrily. "I thought

you got a grubstake from the duchess the other day, Herman."

"Now, Charley, I appreciate you sending me to her, but you know I wouldn't dare use her money on a horse bet."

His eyes softened. The duchess was a sucker for grubstaking the older miners but not a one of them would cheat her.

"Old Phil is whistling for me, Herman. Tell Clarence to put you on a tab for fifty."

"Could you be making it for a hundred?"

"Fifty," Charley growled and stomped to the end of the bar.

"Bit of luck," Phil hissed. "Betting is hot and heavy at the Criterion. Charley Harrison's been going from saloon to saloon signing markers for ten thousand dollars and up. But one big bum started giving him a hard time in his own place, and not over the horse race. When he claimed that Harrison had cheated him out of some gold deal, Harrison spun on his heel and without a word emptied his six shooter into the guy."

"Jamieson?"

"Naw! Too beefy."

"Where's Harrison?"

Old Phil spit without aiming for a spitoon. "Come on, Charley, ain't nobody going to try and arrest him after the farce of his last two trials. He's out picking up more bets."

"You best hang around here for the rest of the night."

News of the latest Harrison shooting had travelled fast and he was not having much luck getting new bets. At one in the morning he staggered into the Mountain Boy's.

"I want bets," he bellowed.

Old Phil looked around. Mountain Charley was out in the storeroom.

"Ain't no gambling allowed by Mountain Charley," he warned.

Harrison drew and fired point-blank at Old Phil, missing him twice. Old Phil spun away and started to draw. Harrison was too quick even in his intoxicated state. He rushed the old man and smashed his revolver into the side of his jaw. As the enormous man began to crumble, his yellow dog snarled and circled Harrison. Without comment, Harrison levelled his gun and shot the animal.

An ominous stillness pervaded the saloon. Harrison had just committed the most heinous offense in the West. The dog had been more than a wife or child to Old Phil.

The bartender jumped the bar, stupidly without a weapon.

"Time you went back to your own place, Harrison."

"All I want out of you is a drink," he growled.

"Not from me! Out!"

Harrison turned coy. "Come on, Lucky. What's a mangy old dog to rile you up?"

"Out!" the bartender insisted.

Harrison was lightning quick. The butt of his gun again crashed into a jaw. Harrison pulled the unconscious Lucky to his feet by the hair and held him against the bar while he screamed his demands for a drink. He pressed the pistol to the man's temple and pulled the trigger four times before it exploded.

Mountain Charley heard the explosion in the storeroom, but Harrison had already reeled out into the street by the time he entered with his own pistols drawn.

It was obvious that no one had lifted a hand to interfere.

"Yellow-livered cowards," Mountain Charley roared. "I'm etching each of your stupid ugly faces on my brain and if I ever catch a one of you in the Mountain Boy's I'll shoot without giving it a thought. Out! I've no bartender, so I'm closed. Phil, get your ass up. We're going after a dog killer!"

The Criterion was locked and barred. They pounded on the doors but no one came to answer.

"My fault, Phil. Should have figured him for the dog killer type right from the first. Well, if he ain't fixin' on comin' out, I've got me a hankering for some target practice."

The two friends backed into the middle of the street and fired volley after volley into the saloon windows.

A half block away, Sheriff Middaugh propped his feet up on his desk and pulled his hat low. He knew what to expect.

Harrison's Criterion gang replied with a fusillade of rifle and shotgun blasts from the upper windows. They were only shooting at shadows as Mountain Charley and Old Phil had long since darted to the back of the building to reload.

Before Harrison could divert his men to the back, the beer barrels in the storeroom were exploding like a cannonade.

Harrison sobered quickly. The two old men had made it sound as if every vigilante in the territory was after him. He split his men front and back to fire at anything that moved.

For a few hours nothing moved. Charley and Phil had slipped back to the Mountain Boy's to take care of the bartender and the dog. They also rearmed.

Harrison was relieved. Not a single one of his men

had received as much as a scratch. He would play havoc with the town come dawn.

However, from dawn to nine his men were like prisoners. During that four hour period Charley and Old Phil shot at the building as often as if they had been an entire cavalry.

"Wonder how he did that?"

"Did what?" Old Phil said with a scowl.

"Listen! Father Machebeuf, gout and all, is ringing St. Mary's bell for mass. Must be nine o'clock."

"Hot damn!" Phil enthused, forgetting his dog and all. "It's the day of McNassar's race."

"And us without a bartender."

"Better a bar without a bartender," he chuckled, "than bartenders without a bar."

In the daylight they could see the aftermath of the shooting.

"Time is short," Charley said. "See you at the race."

They left unseen.

A few moments later Charley Harrison gazed at the destruction in disbelief. There wasn't a thing in his saloon that was worth salvaging.

"Shall we tear the whole town apart, boss?"

"No," he said weakly, "I have partners to account to for this loss. We better make sure we suck every last betting dollar out of the bastards to recoup this loss. Then we will let them know that I own this town."

Bedelia paled. She, like every other soul in Denver, had heard the gunfire. Now, hearing the laggard steps coming toward her rooms, her heart grew faint. "Would that be you?"

"Who else?"

Bedelia shook her head as the door opened. "Enough

to scare a body to death. You've never been this late before. Sit and I'll help you. You look simply tuckered."

Elsa Jane slumped into a chair.

Bedelia expertly peeled away the putty nose and wrinkled jowls and applied creams to Elsa Jane's face, just as she had done every night for the past year.

"Today," she scolded, "You are going to act like a lady and sleep the clock around."

"Going to act like a lady. Mrs. B.," Elsa Jane answered, "but without sleep. Big race day."

"Humph! Big nothing day, if you ask me. Why is it so much more important than your rest?"

"Sneak me back to the house and I'll tell you as I dress. Professor Goldrick is to pick me up at ten-thirty."

Bedelia pursed her lips. "That old imposter. He's no more a real professor than I am a . . ."

"Housekeeper to a duchess?"

For the moment Bedelia was stilled, but a half hour later she was begging Elsa Jane to bet all of her coming wages.

It was an unusually hot day for April. The light breezes failed to cool McNassar's Racetrack, despite the fact that it was nothing more than a starting gate on a treeless plain. The women sweated beneath their elaborate toilettes and the men removed their jackets. The entire oval was crowded tight with wagons and carriages. It appeared as though every living soul from Denver, Black Hawk and Central City had come for the race. Those with an eye for a fast buck were dispensing beer from the tailgates of their wagons.

On the infield sweep of the oval, Josh McNassar

had lined up every available freight wagon he could rent, fronted them with bunting and placed borrowed chairs and benches on their flat beds. One needed a personal invitation to view the race from the "grandstand." Here the beer and wine barrels flowed for free, and to add even a more festive note to the occasion, Josh had "Uncle Billy" Thompson and his five piece brass band play stirring march music.

O.J. Goldrick's fancy little pony cart pulled up to the side of the starting gate and everyone grew quiet. Even those who disapproved of the "beer tax" to help the "Professor" start a school were forced to admit that the Scotsman made quite a dashing and handsome figure in his plaid kilts. However, they were more interested in seeing the woman he escorted—the famous Duchess of Plover.

Goldrick had made it a point to worm his way into Elsa Jane's life. He was a long way from home and thought to make her a "boon companion." He was immediately aware that she was not British, but he admired beauty, charm and daring, and her largess toward his school made her most royal in his eyes.

They walked straight across the now deserted racetrack, for even "Uncle Billy's" band had ceased playing. Goldrick thought the silence had something to do with the heavy cloth satchel he lugged along. Lady Elsa Jane had brought only "Pike's Peak" coins of twenty, fifty and one hundred weight denominations. Goldrick had thought her mad and now feared robbery.

But the silence was for Elsa Jane. Never had she looked lovelier. Her dress of cerise taffeta exactly matched the mass of carnations banked against the high curled upsweep of her honey-gold wig. The gown was cut low and emphasized her perfect bustline. Over her arms and shoulders, a cobweb of white lace floated about her like a cloud. All eyes were riveted on her as they walked slowly across the finely raked gravel.

These were people Elsa Jane knew—the Larimers, the Woottons, the Evans, the Tabors, Sally and Molly, and the pear-shaped Father Machebeuf in his black cassock. She had not known the layout of the racetrack, but realized the bettors she wished to do business with were all on the other side of the track.

"My friends," Goldrick said as his eyes twinkled, "I am sure that you are all acquainted with Lady Elsa Jane."

Elsa Jane sank in a low curtsy, then rose as General Larimer extended his hand to her.

"My dear woman, we see far too little of you outside of your most charming home."

At that instant Elsa Jane decided that perhaps this was really the group of people who would best understand her plot.

"Thank you, General, but this little outing is for more than this marvelous air. I'm highly disgusted over the events of last evening, and I am sure most of you agree."

Larimer colored. He had personally picked the sheriff and took her words as a personal affront.

"Mrs. Humrick, please don't worry yourself over the matter. Sheriff Middaugh is investigating the matter."

"Oh? Is that why he is standing over by the starting gate and Charley Harrison is at his wagon taking bets with both hands?"

"Now, now," Josh McNassar soothed. "Can this not all wait until after we have had the races?"

"No!" Elsa Jane answered sharply.

"No," she repeated in a softer tone. "I have heard of the events first-hand, and I resent the constant freedom this man Harrison seems to enjoy."

Sally and Molly realized that her casual words masked her true feelings. The women had heard of the incident the moment they arrived in town and were amazed that Harrison had not yet struck back at Mountain Charley and the saloon.

"But there is nothing that can be done about it right now," H.A.W. Tabor fumed.

"I disagree, sir. I say that we can run this man out of town within five minutes of the races being over."

"How?" Tabor asked. "He must have a gang of twenty thugs working the crowd to garner their bets."

Elsa Jane smiled sweetly. "And I have a satchel of money here that I am willing to use to beat the man at his own game. We will force the betting right through the sky and ruin him financially when he can't pay off."

"I'm not about to fix the race," McNassar said darkly.

"Who asked you to? I couldn't care less which of the four horses wins. We are going to manipulate the betting and not the manner of the race."

Sally began to laugh. "Elsa Jane, what trick do you have up your sleeve?"

Elsa Jane blinked innocently. "Why, Sally Kallenbrough, what ever do you mean? It's just that simple little ploy that Eleanore Dumont used in Nevada City. Get the betting going so hot and heavy that Harrison can't keep track of all the little bets but will feel himself in a position to come after some of this big money. Besides, if you carefully follow the formula of the percentages on each horse, we can't

help but win money back. Mr. McNassar, we will
need a little time."

Josh McNassar smiled. He was beginning to like
the plan. He didn't mind the gambling, for what was
a race without it, but his whole intent was to keep
his business clean and aboveboard.

"Would a couple of preliminary "purse" races, to
show off the track and all, help confuse matters?"

"So much so that I will put up a purse of five
hundred for one of the races."

General Larimer was not to be outdone. "And I
another. To rid our fair city of that trash and make
it as safe as an Eastern township, the money is well
spent.

Delay and confusion was brought about. The
"Duchess Purse" was open to all, which curtailed
betting by only a few individuals. There was such
a brawling crush of men and horses that it thoroughly
delighted the throng.

The "Larimer Purse" was confined to the best
twenty-five riders and horses out of the previous race.
As the plough horses pulled the heavy flat rake rack
around and around the quarter mile track, everyone
had time to pick and choose their favorites out of
the twenty-five.

The real betting took place throughout the two
preliminary races while the track was being prepared
for the main race.

As the word spread, men raced back and forth
to the bunted wagons.

"What?" Harrison's voice betrayed his astonishment.

"Even the Padre! Look, here he comes again!"

Father Machebeuf ran across the track in his black

cassock. He was having the time of his life. Elsa Jane had quietly told him that she would underwrite his bets.

"Machebeuf!" Harrison growled. "Who's betting?"

"Everyone!"

"I can see that. Who is betting over there and how much?"

"Everyone over there," he said as he pointed toward Elsa Jane, "but mainly the duchess."

"How high is she going?" Harrison's temper was rising. "And who can get in on it?"

"Very high," the old priest said as his voice cracked like that of an adolescent. "Some for twenty and thirty thousand."

"Good God! And these jackasses are complaining about fifty and a hundred. Jake, how much we got out?"

"Sheeet! I can't keep up with it. Every time I turn around they got different figures on different horses. The odds are getting all screwed up."

"Your size bets appeal to me," Father Machebeuf said quickly, to keep Harrison from asking any further questions of his henchman.

"Take it up with Jake. I've got some figuring to do."

"One ticket on which horse, Padre?"

Machebeuf didn't bat an eye. "I wish ten one hundred dollar tickets on Flying Cloud to win."

Jake scowled. "That's a thousand dollars."

Machebeuf rattled a leather pouch to show that he had the money. Jake thought he had a sucker in tow.

"Flying Cloud is down to two-to-one, Padre. Herman's Ace would be better at ten-to-one."

Not for long, Frazer Machebeuf thought. He had just made a similar wager on that horse and the other two. He had placed wagers with other Harrison henchmen on all four horses for place and show.

He smiled innocently. "I am rather partial to the angelic sound of Flying Cloud."

Harrison didn't have time to contact all of his twenty henchmen, but he could see that they were all busy. He figured they must have reached about $200,000. The figure did not worry him, as long as most of the bets were for Flying Cloud. He had arranged for the horse to be pulled up lame at the eighth of a mile marker. However, $200,000 now seemed like chickenfeed. He hungered for some of the duchess's money.

"What is the meaning of this, you flea bag?" the General demanded.

"I only want to place a bet, Your Generalship. Got me a couple of coins."

"Bet?" Larimer asked, stuttering in his amazement. "Across the track with the other ruffians."

"A problem?" Elsa Jane interrupted. "Oh, it's Old Phil. He cleans my stables for me, General Larimer."

Larimer spun away as though he suddenly smelled manure.

"How's it going?" Old Phil winked.

"Well," Elsa Jane whispered. "And with you?"

"Placed all of the saloon money like you said, and are they ever confused. Oh, gotta surprise for you. A gent came into the saloon whilst I was cleaning, lookin' for Mountain Charley. Bartender out of work."

"News travels fast. Where has he been working?"

Old Phil giggled. "Criterion!"

"Well, he will have to wait and see Mountain Charley tonight—if Mountain Charley is feeling like coming in tonight."

"He's here."

"Here? Why?"

"Everyone is going to be thirsty after the race and you've got no bartender to open. I had to let him know in a little way that you were the secret money behind Mountain Charley. Did I do wrong?"

She shook her head and a barely audible "I hope not" escaped her lips.

"Well, this is him. Wilf Guerin. Wilf, this is Lady Elsa Jane."

Elsa Jane turned slowly. The compactly built man doffed a flat-brimmed black hat and smiled a crooked smile.

"I'm at a loss to know what to call you, ma'am."

"Mrs. Humrick will do," she said softly, while carefully studying him. His black hair was brushed back into wings that were shot through with pure silver, but his lantern-jawed face gave no hint of his age. His black broadcloth suit was neat and his black string-tie contrasted sharply with the startling whiteness of his shirt. His nails were clipped short, and his black boots were polished to a high sheen. He had a quiet and self-assured manner.

"Well, Mrs. Humrick, I impose, I'm afraid."

Elsa Jane liked his soft voice and gentlemanly qualities. And he looked like he could take care of himself in any barroom brawl.

"I cannot speak for Mountain Charley, Mr. Guerin, but you would place yourself in his favor if you could open the bar after the race."

"I could be doing that, ma'am. As a family man I can't afford to wait for a reopening of the Criterion."

This pleased Elsa Jane in several ways. Not only would she be stealing a bartender away from Charley

Harrison, but a family man would take precautions not to get himself killed.

"I think you will find, Mr. Guerin, that Mountain Charley will be most generous with your wages, and a profit share if you show an honest daily till. Now, if you will excuse me, I have some important wagers to put down before the race."

Wilf Guerin frowned. He was basically a very honest and loyal employee. He had a mother and an invalid sister to support and had taken the first job he could find. Now he wondered if it wasn't time to change his loyalty.

"Mrs. Humrick, I would advise against you and your husband betting against Charley Harrison. Everyone at the Criterion knows that he has this race in his pocket or he wouldn't be betting so heavily."

His advice pleased her.

"Well, Wilf Guerin, hold onto your hat, for I am going to rip that race right out of his pocket and make his money jingle to the ground. And I would advise you to melt quickly into the crowd, for here comes your former boss."

Harrison didn't see Guerin because he was first accosted by Sally and Molly, who each took quite sizable bets with him.

Wilf Guerin watched it all with growing curiosity and then asked Old Phil what was really happening.

"Damn," he muttered, "that woman has one remarkable business head on her shoulders. No wonder she's quietly invested in a saloon and is taking on Harrison at his own game. Come on, I want a piece of this action."

Sally tapped Elsa Jane on the shoulder.

"Lady Elsa Jane, I would like to present the owner of the Criterion, Charley Harrison."

Elsa Jane turned to the man. His face was aglow with a lecherous grin.

"Criterion?" she cooed coyly. "Is that an eating establishment or hostel, Mistah Harr-eee-son?"

Sally nearly broke out laughing.

Harrison was instantly enamored of her beauty and southern belle charm.

"I'm afraid neither, ma'am. It's a saloon."

"Oh, my," she flustered, raising a dainty hand to her breast, "how wicked and sinful." Then she tittered. "But am'hm just dyin' to see one of them on the inside."

Harrison took heart. He had heard that the man that he had killed in Central City had left a simpering southern wife behind, and he considered simpering on a par with stupidity.

"Perhaps that could be arranged," he said suggestively, "after the race."

"Oh, my, yes, the race," Elsa Jane gushed. "Am'hm at my wits end as to which of those four handsome horses to be betting upon. Aren't those riders most darling in their silk shirts and white britches. Just lak home in Naw Awhlins. Which do you prefer, Mistah Harrison?"

There was no pity in his face as he looked from her to the horses. He turned grimly to glare at the crowds across the track.

"I was under the impression you had been making quite a few wagers, ma'am."

"A few pennies here and there, without knowing what I was about. I wish I really knew what to do."

Harrison couldn't believe how easy it was all going to be. "Well," he gulped, "you won't make as much on Flying Cloud coming in as a winner, but you would have the thrill of having a winner."

"Oh, Mistah Harrison, you are a true gentleman. Winning is all that matters and not the money. I've scads of that. Can you take my bet?"

"What did you have in mind?"

"None of this petty cash," she giggled. "Do you know my daddy once paid fifty thousand dollars for a studman right off of a boat from Africa, and made his investment back in the first ten children produced. Daddy called that petty cash, then. So . . . why not do my Daddy's petty cash double?"

Harrison did not move. He was numbed by the size of the wager. For a moment he thought she and her "uppity" friends were trying to make a fool of him. But the woman opened a satchel by her side and he looked down into a mound of gold coins that boggled his mind.

He laughed. "It is obvious you have the coin to cover the bet, ma'am. As a gentleman, I shall leave it in your care and give you my marker to cover it in return. You did say Flying Cloud?"

"Why, yes," she said, the southern accent suddenly having vanished. "And perhaps this is a good omen."

A rider was coming hard and fast, leaving a flying cloud in his wake.

"I will see to your bet," Harrison said and spun away to race across the track.

"He's fixed the race for Flying Cloud to lose," she said emotionlessly to Josh McNassar, keeping her eyes on the approaching rider. She had the most curious and ominous feeling.

"Haloooo! Haloooo!" the rider screamed. "They done it! Last week! The Rebs fired on Fort Sumter in South Carolina. The Union surrendered it! It's war! It's war!"

"*It's race time!*" McNassar screamed over the rider's

shouts. He would not have his day ruined by such a minor affair. He raced to the starting gate and pulled the Flying Cloud rider to the side.

"I know everything, MacDuff, and I know the capabilities of this horse. I'll be at the finish line."

Elsa Jane made an effort to concentrate. She clutched at O.J. Goldrick's elbow and tried to follow the race, but her thoughts had been pulled away. War! North against South! She wondered where her loyalties would lie. She had been raised on a plantation, but had learned of the cruel side of slavery. Her children and father were in the south. Where was she? This was soon to become the Colorado Territory. Where would it stand in such a war?

"It's Flying Cloud by seven lengths. Herman's Ace for place, and a dead heat for show!"

Charley Harrison buried his face in his hands. "Treachery," he cried, "by every damn last horse."

But he was not above making the best of a bad situation. He rushed across the track to confront the duchess.

"My marker is good, ma'am, but let me first take care of these smaller wagers."

Elsa Jane was now in full command. "Smaller wagers?" she asked with a sneer. "I know of such!" Then she raised her voice. "This man has just admitted he has markers out among you. He carries mine for one hundred thousand dollars. He asks me to wait— to pay his debts to you. Have you chits against him?"

There was no sound in the racetrack.

There was a gasp from the crowd. It sounded like hundreds of people had sucked in their breath at the same time. Harrison turned pale at the sound. He signalled his men to begin paying off.

"You are ruining me," he cried to Elsa Jane.

She nodded curtly, her thin lips pressed together.

"No more than you ruined me, under the hire of Jamieson. You know, don't you, that you will never be able to cover all of these bets. I can't prove that you were responsible for Charles Humrick's dastardly death, or I would have you hanging from the nearest tree. But I can prove the infamy you tried to pull today. Pay them off, you stupid dolt."

Her southern twang was gone and her voice was crisp and clear and commanding.

"I don't think that I can."

"Bullshit!" she snarled. "You will, even if you have to use my money to do it . . . and that will cost you your full knowledge of Daris Jamieson."

"I know nothing," he cowered.

"That is utter and absolute nonsense," she said. "I am a single wolf and they are a hungry pack. Make your choice, you insufferable pig!"

"I will pay," he bellowed, and waved to his men. "Bring the chits and wagers."

The crowd, open-mouthed with astonishment, pulled into a line before one of the bunted wagons. No one spoke as they came to get their winnings.

Not everyone had won, of course, but the main loser was Charley Harrison. By nightfall he was as broke as the day he had arrived.

"What now, boss?"

Amazingly, Charley was in quite a chipper mood.

"Tonight we sleep and in the morning give them a most startling surprise."

Mountain Charley also slept. She was too weary to even look in on the new bartender.

Just after dawn a worried Bedelia reluctantly woke E.J.

"They've got the Rebel flag flying over the warehouse of Wallingford and Murphy on Larimer Street. Next door at the Criterion, Harrison has set up a headquarters, with himself as leader, and is calling this Confederate territory."

"So it begins," Elsa Jane sighed. "Well, go wake up Sally and Molly. I don't think anyone will stop their carriage leaving town."

Bedelia didn't understand her reasoning, but did as she was told. Sally understood fully but had mixed emotions.

"But we are both from the South, E.J."

"Are we? Molly, here, is originally from the North. Does that make us automatic enemies? No, we can't look at either side realistically. The South will die because of this, and the North has been dying for years. Our fortunes are tied up here with the new, and as a new territory we have to look down the road to the day we will become a state in the Union."

Before Sally could reply, Bedelia came waddling in with a panting Old Phil.

"Town's in an uproar," he wheezed. "Harrison refuses to take down the Reb flag and has Middaugh locked in his own jail."

"Who is siding with him?"

"His own men, of course, and about a hundred others who are well armed and mounted. He's got Mayor John Moore to declare martial law with Captain McKee in command. Postmaster McClure is to start going house to house and business to business to collect a Confederate war chest."

Elsa Jane roared with laughter. "War chest, my foot. A very clever way for Harrison to recoup his losses of yesterday. Well, Sal, that brings us right back to Colonel William Gilpin. He's our first official governor of the Territory, and someone has to get back to Central City to inform him."

Sally was worried. "That we can do easily, E.J. But don't you think you should go with us?"

"No," she said firmly. "If Harrison wants to come after me, he'll find that I'm just as good a shot as Mountain Charley."

By nightfall Charley Harrison was far too busy running his new government to think of the duchess. Only a third of the population had been willing to support his war chest, but they were showing themselves to be far more militant than the Unionists, and his little army was growing.

However, the volunteer military company that Colenel Gilpin was hurriedly recruiting in the Clear Creek mining camps was also growing. By midnight he had two hundred men down from the mountains and quartered in the buildings opposite the warehouse and the Criterion. Throughout the night Gilpin recruited men from all over and by dawn the Denver volunteer military company numbered close to four hundred.

From dawn to noon several raids were made on the two buildings housing Harrison's men, but for some reason the Rebels would not fire back.

"Most out of percussion caps, Colonel."

"Go to Wootton and buy more."

"He's out and so is Will Larimer."

"Then go to the warehouse supplier."

The warehouse supplier was Wallingford and Murphy. They were approached with an ingenious proposal to render the Unionists' superiority in firearms useless by sunset. Harrison controlled every percussion cap in the territory.

With an arrogant strut he marched out onto the Criterion balcony and glowered across at Gilpin.

"Sir," he bellowed, "I order the immediate surrender of your men as prisoners of war."

"My men are most busy, Harrison. I have authorized

the military and the police to disarm the whole populace and put their firearm supplies at my disposal. You have one hour to do the same or suffer the consequences of a six hundred gun barrage."

Within twenty minutes loyal Confederates were bringing horses and mules to the back of the warehouse. As the percussion cap cases were loaded on the pack mules, Gilpin held his men at bay. His words had been a bluff, but he would much rather pursue the Rebels on the open trail than have bloodshed in the heart of the city.

Within the hour given them, a hundred loyal men leisurely followed Harrison up Cherry Creek—among them the Mayor and Postmaster.

Gilpin did not pursue. He wisely left that to others while he strove to keep his territory out of the mainstream of the coming blood bath.

18

It became the most frustrating year of Elsa Jane's life. Dispatch after dispatch went forth to Bender's Landing. At first the replies from her father angered her, and then, with the Confederates in full control of the Mississippi, there were no replies at all.

"Utterly maddening. At first he felt that the war would never reach that far west and now I don't know what he is thinking. Shiloh was bad enough, but now New Orleans! Oh, Phil, I've just got to go and get them out of there before the Union moves on Vicksburg."

"You'll be doing nothing of the sort," he grumbled. "I'll be doing it for you. No one is going to question an old reprobate like me."

His offer gave her double relief. She had been playing the role of Mountain Charley less and less

and had given Wilf Guerin more managerial respon-
sibilities for the saloon. It was not to Old Phil's liking, and he was outspoken enough to air his mind
on the matter whenever he could. Sending him to
Bender's Landing would get him out of her hair for
a while and keep her from having to make the trip.

Elsa Jane was tired of travelling. At twenty-eight
she was tired and bored with almost everything. There
was no spice in her life and very few activities.

The Civil War had not only stopped the flow of
immigration, but it had reversed it. Men returned
to their homes in the East and South. Most of the
gulch claims in the mountains washed out, and most
of the hard-rock mines were capped while the men
went to war. The quartz stamping mills were idle.

There were few friends left. The Tabors were off
to Oro City, where he knew he was sure he would
strike it rich.

The Larimers were off to war. After the Union had
control of Santa Fe, the Wootton's realized it would
become the center of commerce for the entire South-
west. Uncle Dick left Nathan in charge of the Denver store, and took Alice to establish a far-reaching
freight line.

Father J.P. Machebeuf arranged for three Sisters
of the Order of Loretto to open St. Mary's Academy
with his gambling profit. A month later he was ordered to Santa Fe. He feared that the constant letters
he had been writing protesting the treatment Elsa
Jane had received by Bishop Landry had gotten him
into serious trouble. To his utter amazement he was
sent to be ordained as the new Bishop of Santa Fe.

Elizabeth Byers was still around, but at last she
had women like Margaret Evans, Sally Kountze and
Helen Moffat to form a club. Elsa Jane was quietly
excluded from their prim and proper world because

of her association with Sally Kallenbrough and Molly b'Damn.

"A note for you from Central City."

Elsa Jane read it indifferently. "A very strange irony, Bedelia. When Coal Oil George died last week they were not aware that he had left a will on file with Murton Mullholland. They didn't find it until yesterday, after Mullholland was shot in his cabin and they began to search his files. Sally thinks I better come right up and sign the claim papers."

"He left you the mines?"

She smiled but there was sarcasm in her voice. "That's the real irony. He's left them to E.J. Forest and Sally Kallenbrough. We are forced back into partnership whether we like it or not." She sighed. "Well, I'd best go."

"As whom?" Bedelia asked.

"With Phil gone, I'll just take the surrey and go as myself."

She had had many dreams while she had controled the mines. Now it all seemed like a great waste. She didn't have the ambition or the guts to return and work the mines. Soon she would have been masquerading as a man for thirteen years. Wilf Guerin ran the saloon efficiently, and without being able to send money to the children it was piling up handsomely in the Kountze Brothers' bank. Once she had her father and children out of the war zone she would figure out a new direction for her life.

Elsa Jane shivered and tucked a hand under her lap robe. A well-built man, past middle age, came riding down the center of the wagon trail. A quick look passed between them and the man drew his revolver.

Elsa Jane tensed. The road had been infamous for

highwaymen in the years past. Cautiously, she moved her hand beneath the laprobe until it nestled about the gun butt resting in her lap. At his signal, she pulled the surrey to a stop.

The man leaned forward in his saddle. "Fancy meeting you here, and all dolled up for a change."

Elsa Jane jumped when she heard his voice. She would not have recognized Daris Jamieson otherwise. He had put on a good fifty pounds, had taken to wearing mountain man buckskins and sported a full beard and mustache.

She eyed him coldly, but did not respond. She needed him a little closer, and at a better angle, before she dared use her own weapon.

"I should have known that you would come hightailing it up to Central City. Pretty clever trick keeping that old coot at the mine as a caretaker. We thought we could outlast him, but Mullholland grew scared after you had to mess into our plans again."

"I messed in? How?"

He spat and brought his horse up alongside the surrey.

"You might as well know all, because this time I'm going to make sure that you die. But I'll make it short, *duchess*," he sneered. "In brief, Harrison and I sorta conned Mullholland into backing the Criterion. I, of course, couldn't be seen, so I went off to teach the Indians a bit about gambling. Harrison had ways of keeping me informed and I wasn't too pleased with what you did to the Criterion and to Harrison. It's made it a very slim year for me and so I had to come back and speed things up a mite."

"I see," she said slowly, moving the revolver barrel into a better angle. "So, it would seem you have two more victims to your credit. I should have realized that when they said Mullholland was shot, but the old man?"

"In his drunken stupor a pillow put him to sleep most naturally. Mullholland got scared and no longer was any help to me."

Elsa Jane threw back her head and laughed.

"You will never change from being an idiot, Jamieson. The old man left a will on file with Mullholland. The claim is back in my name."

Jamieson wilted, but then his eyes caught the movement under her lap robe and his eyes flared.

Elsa Jane fired right through the cloth. The bullet went through Jamieson's wrist and knocked his revolver away. Before he could react, her second shot caught him in the shoulder and spun him backwards off the horse.

He screamed as his horse galloped away. The surrey horse had been trained for gunfire and stood still. Elsa Jane calmly stood up and took better aim. She did not hear his screams. She did not hear anything. She was in a near trance as she pumped the other four shells into his quivering body.

Out of the corner of her eye, she saw a flash of blue as a soldier jumped from his horse onto the surrey. With a chop of his hand he knocked away her revolver and roughly shoved her over into the back seat. She was too stunned to protest.

"Good God!" Captain Liebus Walker called up. "The man is alive and his piece hasn't been fired. Find out who she is, Maxwell."

Amazingly, Jamieson opened his eyes and rasped, "She's a fraud, no matter what she tells . . ." He lapsed away.

"Well?" Walker roared.

Sergeant Maxwell Cushman hesitated. Elsa Jane

was in a state of total shock. She could not believe that she had heard Jamieson speak. She couldn't believe that she had failed to kill him, even at point-blank range.

"Lady," he said gently, "what is your name?"

"I didn't kill him," she mumbled. "Twice I've tried to kill him and I've failed both times."

The sergeant quietly got down from the surrey and whispered her words to the captain.

Walker was a rule-book officer and greatly resented being on frontier patrol when the war was back East. He had counted six bullet wounds in the man's body and knew he would soon have a corpse on his hands. Murder was murder to him, no matter the gender of the one holding the smoking gun.

"It's the same distance either way," he mused, "but the road back to Denver will be quicker. Manacle her to the seat and get him on board. We'll put the whole mess in Major Berthoud's hands."

The law had been put under military command. Major Harvey Berthoud knew little about the people of Denver and didn't care to learn. His patrols were stretched thin between Fort Laramie and Bent's Fort.

For three days he kept Elsa Jane secretly within the military headquarters, a suite of four rooms above a clothing store on Larimer Street.

She was guarded day and night by Sergeant Aston Shaw and was allowed a single meal a day.

"How does it happen, Major, that I have to be with the prisoner all the time?"

"Shaw, each and every hour the victim tells us more and more about the prisoner. This is no ordinary prisoner and we dare not let her escape."

Forgetting she was sitting within earshot, Berthoud

took great pleasure in repeating the story of Elsa Jane's camouflage.

"I can tell you that it all has amazed Dr. Fairplay and greatly shocked his wife, who has been a most caring nurse for the poor victim."

Elsa Jane groaned. Lavinia Fairplay would be most caring in order to gain every morsel of scandal and gossip she could.

When the news reached Elizabeth Byers it was quickly passed along. Elizabeth piously pointed out to any that would listen that she had known right from the beginning that the duchess had been an imposter.

One man listened and acted. The failure of his retention as a teacher, due to a habit of nipping at a liquor bottle in the classroom, had forced O.J. Goldrick to offer his talents to the *Rocky Mountain News* as a reporter.

Lavinia allowed Goldrick to see the patient privately, hoping to get her name in print.

Although the Major had been absolutely convinced of her guilt, he quickly ordered her release after a private meeting with William Byers.

"You may go home," Sergeant Shaw informed her.

"Where is my surrey?"

"Don't ask me."

Nor did she wish to ask Major Berthoud. For three days she had kept quiet and had mentally prepared herself to stand trial. Her only fear was having to counter the lies that Jamieson had poured forth. She knew that Sally might not be too effective as a witness and there was only one man alive who could really help. As she stepped onto Larimer Street, she prayed that Old Phil was quick in his return with her father.

The clothing store owner looked at her with a

mysterious gaze and scurried back inside his store. A second later, curious faces peered out the window at her.

Elsa Jane shrugged it off as she walked up Larimer Street. It happened again and again. People gawked but no one spoke.

"Damn!" she muttered. "Lavinia's got it spread all over town. Look at those old crows tittering to each other. Well, a few more steps and then I'll . . ."

The sign on the Mountain Boy's Saloon door staggered her.

"Why? Why 'closed until further notice'? And on whose order?"

Anger that had been dormant for a year finally flared. She could feel the town's mocking laughter. What right did they have to condemn without all the facts? Hypocrites! Nothing had changed. They were still just as narrow-minded as the original businessmen in St. Louis had been. She had survived for thirteen years by beating them at their own game. Oh, she had had help along the way, to be sure . . . but most of that help now lay in shallow graves. She was alone again, but damned if she was going to be afraid!

"All right, you pious piss-ants," she bellowed in the deepest Mountain Charley voice she could muster, "get your gawking eyes a damn good look!"

She ripped off the disheveled wig and marched on as though wearing sailor's brogans. Carriages came to a stop and women gaped openly, but Elsa Jane looked neither left nor right.

The door of the saloon flew open even before she was halfway up the front steps. An ashen-faced Wilf Guerin stood awaiting her.

"Why in the hell are we closed down?" she roared.

"Thank God you are all right," he sighed, avoiding

her question. "We were not allowed to learn anything until Goldrick came by awhile ago."

"You didn't answer my question," she insisted.

"Other things are more important," he answered dully. "Everyone is waiting for you in the dining room."

"Everyone?"

"Old Phil got back an hour ago."

A surge of joy leapt into her heart and she ran toward the dining room door. Then she stopped short.

Everyone was Goldrick, Sally, Molly and Old Phil. The old man did not look at her, but kept his eyes down on the bowl of food. A cataract of milky gruel cascaded down his beard.

"Well?" she asked more sharply than she meant to. "Where are they?"

"Bedelia . . ." Sally stammered. "Bedelia is bathing and finding clothes for Annie."

"And my father and Charles Peter?"

Old Phil sniffed and looked up at her. His words poured from his cracked lips. "I was most a day late gettin' there, 'n . . . found her, finally, bein' hid out in the old overseer's house by an ole black man named Moses . . . 'n him nearly dead. Did die 'fore we left."

Molly cleared her throat. "I don't think you need to hear it all right now, E.J."

The black lash of fear curled through Elsa Jane's brain and wound itself around her heart.

"I think that I must," she said weakly. "They are gone, aren't they?"

Old Phil nodded. "The slaves rose up without warnin', 'n they were the only three whites on the island, the overseer long since gone to war. Burned and looted everything right to the ground. Miss Annie don't rightly know what happened after her grand-

father ordered the ole slave to take her away. I
. . . I didn't tell her I found and buried them."

Bedelia rushed in, took in the scene at a glance,
then, glaring at Old Phil, walked quickly to put an
arm around Elsa Jane. "Fool," she cried angrily, "utter fool that you are! The child will be coming down
at any moment."

"Then time for a new subject." Goldrick said,
squirming in his chair. "Duchess, through a bit of
journalistic chicanery, Jamieson has exculpated you
wholly from any blame in the attempts on his life.
Byers is printing the entire story in the paper now.
Berthoud is so embarrassed over his role in the matter
that he is having Jamieson removed to New Orleans."

Elsa Jane hardly heard a word. She turned and
kept her eyes fixed on the stairway.

"Child," she thought, echoing Bedelia's word.
"Hardly that."

Annie Forest let her hand rest caressingly on the
smooth marble balustrade as she slowly came down
the stairs. She had resented Bedelia's constant chat-
ter as she had bathed and dressed her in one of her
mother's gowns, but now she was most grateful. She
would not look on the near hairless woman as she
was, but as she remembered her. The marble was
warm where the sun touched it through the skylight,
and its very smoothness confirmed the fact that she
was home and safe. This was her mother's house.

Elsa Jane was overwhelmed. Annie was an un-
qualified beauty. Smiling in satisfaction, Elsa Jane
felt all of the ghosts she had been hauling about for
years bid her a fond farewell. She imagined what
joy she could share with her daughter.

Elsa Jane was alive with the excitement of challenge.
She would hold off her grief for the missing until she
was alone. Let the boobs laugh and sneer at the Duch-

ess of Denver, she thought. She had more important work to occupy her time and mind. She had survived again. Annie had survived. Duchess? That was minor. She would turn that rag-tag town into the Queen City of the plains and Annie would be its princess.

Jamieson had made Elsa Jane famous. Many pioneer women had been in similar situations, but Elsa Jane had fought—and continued to fight.

There was no surprise or envy when the Duchess Mines finally garnered a lion's share of the twenty-seven million that was finally pulled from the mountains around Central City and Black Hawk.

There was pride when the mansion designed by Charles Henry Humrick began to rise on Elsa Jane's Brown's Bluff property, and no one questioned the Kallenbrough million-dollar edifice that was erected nearby.

The talents of Wilf Guerin were put to much better use as general manager of the Forest and Kallenbrough Mining Company. And ironically, it was two years before Elsa Jane had understood what Wilf had meant about being a "family man". It took six more months of convincing by Sally to persuade her that the man was too shy to declare his deep-seated love for her.

She put the entire matter out of her mind twice.

In the spring of 1863 the fire alarm sounded. By dawn of the next day the heart of Denver was a mass of burning timbers. Her love had to be given back to her city.

Construction had finally started when, in May, 1864, a great wall of black water, twenty feet high, came rushing down from Cherry Creek.

Brown's Bluff was safe but again Elsa Jane turned her love to her city.

The marriage of Annie Forest to Nathan Wootton brought about a phenomenon of sorts. The new owner of Mountain Boy's Saloon shaved, donned a suit and sported new false teeth for the occasion. Old Phil had the honor of giving the bride away, and thereafter no one dared call him anything but Mister Phil.

It was going to be lonely for Elsa Jane with Annie moving with Nathan to Santa Fe. She sat with her head bowed as the radiant couple sailed happily down the aisle. Moments later she mumbled hoarsely, "I'm thirty-one years old."

"Time to start living for yourself, I'd say."

Elsa Jane brought her head up. Her eyes were wet but they were clear and unafraid. She met his glance squarely.

"Got any good suggestions on the matter, Wilf?"

"I guess not."

They were silent again as they rose to join the wedding party leaving the church. Halfway down the aisle she stopped and took Wilf by the arm. The tender kittenish quality that had not appeared for years bubbled deep and soundless.

"You know, Wilf Guerin, I think we are going in the wrong direction if we are going to start living."

His smile began in his eyes.